Rising Courage

A VARIATION OF JANE AUSTEN'S PRIDE AND PREJUDICE

HEATHER MOLL

EXCESSIVELY
DIVERTED
PRESS

ESTABLISHED 2001

For Mom and Dad, who let me hide out in their house to write this

"Are you much acquainted with Mr Darcy?"

"As much as I ever wish to be," cried Elizabeth *warmly. "I have spent four days in the same house with him, and I think him very disagreeable."*

Pride and Prejudice Chapter 16

Chapter One

E lizabeth Bennet sat with Charlotte Collins and her sister Maria in Charlotte's parlour in Hunsford parsonage when they were startled by a ring at the door.

"I heard no carriage," said Maria nervously. "Do you suppose it to be Lady Catherine?"

They all exchanged a worrisome look. Since her ladyship's nephews had arrived at Rosings for Easter last week, Mr Darcy, Colonel Fitzwilliam, and now and then Lady Catherine had called every day. Sometimes the men called together, sometimes alone, and on occasion they both came with her ladyship.

"I think it not unlikely," Charlotte said. "It is Tuesday, and we have not seen her for a few days."

Maria professed she was not up to the task of facing such a visitor and fled the room, and Elizabeth was of half a mind to leave herself. When they were honoured with a call from her ladyship, nothing escaped Lady Catherine's impertinent questioning. Elizabeth put away her half-finished letter to her sister Jane with a sigh. It would be an irksome visit.

Mr Darcy might have joined her, and I take no pleasure in seeing him either.

The quiet way her first fortnight at Hunsford had passed had now given way to regular encounters with the proud Mr Darcy. He had called once while Charlotte and Maria were in the village, and they spent an

1

awkward quarter of an hour alone together. Their conversation reminded her of how hastily Bingley had left Hertfordshire last November and of Jane's subsequent heartbreak.

Worse than that tête-à-tête, Mr Darcy now even interrupted her solitary rambles within the park. She had previously enjoyed an open grove that edged a side of the park where there was a nice sheltered path that no one seemed to value but herself. She had only ever seen one other person in the grove—a broad-shouldered man with a disfigured nose who yesterday seemed about to approach her—but then Mr Darcy had come from the other direction, and the man quickly left.

Mr Darcy, however, had turned back with her as he had on two other occasions. She could not say why he walked with her, for he never said a great deal and hardly seemed to take pleasure in her company. Talking with him a little was a disagreeable necessity, but aside from a few formal enquiries and answering his direct questions, Elizabeth did not give herself the trouble of talking or listening to him.

"Why do you look cross, Eliza?" Charlotte asked as they heard the visitors in the hall.

"Oh, I only wish it was not Mr Darcy. He spoils all the pleasure of my walks, and now here he is about to spoil a cheerful morning at home with you."

She could only think on Mr Darcy with hatred and contempt for what he had done to her former favourite George Wickham, and she suspected he had encouraged Bingley to forget Jane, too.

The door opened, and Lady Catherine, Mr Darcy, and Colonel Fitzwilliam were shown in. Her ladyship strode in as though it was her own house, the colonel greeted everyone with an amiable smile, and Mr Darcy sat near to Elizabeth without saying a word.

Mr Darcy seldom appeared animated when he called, and Elizabeth wondered if he joined the others because he had nothing better to do. It was plain that Colonel Fitzwilliam came because he had pleasure in their society. Elizabeth enjoyed his conversations and felt a little satisfaction at his evident admiration of her. It reminded her of Wickham's attentions, although the colonel had a better-informed mind.

"When my nephews said they were calling today, I had to join them," her ladyship said upon entering. She handed Mrs Collins a small bottle. "I have brought you some of Rosings's cherry brandy. Everyone says that mine is the finest in the neighbourhood. It is because I use cherries grown here and only the best English brandy."

Elizabeth noticed Colonel Fitzwilliam and Mr Darcy share a meaningful glance. Mr Darcy even gave a small wince. She supposed the men drank wine at the table rather than their aunt's weak brandy. Charlotte kept a civil expression as she accepted the bottle.

"You are kind, your ladyship."

"I know that you rarely host gentlemen in the evening—the style of living here is above your reach—but you can make cordials with it. Although, Mr Collins will drink it as it is. Darcy, I know, enjoys Rosings's cherry brandy."

Elizabeth, seated near to Mr Darcy, noticed how he shifted his weight. He looked at her before she could turn away, and she knew he saw the half smile she gave at his expense. He huffed, but she could not tell if he was amused or insulted at how she laughed at him.

"Yes, Darcy likes it very much," Colonel Fitzwilliam muttered, smiling. Anyone of sense could tell he meant the opposite, even if they could not see Mr Darcy's pained expression.

"I shall instruct my housekeeper to send you my receipt for ratafia," Lady Catherine went on. "Miss Bennet enjoyed the ratafia I served at Rosings, I remember, and my cherry brandy is its base."

All eyes turned to her, and Elizabeth gave a strained smile. Mr Darcy gave her a look—unseen by her ladyship—as if to say, "Now it is your turn." She had choked down the vile drink and complimented Lady Catherine on it out of politeness. No amount of champagne, gin, or sugar added to that brandy could salvage it.

"Yes, ma'am. The ratafia was very good."

"Then this small bottle will not be enough if it is wanted as brandy for Mr Collins and also to make cordials for the ladies. I shall have a half-anker of Rosings's cherry brandy sent tomorrow, along with my receipt for ratafia."

Colonel Fitzwilliam stifled a laugh, and she dreaded to ask the question. "How much is that?" she asked softly, leaning forward to be heard.

"Half an anker is four gallons."

Her eyes widened as she sat back, and again Mr Darcy looked her way. He pressed his lips together, holding back a smile as their eyes met. He gave her a commiserating shrug. How could they ever drink four gallons of the dreadful stuff?

"Mrs Collins, I have always thought this chair should be placed by that window," her ladyship said while sitting on the chair in question. "Have you considered moving it to take better advantage of the afternoon light?"

Lady Catherine went on to ask many questions respecting Charlotte's house, and as she did not answer them all herself, Charlotte was required to pay attention.

"Well, Miss Bennet," said the colonel, as she and his cousin were left to themselves, "I never feel the loss of cognac so greatly as I do while at Rosings." With Lady Catherine behind him, he made a face as though tasting something horrid.

She smiled widely, but checked her laugh. "It is a shame nothing can be had from France."

"Nothing legally, in any event," Mr Darcy added. At her confused glance, he said, "Kent's proximity to Europe, and the war and high import taxes make Kent a main entry point for contraband."

"What are you talking of?" her ladyship called sharply.

There was never a way to ignore Lady Catherine. "Smuggling, ma'am," answered Colonel Fitzwilliam.

Her ladyship looked quite astonished. "Such business can be of no interest to Miss Bennet. Fitzwilliam, move that table for Mrs Collins so she can see how that would open up the room."

The colonel was forced to do her bidding with many apologetic looks to his hostess, and until it was time to leave, Mr Darcy was his usual taciturn self. When Lady Catherine announced the call at an end, they all rose to part, and Mr Darcy said to Elizabeth in a low voice, "Pour it out the window."

"I beg your pardon?"

"The cherry brandy," he muttered. "No good can come from drinking it."

"I might do, although I fear for the lawn," she whispered.

They exchanged a silent, knowing look with amused eyes, and then she felt a blush on her cheek and a rush of confusion pass over her. As handsome and astute as he was, there was no need to feel such a frenzy over a private joke and a smile. And certainly not with an arrogant man like Mr Darcy.

Lady Catherine and Colonel Fitzwilliam then came near to take leave, she with pronouncements on the future weather and he with his usual friendly manner. Mr Darcy said nothing else as he bowed and left.

Elizabeth walked to the front room to watch Charlotte's guests leave. How extraordinary to share a laugh with Mr Darcy. She had seen him smile on occasion, but she had thought he had too much pride to have a sense of humour. It was a pleasant moment, but she would ignore her racing heart.

Attention, tolerance, comradeship with Mr Darcy was injury to Wickham, and if she was to be on friendly terms with one of them, Wickham was the better man.

~

WHEN DARCY ARRIVED IN THE BREAKFAST PARLOUR THE following morning, he held back a grimace when he saw only his aunt was at the table. As he greeted her and served himself, he wondered how many minutes would pass before Lady Catherine hinted at his marrying her daughter Anne.

Even if I did not admire Elizabeth Bennet, I could never attach myself to my cousin.

Not once in all of his twenty-eight years had Darcy considered his cousin to be worth esteeming. Anne had an unpleasant manner, was sullen if she did take the trouble to speak, asked others to do what she could easily do herself, and was cross and disagreeable, especially if she had not taken enough laudanum that day to make her soporific.

"My mind is full of servants' wages and taxes," Lady Catherine said by way of greeting as she pushed aside her letters. "Both are exorbitant costs. You do not know what outlays I have and the care I must take."

He held her gaze for a breath, wondering if it would occur to her ladyship that, as master of an estate twice the size of Rosings, he had an excellent understanding of the responsibility and expense involved. Lady Catherine only looked as though she expected his assent. Darcy kept his forbearance as he said, "It must be a trial, madam. If you have need of my help or advice on Rosings's management, you need only ask."

His aunt drew back with a disdainful look. He ought to have known better; her ladyship gave advice, she did not accept it, despite having no business habits. As much as he felt an obligation to take care of his mother's only sister—to take care of anyone who had need of him—Lady Catherine refused his help. She was drilled thoroughly in nothing while young, not even music or drawing, and his aunt had not grown up to decide to apply herself with a will to master any subject.

If only that stopped her from sharing her opinion about things of which she knows nothing.

"I am capable, Darcy, of managing my own affairs and accounts," she said crossly, "and I can keep Rosings in fine repair."

He had been thinking more about the land and the tenants. Rosings was a good house, but furnished with disregard for expense. For all the lavish expenditure, it showed not much taste. And Darcy had often thought that a widow who lived only with a grown-up daughter and her companion did not need so many servants. Still, he thought it unlikely that Lady Catherine must pinch many a year to pay for her expenses.

"Besides, once you recollect all that you owe to your family," she added, "I will be more often at Pemberley and can shut up Rosings for months at a time."

Darcy set down his fork. What he owed to his family, as far as his aunt was concerned, was to marry Anne and unite their fortunes. Darcy felt his temper rise. He did not love Anne—could scarcely even respect her—and would never marry her. To say so again would only lead to another quarrel, and for everyone's peace he had years ago decided to end any conversation on the topic.

With practised patience, he said in a tight, low voice, "I will not discuss it."

Her ladyship was not used to having her judgment controverted, no matter how many times Darcy ended this line of enquiry. "It was the favourite wish of your dear mother, you know. The two of you are formed for—"

"When I said I would not discuss it, I also meant that I would not listen to the subject, either."

He held his aunt's gaze until she finally dropped it. After a moment of silence, she said, "While we are alone, I have come across something that you must have."

His aunt drew out a small jewellery box and handed it to him. He opened it to see a ring with a pear-shaped sapphire set next to a similarly shaped diamond. It was an odd pairing, but he supposed there was something pretty in its simplicity and how closely the two differently coloured stones fit together.

"Lady Anne had this made before she died. She had heard that the French emperor commissioned a ring of this style as an engagement gift to his empress. She thought it fitting that her son give such a ring to her niece."

Darcy snapped shut the lid. "I cannot accept this on the condition that I present it to Anne."

"It is already yours; your mother had it made for your sake. I have kept it long enough."

For the sake of familial relations, he reluctantly took it.

"You will do what you must when the time is right," she added.

He started, and since it appeared no other member of the household was going to enter and save him from a conversation he could not stop, he rose. "I am going for a walk, madam."

As Darcy left the house, the ring felt like a lead weight in his pocket. It might have been a more romantic emblem had Bonaparte not divorced his wife two years ago for not giving him an heir. Darcy would give the ring to his sister and tell her their mother had designed it. Maybe he would put it in a drawer where no one would find it until after he was dead. Or maybe he would leave it in his pocket in the hopes that it fell out and got lost.

Although he had not set out for this purpose, his feet carried him to the part of the park that he knew to be Elizabeth's favourite.

I cannot keep putting off leaving Kent just to spend more time with her.

He and Fitzwilliam were supposed to have left the Monday after Easter, and it was now the eighth of April and they were still here. Elizabeth boasted beauty, cleverness, kindness, and he was as bewitched by her now as he had been in Hertfordshire last autumn.

He loved her, he knew. He had known it since he had spoken to her over the instrument at Rosings on Easter. What he had now to decide was whether he was being weak by marrying her. She could bring him no fortune. Her connexions were embarrassing and far beneath his, and his own relations would baulk at him marrying someone of no importance in the world and who was unallied to the family.

He considered the great regard he held for a woman everyone would tell him was a terrible match. They would only see inferior connexions and no fortune. They would not see Elizabeth's amiable disposition, or her lively spirit, or any of her other admirable qualities.

While he considered what to do, Darcy saw ahead of him that Elizabeth was walking the grove. He smiled and called her name.

"What brings you here again?" she asked after their formal enquiries as he turned back to walk with her.

He could not tell her he had to escape Lady Catherine's complaints about expenses, or about his frustration that she would never accept his help, or about the hints that he marry Anne and the expectation that her ladyship would save money by living with them at Pemberley.

"I only wanted a walk," he said.

He asked about her pleasure in being at Hunsford, her love of solitary walks, and her opinion of Mr and Mrs Collins's happiness, and she answered directly. On the whole, it was a companionably quiet walk. It was

7

pleasant not to be forced to talk if neither had anything particular to say. She talked little, and he supposed she must enjoy nature. He felt Elizabeth would enjoy the dales, rocks, and mountains of Derbyshire.

When they were near to one of the gates, Darcy noticed a man by the park paling, close to the turnpike road, enter the grounds. He had the look of a prizefighter, and the sort who would hit a downed fighter or grasp below the waist. Darcy saw the man watching them as he leant against the fence and smoked a pipe.

"Do you often see anyone while you enjoy your favourite walk?" he asked Elizabeth, tilting his head in the man's direction.

She followed his gaze and shook her head. "I saw that man yesterday, but I typically see no one, except you," she added in a low voice.

His heart beat a little faster at her being glad to walk with him, but as the stranger watched them, there was something in his insolent stare that Darcy could not like. If someone wanted to take a footpath through the grounds, they would not stand there, glaring into the park. He was not a gardener, and Darcy could think of no reason for a tenant or villager to be loitering by the gate.

"Hallo," Darcy called. "Do you need to see someone at Rosings?"

"No, sir," he said through a white pipe in his teeth, and the man left through the gate to the turnpike road without another word.

He and Elizabeth walked in silence for a little longer, and he strove to find something to talk of. "Has the cherry brandy been eagerly passed round at the parsonage?"

"Your aunt is too generous for words."

He smiled at her tactful answer. "Lady Catherine is prodigiously proud of it, and talks of it being good enough to sell. Somehow, the tart-sweetness of the cherries is lost, and the only flavour that remains is a woody taste that is further ruined by it being watered-down brandy."

"Let me assure you, it is no better when made into ratafia. I suppose you and your cousin must drink port or madeira after dinner, and her ladyship cannot understand how she never runs out of brandy in the dining room."

"Oh, no, she always runs out." She looked at him askance. "I told you, you must pour it out the window at every opportunity because no one should ever drink it."

She laughed involuntarily and covered her mouth. He felt an absurd delight at amusing her, but they were at the gate, and Elizabeth took her leave before he could say anything else.

. . .

"WHAT DO YOU MEAN MISS BENNET HAS A HEADACHE?" CRIED Lady Catherine. "When does that ever prevent a lady from keeping her evening engagement? I am very displeased by her staying home."

"She really was unwell, your ladyship," said Mrs Collins. "I am certain a lie-down is all she needed."

Darcy was equally displeased, but not for the same reason as Lady Catherine. It was now Thursday, and as he was leaving on Saturday, he had hoped to talk with Elizabeth again. It had only been a day since he walked with her, but he missed her company. How was he to leave in two days and never see her again?

"In persons of a full habit, the headache often proceeds from not being active," Lady Catherine intoned. "I expect young people to be active for their own health. Had Anne's health not been so indifferent, I am sure she could walk to the parsonage and back twice even if she had a headache."

Darcy and Fitzwilliam shared a look, and his cousin lifted his eyes.

"It is likely Miss Bennet was too sedentary today," she went on, "and she ought to have walked to Rosings tonight to restore herself."

"I saw her walking this morning while making my customary tour of the park," Fitzwilliam said.

"Then why did she not come to tea?"

This was, of course, impossible to answer, and so the conversation moved on to other topics, led by Lady Catherine. Darcy ignored them all and paced. His scruples had long prevented him from forming a serious design on Elizabeth, and he now had to decide whether to overcome his reservations and marry her, or leave on Saturday and forget her forever.

She is lovely and kind and clever. I never talk so well as in her company; an hour passes away like a minute.

He felt his passion for her increase daily, and the distance from her embarrassing relations made it easier to forget them. Elizabeth was worthy of his affection. He admired her independent nature, and she was full of energy and quick wit.

He was resolved to lay his heart before her, but he could not call on her if she was ill. If she only had a headache earlier, she might now feel better. Darcy beckoned Fitzwilliam over to where he stood near a window.

"Was Miss Bennet well when you walked with her this morning?" Darcy asked.

He did not like the shrewd look in his cousin's eyes as he asked, "Why?

Do you miss the company of Mrs Collins's pretty friend?" He dropped his voice. "You scarcely say a word when she is near, but I have never seen you look at a woman the way you look at her."

"I only wondered if she was healthy."

Fitzwilliam gave him a long look before saying, "She seemed well. She was reading a letter when I first saw her. We talked a little of your friend Bingley, and of when we are leaving Kent, and on lighter topics. You know her lively manner," he added before walking away.

He did, and it was a great attraction.

Darcy watched his aunt holding court and then slipped from the room. Elizabeth was likely well enough to receive him, and he could not put off proposing a moment longer.

He had gathered his courage to fly in the face of family expectations, and it was time to act. He was the best judge of his own happiness, and he would find that happiness in his own way. Not another day should pass before he told Elizabeth that he ardently admired and loved her.

Chapter Two

Nothing had ever astonished Elizabeth as much in her entire life as Mr Darcy being so in love with her that he asked her to marry him. Despite all of his objections, he had just walked into the parlour last night and proposed as though she had been expecting his addresses. Even now, hours later, she could not recover from the surprise of what had happened, and soon after breakfast, went for a walk.

He was in love with me, and for all of those months!

It was impossible to think of anything else but Mr Darcy. His proposal was gratifying, flattering, and it would have been a match beyond what one might reasonably assume she could reach. Despite that, Elizabeth did not regret refusing him. She proceeded toward her favourite walk, but recollected Mr Darcy sometimes being there and instead turned up the quiet lane. He was the last person she wanted to see.

She felt sorry for the disappointment that her rejection had inflicted. But his abominable pride! Last night, he had openly expressed his satisfaction in ruining Jane's happiness and had not denied his cruelty to Wickham. He was a selfish, prideful man. Elizabeth threw aside all the excitement his attachment had caused and allowed her offended feelings full reign over her thoughts.

After walking two or three times along the lane, she stopped at the gates to look into the park. She thought she saw a gentleman near the grove that edged it and instantly turned away. It was probably Mr Darcy, and her heart revolted against saying a word to him.

She was on the point of continuing her walk when she glimpsed another man moving toward her along the lane. A carriage was swiftly approaching from the other direction, and she stepped through the gate into the park to get out of its way. To her surprise, the carriage slowed by the gate, and the man in the lane quickly came up to her.

He was now close enough to recognise as the man she and Mr Darcy had seen on Wednesday. His nose was much misshapen, and he had a white clay pipe in his teeth. The way he advanced toward her with quick strides alarmed her.

"What do you want?" she called.

He gave no answer, but darted forward and grabbed her upper arms and dragged her toward the gate. Elizabeth shrieked and pulled away as sharply as she could. When that proved fruitless, she kicked at his legs, but that only made the man squeeze her arms harder.

The approaching carriage had stopped by the gate, with one man as postilion and another who jumped off the back and opened the door. She was being abducted!

Elizabeth screamed as loudly as she could.

Was Mr Darcy near enough to hear what was happening, or had he turned back into the park? She tried to drag her feet and pull away with all her might, but the man with the pipe was far too strong. They were now at the steps of the carriage, and Elizabeth kicked her feet against the second man who was trying to capture them and shove her legs inside.

Even though she continued to scream for help, she heard pounding feet, and the larger man holding her suddenly stumbled. Elizabeth realised that Mr Darcy had slammed into the man gripping her arms.

"Run," he cried.

The large man's grip had loosened, and she pulled free to escape, but he caught up to her in a few steps and yanked her back. He pressed her against him, her back to his chest, and Elizabeth fought and shrieked, until she realised that his other hand had pulled a knife that was now pressed to her throat.

"That is enough," he said through the pipe he still had clenched in his teeth. "Tell him to stop."

Mr Darcy had not noticed the knife, and he was tousling with the other man by the carriage whom he had knocked down. Elizabeth tried to speak, but panic made it impossible with a blade at her neck. The man holding her grunted in frustration and called, "Ho there!"

Mr Darcy glanced over his shoulder and started at what he saw. In this moment, the man on the ground jumped to his feet and pulled a pistol from his coat pocket. Elizabeth shrieked involuntarily, and the knife pressed a little harder. Mr Darcy stepped toward them, a hard look in his eyes, but stopped when the blond man he had knocked down by the carriage cocked the pistol.

"Now then," said the man with the pipe, "I only need *her*, but maybe I can take you as well. You might be worth something to him too. You and your betrothed stop fighting and screaming, and we can all get into the carriage without anyone dying."

Elizabeth saw the confusion flit across Mr Darcy's face, and they shared a quick look. Who needed her? And how could anyone have known he asked her to marry him, and why did they assume she had said yes?

Mr Darcy ignored all of this and said firmly, "You cannot take her."

The man flicked his wrist, and Elizabeth flinched in pain. She felt blood trickle down her neck.

"I can do whatever I damn well please. Like I said, 'tis only her ladyship's daughter I need. *You* I can do without."

They think I am Miss de Bourgh. They both had dark hair, and any young brunette at Rosings walking with Mr Darcy might be presumed to be his cousin Anne de Bourgh. Once they knew they had the wrong young lady, maybe they would let her go.

"I...I am—"

Mr Darcy shook his head, and the same moment the man with the knife yelled at her to "shut it."

She glared at Mr Darcy, but he was no longer looking at her. Mr Darcy was watching the man with the pistol, who held it firm and level just out of Mr Darcy's reach. Why should she not tell them they had the wrong woman? They might let them go, and no one would get hurt.

"What shall it be, Mr Darcy? Are you joining us, or do I have Colton put a bullet in your head?"

"Steamer, we don't need the rich cousin," the blond man with the pistol whined. "Let me just shoot him and go."

A sickening thought struck her. If they wanted Miss de Bourgh alive for some purpose, would they just as soon kill her too if they knew they had made a mistake? One man seemed eager to shoot Mr Darcy, and the other ambivalent at best. They might cut her throat if they knew they had blundered so dreadfully.

Elizabeth felt Steamer, the man with the pipe, shake his head. "He wants *her*, but maybe we can get more for the both of them, as long as he ain't much trouble."

The other man riding postilion had pulled a pistol as well and now aimed at Mr Darcy, but Mr Darcy could not see him, as he was facing away from the carriage.

"What shall it be, Mr Darcy?" Steamer called again. "Your cousin is coming with us, but what of you?"

"I will not let you take her."

Mr Darcy's eyes darted across the scene to the knife, to the pistol, and then back to her face. He shifted his stance, looking again at the blond man holding the pistol, and then looked back at her. He seemed to come to a decision, and a very stupid one at that. It looked to her like Mr Darcy was going to risk a bullet to stop the man with the pipe from abducting her.

Elizabeth shook her head, but she doubted he saw it. He might disarm the man called Colton, but he did not know the other man atop the horse was aiming a pistol at the back of his head.

"No!" she cried. "I will go with you, and Mr Darcy will let me go."

He threw her a look that seemed to say he would do no such thing. He might be a selfish man, one who ruined people's happiness, but he was trying to prevent her from being kidnapped. She would not let him get shot, not when it was clear she was about to be abducted no matter what they did.

"There is no need to shoot anyone," she added, staring hard at both men with the pistols, and Mr Darcy looked over his shoulder and recoiled at the sight of another pistol aimed at him. She watched Mr Darcy's shoulders fall as he held his hands out and open in resignation.

The knife point pressing against her neck slackened, and Steamer said, "Now then, Miss de Bourgh"—he let go of her and turned her roughly to face him—"if you would drink this, we can be on our way." He pulled out a bottle and handed it to her.

"What—"

"Laudanum. Take a swig and get in."

Laudanum was an opium tincture made with ten percent opium and ninety percent alcohol. To drink this would entirely dull her senses.

"Don't look indignant, missy. All the village gossip says you are a laudanum drinker."

She had never seen Miss de Bourgh take any, but that explained why Lady Catherine's daughter always seemed to be in a half-dazed state.

"I have no need of this," she said primly.

Steamer gave her a chilling smirk around his pipe. "I was not asking. Drink this so you don't fight us along the way. We want a pleasant ride, don't we?"

Elizabeth steadied her breathing. She had to stay alert, or as alert as her fear would allow. The laudanum would either make her sleep or not know what was happening if she stayed awake.

She held out the phial and said, "I already agreed to go with—"

"Drink it, or he shoots your betrothed."

The man named Colton stepped forward and pressed the barrel against Mr Darcy's head. He flinched but stood his ground, his gaze boring into Steamer with a righteous fury. Elizabeth saw the futility in any defiance; it would only cost Mr Darcy his life. Without blinking, she stared at Steamer and took a full drink. It was flavoured with cinnamon, but it still had a harsh, bitter taste.

She turned on her heel and marched to the carriage, not looking at anyone. She sat facing the horses, and Mr Darcy was about to sit next to her when Steamer shoved him across the carriage.

"No, you sit there," he barked, pointing to the other side.

"I will sit next to the lady."

Mr Darcy's tone and manner might have worked on most men, but not this one. Steamer pulled out the knife and drew back in a swift motion, and Elizabeth cried out, "Stop! Mr Darcy will sit wherever you tell him to. Mr Darcy"—she gave him an imploring look—"please do not give them a reason to leave you dead by the lane."

Steamer sat next to her, his bulk filling up all available space, and Mr Darcy sat directly across from her. Colton shut the door, and the carriage rolled as he hopped onto the back.

"You call your cousin and betrothed *mister*?" Steamer said. "I suspect you've not gone to bed together, either?"

Elizabeth felt her cheeks redden and avoided looking at Mr Darcy. She tried to remember how Miss de Bourgh had addressed him, as Darcy or as Fitzwilliam, but she could not recall a single time she had spoken to him.

"You could not expect Miss de Bourgh to address me so familiarly in front of you," Mr Darcy said in a strained voice. He gave her a quick look and then reached into his pocket. Steamer immediately went for his knife, but Mr Darcy only withdrew a handkerchief and handed it to her. Upon her questioning look, he pointed to his own neck and said, "You are bleeding."

As she blotted the blood, Steamer laughed. "'Tis nothing." He pointed to the bottle she still clutched in her hand. "Drink up, missy."

With a look at his knife, she drank again as the carriage jolted, spilling some of the reddish-brown liquid on her chin.

"Take some more. I hear you typically drink an ounce a day, and Markle might even give you more if you behave yourself."

"Who is Markle and why—"

Steamer cut off Mr Darcy's question by pointing the knife at him. "Village gossip said you were not much for talking, but I might cut out your tongue." He seemed satisfied by the way Mr Darcy angrily pressed his lips into a thin line. Turning to her, he said, "Tie that handkerchief over his eyes before I cut the both of you."

Although she doubted he would stab her to death since it appeared they needed her, she would not risk Mr Darcy being killed. Mr Darcy slid to the side to make room for her to sit next to him, but she still lost her balance as she tried to move across while the carriage swayed. She landed awkwardly, half on the seat and half in his lap. He caught her by the waist to keep her from falling to the floor while she threw out a hand around his shoulder.

She anxiously looked into his face as he fixed his eyes on her. Elizabeth saw there all the same fear that she now felt settling into the pit of her stomach. He gave her a firm look, and tugged her a little tighter and, to her surprise, it gave her some comfort to know Mr Darcy was with her, that she was not alone in this dreadful situation. She could not smile, but nodded and gave him a steady look as though to say she was as well as she could be.

"None of that now," Steamer barked.

They broke apart, and Elizabeth shifted next to him, her heart beating too fast. How foolish of her to be sent into a flutter by Mr Darcy's arm being around her.

"Cover his eyes."

"Stop provoking him," she said into Mr Darcy's ear, tying the knot, "or you will get yourself killed. Why even insist on sitting next to me?"

The blood and laudanum-stained cloth now covered his eyes. He could likely still see the light, but he would have no idea where they were going. *And in half an hour I will be too indifferent to care.* The swaying of the carriage was already making her feel sleepy.

"You just drank enough laudanum to knock you down, and you were getting into a carriage with a man who pulled a knife on you," he whispered, although she knew Steamer could hear. "I had to be near enough to prevent anything worse happening to you while you could not defend yourself."

Elizabeth started at the implication, but still shook her head over it, although Mr Darcy could not see her. She thought to mention that between the knife and the pistols he had not been able to defend her yet, but she supposed that would be unkind.

"Get back over here!" Steamer called.

She tried to move back across the carriage, but it rocked and she lost her balance again, jostling between Mr Darcy's shoulder and the side-glass.

"Oh, just sit over there!" Steamer cried.

She sat and shifted a little away from Mr Darcy, and she saw him stretch out his fingers toward her, then he closed them into a tight fist as though he had changed his mind. She had many reasons to hate this man, but now they would have to rely on one another in this terrifying situation.

Elizabeth leant back her head; she was a naïve user of laudanum and felt the effects already. She was drifting off to sleep, but before she did, she reached out and took Mr Darcy's hand in hers.

DARCY HAD THOUGHT HIS WORST LIFETIME MEMORY WOULD BE Elizabeth rejecting his proposal. Being told that he was the last man in the world she would ever marry had cut out his heart. The letter he wrote defending his conduct, the one still in his coat pocket, had been painful to write, and he had known that seeing her to deliver it would be a strain, but the pain of her words last night tortured him the worst of all.

I thought nothing could ever shock and wound me as much as being told I had not behaved in a gentleman-like manner.

And then he had heard Elizabeth cry out as two men tried to throw her into a carriage.

What wickedness and cruelty were at the root of their abduction? From a slight resemblance based on their hair colour and the fact that she had been seen with him, their abductors thought they had captured their object, but what did they want with Anne de Bourgh? His presence was a bonus, not necessary like Anne's. Ransom seemed a likely motive, but why her more than him? Both he and his cousin had fortunes, both had a wealthy earl as an uncle who could be pressed to pay, so why was she the preferred target?

Darcy's mind raced as the carriage rattled on. They had to escape, but that was impossible until Elizabeth woke up. He was still blindfolded, and about an hour ago, her grip on his hand slackened, and soon after that, her head dipped onto his shoulder. Leaving her behind to seek help was impossible—who knew what they might do to her?

He felt weak and unnerved that he could not protect her. He should have been able to stop them from taking her. What would the kidnappers do when they realised they captured the wrong woman?

They would have to get away before that happened, but they could not escape now. Not with being outnumbered and Elizabeth dosed with laudanum. The man with the pipe, Steamer, still sat across from them, but perhaps while he was distracted later, Darcy and Elizabeth could escape before Colton and the other man on the horse pulled their pistols.

Her head rested on his shoulder, and it was both reassuring to feel her so close since he could not see, and bitterly painful to know she did not want him at all. Not his hand, not his wealth, not his name and protection, not himself; she wanted nothing he had to offer.

Does it even matter if I explain why I was glad to separate her sister from my friend?

Perhaps it did not, but if they survived this trial, she still ought to know what matter of man her alleged friend Wickham was. It was not impossible that they could escape, and she would eventually return home to where her circle included the wickedest man in all of England. She was wrong about Wickham, but it struck him that she was entirely right about *him*.

Darcy's throat was tight with the strain of controlling his feelings. Painful recollections intruded, but it was better to think on those than dwell on the fear of what might happen when the carriage stopped. Grief at being rejected, guilt at not attempting to flatter the woman he wanted to marry, anger at the lies Wickham told all crossed his mind and had their moment of reflection.

He concluded that he had been selfish, in practice, though not in principle. Proud, conceited, selfish, and overbearing. It was a humbling realisation. His conduct toward Elizabeth, toward everyone, was unpardonable.

The carriage then slowed and stayed at this pace before making a few more turns and finally stopping. He felt a sickening sense of dread at what would happen to them now.

A hand roughly tore off his blindfold. Darcy pulled away, turning his head from side to side and blinking at the sudden brightness. His motions had jostled awake Elizabeth, whose bleary eyes slowly took in the scene. He wondered how drowsy and confused she was from the laudanum, but when she saw her hand was still holding his, she yanked it away.

He pushed down his disappointment as the door opened and Colton beckoned them out. Steamer pointed at Elizabeth to leave first, and she awkwardly moved past them to the door. Although she was careful about her footing, Colton did not offer her a hand for balance, and she tripped on the steps and fell onto her hands and knees. Worried what might happen to her if the horses stepped forward, Darcy tried to get out to help her up when Steamer gripped his shoulder.

"You stay where I can see you," he said around his pipe. "Colton will get her."

Colton's help extended so far as to gripping Elizabeth's elbow and hauling her up, and only when he was guiding her on stumbling feet toward a house near to the lane was Darcy allowed to leave the carriage. The man who rode postilion had drawn his pistol, and Steamer climbed down behind him and gave Darcy's back a shove.

"See to the horses, Conway, and send a message to Markle. And let him know we have another."

In the few steps it took to get to the house, Darcy looked around as much as he could. They were in what felt like a small village, but he did not recognise it. They had travelled a little more than an hour, so they were around ten miles from Hunsford, but they could have gone west into Surrey or be still in Kent for all he knew.

Ahead of him, Elizabeth was led into a timber-clad cottage that sat near to what might be the High Street. The other man led away the carriage. Darcy tried to see where the horses might be stabled, might anyone help them, was there an inn nearby, was there a signpost, but Steamer shoved him again, and he entered the house.

Immediately, his eyes sought Elizabeth. They had deposited her in a chair in a cluttered parlour, her typically pretty eyes now empty and lustreless. There were two rooms on the ground floor with beams projecting into the ceiling and a disarray of crates on the floor, and presumably there were offices at the back. He supposed there were only a few chambers upstairs. There was no place to hide in this small house if the opportunity came.

The man named Colton stood next to her and said to Steamer, "I will be at the tavern with Conway. We will be back when we hear from Markle."

Steamer nodded and took a spill from the vase by the fire to light his pipe. They were alone now with one captor, but Elizabeth was still not well enough to escape.

Darcy fought back frustration at Elizabeth's condition. It was not her fault she was too senseless to get away while Colton and Conway left for a drink.

"Help your cousin up the stairs," Steamer said through his pipe. "Kirby!" he hollered.

As they went up the stairs, a boy of about twelve met them at the top. He wore all black, and looked at Darcy and Elizabeth with some surprise. His shoes were scuffed and his hair unkempt, but although his clothes were a little large, they were new.

"Kirby, clear out and return to your mother's." The boy looked at them, and his eyes expressed the question he did not ask. "Never you mind. You had best stay with your mother for a few days."

"What about my books? If I bring them home, my mother will sell them."

"Is she still drinking gin?" Steamer asked.

"When is she not?" muttered the boy.

"Well, leave them here, and go on home."

Kirby gave a frustrated yet acquiescing sigh and approached the stairs.

"I am sorry for your loss," murmured Elizabeth. "For whom do you wear black?"

She had been leaning heavily on the railing, and Darcy had wondered what she was aware of. But even made drowsy by laudanum, even while abducted and afraid for her life, she wanted to console a little boy she did not know. Rather than answer, the boy turned red and ran down the stairs.

Steamer barked a humourless laugh. "We fit him in black in expectation of his father being hanged. Fortunately for you, missy, they sentenced him to two years in Newgate instead. Otherwise, Markle would have had me do something far worse than kidnap you."

Darcy felt his blood turn to ice, but Elizabeth did not react at all. Steamer opened the door to a room with a high porthole window where trunks, boxes, and books covered the floor in every direction. A bed and a washstand were scarcely reachable without tripping. The entire house seemed in an uncomfortable state of litter.

Elizabeth carefully stepped around the mess and made her way to the bed. She took off her bonnet, slipped off her shoes, took off her pelisse, removed her gloves, and left them all on the floor and sat against the headboard, her constricted pupils staring at nothing. Darcy hoped she would not become so sedated that her breathing slowed. Or stopped.

Darcy turned to the man at the door and said, "How long do you intend to—"

Steamer stepped into the corridor, slammed shut the door, and turned the key in the lock.

Darcy's sense of helplessness was devastating. He could do nothing but make sure Elizabeth kept breathing until the laudanum wore off.

Chapter Three

When Elizabeth woke up, she realised she was no longer in the carriage, but sitting on a bed in a cluttered room, and Mr Darcy sat on a box next to the bed. His greatcoat, hat, and gloves were piled on another box, her own things near to his. When she looked about, stretching her neck and trying to reason how she got here, Mr Darcy stood and peered into her face.

When she drew back, he said, "I want to look at your eyes." He said this so purposefully that she met his gaze. He nodded. "Your pupils are not as constricted as they were earlier."

"Have you been sitting there, watching me?"

He nodded. "I wanted to make certain you were breathing normally. I assumed you are not a regular laudanum user and"—he looked down—"I was afraid you might stop breathing."

The care in his voice struck her, and Elizabeth rubbed her eyes to avoid looking at him. "How long was I asleep?"

"You were not asleep," he said, pulling out a watch, "but I would say you have been insensible for two hours."

"No," she cried. "I must have been asleep."

Mr Darcy shook his head. "Your eyes were open, but you saw nothing, and it was plain that you did not hear me. Do you remember leaving the carriage?"

"I was insensible all that time?" She could hardly credit it, but he had no reason to lie to her. "Did you—did someone carry me in from the carriage?" She felt that she would have remembered something as intimate as that.

"No, you walked in on your own. They brought us to a small house in a village I do not recognise, and we are now locked in this cluttered room."

Elizabeth searched her memory for anything that happened after she drank the laudanum and blindfolded Mr Darcy. "I remember a boy in mourning clothes. Did that happen, or was it a hallucination?"

She was afraid of the answer, but he gave a half smile. "He was real. I think he had been squatting in this room, or at the least avoiding his mother's house by hiding in it. The room is a mess, but none of the belongings appear to be a boy's." She looked around and saw that someone had cleared a path to the door, to the box Mr Darcy had been sitting on, and around the bed.

Elizabeth walked to the small round window, but it was too far above her head to see out. She did not bother to try the door.

"How do you feel?" he asked.

"I am alert now."

"I mean, no other symptoms? Stomach not upset, you are not confused, dizzy?"

"How do you—" Elizabeth was about to ask how he knew so much about laudanum use when she remembered what their captors said in the park about Miss de Bourgh.

"Anne, if she takes too much," he said slowly, "her breathing becomes shallow. She often does nothing all day but loll about on the sofa, forgetting where she has left her things, falling asleep now and then, but on rare occasion she has stomach pain or does not breathe well. Mrs Jenkinson has ways of bringing her round, but there is always a fear that..." He blew out a breath and looked away.

"That she will stop breathing?" she whispered. He nodded. "I am surprised you speak openly about Miss de Bourgh's dependency. It is not the sort of thing one admits to outside of one's family."

"Well, until last night I thought you would be my family, so you must forgive my mistake."

He instantly turned away, noisily picking his way through a pile of papers and books stacked on a trunk on the other side of the room.

What an unyielding temper he had. Was he bitter at not having what he expected to have? Mr Darcy had wanted a wife, had asked, and had no anxiety that he would be accepted. What a hateful man. She crossed her arms and sat at the foot of the bed, determined not to speak a word.

Mr Darcy's back was still to her, but she heard him sigh. He idly opened a book and flipped the pages, but it was clear he was not reading a word. He was resentful, but there seemed to be genuine disappointment there, too.

She looked back with regret on the way she lost her patience with him when he proposed. He did have some affection for her, although it had taken her by surprise. She had supposed all his reasons against the match would quickly drive away his feelings, but perhaps she was wrong.

She had hurt him. It would do no good to pain him further, and certainly not now when their forced proximity would require them to get along.

"Mr Darcy, I am grateful that you came to my aid, that you were willing to be abducted with me. Despite your...former feelings..." This was painfully awkward. "I know you must hate me after what happened last evening—"

"Hate you?" He turned to pierce her with a look. His eyes were a pretty colour, more a rich amber than brown. If she had to admit what his eyes expressed, it looked to her that Mr Darcy did not hate her at all. His gaze held hers, and a warmth spread over her and settled in her stomach.

Her rejection wounded him, but he still looked at her with all the fondness a woman might wish for. She felt her cheeks heat, and she looked away. His affection and his wealth were not enough to reconsider her refusal. Mr Darcy was proud and selfish. He had separated Jane from Bingley and had blasted the prospects of Wickham, a man who had been brought up to expect the Darcys' patronage.

How could I trust a man as my husband who treats his friends in such a way?

After an uncomfortable silence, he said, "I have no intention of dwelling on the sentiments and offers that last night were so disgusting to you, so I shall only say that I do not hate you. We have more important matters at hand, and we ought to consider our options."

That was true, and yet she almost considered apologising for disappointing him. She settled for saying, "Before that, I must thank you for trying to prevent my abduction." Not that she believed that his resentment would go so far as to allow her to be harmed, but Mr Darcy had been willing to risk being shot and stabbed for the sake of a woman who disliked him.

He was more generous than she realised.

She hoped he heard the earnestness and gratitude in her voice, but he only bowed. "Our captors knew to look for Anne at Rosings, and knew she was slender and had brown hair, which must be how they mistook you for her. They also knew from village gossip that she is a laudanum user, and they knew she is expected to unite her family's fortunes by marrying me." Mr Darcy paced as he spoke; no simple task as littered as the room was.

Elizabeth wondered if Mr Darcy had told anyone at Rosings that he had asked her to marry him, but said, "But they did not know exactly what Miss de Bourgh looked like. So they had never met her nor seen a portrait, perhaps never been in the house itself."

He nodded. "A ransom seems the likely motive."

"Yes, so we must decide how to best manage ourselves until it is paid and they free us."

Mr Darcy looked puzzled. "Does it not strike you as odd that they chose her over me? They specifically wanted Anne, even though both of us have the same relatives who could be called upon to pay, and I have my own fortune at my disposal."

Elizabeth threw up her hands. "Who could guess? They likely thought a sickly woman an easier target than a hale and hearty young man. The man with the knife made an impulsive decision to take you along."

He tilted his head as though to say he acknowledged her point. "I suppose it does not matter, and we will not remain long enough to find out."

This made no sense to her. "What?"

"We will escape at the first opportunity. The man on the carriage, Colton, and Conway, the one with the horses, left to—"

"Wait, what? Escape?" She was incredulous. He could not mean it. "Have you run mad?"

"The other men are at a tavern awaiting news from whomever is behind the kidnapping. Steamer is the only one here, and we must make a plan on what to do if he unlocks the door."

She shook her head, disbelieving that so clever a man could be so foolish. "I will not cross them. It is madness to think we could get away."

"You got away once when I attacked him."

"I got a handful of steps before the man with the pipe grabbed hold of me again."

Mr Darcy came near, all energy and animation. "That was when I was fighting the other man, and they outnumbered us. If there is a time, like now, when there is only one, we have to overpower him and escape."

"I shall do no such thing!" she cried. "At the slightest provocation, that man pulls a knife." Elizabeth pointed to her neck, and Darcy winced. "And Steamer is a heartbeat away from stabbing *you*; he has made that very clear." Mr Darcy opened his mouth, but she spoke first. "What will he do in retribution if we fail? No, no, I shall do nothing to anger them."

"I tell you, we have to escape." He grasped her hand, startling her with his warmth, but she did not pull away. "You are right; these men are dangerous and won't hesitate to kill me. And we cannot assume that they would return you unharmed if the ransom is paid."

"I have a better chance of being unharmed if I do not cross them."

He dropped her hand and walked a few steps, shaking his head. "I am all astonishment! You mean to say you will not plan a way to escape? That if an opportunity comes, you will not take it?"

"We won't have a good enough opportunity that I would risk my life over. You may do as you please"—she sat on the edge of the bed—"but I intend to be compliant and give them no reason to stab me."

Mr Darcy gave her a pitying look. "They might kill you regardless, and I am certain killing me is likely. For whatever reason, it is Anne de Bourgh they want, not me."

She could see there was a greater threat to his life than hers, but it still did not warrant taking a heedless risk. As though they could get away from armed men determined to detain them. "But they did take you and admitted you might be useful. We will comply," she said firmly, "and stay alive, and then we will be returned."

Mr Darcy swore under his breath, quietly and harshly. She ought to have been shocked by it, but it made him likeable. He was typically so reserved it was a relief to see emotion from him, however little she agreed with his plan.

"I cannot understand why a sensible woman such as yourself cannot see the danger we are in."

"He said he would cut out your tongue!" she cried, standing. "He threatened to have the other man put a bullet in your head. I do understand the danger we are in. Do you think I want to watch you die, especially over some foolish desire to protect me?"

"You will have a scar on your neck from his knife. What else might you or I suffer? That is all the more reason to escape."

She shook her head, and Darcy swore again. "I am afraid to cross them," she admitted in a whisper. "Too afraid of what they will do to me and to you. I could not get away before. I tried, and he caught up to me and held a knife to me." She felt hot tears in her eyes and used her sleeve to dash them away.

There was no sense in crying now, hours after it happened. Mr Darcy gave her a compassionate look. For a moment, she thought he was going to put his arms around her, but he only put a hand atop hers, gave it a quick squeeze, and then let go.

It was foolish of her to want an embrace from a man she had told mere hours ago that he was the last man in the world she could be prevailed on to marry. Wanting comfort was just from the strain of being abducted, and Mr Darcy was the only one here. "Besides," she added, as though she had not stopped speaking, "I doubt we will have a chance to flee. I will comply with them, and you can do as you like."

He threw her a dark look. "You know very well I won't escape alone and leave you behind." He seemed to gather his patience. "Please, Miss Bennet, I shall ask one final time: will you attempt an escape if we can get out of the house?"

"Do you think I want to be responsible for your death if we fail?" Elizabeth wiped her eyes and tried to conquer her fear. "And if they recaptured us, it would likely be my fault. You are stronger and faster than I am, and you would come back for me if they captured me again. And then it would be my fault if they punished you for it."

"No, this is not your fault," he said quickly. "Nothing that *they* do is *your* fault. They do not even have the right woman."

"Do you think that would make me feel less guilty if they killed you before my eyes?"

She saw him stifle his feelings, whatever they were, and sigh. "Very well, we shall comply with our captors." He sat back down on the box next to the bed, crossing his arms over his chest. "Little though I like it," he added.

She remembered Colonel Fitzwilliam talking about how his cousin liked to have his own way. It made her angry on Jane's behalf all over again. She did not want to see harm come to Mr Darcy, but that did not mean she forgave him for all he had done to her friends. Mr Darcy must enjoy surrounding himself with tractable creatures.

It was unfortunate, then, that their being kidnapped together forced him into her company.

"How trying for you not to do as you like," she said, struggling to keep her patience. "You want to direct everything and everyone to your own liking, even your own kidnapping."

"I would choose us to not be stabbed or shot," he said sharply. "But I suspect that is not what you mean. Do you have more to say on the subjects you raised last evening?"

It was irritating that he had so easily understood her. Elizabeth shifted on the edge of the bed to better glare at him. "I do. I suspected you had been concerned in the measures taken to separate Mr Bingley and Jane, but I had attributed to Miss Bingley the principal design of them. Now I know it was all your doing."

Mr Darcy scoffed. "You can think on the separation of two young persons while kidnapped? While you are mistaken for another woman and your life threatened?"

He sounded incredulous. A heartless man like Mr Darcy would not understand how much easier it was to think on Jane and Bingley and other normal things while they held her in this small, cluttered room, after they had abducted her at knifepoint. There was no one to console her, no one to assure her all would be well, and it was better to distract herself by any means necessary.

Even if that meant arguing with the selfish man whose proposal she refused.

"We have nothing to do but wait," she said, looking round the room with an affected careless air, "but I doubt that you can explain yourself to my satisfaction, so we may sit in silence until our captors return."

He rose and went to his greatcoat, picking it up in a swift motion and reaching into a pocket. Then, he hesitated and tossed the coat back down and turned back to look at her. He stared for a long moment and seemed to come to a decision.

"I watched your sister and Bingley at the ball at Netherfield, after Sir William Lucas hinted that the neighbourhood expected their marriage," he said. "Her look and manners were open, but without any symptom of regard, and I was convinced that though she received Bingley's attentions with pleasure, she did not invite them by any participation of sentiment."

"You were wrong," Elizabeth cried, standing and pointing at him. "You acted selfishly, and from pride and caprice! She is heartbroken that he left."

"Then you are right, and I must have been in error." Elizabeth dropped her hand. Mr Darcy admitted to making a mistake in judgment. "If I was misled by such an error to inflict pain on your sister," he went on, "your...

resentment of me, of what I did next to separate them, has not been unreasonable."

She was struck by how he stumbled his words while considering her disliking him, and she wondered if she ought to refute it, even though she was still angry. He was more vulnerable than she realised.

"You were totally unsuspicious of Jane's attachment?"

"The serenity of your sister's air convinced me that her heart was not touched. I thought she had no affection for him, and would accept him only for any pecuniary advantage the match brought her and her family."

That sounded more like Mr Darcy's ill nature, and she was glad she had not told him that she did not resent him.

"Jane is all loveliness and goodness," Elizabeth said, forcing calmness into her voice. "Her understanding is excellent, and she would never marry without affection." She narrowed her eyes in disgust. "It was her having one uncle who is a country attorney and another in business in London that was your primary argument against the match."

"No," he cried, coming near. "I told you last night that, yes, her inferior connexions could not be desirable to a man of Bingley's situation—"

"Or yours, as you kindly told me—*during* your proposal."

He flinched, and it gave her a satisfaction that she was not proud of. "Or mine," he repeated quietly, "but I overcame that in my own case—little it mattered." He stared at her before continuing. "But in both instances, it was the behaviour of your youngest sisters and your parents that gave me greater pause."

She remembered how her family had behaved at the ball at Netherfield and turned away.

"The situation of your mother's family," he went on, "was nothing compared to that total want of propriety so almost uniformly betrayed by herself, by your younger sisters, and occasionally by your father."

Elizabeth sat on the bed again, feeling her cheeks heat in shame. The justice of Mr Darcy's charge struck her too forcibly for denial. Her sisters were wild for anyone in scarlet or too pedantic to be pleasant, her mother was vulgar, her father sarcastic. She had even wondered at the ball if her family had made an agreement to expose themselves as much as they could during the evening.

She covered her face with her hands and wished for all the world that Mr Darcy was anywhere else. He was right about her family, and it mortified her.

"I am sorry to pain you." He sounded apologetic. "I should add," he said hastily, "that you and your eldest sister have always conducted your-selves so as to avoid any share of that censure."

The compliment could not console her. She still refused to raise her eyes, but she could hear Mr Darcy rub his hand through his hair as he walked past her, back and forth, over and over.

Mr Darcy's judgment was wrong, and he acted wrongly, but Jane's disappointment had also been the work of her own complacent air and her nearest relations' behaviour. Their improper conduct had influenced his interference as much as his concern that Jane did not love his friend.

"Although I pointed out to Bingley the certain evils of such a choice," Mr Darcy said, "I do not know that it would have prevented the marriage, had it not been seconded by my assurance of your sister's indifference."

After a long stretch of silence he added, "I wanted to preserve him from an undesirable connexion, but more than that, I wanted to preserve him from an unhappy marriage."

It struck Elizabeth that she must have captivated and subdued Mr Darcy's heart for him to ask her to marry him. If he wanted his friend to be happy in his marriage, to be loved and respected, he undoubtedly wanted the same for himself.

He wanted a marriage of equal and ardent affections, and had thought he would find that with me.

"There is," he said, coming near, "one part of my conduct on which I do not reflect with satisfaction." He seemed about to sit next to her on the bed, but then changed his mind and stood before her. She was not ready to look into his eyes and stared instead at his shoes. "I concealed from Bingley your sister's being in town this winter. I knew it myself, as it was known to Miss Bingley, but her brother is ignorant of it. Perhaps this concealment was beneath me," he added softly.

She finally looked at him, standing before her in this dirty, crowded room, still looking imposing and noble even though he was a captive. But she could not see any hauteur, any arrogance in his face. He was not gloat-ing, satisfied in his success.

"I had thought you prideful and capricious," she said, feeling ashamed.

"It was not my pride, or caprice, that caused your sister to suffer, but my concern for my friend's happiness."

While she disagreed with his conclusions, she had misjudged his reasons. When she only stared, he added, a little stiffly, "On this subject I have nothing more to say, no other apology to offer. I wounded your sister's feelings, but it was unknowingly done."

His interference came from concern. Mr Darcy had thought he was acting in the service of a friend, and Elizabeth had to reconcile herself to his not being as hateful as she had always imagined.

"You are sorry for hurting my sister?" He nodded. "Then you should reunite them," she said softly. He raised his eyebrows in question, and she went on. "If—*when* we are released, you could confess all to your friend."

"He will be angry," Mr Darcy said with a sigh.

At least that was not an outright refusal. "If your friend loved Jane, tell him that you were wrong, that she did and still does cherish a tender affection for Mr Bingley." She tried to force cheerfulness into her voice when she said, "Any anger at your interference might be offset by the assurance that Jane loves him."

Mr Darcy gave a half smile. "Well, if we survive this ordeal—since we are to wait out our captors and hope for a safe release—then I will tell him I concealed your sister being in town these three months, and that I believe myself mistaken in supposing that your sister was indifferent to him."

She smiled at him in return. "We will survive the ordeal. A ransom will be demanded and paid, and we will be restored to our loved ones."

He did not look as though he believed it. "If you intend on complying and not escaping, then we shall have to assure our captors that you are, in fact, Anne de Bourgh."

After she assured him that she could, they lapsed into silence. She had been wrong about Mr Darcy's reasons, and as proud as he was, he had not been as unfeeling a friend as she had presumed. It pressed uncomfortably on her mind that he had lost his patience last evening when they were discussing Wickham rather than Bingley and Jane.

What if there was more to their history, too? She feared her friend Wickham's account of Mr Darcy was not entirely right. Was there a part of that story and Mr Darcy's motives that she likewise misunderstood?

If he spoke honestly about his interference with Jane and Bingley, perhaps he would answer if she asked about his relationship with Wickham. Before Elizabeth could speak, the lock turned in the keyhole, and the door opened.

Chapter Four

The last thing Darcy wanted to think about was rejected marriage proposals or failed love affairs or the defects in his own character. All of those subjects needed their moment of reflection and proper action, but now he wanted to fight whomever was about to open that door. If Elizabeth had been willing to risk escape, they might have planned what to do in this situation. They might have taken them by surprise, and then run into the village to find help and sanctuary.

Instead, over the past hour he had to address, in his own heart, how he had hurt a young lady who did not show her feelings, how he had lied to one of his closest friends, and that he had failed to flatter the woman he loved.

Elizabeth had stood when the lock turned, and Darcy shifted to stand in front of her. But instead of Steamer, a boy opened the door, the one in mourning clothes too large for him. He was awkward, not quite a little boy but not close to being a man either. He entered, and behind him a maid followed and placed a water pitcher on the cluttered washstand shoved into a corner.

As she lit two candles on the mantel, the boy said, "Steamer said I was to let in the daily girl. He is at the bottom of the stairs. He, he also said if you knock me down, he would come up here and..." The boy gave an embarrassed look to Elizabeth and then turned to Darcy. "He said he would stab you and then he would, to her..." He dropped his voice to a whisper. "Do I have to say it in front of the lady?"

Darcy shook his head, not daring to look at Elizabeth. This vague threat, delivered by a child, was alarming. It was not helping her point that they stay.

The maid edged around the boy, saying she would be back with the tray. The boy stayed by the open doorway and Darcy asked, "Why were we taken?"

The boy shrugged, and Darcy wondered if he was lying or truly did not know.

"Who is in the house now? Who lives here? What village are we in?"

The boy looked out the door and shook his head. Steamer might have told him not to answer questions. Darcy tried to check his impatience at being so entirely out of control.

"Are we occupying your room?" Elizabeth asked in a pleasant voice that felt unsuitable for the situation. The boy shrugged again, but this answer seemed to convey that he did not mind rather than that he did not know. "I am sorry to have taken your space. Where must you stay now?"

"My mother's. She is the barmaid at the Old Bell. We have rooms upstairs, but Colton and Conway stay there when they come to the village, so I have to sleep in the offices in the stable now."

Darcy shared a look with Elizabeth over the boy's head. She gave a quick nod, understanding that he wanted her to keep him talking.

"'Tis a shame you have lost your room both here and there. Why is there no other space in this house for you?" He shrugged. "How many others live here?"

"Just Steamer, when they are in the village. My uncle stays at the tavern when he passes through."

"Is your uncle Mr Markle?" Darcy asked as gently as he could.

The boy nodded, ducking his head.

After a silence, Elizabeth tried again. "Do you see him often? Is he expected soon?" One might have thought she was hosting a morning at home and making chat with the neighbours.

The boy pushed up the sleeve of a coat that was too long. "I don't know. Colton sent a messenger, but Mamma and I have not seen him since" —his voice dropped—"my father..."

"I am sorry for your loss," Elizabeth said. Darcy knew she had forgotten talking with the boy while she was under the influence of laudanum.

"He is not dead, like Steamer said," the boy answered defensively, "just gone. I like the clothes because they are new, and clean." After a pause, he said, "My uncle bought them when my father was captured—we all thought he would be hanged—but he is only in Newgate." He rubbed a hand across his sleeve, looking at it. "I enjoy having a new coat."

"Perfectly reasonable," Elizabeth said, nodding. This was the most he had said thus far. "Are your father and uncle gone often? What line of work are they in?"

They were interrupted as the maid entered with a tray and looked around, undoubtedly wondering where to put it in a room that had not one flat, uncluttered surface. She looked to the boy to direct her, but he did not understand her looks and she simply laid the tray on the floor next to the bed.

"You were saying what your father and uncle do?" When the boy only looked at his feet, Elizabeth asked, "Do you want to go into the same line of business?"

"I don't want to be a free trader," he whispered.

Elizabeth turned to give him a questioning look, but Darcy shook his head. The boy seemed nervous, and whatever a free trader was, he did not want to discuss it.

The maid left, and the boy fidgeted with the key. Darcy saw him look toward the detritus. He followed his gaze to a pile of books. "Did you want to take a book with you?"

The boy's expression shuttered, and he shrugged again.

"If they are your things, you must take them," Elizabeth added, smiling.

"No. Mamma would only sell them if she saw them. My uncle lets me read in the kitchen when he comes." He scuffed at the floor with the toe of his shoe. "Steamer mocks me if he sees me reading."

"Well, if you like to read, then you must come as often as your mother can spare you."

The boy scoffed. "She is drunk on gin half the time. She won't notice if I am gone or—"

"Kirby!" Steamer roared up the stairs. "How long does it take to lock a door?"

The boy flinched, and Darcy wondered if he was likely to be struck. He ran through the door and turned the lock. They heard his feet pounding down the stairs two at a time.

Elizabeth perched on the edge of the bed again. "He does not seem to know anything about us."

Darcy agreed. "He told us a few things. No one lives in this house, wherever we are. The other men take rooms at the tavern. Steamer sleeps here sometimes, and this man Markle is rarely here."

She nodded. "They do not keep a maid; they must have someone from the village to come in when they are here. But what purpose does the house serve if a boy spends his idle hours reading here and no one regularly lives here?"

"A better question is why are we being held here, and how long do they intend to keep us."

Elizabeth shrugged and rose to stretch her arms over her head. She looked around for some place to walk and sighed in frustration. "He appears to not be wealthy, and his father a criminal and his mother a drunk."

"I am more interested in the uncle and why the father is in jail. It might be behind our kidnapping. While you were under the influence of laudanum, Steamer said that if Kirby's father had been hanged, far worse would have happened to Anne than merely being kidnapped."

He said this to convince her to escape, and hopefully not frighten her more than she was, but Elizabeth only threw up her hands. "What could Miss de Bourgh possibly have to do with a gang of criminals?"

Darcy rubbed his face, desperate to pace but trapped by the clutter and the tray on the floor. "Maybe it is more a punishment to Lady Catherine? Injuring Anne injures her. But I have no idea what Steamer's or this Markle's connexion with her ladyship could be."

He did not expect an answer, and Elizabeth had none to give. After a silence she asked, "Am I to understand they sent a message to this Markle and are awaiting his reply?"

Darcy nodded. "It sounded from the boy that they are expecting him in person."

"So, they have sent no message to your aunt yet? They are waiting for this Markle? Why would they not demand a ransom immediately?"

"To show they are the ones in control. Or Steamer can take no further action without consulting this other man."

Elizabeth fell onto the bed, looking oppressed. "When do you think everyone will know we are missing?"

Darcy thought back over the morning. "They took us around eleven. I left Rosings at ten thirty to find—" There was no point in mentioning his letter of explanation now. "I left for a walk at half ten, but it will be a while before anyone worries for me. Fitzwilliam and I intended to take leave from the parsonage today, but if he cannot find me, he will just go alone. Likely, no one will be alarmed until I fail to dress for dinner."

"Those at the parsonage will be worried for me by now, although I often take a long walk. Mr Collins will call at Rosings to express his alarm before you are known to be missing." She sounded extremely worried.

"There will be a great cry when we are discovered to be gone," he agreed.

She was giving him a look he could not understand. Why did she look so distressed now? "And what will everyone at Hunsford think when they realise we are both gone?" Her voice raised in pitch.

"They might think we suffered an accident or—"

She leapt to her feet. "If there is no message from our abductors, they might think we have run off together!"

Darcy struggled for composure at her horrified tone. "Well, you will certainly disavow them of that notion after they free you. I suspect you will be quick and confident with your assertions that you would never, ever throw yourself under my power, leave all of your friends, and elope with the likes of one you hate."

He turned away, trying to put some distance between them, and almost tripped over the tray. He was tempted to kick it and let out a curse, but stepped over it to sit on the side of the bed with some of his dignity in place. As though this situation was not dreadful and frightening enough, he was now trapped in close quarters with a woman who not only refused him, but detested him.

After a few awkward minutes had passed, he felt a gentle hand on his arm. "I do not hate you," she said, and he felt the heat of her touch through his sleeves. It made his heart beat a little fast. "I admit I was wrong in assuming the worst of you regarding Jane and Bingley, and you seem willing to correct that error." Before he could agree, she dropped her hand and added, "I still feel that you have been arrogant in all of your dealings with those outside your circle, and have a selfish disdain for their feelings as well, but please do not think I hate you."

Darcy shifted on the bed to look at her, feeling indignant. "If people will make me out to be so proud and selfish, they are very welcome, and I shall take the liberty of caring very little about it." When had he ever been concerned about what other people, what strangers, thought of him? She opened her mouth, but he interrupted her, saying, "And how disdainful of others' feelings could I truly be if I will risk my friendship with Bingley for the sake of your sister's happiness?"

"You were disdainful of Mr Wickham's feelings," she murmured.

When would his animosity toward the man who nearly ruined his sister settle into a cool indifference? "This is not the time to talk about that man, and I will thank you not to mention his name again!"

His severe reply silenced her, but he knew he had not been completely honest. Although he rarely cared what strangers thought of him, he had already conceded that she had not been wrong about his nature. About Wickham, she was completely wrong, but Darcy knew that she had been right about his own manner.

"I realise, Miss Bennet, that I have for all my life been wishing to think meanly of others' sense and worth compared with my own, and I know I ought to do better by them." He addressed his next words to the wall in front of him. "I do not deserve that you have taken so marked a dislike to me, but I assure you that your words, 'Had you behaved in a more gentleman-like manner' have made an impression on me." He gave a wry laugh. "I might even say tortured me, but hyperbole seems inappropriate given what has happened to us."

At the foot of the bed, Elizabeth fell onto her back, her feet tapping against the floor, looking at the ceiling and not at him. "You are right," she said. From where he sat on the side of the bed, he now had a clear view of her face. "You could not be so selfish if you will confess all to Mr Bingley based only on my say-so. My dislike of you was based on something trivial, never amended as I knew you better, and it was wrong of me. I am sorry."

"What," he asked haltingly, a little afraid of the answer, "what was the basis of that dislike?"

"First impressions, you know, are generally longest remembered."

Darcy clearly remembered the first time he spoke with Elizabeth beyond common courtesies. "I did not have courage enough to speak to you until a party at Lucas Lodge." He could not remember saying anything offensive to her that evening. He had even asked her to dance.

She gave a little laugh. "For one so resolute, someone with such clear opinions, you lacking the courage to do anything surprises me. We did not *speak* at the assembly in Meryton, but you did look at me, and—"

"I remember. You were watching the dancers."

He had felt something when she looked at him then, sitting alone and not dancing—and she was just as pretty as Bingley had said. He had not wanted to dance, he had not thought her deserving of his notice, but he had still felt *something*. An initial attraction, perhaps, something he had later thought was a genuine connexion.

"Yes, but I should tell you that most of the room disapproved of you by then. I was not alone in thinking you acted as though you were above your company."

"I remember what you said at Rosings," he said flatly. "Apparently, my dancing only four dances was a great crime."

"The greater crime was declining being introduced to any other lady and speaking only to your own party. You were decided to be the proudest, most disagreeable man in the world."

"And this is why you said that from the first moment of our acquaintance..." He did not want to repeat the words she had said. Hearing them only once had imprinted them into his brain forever.

"No," she said through a sigh. "This paints me as a vain creature, Mr Darcy, so be prepared for what little remains of your affection for me to be driven away. You then looked at me, as you remember, then coldly withdrew your gaze to say to your friend, 'She is tolerable; but not handsome enough to tempt *me*; and I am in no humour at present to give consequence to young ladies who are slighted by other men.' That left me with no cordial feelings toward you, but I regret how I allowed that to cloud my judgment."

Conscious and ashamed, Darcy sat back. Ashamed that he had thought such a thing and ashamed for having said it. He was sensible now of the extent of what his own actions had cost him.

"I am damned sorry I said something so unkind," he said gently, "and so untrue. There is no excuse for it."

Still lying on the bed, she turned her head just enough to look at him. "No, I was vain. Mortifyingly vain—"

"I think you very handsome," Darcy said quickly. "You might not believe me, but within a month of knowing you—" He leant a little closer, balancing on his hand so he could better see into her face. "Once I had taken proper notice of you..." He could hardly say what he thought of her eyes, her figure, her playful manner now. "You are a handsome woman, and nothing excuses my shocking rudeness."

Elizabeth's cheeks turned pink as she turned on her side, propping her head up on her hand. "It would speak all the worse of me if I was now flattered to be thought handsome when I held such a grudge for being thought just tolerable."

"But that is what I failed to do," he said. "I *ought* to have flattered you when I asked you to marry me. I ought to have aimed to please a woman who is indisputably worthy of being pleased."

He heard her gasp. "Well, I am sorry for how uncivil I was last night, and for holding a grudge against you for your neglect at the assembly." She gave a weak smile. "We have more important concerns right now, and everything about that assembly, at least, ought to be forgotten."

"I did not remember precisely what I said, but I believe your version of events. I can imagine it being the sort of thing I would say, and am resolved not to be that manner of man in the future." His heart was beating faster when he added, "But most clearly, I remember your eyes, with a kind of teasing smile in them."

They were very near to one another now, stretching across diagonal sides of the bed, their faces nearly meeting at the middle. He wondered if she would as soon forget his proposal, and if, should they survive their kidnapping as Elizabeth felt certain they would, there was any way he could earn her good opinion.

Elizabeth's gaze dropped to his mouth and then slowly lifted back up to meet his eyes. Darcy was certain all the air was driven from his lungs. He opened his mouth to speak, but she then blinked and sat up, standing from the bed and looking every which way until her eyes landed on the tray.

"We should eat something, don't you think?" she said in a high voice. "I doubt they will poison us, and who knows if they intend to feed us again."

He gave her a long look, but it was clear she would not acknowledge what he was sure they had both just felt. Silently, he rose and looked at the tray near his feet. A teapot and two cups were next to two crockery pots and some spoons. There was no space to arrange the boxes into chairs and a table, and Elizabeth must have realised the same because she sat on the floor by the tray and arranged her skirts around her.

"What do you think they brought us?"

Darcy picked up one pot and poked at it with a spoon. They were clearly not to be trusted with anything sharp. "Potted something." He scraped aside the butter and tasted it. "Salmon, I think." After swallowing, he said, "I think it has been kept closer to months than weeks."

Elizabeth gave a pained smile and tried her own. "I think mine is a small bird, but I cannot tell which one."

"Would you like to trade?" he asked, holding out his with a wry smile.

She wrinkled her nose. "Neither will be good. It is the sort of thing we would bring to eat in the carriage."

He nodded. "It brings back memories of changing horses at an inn."

Elizabeth poured tea for them both from a chipped pot. "They have left us no sugar, I am afraid."

"I do not take sugar in tea or coffee."

"Do you fear for your teeth? I rarely see them, but I would say they look rather good."

He was being teased, but he answered truthfully. "I am so harrowed by statements of West Indian slavery that I have given up taking sugar."

Her playful expression fell. "The slave trade has now ended, thank goodness, but the practice is still in place. Slavery, however it may be modified, is still slavery."

"And it is much to be regretted that any trace of it should exist in countries dependent on England. My parents joined the abolitionists, and Pemberley prohibited sugar years ago."

"You have entirely given it up? I am trying to recall if I have seen you eat custard or a tart or a cake."

"I only buy sugar from the East Indies. I cannot be so particular when I am eating at someone else's home and harass my hostess about her desserts, but I can at the least refuse the sugar they put on the table."

"And if someone asks you why you take no sugar, I am certain that you would answer."

Elizabeth was giving him an approving smile. Darcy realised he was not accustomed to receiving such a look from her. "Lady Catherine claims she only uses East India sugar, but she is more concerned with appearing to be aligned with that cause rather than having any strong feelings on the cause itself. It is not as though one can tell by the taste where the sugar comes from."

"Do you think she puts a great deal of sugar in her cherry brandy?" she asked, laughing.

He made a face, and she laughed a little more. The memory of Lady Catherine's awful brandy made the potted whatever it was taste more tolerable. "Let us hope she never takes it into her head to make elder wine or mead," he said drily. "I highly doubt the amount or origin of the sugar is that brandy's problem."

"Since you are so principled, you must have few cakes at Pemberley. East India sugar is expensive."

He smiled. "You would be amazed what my cook can produce with honey."

"You have a sweet tooth?" She seemed amused, as though she had discovered a secret. "Do you have many beekeepers?"

"Just Charles Farber and his son. Their family has four acres for tending the bees, and has done so for several generations. His grandson, I am told, has no interest in the tenancy, but he is about three and terrified of being stung. I can suppose his opinion will change."

She laughed again, and Darcy was charmed by her amusement.

"You must have hundreds of people in your care." He nodded. "And you know their internal characters and circumstances in addition to their manners of business?" He nodded again, and Elizabeth fell quiet, giving him an appraising look with a soft smile.

After a stretch of silence while they finished their food she said gently, "They will all worry for you, when they hear what has happened."

Darcy set down his teacup carefully. "Let us hope that by the time anyone at Pemberley, or Longbourn, hears about this, we will already be on our way home to our loved ones."

She gave a confident nod, but Darcy felt unsettled. By now, Rosings and the parsonage knew they were gone, and even if they did believe for the rest of the day that they had run off together, a subsequent message from this Markle would make the truth of their abduction known.

And I still have little reason to believe they will return us alive.

Chapter Five

There was something equally charming and odd about sitting on the floor and sharing a meagre meal with Mr Darcy. They talked about their homes, their friends, books and music, and even what dessert each liked best. Elizabeth saw more of his wry sense of humour that she had only recently seen hints of, and he talked fondly of his sister and cousin. He was attentive, listened more than he spoke himself, but was quick with an astute reply when he did speak.

She enjoyed talking with him—he was clever and well-informed—and it was far better to have a discussion and distract herself as best she could from the fact that they were locked in this small, miserable room.

Mr Darcy rose to put the tray nearer to the door, but it did little to give them more space. Elizabeth looked round and realised that the room was rather dark; she asked him to check his watch and was surprised that it was only seven.

"I think it is because of the window," he said, pointing to the small oeil-de-boeuf window near the ceiling. "The sun has dropped below it. There are only a few candles; we shall not have much light in another hour." He peered out the window for a moment, but it was too high even for him to see anything but sky. "I know you won't discuss a plan for escape, but we ought to consider what is to be done once we face this Mr Markle."

"You mean how to assure our captors that I am Miss de Bourgh?"

He blew out a long breath before saying, "I am afraid they will kill us both if they learn they kidnapped the wrong woman."

"I need not convince them for long," she said confidently, "and it is clear they knew little about your cousin, or even what she looks like other than she has dark hair."

"Steamer and the other two might not know her, but we do not know what this Markle knows."

"It will not be difficult to pretend to be Miss de Bourgh," she said, forcing brightness into her voice, "if they know anything about her manner, they must know she is often silent. I can defer to you if they ask me anything I cannot answer. Most men assume a woman will be meek. Or I shall pretend to be too frightened to reply."

Mr Darcy gave her a penetrating look as he sat on the box near the bed. "Is that not likely to happen? Because I feel no shame in admitting the truth of it in my own case, and I still think we need to be ready to escape if the right moment comes."

She had to reply without showing one symptom of the fear that might overpower her if she thought of it. "I do not think we will have that chance, and I will not risk not getting away and suffering further punishment." She steadied her breathing. "Mr Darcy, I am not going round and round with you again."

She saw him struggle to keep his patience before giving a nod of agreement. After watching the small features of his face shift and change, Elizabeth realised he was not impatient with her. Or at least, not only impatient with her. Mr Darcy struggled with being inactive, in having no control, and in having nothing at all to do but wait in fear.

She had to cheer him and keep his attention occupied. "Our time is better spent telling me about your cousin so I can pretend to be her."

"She is as you saw her at Rosings," he said, throwing up his hands. "Mute, overly demanding of the servants, and unconcerned with any conversation happening around her."

Elizabeth could not disagree with any of that. "Is there anything they might expect from Miss de Bourgh, something she might know or have an interest in, that I ought to be able to speak on?"

"Anne is a laudanum drinker," he said sadly, "with no inner life. She rides in her phaeton, but does not drive it herself. She has never had to express an opinion because her mother does it for her. She does not apply herself to anything and has never wanted to—as best as I can tell, for she says so little for herself."

Elizabeth regretted thinking that the sullen woman would have been a good match for Mr Darcy. He needed someone to draw him out in conversation, to give him a little liveliness. She twisted her fingers, not liking the settling realisation that someone with her play of mind and willingness to give her opinion would have suited him well.

After sitting a while in silence, she at the foot of the bed and he on the box, he finally said, "Our captors will almost certainly write to Lady Catherine, and given the uproar our absence will have caused, she will of course then realise that they took *you* by mistake."

"Do you think she might not pay?" she asked, not believing it. It would take years, but her father would pay back Lady Catherine.

Mr Darcy sighed. "I think she would, and she would want to be thanked for it by everyone she meets for the rest of her life. She adores being of use, and saving the two of us and being able to boast of it would appeal to her." He looked away. "I cannot believe my aunt would not pay, but the fear is still there."

There was still the disturbing possibility that everyone at Rosings might think they had eloped. "Does anyone know that on Thursday you intended to..."

It took him a moment to understand her hint. He even blushed a little. "No," he muttered. "No, I told no one."

"That is good news. Lady Catherine would not pay for my return if she thought you had at one time intended to present me to her as her future niece." She added a weak laugh but with little feeling behind it.

"I do not want to believe my aunt capable of such cruelty, even if you had accepted me."

He said it plainly, calmly, but she heard the disappointment in his voice. Did he still wish that she had accepted him?

What might my answer have been had he not wronged Jane, had he not been arrogant, if he had not called me 'tolerable'? She looked at him, but he avoided her eye. It did not matter that he was handsome, clever, and not as selfish as she had thought. She could not forget that a significant shade of Mr Darcy's character was unfolded in the recital she heard from Wickham.

Any man who wilfully deprived someone who had been brought up to depend on his family's patronage was depraved. She could never commit herself into the care of a man capable of that.

But thus far Mr Darcy had proven himself to be loyal, considerate, and not at all like a man who would even treat an enemy the way he treated Wickham. Who was the real Mr Darcy? The one she had seen today, the one who wanted to be a better man, the one she found herself enjoying knowing better—or the one Wickham said ruined his prospects out of jealousy?

She was not about to mention Wickham now, however; not after the way Mr Darcy had silenced her before Kirby came in. Now was not the time for an argument. To avoid any further mention of Wickham, Mr Darcy's proposal, or whatever his feelings were, Elizabeth changed the subject. "What if they ask a grand sum, one Lady Catherine might not be able to pay for the cousin of her parson?"

"My uncle, Lord Fitzwilliam, will pay," Mr Darcy said.

Elizabeth felt herself breathing faster. "For *you*. What if Lady Catherine writes to Longbourn to ask for the money rather than front the money herself? My uncle Gardiner might be able to spend a few thousand to recover me, but not my father." She knew she was talking faster but could not help it. "We have no money—you know that—and what if the kidnappers will not wait while Lady Catherine arranges for anyone connected to me to come up with the money?"

Mr Darcy rose from his seat and took her hand. For a long while he said nothing; he simply held it, gently stroking his thumb back and forth. His touch was a comfort, an anchor in her swirling sea of fear and confusion. She felt herself calm, and the wave of panic receded.

"We cannot control any of that," he said, "and worrying will do us no good. There are people who will pay the ransom, even though they will know it is for *you* and not Anne. And you cannot think that I will not do everything in my power to convince these men that *I* will pay for your release." He gave her hand a squeeze before letting go. She missed its warmth immediately. "We have other things to think on that we *can* control. Now, are you ready to answer to the name Miss de Bourgh? You are twenty-nine, you are an heiress, and you cannot exert yourself to do anything."

She recovered enough to smile a little. "Are you ready to call me Anne instead of Miss Bennet?"

"I shall do my best, although aside from your hair colour, you bear no likeness to such a dull creature."

She knew what he was doing. "How uncivil of you to say," she said, endeavouring not to laugh. "How does she address you?"

"She has called me 'Darcy' since we were children, even while alone, rather than 'Fitzwilliam'. And I do not think she has begun a conversation with me in nearly as long."

That did not bode well for a happy union. "Everyone believes you will marry her, you know."

"Everyone?" he repeated. Elizabeth realised he meant that *she* knew better, and she felt her cheeks burn. "Lady Catherine certainly believes it and speaks of it as often as she can to whomever will listen. My family wants to believe it, although after my parents died, I told them all that I would not marry her. I even told Anne." He thought for a moment. "Fitzwilliam knows I won't marry Anne. I think he guessed that I admired —well, it is no matter. Despite my family's wishes, I have no intention of marrying Anne, and they refuse to accept it."

"In a prudential light it is a good match. Your second son inherits Rosings, and Miss de Bourgh is already an heiress of tens of thousands of pounds."

"If one looks at marriage as a balance sheet, it seems perfectly reasonable, and as a child I suppose I had been conditioned into thinking I would grow up to marry Anne." Mr Darcy shook his head. "But when I was old enough to realise what a life association meant, I shrank from the prospect."

His expression made it look like he had actually been repelled. "The pressure from your family to marry her must be great." She realised Mr Darcy was serious when he mentioned the family obstacles to overcome if he married *her*.

"It is a good match for my *family*, but not a good match for my happiness, and fortunately, I am not in a situation where practicality and finances must be the deciding factor." He gave her an earnest look as he came nearer. "Anne is a brittle shell: shatter her, and she is empty inside. Some might say the money, the connexion, the family approval, it would all make it worthwhile. But I could never bear it."

"Of course not." There was no chance of him forming a rich life with Miss de Bourgh. Now that she was paying attention to Mr Darcy—forced into paying attention—it was plain how unhappy he would be with a woman like his cousin. "There is no true partnership there, and a person like you would be miserable in an empty union."

"You are not such a person either." He said it like he knew it to be true, down to his bones.

"No," she whispered. She had refused two respectable offers—one splendid, if she were honest—because she did not love or admire the men who asked her. But now, despite whatever it was that had caused his terrible breach with Wickham, she felt she could now respect Mr Darcy.

"What manner of marriage do you want?" he asked tenderly.

The room was now dim, and Mr Darcy was standing very near to her. He might have the right to ask her to marry him, but she had the right to refuse, and there was nothing else about his proposal to discuss. The matter was closed. But something about the room, their isolation, their frightening situation, it all combined to make her want to answer his impertinent question.

"My parents have no affection for one another, and no respect, either. My mother was attracted by security and status, and my father by a pretty face. They live in the same house, but there is nothing between them, Mr Darcy." He touched her arm, running his hand up and down as a slight reassurance. She was uncertain he even realised he had done it. "They have given up on one another, and their daughters suffer for it. We have no means of support after my father dies, and little guidance or attention while they are still with us. I would never want a union like theirs."

He nodded slowly. "You must have always known that you needed someone who would see you as their equal partner."

"I want someone who will respect me, someone I can trust to take care of me." The truth had burst forth from her heart. "I want to be treated with dignity in public and in private, and I want someone who I can trust will have as much admiration and love for me in twenty years as he does on the day we marry."

"And someone you can love and respect in return."

His gaze never left hers, and her breathing hitched. In this moment, she wanted to believe that he was such a man. Mr Darcy's chest rose and fell, and she wondered what he was feeling as his amber eyes pierced hers. If he leant down and kissed her, would she put her arms around him and kiss him back?

Elizabeth turned her head, and the moment was gone. Why would she presume that Mr Darcy was the type of man who would respect and confide in his wife? He cleared his throat and stepped away, and she busied herself with lighting another candle with a spill from the vase. Her flustered movements made it take three tries.

What was she thinking, imagining kissing Mr Darcy? All thoughts of affection following the esteem she was beginning to feel for Mr Darcy had to be pushed aside. Someone had kidnapped them for ransom, and she still did not feel brave enough to ask what had happened between him and her friend Wickham.

The air still felt thick when she felt ready to face him. He was looking at his watch when he said, "We should try to sleep."

"It is not that late."

To her surprise, he started untying his cravat. "I am too worried to read whatever books are here in what little light we have, and I do not want to talk any longer." He tugged sharply, and the linen snapped in his hand.

This did not feel like a slight against her, although if he had said such a thing in a drawing room yesterday, she would have been insulted. Maybe he did not want to talk about what they both wanted in a marriage partner.

"Besides," he went on, taking off his shoes, "we do not know when that door will open or what will happen when it does. It has been a terrifying day, and whatever sleep we can get would do us both some good."

That made sense, but she was distracted by Mr Darcy arranging the pillows. He tossed one to the far side of the bed and placed the other nearest to him. She suddenly realised what he intended to do. "You should sleep on the floor," she cried.

He gave her a look as though she were stupid. "There is literally not enough space to lie down anywhere in this small, crowded room but there," he said, pointing at the bed.

"I do not want to sleep next to you."

Mr Darcy looked up from his coat buttons in complete shock. "Are you afraid of me?" he asked, incredulous.

Her stomach dropped. "No!" The thought had never crossed her mind that he would harm her. "I simply am not in the habit of sleeping next to a *man*." How could he be so calm about sharing a bed? "Is it your habit to often sleep next to women?"

Mr Darcy said nothing, only tilted his head slightly, and the unintended meaning behind her impulsive retort flashed across her mind. This was now a thousand times worse, and if the entire house fell down around her at this moment, she would not mind it at all.

"Well, Miss Bennet," he said deliberately, "if you had given me a different answer last evening, that might be a question I would consider answering."

She was absolutely certain her cheeks were on fire, but there was nowhere to hide and no way to avoid him. She could not grow nervous. She had to show a little courage, if only to prove to herself that she would survive this ordeal with her dignity.

"You are right that this is the only sensible place for us both to sleep, but you could be a little kinder," she said, trying to sound calm. "How many single women find themselves having to sleep next to a man, let alone one whose proposal she refused?"

Mr Darcy did not answer. He had removed his coat, and seemed to debate what else to remove, his hand hovering near his waistcoat buttons. Her heartbeat darted in those few seconds, and she wondered what his arms and chest looked like under his shirt. In the end, he only removed the pocket watch before forcefully pulling back a corner of the blanket that covered the bed.

She saw how his complexion had reddened when he finally looked at her. The pause was, to Elizabeth's feelings, dreadful.

"If you think I am not as affected, as distressed, to be here with you in such an intimate way, then it is a good thing that you refused me because you do not know me at all."

He got in, turned his back to her, and wished her good night.

She felt absolutely stunned, and she was determined not to climb into the bed until she was certain Mr Darcy was asleep. She would wait for hours, and she perched on the edge of the bed, staring at the flickering candles.

She would never have guessed what emotions and passions lay beneath Mr Darcy's unbending pride.

There was no doubt of his having superior abilities and understanding. And he was not as ill-tempered as she had previously thought. But aside from the complete awkwardness of the situation keeping her awake, Elizabeth was distracted by the fact that Mr Darcy had a temper to love, and she had been too late to see that he also had a temper worthy of being loved.

It was a shame that he had done such a despicable thing to Wickham. But how could Mr Darcy be friends with an amiable man like Bingley, speak so affectionately about his sister, go to such lengths to try to protect her from their kidnappers, if he was as selfish and hateful as she previously thought?

I like him.

Elizabeth chanced a quick look at him, but he was still turned away from her. She could not reconcile the man lying on the bed behind her who had ruined Wickham's prosperity with the man who spoke so endearingly about the sort of life partner he wanted.

When she knew Mr Darcy slept from the deepness of his breathing, she blew out the candles. Somehow, even from here she sensed the relaxation of his body.

Still wearing all of her clothes but her shoes, Elizabeth laid on top of the bed and stayed as close to its edge as she could. In all of her immodest and curious imaginings of sleeping with a man, of him lying atop her, and whispering and doing all manner of bold things, she had never imagined the man being Mr Darcy.

It was no longer so laughable a thought as it was yesterday.

The strain of the day was the only reason she could sleep so near to him. As she closed her eyes, she wondered if he reflected with regret on how he had destroyed Wickham's prospects as much as he genuinely regretted ruining Jane's happiness.

~

When he woke early the following morning, Darcy sighed at the sight of Elizabeth on the other side of the bed. She was curled up as tightly as possible, at its very edge, and had even refused to sleep under the blanket. There was no tone, gesture, or expression given now, just the simple rise and fall of her chest. Somehow, Elizabeth looked pretty, graceful, and intelligent even in her sleep.

I still admire her and love her, despite my feelings not being returned.

Darcy rose to dress and rummaged through the battered washstand in the corner but only found old toothpowder and a few cloths of dubious cleanliness. It was better than the alternative, and he poured out enough water for himself. Running a cloth over his stubbled face, he thought about his conversations with Elizabeth last night.

She did not know his character. He would always consult his wife's wishes, never open her to criticism before others, take care of her for as long as she lived, and love her with undying devotion. He could not alter his broken heart, or conquer his fear over what would happen to them here, or lessen his anger at Wickham, but he could show her that he had heard her reproofs.

His letter still sat in his greatcoat pocket. He ought not to have lost his temper yesterday when she mentioned Wickham's name. Darcy pushed aside the fear that their time was short, that their captors would kill them, and that he would rather have Elizabeth die not hating him and not holding Wickham dear to her heart. She did not think that he was the man best suited to make her happy, but was there enough time for her opinion of him to improve?

He turned from the dusty mirror with a scoff. Here he was, in the midst of a kidnapping, wondering if there was any chance she could love him. When this was over and they were safe, he would tell her what Wickham was truly capable of and disabuse every lie that man had told her.

Elizabeth was still asleep, and as quietly as he could he scoured the room. It was cluttered with things that appeared to be cast off or dumped from other places, but Darcy looked for anything that could be used to overpower their captors. However, he found not even a pencil.

Darcy sighed and sat on the bed, leaning his head against the headboard. *Not that it matters, because even if I found a weapon, Elizabeth thinks appeasing these villains is the way to get home.*

He dozed for a while until the sound of a carriage jolted him awake. He heard the front door open and voices downstairs. Darcy reached out and shook Elizabeth's shoulder. She woke instantly, looking all round and then fixing on him.

"I think Markle is here."

Elizabeth gave him a nervous look before nodding determinedly and sitting up. She had only to put on her shoes, but he still refused to watch, and pointed vaguely at the washstand. There was not much there, but he heard water splashing as he looked at the window no one could see out of.

"Have you been awake for long?" she asked, her voice still thick with sleep.

He checked his pocket watch. "An hour, maybe. I thought it best to be ready for whatever happens when they unlock the door."

"I am prepared to be your cousin," she said. He looked over his shoulder and saw that she was pinning her hair so he turned back around. "Let us hope they do not expect me to drink more laudanum."

"That would not do at all." Elizabeth would have to be alert for this to work. "We should try to learn what we can about these men and what they want."

When he heard her move from the washstand he turned. "What do you think this Markle's connexion is to Lady Catherine?" she asked, now standing next to him.

Darcy shrugged. "Steamer seemed to believe she had wronged him, and there is some connexion with that boy's father being in prison. If they do not know that Anne is sullen and silent, perhaps you can draw Markle out and learn what his alleged grievances are."

"I am uncertain I can do that," she said, lowering her eyes.

This surprised him. "You are possessed of a lively humour and a sweetness of temper that make your personal charms only a secondary object to your sensibility. Despite how afraid you must be, I think you very capable of getting Markle to talk."

She looked taken aback, and while she blushed at first, her expression then became drawn. "You are kind, very kind to say so, but I am not accustomed to anyone relying on me, certainly not when I am pretending to be someone else while I am kidnapped." She bit her lip. "What if I cannot get him to admit to anything, and what if I cannot keep up the pretence that I am Miss de Bourgh?"

"Do not worry about that," he said, laying a hand on her arm. He started when he realised what he had done and was embarrassingly glad that, after their conversation before bed, she did not pull away. "Like you said, be silent if you cannot answer about being Anne. And we will both do our best to learn what we can."

"I suppose my fear only makes you eager to press your point to attempt an escape."

Drawing his hand down her arm, he hesitantly took her hand. "We have to rely on each other, completely," he said. "The only thing we can trust in this affair is each other. Whatever we do, we do it together. You don't want to risk escape, so we stay and comply."

She squeezed his hand, and sat on the end of the bed, facing the door, pulling him down next to her. Still holding his hand, she added, "Besides, now there is another man here, and it would be harder to escape."

"So, now we wait."

"Now we wait."

Remaining in silence normally was nothing to trouble him, but today was not an ordinary day. After a few tense moments, Darcy could no longer bear the silence and asked, "What will your friend Mrs Collins be thinking by this time?"

"She must have been beside herself when I never returned from my walk."

"I hope Mr Collins did not give her a glass of Rosings's brandy to calm her nerves."

Elizabeth laughed as though she could not help it. "That would not make her feel any better." She took a slow breath and let it out. "I am sure she worried for me until she was told that you were also missing. What is the likely reason for a single man and woman to be absent overnight? She would keep her thoughts to herself, but I am sure Mrs Collins is feeling quite smug in her conclusions."

"How do you mean?"

Looking down at their joined hands, she said, "She once or twice suggested the possibility of your being partial to me, but I always laughed at the idea."

He considered this for a while. Elizabeth had not been wishing for his addresses, certainly not expecting them. He had been a terrible suitor. "Well, the truth will become apparent soon."

"You do not think Mr Collins wrote to Longbourn to say that we ran off together? I know the truth will come out in the end, but I hate the idea of my father's anger and my mother's enthusiasm."

Mrs Bennet would talk to all and sundry of the jewels and pin money Mrs Darcy would have when she returned from Gretna Green. "I doubt that Lady Catherine would be eager for that rumour to get abroad. She likely ordered Mr Collins to stay silent for the present. He seems the sort of man to follow such a directive."

"True," she said with a sigh. "And Mr Collins is not the sort to pursue us."

"My cousin might," Darcy mused. "Lady Catherine might demand that he speak to every tollkeeper on the road north and try to find us."

"Colonel Fitzwilliam must wonder at the idea of any woman eloping with you." Darcy narrowed his eyes, but she shook her head. "No, I mean you are the sort of man no father would refuse. Why would you need to elope? You could ask any—"

She broke off, of course remembering that he could not ask *any* woman and be accepted. "So, now I am an eligible man?" he said as lightly as he could and trying to smile.

Elizabeth's cheeks were pink, but although she avoided his eye, she did playfully push her shoulder into his. He smiled. It was a friendly gesture, something she would not have done two days ago.

Were they friends? He might have thought they were before Hunsford, but she had only thought of them as acquaintances, and with no fondness between them. But now they had a connexion, a closeness, a companionship through this experience that he felt certain nothing could break.

"How distressed will your family be if they think you eloped?" she asked while stroking his fingers with her other hand. He wondered if she realised what she was doing. "Lady Catherine would be enraged, of course. What about Colonel Fitzwilliam? Would he be afraid you had been taken in by a poor woman?"

Darcy thought that before what happened last summer at Ramsgate, Fitzwilliam would have laughed until he turned blue at the idea of him eloping, and from Lady Catherine's house, no less. Eloping could not be as amusing a prospect now, but this was not the time to tell Elizabeth what had happened to his sister and Wickham.

"Fitzwilliam would be astonished," he finally said, "but like your friend Mrs Collins, I think he suspected my partiality, so only the act of fleeing to Scotland would shock him, not my choice."

They heard people moving around the house, and the general noise and conversation below them grew louder. He and Elizabeth exchanged a worried look. She squeezed his hand, and he gripped hers tightly and held it in his lap.

"Would Miss de Bourgh be disappointed if you married elsewhere?" she asked, as though their conversation had not just been interrupted by the realisation—and fear—that they would soon face their violent captors.

"Only in the way a child is disappointed when another child takes their toy that they were not even using." She laughed at his wry reply. "Anne must accept that I won't marry her. I have told her, and my behaviour toward her should also speak to that, but until I leave the registry with a bride on my arm, she assumes she can have me because her mother said so."

Despite the tread on the stairs, Darcy hoped it was not impossible that someday that bride could be the woman next to him.

The door was unlocked, and once again a maid came in to clean and Kirby stood to the side. He shifted his feet and avoided meeting their eye. "My uncle is here," he said, gesturing with his shoulder toward the door. "He says you are both to come down, and to not give him a reason to send Steamer up to make you."

They both rose, and Darcy gave her hand a firm squeeze, reluctant to let it go.

"Ready, Anne?" he asked as steadily as he could.

"Ready, Darcy."

Chapter Six

E lizabeth went down the stairs, with Darcy and the boy Kirby directly
behind her. She had hazy memories of entering the house, and it took
her a moment to orient herself. One entered the house almost directly into
a parlour, but that room was just as cluttered as the upstairs was. To her
right was a dining room, and in there were all the men involved in the
crime.

She noticed Darcy take a long look at the front door, but Kirby came
up behind him and herded both of them into the dining room before
sidling off to sit in the corner. The men with the carriage from yesterday,
Colton and Conway, were standing on either side of the door. Steamer, still
with a clay pipe clenched between his teeth, leant against the far wall with
his arms crossed over his chest.

An unknown person sat at the head of the table, elbows on it and chin
resting on his hands.

Markle seemed about thirty-five with a hardened look. He was blue-
eyed like his nephew, and not tall, and when he looked up, he gave the
appearance that a brutal life had cut up his youth. He did not rise when
they entered, only stared at her with a gaze that passed a chill down her
spine.

"Miss de Bourgh, I trust you slept well?"

The rest of the men laughed, and she supposed they had all taken
amusement in forcing her and Darcy to share a bed. Elizabeth curtly

nodded. One of the men by the door pushed Darcy into a chair, and Elizabeth reached for one next to him before they forced her into it.

"No, you come here," Markle said. His voice was as cold as his look. She wanted to sit by Darcy, as far away from this man as possible. But that would only lead to Steamer drawing his knife. Compliance was the key to their survival. She came around the table and stood before Markle.

"You are rather young-looking. I thought you were near to thirty."

She had not expected anyone to disbelieve that she was Anne de Bourgh before she opened her mouth. Elizabeth looked at Markle steadily and said, "I am near to the same age as my cousin Darcy."

Markle turned his frigid gaze to Darcy before snapping it back to her. "I understood you to be a sickly opium eater approaching the years of danger. You are heartier and more good-looking than reported."

She wanted to say, "That will not do for a compliment," but she supposed Miss de Bourgh would be silent, or perhaps give a haughty glare reminiscent of her mother. Elizabeth only stared.

"You are pretty, and rich, so why have you two not married yet?"

She had not expected this question, and while she struggled for an answer Darcy said, "Every man must have time to sow his wild oats."

Markle made a thoughtful sound, then leant back and looked up at Steamer. "You got the right girl, did not you?"

"Of course I did! I watched the park every morning last week, and she was in the grove, often with him," he added, pointing at Darcy. "And good thing too, because we never could have grabbed her from the house or got near the phaeton."

"I wonder, Steamer," he murmured. Elizabeth felt a wave of terror wash over her. What might they do if they learnt Anne de Bourgh was safe at Rosings?

"'Tis her! Besides, she stopped us from killing Mr Darcy. Hardly would have tried so hard if they were not cousins—and lovers. They probably enjoyed a good frig last night."

Darcy huffed, and she was certain he had a retort about that insult. She threw him a cautionary look, and he sat back, grinding his jaw. She little liked their coarse talk, but they would have to endure it to return home safely.

Markle rose and came near, and Elizabeth instinctively drew back. "You do not look a thing like Lady Catherine."

That put to rest whether Markle knew her ladyship. Fearing he would grow to suspect her, Elizabeth said, "I favour my father more than my mother."

"I got the right girl," Steamer cried. "She even took the laudanum yesterday."

Markle ignored him and asked, "What does he call you?"

Elizabeth gave him a questioning look. "Who?"

"Who do you think?" he said impatiently. "You are betrothed to that man, are you not?" he asked, pointing at Darcy. "Your mother made hint of it every time we met. She could not wait for your families' fortunes to be combined."

She pressed her lips together, nearly saying 'Mister' before she spoke his name. "Darcy and I are promised to one another."

"Were you about to give him his title?" Markle's dark look hinted at amusement as his lips turned up for a moment. "Now, that does sound like Lady Catherine's daughter." She was surprised he noticed her mistake. This man was shrewd. "What does he call you, when you are alone?"

The other men laughed again, and a crass comment begun by Steamer brought a blush to her cheeks, but Markle raised a hand, and they stopped.

"Your betrothed," he said, gesturing at Darcy. "If you are Miss de Bourgh, what does your future husband call you?"

Elizabeth swallowed thickly. Surely Darcy had no pet name for his cousin, and if he did, this man could not know it. Miss de Bourgh rarely spoke, so she stayed silent.

Markle took two steps forward and grabbed her left arm, causing her to wince. "You will find I am not a patient man, and if you—"

"Nan!" Darcy cried. All eyes turned to look at him, including her. He stared at her. "I call her Nan when we are alone."

"What a sweet pet name," Markle said in a tone that was nothing sweet. "Not Annie or Nancy, but Nan." He let go of her arm with a rough shove and took his seat. Elizabeth wanted to rub her sore arm, but would not give him the satisfaction.

"What is it that you want with us?" Darcy asked, his frustration clear.

"Not 'us'," Markle said harshly. "*Her*. I don't want you at all." He glared at Steamer, who only shrugged. "But my associate made a decision, and now I am left to deal with you, so keep your mouth shut or I will let Steamer put his knife in you."

Elizabeth's stomach roiled. This was why they had to agree, be compliant. Submitting was how she and Darcy would get home. Darcy would be killed over a trifle if they were not careful. But they should learn what they could in the hopes of their captors being brought to justice later.

"Then what is it you want with *me*, Mr Markle?"

He smiled, and it did nothing to ease her anxiety. "Your mother and I had a business arrangement. I will do you the credit of assuming you knew nothing about it, otherwise I would let Steamer here do as he likes with you." A cold sweat broke out across Elizabeth's body. "She reneged on our deal, and people got hurt. Her ladyship won't make that mistake again."

"She will not," she said as mildly as she could, "not since you have proven how you can hurt her."

Markle's expression shifted; he gave her a satisfied look. She would appease him if she could. "Yes, I can. Just as she hurt me and mine."

"How did my mother hurt you? I do not remember ever having the pleasure of seeing you at Rosings."

He scoffed. "We met where it was convenient for *me*, not for her. Or at the distillery. Do not labour under the impression that she was doing me any favours."

"What do you want with Nan, now that you have her?" Darcy asked.

She wished he would stop talking, but at least Steamer did not show any indication he was going to stab them. Perhaps he would not lash out in violence with his superior here.

"She will write a letter to her mother, calling her to task for her offence and demanding that she pay for your release." Markle beckoned, and the man who had ridden postilion, Conway, came with a travel writing box. "Sit," he said, pointing to a chair on the opposite side of the table from Darcy.

Elizabeth dipped the quill in the ink, and after writing, 'My dear mother,' she asked, "What would you have me write?"

"Tell her ladyship about your abduction, and that since she chose to alter our deal and Ramer got arrested and the load was lost, she owes us recompense."

She did not know what this meant, and could not comprehend Lady Catherine's connexion to any of this. She added that she was sorry that she had missed supper Thursday evening because of her headache, to leave Lady Catherine in no doubt as to who was taken. After succinctly describing the abduction yesterday, she said, "Will my mother be able to make sense of this? Will she even believe it?"

"She will if I include your finger with the letter," Steamer said around his pipe.

Elizabeth clenched her fingers on instinct, dropping the quill, but Markle said, "No need for that. Nan here is eager to do as she is bid. Maybe I will give you a bottle of laudanum if you are a good girl."

"That will make it easier for her cousin to have his fun with her later," replied Steamer.

The men all chuckled, and Elizabeth refused to look at Darcy. Although they were as far apart as the table allowed, she could feel his fury. As though Darcy would countenance such a thing. She hoped he kept his patience. *I cannot allow it to show how deeply their comments bother me.* Darcy would act foolishly to defend her, or the men would see how their words affected her and do far worse.

When she had to reference Markle's lost load, she hesitated. Darcy wanted to know what had happened, and she could admit her own curiosity. "Should I say anything about these lost goods so my mother knows what you mean?"

"Is anyone else running brandy for your mother?" He barked a laugh. "Anyone else she defrauded shall have to wait their turn."

This made no sense to her, but Darcy cried, "You are smugglers?"

Markle fixed his eye on him. "Free traders," he said pointedly. "And you had best not look at me with that so high and so conceited manner. All households purchase contraband—tea, sugar, tobacco, spirits—even if they don't know it."

Darcy looked about to argue, so Elizabeth quickly said, "Why would my mother need to smuggle anything into England? She is a wealthy woman who can afford to pay duties on—"

"Stop talking about things of which you know nothing, Nan," Markle said.

Elizabeth stared at her paper. Lady Catherine could not be involved in a smuggling gang. There had to be another explanation. "I would not wish for my mother to claim she has no knowledge of what you say," she said carefully. "If I lay it plain in this letter, she cannot deny it, especially if she must show it to anyone in order to raise the funds for our release."

"Want to help me shame your own mother, do you?" Markle asked, laughing again.

"I only want Darcy and me returned safely."

"That is up to Lady Catherine." After a pause, he said, "Kent is a prime location for smuggling, always has been. Proximity to Europe, good roads to London. Tidal waterways in the north, coves in the east, shingle beaches and marshes in the south—all good places for a landing to bring goods ashore. Britain is a market for wine, brandy, silk, and France needs raw materials and gold." He pointed at her. "And your mother needs money."

Elizabeth refused to look at Darcy to see if this was true. Miss de Bourgh might refute such an accusation, but she thought it best to be silent.

"I cannot believe it," Darcy whispered. In a louder voice he said, "How did you convince my aunt to enter into a smuggling scheme?"

Markle laughed. "*She* approached *me*. You can leave off that shocked expression, Mr Darcy. I am in a secure enough position to conduct business in broad daylight." He opened his hands wide and gave a chilling grin, full of pride. "There are free traders conducting business in towns across Kent, without a word of contest from the constables and villagers. I have business with great houses across the county, and she learnt my name and arranged a meeting."

He sounded pleased with himself, and Darcy clearly had no idea what to say. Elizabeth poised the pen over the paper as though eager to write and asked, "What was your arrangement with my mother?"

"Lady Catherine's role was to provide watered-down brandy from Rosings and arrange for it to be cleared to be shipped to another English port. After taking it on board, my crew would actually go to Dunkirk or Gravelines, with Bonaparte's blessing, unload her awful brandy, take on French brandy in equal quantity, and then take that valuable cargo to the cleared port."

Elizabeth dutifully wrote, not understanding any of this. She understood how import duties on goods led to a clandestine market, but she did not comprehend what this had to do with Lady Catherine's cherry brandy. Darcy, however, seemed to realise it all.

"She provided the filled containers as a decoy, and she financed your initial purchase of the French brandy?"

"Paid in guineas. And she paid for the bribes and permits for the excise officers, too. Those permits are often fifty guineas a piece."

"Guineas?" Darcy repeated. "She paid the French in guineas, through you? You are accusing my aunt of treason." He shook his head. "You are guilty of the same yourself."

Markle then shouted a vile suggestion as to what Darcy could do. Elizabeth started, and Darcy glared in silence. "Her ladyship was an equal partner in our arrangement," Markle said, anger still in his voice, "and what cost her one thousand pounds, I could sell for three."

Elizabeth gave Darcy a questioning look. "What has this to do with treason?"

"It has been illegal to export English gold to France since 1797. The French are hoarding coins, and our economy has been weak during the war, propped up by credit, with little gold in reserve."

"All the more reason people like you need people like me," said Markle smugly.

"No respectable person would willingly purchase wares that had never paid the king his dues."

The entire room laughed save for her and Darcy. "Tobacco, tea, coffee, sugar, spirits, silk, lace"—Markle counted on his fingers—"all come into this country and are bought with no duty by people just like you. You think it is only unscrupulous shopkeepers who buy from me and not houses like yours? By your own housekeeper?"

Darcy shook his head. "You think people have the right to shun paying any duty on their goods?"

"Absolutely I do." The other men in the room nodded. "We are free traders. Everyone benefits from cheaper prices."

Darcy had no answer, but comprehension to the scheme rose over Elizabeth. *It was a racket!*

Lady Catherine bribed excise men for permits to ship her bad cherry brandy across England, and she also funded the purchase of contraband French brandy to be shipped in its place. The brandy was bought and swapped in France and then smuggled into England and sold. They paid a low, tax-free price for what the excise men thought was English brandy, but in fact it was fine French brandy that had not paid a penny of taxes.

Her ladyship paid a thousand pounds to buy the French brandy, plus fifty guineas per permit and whatever bribes were also needed, and Markle swapped her cherry brandy with quality spirits from France, and sold it here for three thousand pounds. If they profited two thousand, Markle likely got five hundred, and Lady Catherine got her initial investment plus another five hundred pounds.

"What went wrong?" Elizabeth asked curiously. "If you had this clandestine arrangement with my mother, why did you kidnap me?"

She regretted asking when she saw the harsh expression in Markle's eyes. He rested his elbows on the table and fixed his eye on her while fear settled into her stomach.

"For the sake of fifty or a hundred guineas, she ruined the entire deal. Your mother decided she did not want to pay for new permits and certificates. She thought she knew better and reused ones from a previous shipment."

"You have done this more than once?" Darcy interrupted.

"Every month for six months," Markle said. Turning his gaze back to her, he continued. "Until she thought she could scrimp. Colton and Conway collected March's shipment and took her permits without reading them, assuming all was as it should be. They loaded the ship, captained by my brother-in-law, Ramer." Here he looked to the boy Kirby, who sat on a stool in the corner, his eyes on the floor. "Ramer cannot read well and did not know that he did not have permits for the load on his ship. The navy stopped him, and when his certificates were found to be invalid, they discovered he had one hundred gallons of foreign brandy, being uncustomed goods, and was liable to pay duties that had not been paid or received.

"Ramer offered to resign half the goods and let the navy who caught him off the coast keep the other half, but they refused. He fought for his goods and pulled a pistol. He was tried for attempted bribery and tax offences, and violence as well. We thought they would hang him on account of the fight he put up, but now he is in Newgate for two years! My sister is back to drinking without his income, and I lost a full load and a member of one of my crews." He pointed at her again. "And all because your mother thought to save a few guineas!"

Elizabeth did not have to pretend to be Anne de Bourgh to stay silent. She wrote as best she could about Markle's fury at her ladyship's refusal to pay for the permits and bribes, and his distress at the arrest of this Ramer.

He leant down the table to see what she had written. "Tell Mamma that if she wants your return next week, she will have to pay handsomely for it."

Next week? When next week? Today was Saturday. Why would it take long to secure a banknote and see them returned? Did Lady Catherine even have the money to pay them?

"If you want prompt compensation, you know that our uncle, Lord Fitzwilliam, is one of the wealthiest landowners in England," Darcy said, likely thinking the same. "His lordship will pay handsomely for our swift return."

"I don't want his lordship's money!" cried Markle. "Your aunt's actions caused my brother-in-law to end up in Newgate. Kirby might not have lost his father to the gallows, but it is bad enough he is in jail. I lost a hundred gallons of brandy. I want *Lady Catherine's* money. And if she has sleepless nights over her daughter's welfare, all the better!"

Markle exhaled sharply and added, "Now, Nan, write that since she lost me a crew member and an entire shipment, if she would like you and your cousin returned unharmed, she can expect to pay ten thousand pounds. Tell your mother you will write again regarding the arrangements if she returns a favourable reply."

"If my aunt entered this smuggling scheme, it must have been for the money. What makes you think she can pay you ten thousand pounds?" Darcy asked. "I am in a far stronger position and will—"

"Shut it!" he cried. "The point is that your aunt pays, and if you suggest otherwise again, then I will have Steamer share a bed with your cousin instead of you!"

Markle leant back in his seat, clasping his hands behind his head. "Your aunt's access to money is not my problem. She crossed me, and I want what I am due. Her ladyship made three thousand pounds through our arrangement, and I do not care if she has to beg, borrow, or steal to get the remainder."

This affair was deeply personal to Markle. Elizabeth finished the letter and hoped Markle did not notice her falter when she had to sign her name Anne de Bourgh. Their captor was rough and rugged to the last degree. He felt wronged, disrespected in his profession, and had no qualms with using violence, fear, and coercion to achieve his end.

Was Darcy right to want to attempt an escape?

Was Markle to be trusted to return them if he got his money, or would he kill them both and tell himself that it was a righteous justice in return for his brother-in-law being jailed and Lady Catherine betraying him?

While Markle folded and sealed the letter, Steamer pushed off from the wall and opened the cabinet with the chamber pot. Rather than use it in the cabinet, with his back to her, he pulled it out and turned sideways so she would be certain to see everything.

"You are excessively rude, Mr Steamer," she cried, averting her eyes.

They all laughed, Conway even crying out, "How do ye do, Mister!"

She looked quizzically at Darcy, not at all understanding why they were so amused. Darcy said, "Steamer must be only a nickname." When she continued to stare at him perplexed, he added, "On account of his pipe."

Darcy reached across the table and busied himself with closing the writing box while the other men laughed. Steamer finished with the chamber pot and did not bother to fasten his placket. "What is the matter, Nan?" he taunted. "Have you not seen a man's yard before? Want to touch mine?"

"I think it closer to an inch than a yard," she cried, disgusted by their coarse talk.

Conway, Colton, and Markle all laughed heartily, but Steamer's eyes filled with a dark rage. He stormed toward her so quickly Elizabeth leapt up to back away. Steamer brought his right arm across his body as he came near. She heard Darcy's chair scrape back, and he called out, "Don't!"

Elizabeth did not have a moment to even raise a hand to defend herself. Steamer whipped out his arm, and the back of his hand connected with her cheek with a resounding crack. The blow brought her to her knees as her neck snapped to the side. Lights spotted across her eyes as her teeth rattled together.

She heard Darcy yelling, and then someone was punched. Probably Darcy. Her mind spun, and her vision along with it, and she had to brace a hand on the ground to keep from tipping over. She had never been struck in all her life. The pain was alarming, and so was the terror at wondering what Steamer would do next.

"That is enough, Steamer," she heard Markle say, although she could not focus her eyes on anything but Steamer's shoes and the ground in front of her. The shoes moved away, and she heaved a sigh of relief. Markle would not allow further violence against her. "Get up, Nan."

Elizabeth fought against the pain in her teeth and neck, and the confusion of being smacked to the ground. Her cheek throbbed, and she fumbled to rise. Another moment, then she could figure out how to keep her balance and stand again.

"I said, get up!" Markle yelled. A fist plunged into her hair, and grabbing a handful, Markle tried to yank her upright. She gave a shriek that felt ripped from the pit of her stomach. Her neck twisted again, and she heaved herself up to make the agonising pain stop. "If I tell you to do something, you do it."

Markle's hand still held a cruel grip on her hair. Her head was bent at a terrible angle and tears streamed from her eyes. Darcy was yelling for him to stop, along with a string of curses and oaths to make them pay that would never happen. It was useless on his part to try to defend her.

Markle bent his face close to hers, staring into her eyes. He was not much taller than her, but seemed to relish the control he had in this moment. His blue eyes looked soulless.

"Nan, do you understand? If I say to do something, what happens?"

"I do it," she said through pants of pain.

He let go of her hair with a shove, and she had to brace herself against the chair to keep from falling to the ground. Although she had not eaten since last night, she felt waves of nausea come over her.

"Colton, take this to Hunsford and find some boy in the village," Markle said, handing him the letter. "Tell him to deliver it and wait for an answer, and then watch the house to see what happens. See if she sends for her banker in town before you come back. Make certain you are not followed."

Elizabeth took large breaths in and out, but she still felt terror settling in her stomach. Her hands were shaking, and tears of excruciating pain and fear blurred her vision.

"Do you want me to return here, or meet you at the next house?" Colton asked.

Elizabeth tried to look at Darcy, and moving her head made her feel sick. He was back in the chair, with Conway pinning him down by the shoulder, holding a pistol to his head. Darcy had been right. There was no guarantee Markle would let them go if he got his money.

"No," Markle said as though considering the answer. "We shall move them tonight, so you might as well go ahead to the next safe house. I need to see about the load from Holland and will meet you there."

Elizabeth kept her balance now without the chair's help. She met Markle's eye, and did her best not to flinch.

"Kirby, lock these two upstairs, and then go down the street to find some breakfast for us. Then you can go home, unless your mother has been drinking too much."

Kirby moved to the door and then turned back, asking, "Breakfast for them, too?"

"Of course," Markle said, giving her a smirk as he answered his nephew. "We are not barbarians, are we, Nan?"

Bile rose in her throat, and she staggered to the stairs ahead of Darcy. Elizabeth only just made it to the basin on the washstand before her stomach heaved.

Chapter Seven

E lizabeth had stumbled up the stairs ahead of him, and by the time Kirby locked the door behind Darcy, Elizabeth was retching over the washstand. Darcy burnt with an indignant rage, an implacable hatred he had not known he was capable of feeling. What manner of human being would brutalise a woman?

When she was done, Elizabeth sank to the floor. Darcy watched her cautiously shift to put her back against a box with her legs stretched in front of her. Her eyes stared at nothing.

He hated feeling helpless. Steamer and Markle's cruelty was terrifying, and he had been powerless to stop it. The sound of the hand smacking her face would remain forever seared in his mind. Darcy was on the verge of punching a wall at the frustration that his influence, his money, his connexions, his own will had been utterly useless.

What kind of man am I if I cannot protect Elizabeth?

He looked at her and saw that her cheek was bright red and, although she had stopped crying, tears still streaked her face. Darcy dragged in a deep breath through his nose and briefly closed his eyes. His anger was what was useless. He could at least take care of her now.

Although he would never say so aloud, Elizabeth looked in complete disarray. There was a scab on her neck from where Steamer cut her yesterday. Her hair was falling from its pins, and there were tears on her face and saliva on her lips, but the most startling thing was the vacant look in her eyes.

Darcy moved to the washstand next to her, and she showed no outward sign that she saw him. She could probably hear him, unless she had retreated inward farther than he realised.

"I am getting a cloth. There is still some water in the pitcher." He decided to narrate what he was doing, speaking as soothingly as he could. "I am going to clean your face; is that acceptable?"

She said nothing, but she did not pull away. Darcy lightly wiped her mouth, then waited to see if she reacted. Elizabeth still stared at nothing. "I am glad your lip did not split open when Steamer struck you." No reaction at all. "I have never wanted to hit a man so badly, not even when—"

Now was not the time to think about Wickham and his sister. He wet the cloth again and wiped away the tears on her cheeks. Elizabeth blinked her eyes, but she stayed silent. He wrung out the cloth and then took another look at her. Her hair was limply falling down one side of her head and, combined with the red splotch on her cheek and her dead-eyed look, it was haunting.

The need to do something for her, anything, felt like it was clawing out of his skin. He could at least help with her hair.

"I saw a comb in the washstand when I was looking for a weapon. It is a gentleman's comb, and is missing several of its teeth, but it is better than nothing." He knelt next to her and waited for any indication as to what she wanted. "Elizabeth, I am going to take out these pins. Is that acceptable?" No reaction. "Tell me if you want me to stop."

He took out a few hairpins. Her hair had lost its curl now. She probably wrapped it at night. It fell to below her shoulders and had a slight wave. Darcy set the pins in her lap and tried to comb out the tangles without hurting her.

Darcy wondered what had hurt more: being backhanded by a boxer, or being yanked to her feet by her hair. Both had looked and sounded brutally painful.

He finished combing and moved to look into her face. "I am sorry, Elizabeth." He knew he was pleading. He needed her to know how urgently he had wanted to preserve her from this suffering. "I wish I had protected you. I tried to get around the table to stop Steamer, but Conway drove his elbow into my stomach before I could get to you. And then Colton pulled a pistol and...I am so sorry."

She was still silent, and he hung his head. It was not up to her to absolve him, and certainly not now when he should be taking care of her.

"Well, let us see if I can put your hair back up. You might laugh at my attempt. I will try my best, but I think it beyond my skills." After a few tries to pin her hair, he decided he was only making it worse. He took out the pins he had managed to place and put them along with the comb back on the washstand. "I daresay you will do a far better job yourself when you feel ready."

He gave a weak smile, but she still did not give any sign she heard him. It was as though the candle inside her had been snuffed out. Darcy regarded her with tender concern, although he doubted she noticed. He wished he was master of the art of bestowing consolation. What comforting words of his could afford her any relief after what had just happened?

Her hands lay limply at her sides, and he took her right hand in both of his. "Is it possible to withdraw your mind from the contemplation of your sorrows, my dear? How can I help you?"

After searching her face for some sign of alertness, he raised her hand to his lips and pressed a fierce kiss to her fingers. "I would do anything for your comfort, you have to know that."

But what could he do? He was helpless to preserve her or protect her, everything was out of his control, and Markle was inclined to impulsive violence.

Darcy pressed a final last kiss to her hand before letting it go and placing it gently on her lap. "We will find a way out of this," he whispered. He tried to hide the pessimism from his voice in light of Elizabeth's clear despondency and shock at both their situation and the brutality she just suffered.

He wanted to put his arms around her, but his heart could not handle the loss if she pushed him away. Besides, wherever she had gone in her own mind, she seemed in no place to consent to his embrace.

He felt embarrassed that he had tried to take care of her at all, that he had actually touched her hair. His instinct had been to protect her, and now it was to comfort her, but he doubted she wanted it. She might be reluctant to be touched at all after what had happened downstairs.

Darcy rose abruptly and sat on the bed, not looking at her. He ran a hand across his coat sleeve, where underneath he had concealed a quill knife from the writing box while the smugglers were distracted. Who knew if he would have the chance to use it.

After more silence stretched, he laid back and stared at the ceiling to consider what he knew. Lady Catherine had been in league with smugglers, and she might not have the money to pay their ransom. How could he believe that his aunt, as officious and arrogant as she was, had aligned herself with criminals?

It could only have been for the money.

Had her eagerness to see him wed to Anne been because she had misspent her fortune and now had nothing left? He thought over his aunt's complaints about expenses, about how eager she was to live mostly at Pemberley after he married Anne, at how adamantly she spoke of Anne and him being destined to unite their splendid fortunes.

A thought struck him. Lady Catherine might have spent Anne's money too. His cousin might not have a fortune any longer, and who but a family connexion with his own wealth would marry a woman like Anne who also had not a penny to her name? That was why his aunt had pushed so hard for their union.

Darcy ran his hands over his face. His aunt must be desperate for funds to have entered this scheme. She had to have hoped to make money quickly and did not realise what these men were capable of. These smugglers were brutal. Markle was short-tempered and demanded respect. He was capable of violence, but had men like Steamer to cheerfully carry out that violence for him.

Darcy could believe Lady Catherine had mismanaged her money, and could believe her arrogant enough to think she knew more about smuggling than the smugglers themselves, but he could not imagine that his aunt had any notion they were capable of kidnapping. Or murder.

"We have to escape."

He spun his head. Elizabeth still stared at nothing, her unfocused gaze somewhere far away from here.

"Do you mean it?" he asked, not even certain she had spoken aloud on purpose.

"You were right, Darcy." Her voice was only a whisper. "We cannot trust them to let us go if your aunt gives them the money. We have to escape."

How awful that Elizabeth had trusted that these men had some goodness, that they would free her in return for money, and now that faith was shattered. She had to be terrorised before she could see it clearly.

"If we intend to get away, we must make a plan," he said, sitting up to better look at her. "And be ready to act with some violence ourselves, if need be."

She finally met his eye with a steady stare, the intelligence in her gaze restored. Elizabeth nodded. "I can do it."

Darcy nodded in return, feeling relieved that she had returned to herself and was willing to risk escape.

"You had more discernment than I did," she said, looking uncomfortable. "You saw it plain yesterday, and we might have had a chance then, if I had known..."

"Do not apologise for being a sincere person with integrity." He moved to sit on the floor across from her, facing her, bending his knees so his legs fit in the tight space next to her between the box and the bed. "We will get another chance, and this time we will be prepared to take it."

She said nothing, but at least the brightness had returned to her eyes. "What can we do to overpower men like that?"

Darcy reached into his sleeve and pulled out the quill knife, holding it out to her.

Elizabeth's eyes widened. "You have not had that this whole time."

He shook his head. "When Steamer used the chamber pot, and they all laughed about your mistaking his nickname, I put away the writing supplies." He took back the knife. "And I took something for myself." He held it against his thumb. "It is not very sharp, but it is more than we had before."

"Clever of you," she murmured. "They are all armed and so violent." She sounded as though wanting to be given some hope.

In truth, he had little to give her—as desperately as he wanted to—but he had been considering their options. They typically sent the boy Kirby to unlock the door, but harming him was out of the question no matter who his uncle was. "I am uncertain what you heard after Steamer struck you, but Colton has gone to Hunsford with the letter, and they intend to move us to another house."

She brought a hand to her cheek, touching it gingerly and wincing. "Perhaps we can escape when they stop to change the horses."

Darcy thought over how complicated escaping from a carriage would be. "No, we will have better luck if we got out of the house here. Someone in the village is bound to help, especially if it is *you* they see."

Elizabeth's intelligent gaze hardened. "If we escape, we do it together." He nodded, but she leant forward and said, "Promise me."

"I promise, but you have to promise me in return that if something happens—if you can get away and I cannot—do not stop running." His priority was for Elizabeth to be rescued.

He saw how she stared at him, weighing her answer. "I promise." She sat back and sighed. "I am terrified to stay here. I know that we have to get away, but I am just as afraid to attempt escape and fail."

They both had seen enough to know what might happen to her if they did not get away.

"We have to be brave," Darcy said firmly.

She gave a sad little laugh. "Bravery is not as exciting as the novels and poems make it seem."

"Or easy. But have courage, my dearest Elizabeth."

Her name and the endearment fell from his lips before he could stop it. Darcy hoped she did not find him condescending or insulting. A faint breath escaped from her lips, and then she lowered her eyes. She might have blushed, but with the injury to her cheek and her previous tears, he could not be certain.

"How did you come up with Nan?" she asked when she could meet his eye. "Markle wanted an answer, and I had nothing in mind."

He knew for certain that he blushed. "Oh, well, I thought of my mother. Her name was Anne, and although in front of the servants and in public my parents addressed one another as 'Lady Anne' and 'Mr Darcy', when they were alone my father called her 'Nan' and she called him 'my dearest George'."

It felt strange to relate something so personal, something he had not thought about for a long time. Elizabeth gave him a soft smile. "That is very sweet."

After a moment, she laughed but said nothing. They sat facing each other, their legs outstretched alongside each other and almost touching, and Darcy tapped his foot against her hip to prod her to say what was funny. "I am struggling to imagine Lady Catherine as a young girl, being called Cathy and running around with a little girl named Nan."

At the mention of Lady Catherine, Darcy's spirits fell. A flat, heavy feeling settled over him like a fog. "How do I apologise for what she—"

"You don't," she said plainly. "You are not the one who went into business with violent smugglers, or who tried to cheat them. You did not kidnap anyone, or threaten anyone, or illegally run any goods."

It was gracious of her not to hold him accountable for Lady Catherine. He wondered if she thought about how he had judged her entire family, weighed them in the balance before deciding that he would lower himself to marry Elizabeth. Darcy managed to nod in reply as he ran a hand over his stubbled jaw. He cringed in mortification of all that he said to her two nights ago.

Her rejection had been a blow to his self-respect and, worse, to his self-belief. She cut to the core of who he was, and it was a painful lesson. *A lesson that will make me a better man.*

"What are you thinking about?"

He supposed she asked to not have to think about being struck in the face, or being yanked about by her hair, or being threatened with having her finger cut off. Or think about any of the lewd suggestions the men downstairs had made. And neither did he want to talk about his aunt.

Darcy answered her honestly. "I was thinking about what you said to me on Thursday night, particularly 'had you behaved in a more gentleman-like manner.'"

Her curious expression fell. "I was wrong about your inducements behind Bingley and Jane's separation, and I am sorry I spoke harshly." She laid her hand on his leg, just above his ankle. "I think until yesterday I hardly knew you at all."

She removed her hand, and the feel of her touching him faded, long after the gentle pressure had been physically removed. "Elizabeth, you should know, in case—well, no matter what, you should know that you were right about me. I certainly have a great deal of proud scorn or scornful pride or what have you in my disposition, which is no mark of a good character." It was mortifying to admit, but he owed it to himself and to her to be honest. That was how he could change. "I have immense work ahead of me."

Elizabeth watched him with absorbed attention. "I think," she said slowly, "that you must have a great character—a far better one than you give yourself credit for—to recognise a fault and decide to improve it." She looked at him steadily and then smiled. "Besides, you seem to find friends, real friends, of intellect and character to admire you. I suppose I could at least trust Colonel Fitzwilliam and Mr Bingley's good judgment. They would not be friends with such a man if he did not have some goodness."

He felt a sort of comfort in this give and take of her teasing, so much so that he dared to ask, "And what about you?" She gave him a quizzical look. "Are you willing to call me your friend?"

"Would you want me as your friend," she asked, looking more at his waistcoat than at him, "after how I spoke to you on Thursday?"

Darcy stretched forward and pushed a wayward strand of hair behind her ear. He wanted ever so much more than that. Giving her a fond smile, he said, "There is not a creature on the face of the globe who will remain more your friend than me."

The bright smile she gave him caused a slight easing of the misery inside his heart. Maybe he ought to tell her now about Wickham's true character. He wished he could tell Elizabeth that he still loved her and would do whatever was necessary to earn her good opinion and progress their tentative friendship to a more lasting, affectionate union, but he would not harass her with his own hopes. But he could warn her about Wickham.

Darcy was about to rise to get the letter out of his greatcoat pocket when he heard the key turn in the lock. They both started and stumbled awkwardly to their feet, Elizabeth's face draining of all colour. When the door swung open, it was only the boy Kirby, holding a laden tray and struggling to hold the door open and balance it.

Elizabeth took the teapot off the wobbling tray, and the boy shut the door and set down the tray. Kirby stood there, staring at Elizabeth. Darcy could not understand why he stayed, standing in silence and looking as though he did not know what to do.

"Thank you for the food," Elizabeth eventually said, sitting back down by the tray. An assortment of buns was piled on a plate along with the tea things. Again, there were no knives or forks.

Kirby shifted his feet, and from his pocket he pulled out something wrapped in oilcloth. "Here." He thrust the bundle at Elizabeth, who unwrapped it carefully.

Darcy saw it was a chipped block of ice about the size of her fist. "The manor outside the village has an icehouse," Kirby mumbled, before gesturing to his own cheek. Darcy wondered how often this boy had been struck by those who were supposed to care for him. The imprisoned father, the gin-drinking mother, the violent uncle might all have hit him.

Elizabeth might have thought the same, because she gave him a compassionate look. "Thank you, young man."

It was good of her to call him "young man." Kirby looked proud, although to Darcy he looked more like a little boy than a young man. Her sincere thanks and admiration would mean more to a boy like that than even a coin.

While Elizabeth placed the ice in a cloth from the washstand and held it to her cheek, Darcy looked at Kirby. He was avoiding their gaze, looking at the plate of buns almost as longingly as he had looked at the books yesterday. "Why do you not take one?" Darcy asked.

The boy shook his head. "I ate one on the way from the baker's; he gave me an extra."

He was a skinny boy, but perhaps it was the oversized mourning clothes that led to his underfed appearance. Darcy sat by Elizabeth, took a bun for himself, and tossed another to Kirby. "Eat it, if you insist on watching us."

Kirby nodded, tearing off a piece and chewing quickly. "I am just to stay while you eat, and then take the tray. Uncle said you would not thrash me, and he does not want the door opening often."

Darcy wondered if the boy had little love for his uncle. He had said he did not want to be a free trader, and now Darcy knew Kirby meant he did not want to be a criminal like his father and uncle. Perhaps he could get more information out of him, especially if the men's cruel treatment of Elizabeth troubled him.

"From what great house did you get the ice?" he asked.

"You need not trick me." The boy talked around the food in his mouth. "You are in Shoreham, but they will move you soon."

Elizabeth turned to him. "Darcy, that is only several miles from Hunsford. Someone in the village might help—" She stopped, not wanting to say more in front of Kirby.

The boy knelt on the floor near to them. "None here shall help you," Kirby whispered. "The small villages on the way to Gravesend on the Thames are along smugglers' routes. Everyone looks to the wall when smugglers go by."

"Not the constables, surely," Darcy said.

"If you were to go into Shoreham's High Street, if you tried to run, within five minutes, there would be a signal to the townsfolk to muster their horses."

Darcy gave Elizabeth a look to not talk about their escape now. The boy seemed unlikely to betray them, but who knew what he might say to Markle while under duress.

"How did your family become free traders?" Darcy asked.

"Uncle was a deckhand on a smuggling ship, paid in contraband, and over time he amassed enough to buy a boat and run a crew of his own," Kirby said, swallowing the last of his bun. "He now has two ships, two crews. My uncle makes several runs to France and Holland a month. He needs five men to run his one-tonne cutter, so with my father now being in Newgate, he expects me to take his place."

"And you do not want to?"

"Have no choice," Kirby mumbled.

"What would you rather do if you need not become a smuggler?" Elizabeth asked. She had set aside the ice to nibble on a bun. When the boy shrugged, she pressed him. "I am certain you have thought of it, a clever young man like yourself."

Kirby muttered an answer Darcy could not hear, and Elizabeth gently asked him to say it again. "I said I want to study the law. But I have no tutor, and no one to help me with the fees, and my uncle and father expect me to learn to man the gaff rig on the cutter."

There was such resignation in his voice. Darcy hated to see a child of twelve feel such hopelessness, to have accepted he was destined to a life of violence and crime.

Darcy went to his greatcoat pocket, shifting aside the ring box from Lady Catherine and the letter to Elizabeth. He pulled out a small pocketbook and removed one of his cards. "Take this, and put it away. In fact, commit it to memory and then burn it."

"Why do I need to know your name and direction in town?"

"Because if our ransom is paid, if they return us, I will help you. Do not tell your uncle, or your mother, or any of your uncle's gang. If you decide this is not the life you want, I will see that you are sent to school, and I will help you to enter the law when you are old enough."

Kirby gave him a doubting look, and Darcy held the card out closer. He took it, shoving it into his pocket. "Because I brought her some ice?"

If he knew where to find ice to tend to his bruises, what adult had this boy ever been able to trust? "No, it is because you are a promising young man, Master Kirby."

The boy pushed up his too-long sleeves and shrugged as though not really believing it. He bent to pick up the tray, leaving the teapot and cups behind on the floor.

There were two buns left on the plate, and Kirby handed one to Elizabeth, who took it with a smile. He held the other out to Darcy, who shook his head. Kirby lifted the tray and went to leave, but turned back at the door.

"A few months ago, just up the road near Eynsford, a revenue officer met up with my uncle's crew," he mumbled. "They were moving tea from one barn to another up from the coast, and the load was seized from Colton and Conway. My uncle raised men from all round, and they hunted down the revenue man and threw him in a well. On his command, they all took turns throwing stones onto him until, um, until they did not need to anymore."

Elizabeth gasped and Darcy's stomach dropped.

"And then, when a farmer near Shoreham told a neighbour he would tell a constable what my uncle had done, the neighbour told my uncle, and they burnt down his barn. When he was in it," Kirby added, although Darcy had not needed the clarification. "I doubt you could get past Steamer, but you ought to know that no one in Shoreham will help you if they think you are fleeing a free trader gang. They would bring you back and not lose any sleep over it," he added, before unlocking the door and passing through.

Chapter Eight

They were both silent after Kirby left. Elizabeth watched Darcy try to pace, but the teapot on the floor was in the way and their room was in cluttered disorder. He eventually sat on the bed, staring at the wall, and Elizabeth stayed on the floor, picking at a bun that was now tasteless.

She had been aware of what Darcy said and did for her after they were returned to their cell. There was a gentleness and, she dared thought, an affection behind his care. He had called her "my dear" while he comforted her. From all she had come to know about him, it felt unlikely to be an unconscious display of a former affection. Every word and action he took showed that she was still cherished by him. But would that affection last, or would it fade once this dreadful ordeal was over?

Her horror at what happened downstairs had only receded because of Darcy's help, but Kirby's admission about how far Markle's cruelty spread brought it back. Equally horrifying was how the local people accepted his crimes and violence, or at least turned a blind eye to it in fear.

And Darcy offered to help his nephew if he wanted a different life.

Was his kindness to Kirby something Darcy would always have done, or was it evidence that Darcy now wanted to be a better man, and more caring to those outside of his circle? How could a man that generous also be a man who denied Wickham the living that his father had always intended for him? Had Wickham not told her the entire story? Or worse, had Wickham lied?

Her heart whispered that Darcy had always been a good man.

And she admired him, and he did not want to hear mention of Wickham, and now was not the time to raise questions. Pushing aside her curiosity and her fondness for Darcy, she said, "That was a generous thing you did for the nephew of the person who kidnapped us."

"You cannot think the boy has anything to do with it," he said, still looking at the wall.

"Of course not, but most men would not offer to educate a stranger."

She heard him sigh. "I doubt Kirby has the courage to accept my offer, or that his uncle would not come after him if he suspected where he went, but if Kirby wants to be an attorney or a barrister, someone ought to help him."

She smiled, although he could not see it. "Most would think that someone must help him. Few would take that upon themselves."

He looked over his shoulder at her. "You think it odd given the precarious situation I am in? Since I cannot help anyone at the moment?"

This was not a man accustomed to feeling out of control. "But we are going to escape, so ultimately you can help this boy if he chooses it."

"What manner of child from a family of gin drinkers and smugglers decides he wants to study the law?" he mused. "It is a fascinating juxtaposition, is it not?" He did not pause for an answer. "He hides from the taproom and his drunken mother to read discarded books in a smuggler's shelter, and he wants to enter the law, possibly to punish the people who were supposed to take care of him."

There was nothing she could say, so Elizabeth watched Darcy think. He had a strong but calm attitude and carried himself with authority, and yet treated anyone who might depend upon him with kindness. His sense of honour was more heavily ingrained than she had seen in most gentlemen. Darcy thought he had a duty to this neglected child.

Kirby told them they would never escape the house, and even if they did, no one in this village would give them sanctuary. Elizabeth squeezed her eyes shut and breathed slowly. She could not give in to fear. Staying to be further victimised or killed was not an option.

"We ought to talk about something we can take action on now. We need a plan to escape."

Darcy agreed. "I think we flee before they move us someplace else."

"But Kirby hinted that no one in the village would help us."

"I do not judge them harshly." He inhaled a deep breath and would not look at her. "The people here benefit from cheap goods, and they are afraid of the violent men who provide them. And would be too afraid to give evidence against them. But our best chance is for *you* to be seen, and likely in some state of distress."

Kirby's warning about the local populace stayed in her mind. "What if we waited?"

He shifted on the bed to better look at her. "Waited for what? There is no one coming to rescue us."

"If they are moving us to hide us in another place, far from here, what if we escape then?"

Darcy scoffed. "Our chances of survival lessen each time they move us from one place to another."

Elizabeth shook her head, warming to the idea. "We cannot hide here in Shoreham, and no one will aid us. But we would have better luck in a larger town."

"No, we should attack our captors here, *before* we get in the carriage," he said firmly. "Then we do not have to overpower anyone just to get outside. You merely have to get away to where someone will see you. Not difficult because I think we are on the High Street."

"I don't think anyone will help just because I am a woman," she cried. "Markle's sister lives here, and he is known in Shoreham. Here the villagers might all look the other way out of fear, but in a town, someone is bound to aid us."

Darcy stood, shaking his head. "His gang is known all the way to the coast."

"Not with the same strength that they are known here in Shoreham." Elizabeth did not like looking up at him, and she scrambled to her feet. "We would have better luck if we overtook them in the carriage or when we change the horses in a larger town than we could in Shoreham."

"Unless he drugs you and blindfolds me."

She felt herself grow furious. Darcy had wanted to escape, and now when she saw the wisdom in it, he failed to see their best hope was to escape in a larger town. "Why are you afraid to take a risk now? The way I see it, we have no options here, but we at least have a chance in a town farther from one of their safe houses."

Darcy practically vibrated with some elemental force, and he took a long time to answer. "No. We overpower them as soon as they attempt to move us. The moment that door opens," he said, pointing, "the goal is to get you onto the street."

"This area is under his gang's control!" she cried. "Kirby told us as much. Ten miles away could be completely different. Ten miles away, someone could help us, or we could find somewhere to hide, or send a message for help, or hire a carriage ourselves. Here we have nothing." Darcy's face was of repressed apprehension. Elizabeth looked at him curiously. "Do you not like my plan because it is not yours?"

He now looked excessively shocked. "That is what you think of me? That I need to control everything? So arrogant as to not think a woman can be sensible?" He shook his head. "Do you not credit a single thing I say and refuse to escape at the first chance you get because I am the man who made himself agreeable nowhere, and who had refused to dance with you?"

"I do credit your opinion, your intelligence." That he still believed that she thought so little of him disappointed her. "I have greater respect for you now that I know you better, and since you swore to be less selfish and to reunite Jane and Mr Bingley. You even tried to preserve me from being kidnapped, from being harmed. You cared for me after what happened downstairs."

"Do not thank me for *that*," he cried. "If you cannot believe me capable of that, you must think me the most despicable creature on earth!"

She shook her head. "No, I don't, truly I don't. I—" She looked into his eyes and wondered what she felt for Darcy. She was not passionately in love with him, but she cared more for him now than she had two days ago. She liked him now very much. Could she come to love him? He was certainly deserving of being loved, and had blazing attractions she could no longer discount. As she looked at his face, regretting that she had injured him, her gaze dropped to his lips. She wondered what they would feel like on hers.

Elizabeth blinked and looked away. Now was not the time to investigate how deeply her heart was engaged. "I just don't understand why you want to escape from Shoreham when we have no place to go, nowhere to hide, and no one to help us."

"Steamer is a brute, impulsive and vicious," he said, pacing the few steps available to him at the foot of the bed. "Conway and Colton are followers—they are not going to take action on their own, but they are not afraid of violence, either. Markle is willing to commit violence himself, but he has others to do it for him, and we cannot trust him to keep his word. That is why I want to escape immediately. Think of me what you will, Elizabeth—ungentlemanly, selfish, proud—but you cannot believe I want to see further harm come to you."

"I think better of you than I did before," she said softly, "so please stop assuming such hateful things about how I see you. I know you are a good man." It was the truth. Despite whatever had happened in the past with Wickham, the man standing before her today was a respectable, trustworthy man.

He nodded but stayed silent. Darcy's face was pale, and he shook with some barely contained energy. He seemed more distressed than frustrated about being powerless.

"You are terrified," she whispered.

Darcy took two quick steps toward her. "Of course I am terrified!" He gripped her arms and bent low to look into her eyes. "I have seen you brutalised in front of me, over and over, and I could do nothing to stop it! And they hinted at violating you. They will probably kill you after they get their money. And they will certainly kill you if they learn you are not Anne." His tight hold on her arms lessened, but he did not let go. "The *instant* there is a chance for you to get away, you take it."

"A chance for *me* to get away?"

"Yes," he cried.

"Why would you value me any more than yourself?"

Darcy tilted his head, giving her a look as though the answer was obvious. And after a heartbeat, it was. He loved her. He still loved her, and he would put himself in harm's way if it meant she was safe.

All the air seemed to escape from her lungs, and she found it difficult to speak with her heart residing in her throat. Their eyes met, and her lungs constricted further. For a moment, she thought he was going to kiss her, and her heart raced in anticipation. But Darcy seemed to realise that he was still holding her arms, and he dropped them slowly.

"We will both get away," she said gently as the flash of some sort of feeling between them passed. "This is not your fault, and I won't leave you behind, so you had best get accustomed to the idea that either we both escape or neither of us do," she added as lightly as she could.

Darcy's face was taut, and he crossed his arms over his chest, sighing as he stepped away. He nodded vaguely as though he had heard her but did not agree. "My priority is to see you returned to your family, and as whole as you are now."

"And mine is for us to escape together."

He might have left the room, or paced, or stared out a window, but the man had no way to retreat. As frustrated as she was, Elizabeth sat on the bed facing the washstand and gave him as much privacy as she could.

Her vexation with him came in waves, like when he insisted he would sleep in the bed or over his need to manage everything. But it receded just as quickly. It used to be a constant in her heart that Fitzwilliam Darcy was entirely unlikeable. And now he was more likely to rouse her interest or make her smile than do something to remind her of her previous ill opinion.

She not only admired his good qualities, she not only respected him, but she genuinely enjoyed his company and wanted to hear his opinion. She cared for his happiness. As she had sat on the ground, stupefied by fear after her savage encounter with Markle, Darcy had shown her unparalleled kindness.

If he had not talked calmly, if he had not shown her such genuine care, she might still be sitting on the floor, lost in her own terror.

Darcy had turned out to be one of the most right-minded men she had ever known. He worried for the future of the nephew of the man who had kidnapped him. He was principled enough to care where his sugar came from. He showed her attention, fondness, and his protection—as far as it went here—even though she had refused his proposal.

Elizabeth looked over her shoulder at him while his attention was elsewhere, somewhere turned inward. Darcy was quite handsome, but he did not carry himself like some men who knew they were attractive. His confidence and pride made people notice him as much as his fine face and figure.

His pride was not as unearned as she once thought.

He must have felt her watching and looked up from his reflections. She ought to have looked away, but she held his gaze, trying to read what he was feeling. Her heart turned over as he gave her a fond smile. Darcy's smiles were like lightning flashes at night, vivid and fleeting, brightening the darkness before vanishing.

He often smiled at her like that. For all of her assumptions that he was unpleasant and disliked her, she could now remember that in Meryton, in Hunsford, when she stayed at Netherfield, Darcy had smiled warmly, at *her*.

She needed him to know that she did not blame him for his aunt or what happened to her, that she did not hate him—that she now admired him. Would he let her put her arms around him? It was not because he was the only person who could understand her fear, or because he loved her. Gratefulness and companionship were not love, but Elizabeth grew more certain that what she felt for Darcy was a deep affection.

What would it be like to kiss him?

She felt her cheeks redden, as though Darcy had any idea what she was thinking.

She liked him so much now, but what about how he had behaved in his past? How could a man who was generous, was willing to take criticism, was humorous, attentive, and likeable, a man who cared so deeply for her, how could he also have callously ruined Wickham? Although he loved her today, was he capable of resenting her, of cutting her off from her family, of eventually hating her? The Darcy of two days ago might, but she could not believe it of the man she knew now.

Elizabeth laughed to herself. It was not as though Darcy had given her reason to think he might ask her again to marry him. But Darcy was here. He cared for her well-being, and she cared for his. They had to work together, but she wanted him to know that she now had a genuine fondness for him.

Elizabeth walked over to him, ignoring his startled gaze at her being so near, and put her arms around his shoulders.

"Thank you," she whispered, resting her cheek against his chest. "I know you do not want it, that you would never admit that you rendered me the slightest service, but thank you."

He stood very still, and inhaled a deep breath before carefully putting his arms around her waist. She felt the beat of his heart, the steady rhythm of his breathing, and enjoyed the feeling of being pressed against him. Then she felt him relax against her and hold her a little tighter.

"I know that I promised we would escape together," he said softly, "but you also promised me that if you had the chance to get away without me, you would take it."

"I don't want to leave you behind." She knew what would happen to him if she escaped and he did not. Markle would have Steamer kill him, if he did not do it himself. Her heart clenched at the thought.

"Elizabeth, I would not be able to outlive the loss if you died and I might have prevented it."

His heat and his nearness invaded her thoughts. She remembered her hair was still down when Darcy brought a hand up to stroke his fingers through it. She was tucked under his chin, and he probably had not realised what he was doing. Elizabeth closed her eyes, settling into him as he held her closer.

"I have never been more aware than I am right now of what I lost when I refused your affections," she said through the emotion in her throat.

She felt him sigh, and then he pressed a kiss to the top of her head. She tilted back to better look at him, and Darcy brought his hands to either side of her face. He drew a quick breath as if to say something, but instead his thumb started brushing her cheek, the one that had not been struck. His attention shifted from her eyes down to her mouth, and then quickly came back up. With her heart racing, Elizabeth nodded, leaning a little closer toward his lips.

The key turned in the lock, and she started. Darcy shifted her behind him as the door pushed open and Markle entered. In one hand he held a pistol, aimed at the floor. His gaze sharpened as a smirk crossed his lips.

"Am I interrupting, Nan? What would your mamma say?"

Elizabeth stepped out from behind Darcy, but did not give him an answer.

"By all means, you need not stop on my account," he continued. "Although, if Darcy does not satisfy you, any of the men are eager to swive. Shall I send one of them up?" He gave her a cold look. "Or all of them?"

"What do you want?" Darcy asked.

Markle ignored him and kept his stony gaze on her. "We are moving you both tonight, Nan, to a place near the coast." He pulled out a bottle from his waistcoat pocket. "And I need you to be agreeable for the journey. It will help keep Mr Darcy in line."

She assumed it was another opium tincture. "You do not need that," she said as calmly as possible.

He levelled the gun at her, cocking it. "Remember what I said earlier. If I say to do something, what do you do?"

Elizabeth felt a cold terror pass over her, her scalp stinging in pain at the memory. "I do it," she whispered.

Darcy stepped forward, and Elizabeth threw out her arm and clutched his sleeve. This was not the time. She held out her hand, and Markle gave her the laudanum.

"Drink it."

She was afraid he would insist on watching her. She took a long swallow. Markle continued to stare, gesturing with the pistol that she should continue. Elizabeth brought it to her lips again, only taking a sip and wincing. "I cannot drink it all now," she said in as sorrowful a voice as she could make. "Will you leave it with me?"

Markle gave her a flat look. She could not be certain if he was about to shoot her or agree. He was unreadable, and both seemed equally possible.

"Is it because you want to be awake for what Darcy has planned for you after I leave?" he asked. "Drink it all now, in case you don't want to remember it. He might not be any good."

Answering his taunts would not help. Elizabeth refused to look at Darcy; she could feel the anger rolling off of him. "I will drink it, but I cannot drink it all at once. This is as much as I might drink over the course of a day." She took another small sip.

Markle lowered his arm, held the hammer, and pulled the trigger to drop the hammer to a half-cock. Elizabeth closed her eyes in relief.

"Before Steamer puts you in the coach, you had better be half asleep." He gestured with the pistol at Darcy. "Or he will suffer for it."

Markle strode through the door and locked it behind him. Elizabeth heard Darcy blow out a breath as he sat on the bed. She ignored him as she lifted each lid on the trunks within reach, trying to find one that was unlocked.

"Elizabeth, if you will be soporific from laudanum, we are out of time."

Elizabeth found one that opened. Whatever had been resting on its lid fell behind it as she lifted it, and she thrust two fingers down her throat.

"We must run the next time the door opens," he went on, "even if that means I get shot or—"

The bun she had eaten and the laudanum came up violently. She might have forced herself a second time, but she hoped just once would be enough. She dumped the rest of the laudanum into the trunk and replaced the lid, sinking against it to catch her breath.

When she turned around, Darcy was looking at her in a way she could not make sense of.

"Have I appalled you?" she asked, a little embarrassed. "I have to be alert for—"

"You impress me."

She gave a shaky laugh and took a drink of cold tea. It did little to distil the taste in her mouth, so she went to the washstand and did her best with old toothpowder and a cloth. While she was there, she saw her reflection in the dusty mirror and did her best to put up her hair with the broken comb.

As she made herself as neat and clean as she was going to get, she looked at Darcy in the mirror's reflection. He was sitting on the bed, watching her but not meeting her eye.

What could we say to one another after being in each other's arms?

Elizabeth could turn around and say that she wanted to kiss him, that she wanted to know him better, that she was falling in love with him. As she looked at her swollen cheek and wan reflection, she knew instead they had to think on what to do next, to be ready for whatever had to happen tonight so she and Darcy could escape.

Chapter Nine

There was something inherently strange about being held a prisoner and wanting to kiss a woman who had just made herself be sick.

While Elizabeth busied herself at the washstand, Darcy wondered what to say about his almost kissing her. A few days ago, she made it clear that she would not marry him, but did a few poignant conversations and an experience that would inevitably tie them together—assuming they both survived—change her mind? She had some admiration for him, but was it only from their being forced together?

Darcy avoided catching Elizabeth's eye in the mirror as he considered her feelings. If there was a sincere affection for him there, what would happen when they were safe and only saw one another across a crowded drawing room?

She turned from the mirror and sat next to him, facing into the room just as he was. She seemed uncomfortable, but was that because she had just forced herself to throw up or because they had almost kissed? The silence pressed on him, and he hardly knew if he ought to take her hand or move away.

Their mutual discomfort felt like a third person in this tiny cell.

"We need a plan to escape," he said abruptly and far too loudly. It was best to focus on getting away, and it was useless to wonder if Elizabeth might want to marry him if they survived.

Out of the corner of his eye, he saw her nod. "We let them put us into the carriage?"

Part of him wanted her to get away now and take the slim chance that someone in this small village would help her, even though it was in the stranglehold of a smuggling gang. But if she refused to flee without him, what was the point? "Yes, and we need to decide when and how we escape from it."

Even if they got the door open, jumping from a moving carriage was a certain way to break a leg, or worse.

Elizabeth shifted on the bed to look at him. "Where do you think they are taking us?"

"Markle said to near the coast," he mused, "but if he intends for us to arrive there tonight, then I doubt we are going to the Channel." After picturing a map of northern Kent in his head, he added, "Maybe an estuary on the Thames since they are smugglers. Gravesend, maybe."

"How far is that?"

"Twenty miles, I think. They must change or bait the horses, especially since the roads are muddy this time of year and it will be a strain on them." He met her eye for the first time since Markle interrupted them and felt a heat rise in his cheeks. Looking away he asked, "Have you any idea where they might stop?"

She gave a dry laugh. "I have never been anywhere, Darcy. You are more likely to guess such a thing, with all your travelling and what is fifty miles of good road."

He gave her a half smile when she playfully nudged his shoulder. He was being teased, but it felt like there was a kindness behind it, that it came from a place of friendship rather than mockery. After considering it for a moment, at where the crossroads and a few coaching inns he knew were, he said, "If I was in Shoreham, going northeast, then I would change them at Dartford, about fifteen miles from here."

"Then we escape when we change the horses at Dartford." Her countenance brightened. "Anyone in the stable yard could help us and stop Steamer and the others from apprehending us again."

Doubt overtook him. "It is a larger town, not likely to be beholden to smugglers like a small village, but I do not think we can trust anyone to help us."

She threw him a dark look. "Dartford will be safer than here. I thought we already decided—"

He held up a hand to interrupt her. "I do agree, but I do not think it wise to call attention to ourselves." Darcy rushed ahead in case she was inclined to argue. "I am unwilling to trust anyone along their smuggling route. But in a coaching inn, in a larger town, we can find someone to send a message to Hunsford, or hire a carriage ourselves, but using our names and admitting a smuggling gang wants us is reckless."

"Very well." Darcy blinked, and Elizabeth laughed. "You look surprised. Did you think I would argue for the sake of being contrary? I agree it is sensible to not admit to who we are."

"Well, in the past you have enjoyed arguing with me for the sake of being contrary, and I did not know how far that pastime went." She smiled, blushing a little, and it charmed him. He smiled back, but the moment faded as they remembered their situation. "Anyone might be a sympathiser or someone who could be bribed. We have a better chance in Dartford, but I cannot assume we will be safe enough to use our names or admit they kidnapped us."

She sighed but nodded knowingly. Elizabeth turned her neck from side to side, as visibly as uncomfortable on the bed's edge as he was. He supposed it was still better than the floor. "When do you think they will move us?"

"Markle said tonight." He pulled out his watch, and took a moment to wind it. "It is almost one. We shall have a long day, but it gives us time to plan. If it is in the middle of the night, it will be impossible for us to hire a carriage after we escape. Maybe the mail coach or the day's final stage coach will come through, and we can take it wherever it is going."

She scoffed. "Have you ever ridden a stage coach in your life?"

He gave her a sideways look. "Have you?" He would not believe it if she had.

"Oh yes, and I prefer to sit on the top if I can."

He laughed, shaking his head. "Well, you may jest, but if it means we can escape from this area of Kent, then I will ride on the top of the stage coach to wherever it is going, even if it is raining."

"No one will hire out a chaise or a room on credit, not even if you announced that you are Mr Darcy of Pemberley. And we will be two nameless travellers who appear in the middle of the night."

They exchanged a worried look and then opened their coin purses to find only eight shillings between them. Darcy ran a hand across his jaw. Elizabeth watched him, her gaze absorbed by his fingers running across the stubble on his chin. She was probably lost in thought or equally annoyed at how little money they had.

"It is not enough to hire a post chaise," he said, trying to keep his frustration at bay. It was scarcely enough to pay the tolls and tips to London. "It is enough to take a room and to hire a messenger to ride to Rosings, although we shall be poor tippers."

Elizabeth opened and closed her mouth, hesitating before finally saying, "What will you say to her? Do you want Lady Catherine to know that you are safe?"

"I want Fitzwilliam to know where we are. *He* I can trust, and assuming he is at Rosings, he will leave for Dartford as soon as he reads my signature on the bottom of the page. Lady Catherine..." His aunt would not condone what had happened, but how would he navigate the now churning waters of that relationship? "I hardly know what I will say when I see her," he muttered.

Elizabeth ran a hand up and down his arm, a comforting gesture that only made him want to hold her as close to him as was possible.

"Part of the reason she pushed so hard for my marriage to Anne must be because of her dreadful financial situation," he mused. "All of her talk about what my mother wanted and that I have a duty to my family, and she was primarily concerned with her own wealth."

"You must often struggle between duty and inclination." Her voice was kind, more kind than he deserved given what he had said to her during his proposal.

"As far as Anne goes, it was a short-lived struggle. I do have a duty to my family"—he turned to look her fully in the face—"but a wife means a contract of a different sort. An honesty and a loyalty above all else, a true partnership."

"Darcy," she whispered.

"And I could never have had that with Anne."

Could she hear the longing in his voice? Her dark eyes were gentle as they swept down to his lips and then back up to his eyes. His heart rate increased with every breath, and he felt something might be unleashed if only they would let it.

Elizabeth stared at him, lips parted, leaning forward slightly, but then she hesitated, exhaling lightly. Darcy dropped his gaze, and the moment passed. It seemed that her feelings for him had changed, but could she properly investigate her own heart and mind in such a situation?

He cleared his throat as she shifted on the bed, rolling her shoulders and stretching her back. He did the same, wishing that the next time he was kidnapped that his cell had a chair.

She gave him a long look and then came to some decision, grinning. "Right then, move here, sit on the bed this way." She gestured for him to move to the centre of the bed with his legs stretched out. Elizabeth then moved behind him, and leant against his back, both of them bracing each other up. "You make a fine chair back."

"I live to serve."

She laughed, and she was right that this was more comfortable. He missed being able to look into her face, but the feel of her against his back was a comfort.

"You are right, of course, to consider your own happiness. I suppose duty was ingrained in you at an early age," she said gently from behind him. "You have so much responsibility for your age. You were young when your father died?"

"I was about your age, twenty-two," he said. "My life was beginning as my father's was ending. I could ease his final days by assuring him that I was dedicated to Pemberley, to my sister, and to being a man he would be proud of."

"I am sorry that I mistook your character for so long," she said after a short silence, "but I know your father would be proud of you. And given your feelings toward Miss de Bourgh, he would not fault you for marrying elsewhere."

It hung in the air that Darcy had wanted to marry Elizabeth, still wanted to if she would have him. His father would have liked her, he was certain. She had common sense, was quick and decided, cheerful, and charming and beautiful.

Darcy ran his hands over his face. Now was not the time to think of romance, not with smugglers roaming the countryside abducting innocent people for ransom. Even if Elizabeth confessed that she was not Anne de Bourgh, Markle had shown enough impulsive violence that made Darcy fear he would kill her out of anger.

If they did not escape in Dartford, he was certain they would kill Elizabeth. Markle would use her to get the money from Lady Catherine, and then he would murder them both. And Markle and his gang would not blink an eye before returning to running their illicit sugar and brandy and tea.

"What are you thinking about?"

"I was thinking about sugar" was what he managed to say, not wanting to speak of their prospective murder.

"I am hungry too, but I am surprised that even you want a dessert in the middle of the day." He envisioned the fond, teasing look, even though he could not see it.

Darcy smiled. *She braces me up.* He hoped he might do the same for her. "No, I was thinking about what Markle said about everyone buying contraband, even if they did not know it. It made me wonder how pervasive such goods are."

"You wonder if you had bought West Indian sugar without realising it?"

He nodded. "If you purchase the commodity, you participate in the crime." Slavery was institutionalised manslaughter. "The East India sugar I insist my housekeeper buy might be smuggled from the West Indies."

"You seem determined to feel guilty about something."

He shrugged. She was not wrong. The feeling that he ought to have done more, done better, was pervasive. "You are a lively woman; you do not strike me as the sort to dwell on regret."

He could tell by her movements that she had dropped her head. "Well, I may not dwell on my regrets, but I do have them."

He lacked the courage to ask if any of her regrets had something at all to do with him. Besides, it would be a selfish question, and he was resolved to be less selfish. "We ought to make better use of our time than thinking of the past."

"Then do we escape from the carriage in Dartford, or while the carriage is moving before we get there?"

He thought for a long while, and Elizabeth did not seem to mind. She just leant against his back, slowly breathing in and out. It was pleasant, consoling, to feel her breathe against him and know that she was, at least at this moment, safe.

"If we escape the carriage in the inn yard," he mused, "what if Steamer convinces them we are guilty of something? Young lovers running away or servants caught stealing. He could convince a constable to turn us over to him. Steamer might even bribe or threaten someone to look the other way."

"Then we escape from the carriage before we get to Dartford. We walk the rest of the way and make it appear that we arrived at the inn yard like any other traveller." Elizabeth pressed into him, making her point.

"You intend for us to jump from a moving carriage, without breaking any bones, and without the carriage stopping to retrieve us?" he asked in disbelief. "We shall have little luck getting past Steamer anyway if he rides with us as he did last time."

"I assumed he would. What if we throw *him* from the carriage?"

It sounded as though that was what Elizabeth wanted to do all along. "What about the door?" Carriages had no handles on the inside. The only handle was on the outside, so whomever folded up the steps also closed the door.

"I can lower the glass and pretend to need the fresh air. I should be strong enough to reach out and lift the lever." The idea had merit, assuming Steamer did not run either of them through with his knife in the attempt. "When I lean out, it would force him near the door to pull me back. Or, if he objects to my lowering it, I can refuse, and he will come nearer to stop me. Either way, he puts himself by the door right before I open it."

It would only work if Elizabeth threw open the door at the exact moment Darcy pushed him out, and did not fall out herself. "He is a large man, built like a boxer and broad-shouldered." If Steamer had been a boxer, he had not been a successful one; his nose had been broken and his left ear portrayed the vigour of his opponents. But that was not to say he was not capable of fighting and harming Elizabeth in the process.

Elizabeth sighed. "If you dislike this plan, then please come up with your own."

"I do not dislike it," he said quickly over his shoulder, "but we must plan every step to the best of our abilities, and one shove won't be enough." He pulled the slight quill knife from his pocket and passed it behind him. "I shall have to injure him, throw him off balance and distract him, and then push him out. You will have to throw open the door and then get out of the way so you don't fall too."

A thousand things could go wrong.

He heard her turn the knife over a few times in her hand, but she was quiet. After more silence, Darcy said, "He is certain to be wearing a coat. I shall have to aim for someplace vulnerable."

"Do we kill him?" Elizabeth whispered.

She said "we," but it would be Darcy who stabbed Steamer and threw him from the carriage. It hardly sounded difficult now, not when he remembered how Steamer had brutalised Elizabeth and threatened him. But practice differed from theory, and any hesitation on his part could be fatal to them both.

"I won't intend to kill him," he said quietly. "The goal is to incapacitate him and throw him from the carriage and let the fall take care of the rest."

She passed the knife back to him. "That solves one of our problems, but how do we get the carriage to stop before we arrive in Dartford?"

"Conway rode postilion last time. An experienced rider will stop the horses when he feels the change in weight and knows something is wrong. Let us assume he stops and Steamer is no longer relevant." If Steamer could fight after the fall, there was no hope he and Elizabeth could overtake an angry man with a knife and a smuggler on horseback with a gun. "Do you think we can rush out and overtake him before he draws his pistol?"

He felt and heard Elizabeth heave a sigh. "No. When you tried to stop them from abducting me, Conway was on horseback, and he pulled a pistol, but you could not see him." Through his back he felt her breathing faster. "It was terrifying. I could not alert you and I could not stop him from shooting you. There was no way he would miss from there. He would have shot you in the head and you would have died in front of me."

Coping with the fear and shock of their abduction was going to take a long time. "No one better than me understands how helpless you feel." Darcy reached back to where Elizabeth's hand rested on the bed. He gave it a squeeze. "But now we can do something about it. Focus your thoughts on that."

She tilted back her head to rest against him, and when she righted her head, he let go of her hand. The desire to hold her, to protect her, had not waned. If they managed this and Steamer was no longer a threat, he would gladly take a bullet if it meant Elizabeth would get away from Conway.

"If Conway dismounts and looks into the carriage, we could surprise him there," Darcy suggested as an idea formed in his mind. "He looks inside expecting Steamer so his pistol might not be drawn, and I overtake him and steal the carriage."

"How?"

"The carriage stops after we toss out Steamer. It might take the rider fifty yards to come to a stop, and in the dark Conway won't see him. Conway dismounts, looks into the carriage, I surprise him, take the pistol, and then get past him to ride the horses to Dartford." Conway was a follower, not one who made decisions. He would stay with Steamer, who would hopefully be too injured to follow. Without his pistol or instructions, Conway would not be the same sort of threat Steamer was.

"And what do I do?"

This was the part he did not like. "You keep Conway from re-entering the carriage as I start moving the horses. There is a bolt in the door to keep anyone opening it. You get back inside and shift it into place. It would help if you had a knife to keep him from grabbing hold before you can lock the door and put up the glass."

"Then we need a second weapon. Maybe they will bring us cutlery when they deliver our roast lamb for dinner."

He laughed. "Bold of you to assume they intend to feed us again."

Elizabeth joined in his laughter. "I am counting on it. I had to cast up my breakfast to lose the laudanum, so I will even take mysterious potted meat again."

This gave him an idea. "Do you still have the bottle?" She passed it back to him. It was a teardrop-shaped crystal bottle, slightly larger than a ladies' perfume bottle, with a little silver cap. "I think I can break the bottom," he said, "and you can hold the neck to keep Conway from getting back in."

"You want me to wield it like a knife?"

"If I can break it into a large enough piece for you to hold."

Elizabeth was silent, and he wondered if she was afraid to stab Conway. "Never mind," he said. "All you need to do is shut and bolt the carriage door once Conway dismounts. I can get the horses moving swiftly, and he will fall off."

"What?" she asked, confused. "No, no, I can do it."

"You hesitated, so I thought—"

"Darcy, I hesitated to ask you how a laudanum addict must act."

Realisation dawned. She did not want to distress him by mentioning Anne's opium use. Thanking her for thinking of him felt wrong. She would not want to be thanked for showing him a kindness. "I think the best way to act is to be in such a state of indifference that you take the least interest in anything." He thought for a moment. "The only problem might be your eyes."

"What is wrong with my eyes?"

Good God, not a thing. "They have to look as small as pinholes." He blew out a breath. "How will you possibly look as though you have lustre-less eyes?"

She was quiet, and Darcy wished he was looking into her eyes right now. "Darcy," she asked slowly, "do you like my eyes?"

He could scarcely hear her question; it was uttered so softly. His throat felt impossibly dry. "Yes, I do. They are beautifully expressive. It was one of the first things I admired about you, before we ever spoke."

In the silence that followed, he wondered if she was blushing, or angry, or flattered. "Thank you."

The feel of her back pressing against his was now immensely distracting. She sounded pleased, but he wished she was in his arms and he could see her expression.

She blew out a breath. "I can act unconcerned, and it will be dark. Hopefully no one will look carefully at my eyes."

They talked through their plan again and again. How would Elizabeth act, when would Darcy signal for her to move to the window, all the way through to how many times might Elizabeth have to stab Conway's hands with the broken bottle. The horses would need to rest so they could not take the carriage any farther than Dartford. They would take a room in the coaching inn while they awaited a stage coach and while Darcy sent a messenger to Fitzwilliam.

After another hour, Elizabeth asked, "Why is Markle moving us at all? It is not as though anyone knows where to find us."

They were being moved so they could more easily be killed. They likely wanted Elizabeth to write one final letter, or they needed her finger to send a more gruesome message to Lady Catherine, and once the ransom was paid, they would both be killed and their bodies dumped in the Thames.

"It does not matter, my dear," he said as calmly as he could. "We have a way to escape now and that is what we must think on."

He did not voice his doubts about every possible thing that could go wrong.

Chapter Ten

E lizabeth had long been resigned to the truth that, as a woman, there was little in her own control. She could not travel without a man to accompany her, she could not enter a profession and still be genteel, and she could not manage what little money she had on her own. While she often bristled against these strictures in her own mind, she had accepted her place in the world and was resolved to act with as much agency as she was allowed.

Now, in this wretched, terrifying situation, she had no power at all, but at least she had a plan for her escape. That was enough to prevent her from giving up in despair. She could cling to that. She was not entirely helpless or hopeless, and it made her feel better to be in accord with Darcy.

Perhaps some of this strength, this resolve, had not only to do with having a scheme, but it also had to do with the man leaning against her back. She was not alone, and while they might not be equals in fortune or family, she was Darcy's equal in every other way that mattered. In intelligence, in generosity, in courage. Maybe also in warmth of affections.

Darcy still had an affectionate ardour for her, but was it enough for him to repeat the offers that she had rejected? Her own feelings had been far from equalling his two days ago. On Thursday, she would have said that she despised him, but she knew now that her feelings would someday soon match his.

Does every glance, every caught breath mean what I think it does?

"What shall be the first thing you do when you are restored to your family?" Darcy asked.

They had been quiet for a while, and she smiled that he was the one to begin a conversation. And not one about how to escape or about the horrid thing happening to them. She wanted the distraction, too, both from wondering what name to give to what she felt for Darcy and what would happen when they tried to escape.

"If we go to London, which would be my preference, and after I see the Gardiners and Jane, I want a bath." She laughed, and she felt him exhale his own soft chuckle of amusement. "I want to change my clothes and clean every inch of me."

"I want to shave."

Elizabeth heard the scratching sound of him running his hand over his jaw. She had never seen Darcy with whiskers, only the faint hint of them after the Netherfield ball when it was four in the morning and he had probably shaved the morning before. He seemed to dislike the feel, given how often he brought his hand to his face, but she thought it gave him a handsome and roguish air.

Her stomach rumbled, and she gave an embarrassed laugh.

"I am hungry too," he said.

"What will you eat when you get to town? Kidnapping victims get to eat whatever they like, I am certain."

"Like how children who have had a tooth pulled or a collarbone set get their choice?"

"Of course." She thought a moment and asked, "Which one happened to you?"

"Both," he said over his shoulder. "Due to milk teeth not falling out on their own and later a fall from a tree. The tooth was far worse."

"I have never suffered either. You would have thought with all my childhood running and rambling that I would have broken or sprained something, but I never did. Now, after this, I intend to eat curry, an entire platter of it. My aunt's cook makes a curry of rabbit with preserves of olives. They need not bring me a plate; they can simply give me a fork and set the platter at my place."

Darcy laughed, but she was not joking at all. "Please invite me to this dinner because I need this image in my mind for the rest of my life."

She wondered if he realised that meant he would have to call in Cheapside and be known to people in trade. "You are always welcome," she breathed. In that moment, she knew how much she wanted Darcy to call on her when this ordeal was over. In a livelier manner, she said, "What shall you eat? You want something sweet, something made with honey, I know. Come, you must tell me."

"My cook at Pemberley makes a saffron cake," he said. "She adapted the recipe to use honey instead of sugar when my mother joined the abolitionists. It has cinnamon, honey, and rosewater."

"It must be so sweet!" she cried, cringing.

He laughed. "You shall have to try it." While she wondered if she would ever see Pemberley, he said, in a more serious voice, "Who in your family are you most eager to see?"

She sensed he was not merely making conversation; he wanted to know. "I want to see Jane," she said. "My parents will not be a comfort to me. I want them to know I am well, of course, if they even know the truth yet, but I do not want to see them too soon."

"Why not?"

This was painful, but she wanted to answer him. "My father won't show his fear or concern, and will make a joke of it to ease his own mind. And my mother will only wail about her own anxieties. I know it might sound strange to not turn to one's parents, but neither of them will be able to show their concern, to listen, to take care of *me*."

"But Miss Bennet will?"

"Jane is so kind and patient, and my aunt Gardiner is elegant and intelligent. If I was more like the two of them, I would be a better person," she said with a laugh. "They are the ones I turn to for solace, to hear advice. Jane is never critical; she listens well and loves unconditionally. Mrs Gardiner also listens well, and while she remembers what it is like to be young, she gives sound guidance from someone who has come out the other side wiser."

"Your aunt sounds like an amiable woman, well worth knowing. I would like to meet her."

She felt surprised, but then wondered why this should surprise her, given what she knew of Darcy. It would have astonished her *before*, but she had no reason to doubt him now. "I promise to introduce my aunt and uncle to you."

"I am saddened to learn that your parents are not to be relied upon in times of crisis," he said, "that they will not or cannot give your feelings the care and attention they deserve. Still," he added brightly, "you are lucky to have a sister and aunt who love you so thoroughly."

Did Darcy still love *her* that thoroughly, enough to ask her to marry him again?

"Who do you turn to?" she asked quickly. He seemed so decisive, so confident, it was a little hard to imagine him asking for guidance or succour.

He was quiet for a while, and Elizabeth wished she could see his expression. "It might be unexpected, but I used to turn to my father for comfort and my mother for advice. She was serious while he was benevolent. Both were level-headed and reasonable, but my father listened better. My mother wanted to solve the problem. Both temperaments had their uses, of course."

"And now?" she asked. "They have both, I understand, been gone for a long time."

Darcy grew quiet again, and she wondered who he relied on. She supposed that a wife, that true partner he spoke of, might offer him both genial comfort and sound guidance. Regret at what she had thrown away pressed on her heart. Darcy had acted wrongly, of course, but so had she. She had judged too harshly.

Now was not the time to focus on what might have been or what could be. She tried to be lively as she said, "I refuse to believe that even the great Mr Darcy has no one he turns to in times of grief and woe."

"For things relevant to Pemberley, my steward is a capable man for day-to-day concerns. For more lasting estate ones, my uncle. For personal matters, well, I typically keep my own counsel. I suppose Fitzwilliam listens, although he shows his care by mocking me."

She smiled, and from his voice it sounded like Darcy did too. "I think he is fond of you. If you write to him when we get to Dartford, will he come?"

"By the time he gets it, I hope to be on a coach to anywhere, but yes. He would drop anything in an instant for my sake." He sighed heavily, and it sounded like he had brought his hand to his face again. "I hope he knows I would do the same for him." He grew thoughtful, and then said, "I have several dear friends, but Fitzwilliam is the one to abandon everything if he thought I needed him."

"No one would jump in a carriage at a word from me. Ladies do not have the same agency as men do, however much they wish it. My uncle, in a dire emergency, could be relied upon, but he has a wife and four young children who must always come first. My father?" she mused. "Maybe, if there were no other option but for him to act, but decisive action, and for the sake of others, is not in his nature."

She did not care for the sadness in her own voice and hoped that Darcy had not noticed. Everyone needed someone in their life who would drop everything and rush to their side, someone both capable of it and willing to do it. Did Darcy want to be that person for her? He was surely capable of that sort of wholehearted devotion.

Then why had Darcy denied the living to Wickham when that was what his father had wanted? He must have had an excellent reason, something more than the jealousy Wickham had mentioned.

"We shall try to get a stage coach to London so you can be with your sister and aunt," he said firmly. "I would not wish to go farther into Kent or Sussex where these smugglers operate if we have a choice. We would be safest in London to be sure, and you want to see Miss Bennet." He hesitated then said, "And I have to talk to Bingley regarding her."

There was no need to go over all of that again. "I think after I bathe and eat and cry in my sister's arms, I want to be outside, Darcy. I almost feel like the walls are closing in."

"I understand that." She felt him turn his head to look up at the useless window. The room was cluttered, there was no space to walk, and the sole window was too high to see out of. "I will go to Pemberley as soon as I can. I want to be amongst hills and open spaces."

"Tell me about it, please."

"You will soon grow tired of me talking about Pemberley."

"I want to picture it," she insisted.

"Very well." He described the park, the woods, his favourite walks, where he rode, the different holdings. The park sounded large, and with a great variety of ground. Valleys, hills, streams were described in such a way as to put a beautiful picture in her head. There was affection in his voice, and pride too. He would not give her much information on the house, but he described the tenants and land of his home in loving and vivid detail.

What might it have been like to be mistress of such a place? She had assumed Darcy would have kept her family from her if they married, but now he wanted to meet the Gardiners because they meant a great deal to her.

Would she ever see the Gardiners and Jane again? She felt her mind slip back to fear, and she did not want to think about what would happen after the door opened. "Let us play a game," she cried.

He paused for a heartbeat. "I do not think we have room for move-all or blind man's buff."

"I meant a word game," she said, turning. He shifted too, and now that they were no longer supporting one another, she had to look into his eyes. It was strange to sit on a bed with Darcy, and it brought to mind all manner of stimulating things not appropriate for the time and place.

He stretched and moved to the headboard, sitting tailor-wise. "What do you want to play?" he said with no patience.

She moved to sit next to him, folding her legs likewise and arranging her skirts over them. "Darcy, you are a clever man. You cannot think I want to play a game right now for the sake of amusement."

"Of course," he murmured. He looked chagrined. "I feel the same way. A distraction would be good. Choose a word game, something to tax our attention or some game of memory."

She thought, then said, "I will enigmatically describe a city, and you must guess it." He nodded, and she thought for a while. "Contention, plus what belongs to a lamp."

"Warwick."

"You guessed that far too easily," she cried. He shrugged, and she said, "What about 'merchandise'?"

"Ware." She threw him a surprised look. "What?" he said smilingly. "That was easy, and also a city very near to you."

"I have one you shall not guess. Gain this city, and you name another." He was quiet, but she could see he was thinking. "Do you give it up?"

"Winchester."

She threw up her hands. "I thought I was clever."

"You are," Darcy said quickly. He gave her a teasing smirk. "Perhaps I am cleverer."

Elizabeth narrowed her eyes. "I am a kind person, so I will allow you to think that. Your turn; you try to fool me."

"What tree is of great use in history?" She thought for a moment, and Darcy said, "A date."

"That is not fair," she cried, swatting his arm. When she realised what she had done, she was about to apologise, but Darcy laughed. Maybe he was as at ease around her as she was with him. She smiled and said, "That is not fair because I did not cry to give it up. It does not count, and you must go again."

"What tree is a lady's name?"

"Olive. Ha, no forfeit for you."

"What small tree is a letter of the alphabet?"

She ran through all the letters. "A tea tree!"

"What tree is a city? You should do well with this one," he added teasingly.

She thought for a long while, and Darcy brought out his watch and told her it was nearly four o'clock. "Very well, you may tell me."

"A cork tree." She groaned. "You owe me one forfeit, Elizabeth. Shall we keep a tally?"

They went back and forth, taking turns to quiz the other on naming trees and cities. It was a more pleasant time than she had thought it would be. Darcy did not give up once, even if it took him several minutes to give an answer, much to her annoyance. By the end of an hour, he had missed none and told her she had missed three.

"No, not three," she said, pointing at him. "A date does not count because I did not admit to giving up. You gave the answer too soon."

Darcy smiled. "Very well, then you owe two forfeits. We ought to have played for money," he said, laughing. "I might have made out well if we kept this up."

"I will pay my forfeits and keep my coins. Besides, to not do so is to ruin the game. What are your favourite forfeits to demand when you play with your friends?"

"Hmm, if I am playing with Fitzwilliam, he must keep a serious face for five minutes. It is a horrid struggle for him. What do you make your sisters do?"

"It depends on which one. Lydia might recite a proverb or Jane repeat some phrase five times rapidly without her tongue tripping up. They are sure to fail and make us all laugh. 'Kneel to the wittiest, bow to the prettiest, and kiss the one you love best' is also a favourite among our Meryton circle."

"Are all three forfeits paid to you?" he asked, giving her a steady look.

Her pulse pounded in her ears. "What do you mean?" she breathed.

"Elizabeth," he said in a low voice, "you must be the wittiest, the prettiest, and the most beloved."

It was clear to her that he had not spoken in jest; he was entirely earnest. Had she not considered what sort of partner she wanted for herself? Into her head slipped the image of a life with Darcy. *I can see myself loving this man.* Her heart skipped a beat at realising the depths of her own attraction. Would she regret it if she did not show him that she cared for him, too, even if it all came to nothing when this was over?

She rested her fingers on top of his hand; when she met his eyes, his pupils dilated. What did he feel in this moment? What she felt was complicated. Admiration and attraction, but was it the depth of love that Darcy felt for her? Not yet, but it was certainly there, and she certainly wanted to kiss him.

They stared at one another for a few shallow breaths. Darcy's fingers trembled as he touched her face. He slid his hand back, cupping it around the back of her neck. They both slowly, deliberately, leant toward each other and brushed their lips together.

His lips were warm and soft on hers. Elizabeth closed her eyes and sank into it. Kissing Darcy was the loveliest feeling. He was gentle and tentative, even now as both of his hands held a firm hold on her face, tilting her head so he could better fit his lips against hers.

When he stopped, she opened her eyes, and Darcy's rich amber eyes shone back. Some silent question was conveyed in his look, and in an instant, they eagerly reached for each other again.

This time, he deepened the kiss, and she moaned slightly as his tongue entered her mouth. She revelled in Darcy's ardour even as it amazed her to learn he could be passionate. Pure excitement flashed through her, and she felt all the tension and emotion that had been between them for the past two days. He pressed harder against her lips, his tongue sliding against hers.

She wrapped her arms around his shoulders, gripping him tightly. She had thought about kissing Darcy several times over the past day, but the reality of it was warmer, more ardent than she had imagined. She felt breathless, and was determined to make up for lost opportunities. The soft moan he made when her tongue found his and stroked against it filled her with disorienting delight.

His breathing was ragged when he bent to kiss the tender skin beneath her ear, spending so much time along her neck that it felt like he was concentrating on learning how sensitive she was. When he traced the edge of her ear with his tongue, she released her breath in a satisfied moan.

He drew back, and a small sigh escaped him as he pressed his forehead against hers.

"This is the worst moment in the world to be doing this."

At his tone, Elizabeth had a moment of panic that he regretted kissing her. She sat back from him and felt his gaze move over her even though her eyes were fixed on his waistcoat buttons. When she finally lifted her head, his eyes were dark and affectionate.

"But later?" she asked.

Darcy nodded, and she felt her anxiety fall away. "Later, when we are safe."

His voice was tight with what she finally realised was restraint. He was intently gazing on her, and it made her eager to know how much ardour Darcy was capable of. With a final longing glance at her mouth, he stood with a resigned sigh.

～

DARCY ROSE FROM THE BED TO GIVE HIM AND ELIZABETH AS much space apart as their cell of a room would allow. Not that he wanted to be away from her. He wanted to draw her back into his arms and kiss her again. No one had ever kissed him with such warmth, with such need. Elizabeth was just as perfect and sweetly passionate as he had imagined, and how awful that he had to learn that truth for himself when they were likely to be murdered.

And after she had said he was the last man in the world she could be prevailed on to marry.

He ran a hand over his stubbled jaw, hating the feeling of it, as he found the laudanum bottle on the washstand and snatched it.

"What are you doing?"

He had to *do* something, and kissing Elizabeth senseless was not an option. "Breaking the bottle so you can use it as a weapon."

She rose from the bed. "Put on your gloves. I don't want you to cut yourself." She found where his things were piled on a box and brought them to him. The outer edge of her lips was still pink and swollen from kissing him.

Elizabeth had character and sense and was not the sort to marry without love. But what did that say about kissing? Was it an impulse in a lonely, frightening moment, or did she feel something genuine for him?

"Did you need my help?"

He had been staring as she held out his gloves. Shaking his head, he put them on, walking to a crate in the corner to push off the detritus and lift the lid. With a swift tap he hit the base of the tiny bottle against the edge. The glass tinkled and left a few jagged edges behind.

He felt her watching him as he checked his work. The sharp edges, however small, would do damage against the hands or eyes of anyone who got near to her. He handed it to her, gesturing to her pelisse, and she hid it in the pocket.

"Let us walk through the plan again," he said, taking off his gloves. It would not do for him to think about begging Elizabeth to marry him and pressing her back into the mattress to indulge in everything he had longed for.

He replaced the lid and leant against the stack of crates as Elizabeth talked over every step of their plan, all the way to arriving in the inn yard.

"If Markle moves us too late, we will miss the final stage and mail coaches. Tomorrow is Sunday," she added.

"You know coach schedules are mere suggestions at best. We might not miss it after all."

She threw him a look. "Yes, we will."

"If we miss the coaches, I was going to find someone to take a letter to Fitzwilliam at first light anyway. He will come to get us, and we can stay in the coaching inn. We have enough to pay for a room."

She nodded to herself, and then asked, "When should I lower the glass and try for the carriage door?"

Darcy crossed his arms and blew out a breath. No decent postilion would push the horses faster than seven or so miles an hour, and certainly not at night. "If we make five miles an hour, and perhaps it is fifteen miles to Dartford, we might have three hours to wait for our moment."

"If I am to be completely disinterested from laudanum, I cannot always be looking at my watch."

"I can look at you when it is time to lower the glass."

"Will that be the only time you look at me the entire coach ride?" she asked softly. "I do not think I could bear that."

Her gaze was steady, serious, and he hoped their shared look meant to her what it meant to him, that he could scarcely bear the thought of not being near to her, not looking at her, not being with her for the rest of his life. "Well, I will cough to get your attention when I think we are within a few miles of Dartford."

They both heard a sound in the hall at the same time. Darcy pointed to the bed and whispered, "Pretend to be tired."

She hopped onto the bed and lolled her head against the headboard just as the door opened. Thankfully, it was only Kirby and the maid, exchanging water and pots and candles like yesterday. While the maid moved about, Kirby glanced at Elizabeth.

"Your face looks better," he said kindly.

She gave a faint smile but did not raise her eyes.

Kirby set down a tray, but he seemed more nervous than he had been this morning. He looked neither of them in the eye. He was neither friendly nor curious. Darcy wondered what might happen to the boy if Steamer or Markle suspected him of talking to them.

When the maid finished, Kirby let her pass, and before he locked the door, he turned back. Darcy watched him shift his feet and push up the sleeve of his too-long coat before whispering, "She took the laudanum?"

Darcy nodded, and Kirby blew out a relieved breath.

"Good. It would not do for my uncle to be cross with her."

The boy left, still refusing to meet his eye, and Darcy felt certain that Kirby knew that after Markle had strung along Lady Catherine and bled her dry, he and Elizabeth would be murdered and their bodies thrown in the river.

Elizabeth rose from the bed to see what had been left for them: a pitcher of water, two cups, a plate of cheese, and bread that must have been baked yesterday. The cheese had been sliced, and they would have to tear the bread with their hands.

"So much for getting a knife," she said through a mouthful. "Or roasted lamb."

They ate quickly and silently, and seemed lost in their own thoughts for a long while. There was nothing else to say or to plan or to distract them from the fact that soon they would have to fight for their lives. Elizabeth idly flipped through one of Kirby's books, and Darcy silently composed in his head the letter he would write to his cousin. They occasionally heard men's voices coming from the rooms below.

After checking his watch, Darcy said, "We should try to sleep. I know it is early, but we don't know when they will take us. We will need whatever energy we can muster."

Elizabeth agreed and gave a half smile. "I have to be ready to act dull and disinterested."

They both knew she would have to do more than that, that their entire scheme depended on her lowering the window and opening the carriage door.

They stood on either side of the bed, looking at it and then at each other before both of them looked away.

"We ought to stay dressed," she said, smoothing her skirts.

"Yes," he said, clearing his throat, "we need to be ready to move in a moment."

Darcy toed off his shoes and pushed back the pillow on his side, getting in without making eye contact with Elizabeth. She left up her hair and, rather than rest on top of the blanket as she had last night, climbed in next to him. He laid on the pillow, staring at the ceiling in the dim light, feeling Elizabeth's tempting presence surround him.

After a while, he heard her turn on her side, facing him. When he looked at Elizabeth, he thought he saw the same longing in her eyes that he had seen when he kissed her this afternoon. The tension that hung between them seemed to build impossibly stronger.

"May I kiss you one more time," he whispered, "before we go to sleep?"

Elizabeth nodded, looking pleased, and eagerly reached out to him. The light touch of her fingertips against his cheek was enticing, and he wanted to feel her touch him everywhere. She gave him a serious kiss, with parted lips, and his pulse accelerated. The same shocking passion he felt when he kissed her before shot through him again.

His heart drummed away at how she deepened the kiss until their tongues touched. Her mind and body had no hesitation when he tugged her against him so they were hip to hip, and he lightly curved a hand over her breast. She kissed him with languid intimacy, and it felt like her kiss seeped into his blood to course through him.

Common sense told him to stop and not pull her on top of him, and by mutual, silent agreement they moved apart and rolled onto their backs, and her hand clasped his in the dark.

Chapter Eleven

T he sound of the door being thrown open startled Darcy awake. He
was already sitting up by the time Steamer strode in.

"Rise and shine, Nan!" he said in a menacing voice, coming up to the
foot of the bed and shaking Elizabeth's legs. "Get up before I get in there
with you."

She woke and swiftly drew her legs away from him with a gasp. Darcy
put on his shoes, coat, and gloves while Elizabeth rose to move past
Steamer.

"Do you need help with that, Nan?" he asked, throwing out his hand to
stop her from taking the pelisse Darcy held out. "I can do up your
buttons."

Elizabeth shook her head, keeping her eyes down. Darcy edged in front
of Steamer to put himself between him and Elizabeth to keep him from
touching her. He fastened the buttons for her, and after she placed her hat
atop her head, Darcy tied the ribbon under her chin. It was best to pretend
she needed help because she was slow and dull from laudanum, but Darcy
saw that if anyone looked into her eyes, they would know she was alert and
terrified.

With his back to Steamer, Darcy gave her a questioning look, wanting
to know if she was truly ready to do this. She reached into her pelisse
pocket and gave him a quick nod. He guessed she had her hand clenched
around the little broken bottle.

Steamer stretched around him to yank Elizabeth by the arm and toss her toward the door. She stumbled, and it took every ounce of his strength not to lash out against Steamer. Darcy looked at his watch as they went down the stairs and out the door. It was after eleven; they had managed a couple of hours of sleep.

In the dim light of the coach lanterns Darcy saw Kirby by the lane, staring at the carriage. He tried to catch his eye, but the boy turned away. Darcy did not see Conway, but he supposed he would eventually mind the horses.

"Where is Markle?" Darcy asked.

Steamer flung open the carriage door and folded down the steps before giving him a rough shove. "Never you mind. You will see him tomorrow night. He ain't done with you yet."

Darcy got in, facing the rear, and Elizabeth sat next to him. Steamer sat across from them facing the horses, with his arms folded and giving them both a forbidding stare. At least this time there was no argument over who sat where, he was not blindfolded, and Elizabeth was already next to the door. Someone shut the carriage door—Darcy could not see who in the dark—and the carriage moved.

Elizabeth let out a sigh and closed her eyes, and Darcy wanted to put his arm around her and draw her against his chest, but attracting Steamer's attention in that way would be foolish.

"What is the matter, Nan?" Steamer said to her. "Did you not enjoy your time with your cousin? Was he not very good?" Elizabeth blinked at him, and then closed her eyes. Steamer barked a disdainful laugh. "No need to worry. Laudanum makes the memories fade."

He could feel the tension in her body at Steamer's taunts, but she pretended to be tired and stayed silent. Or she was silent from fear.

While the miles passed, Darcy wondered what Elizabeth was feeling. Did she feel the same hatred toward the men who had abducted and tormented them as he did? Was she gripped with terror at what would happen if they could not get away before they arrived at their smuggler's stronghold on the river? Was she near to trembling at the idea that they would be murdered if they failed to escape, that no amount of money in the world would convince Markle to spare them?

Anticipation of what they had to do felt like it was bursting out of him. He clenched and unclenched his fingers for hours, bouncing his legs and shifting his arm to feel where the quill knife was hidden in his sleeve.

Darcy checked his watch, ignoring Steamer's shout that he put it away, that it was a damned new moon and too dark to see anything.

I have to drive this tiny knife into that man.

When the time came, any hesitation on his part might cause Steamer to hurt Elizabeth or for her to fall from the carriage instead, or it might lead to them arriving in Dartford still in their captors' grasp. And all of that meant Markle would kill them.

This entire carriage ride set his teeth on edge. What might go wrong? Simply everything. He continually thought about how to both protect Elizabeth and throw Steamer from the carriage. The wait to get nearer to Dartford felt interminable. He was tense with nerves at the waiting and at not being able to speak to Elizabeth. They exchanged a few glances during the ride, but she seemed to be turned entirely inward.

He supposed that was good, given that she was supposed to be inebriated from laudanum.

With his heart racing, Darcy looked at his watch again. They had been on the road over two hours. Steamer did not yell at him this time. His eyes were closed, but he was likely not asleep in the jolting carriage, but perhaps lulled enough to give Elizabeth more time.

Darcy closed his eyes and drew in a long breath, and then he coughed.

Elizabeth's eyes flew to his, an expression of anxiety on her countenance. There was a moment of suspense where he wondered if she would act after all. Then she reached for the strap on the door's window and unhooked the frog holding it in place.

Rather than lower it carefully, she let the strap run through her hand and quickly brought the glass all the way down. The road noise increased and the wind rushed in, and Steamer cried, "Raise that side-glass!"

"I am very hot," she said weakly, resting her hand on the window frame and then putting her chin on her hand, facing out into the night.

"That is enough," he said after a moment. "Raise it up now."

She shook her head, still looking out.

Steamer reached for the strap that raised and lowered the side-glass, but Darcy called out, "Leave her be. You would not want her to be sick in the carriage."

"She had better not, or she will get her brains knocked out!"

While they talked, Elizabeth reached the hand that had been resting on the window frame down the outside of the carriage. She was reaching for the door handle and within seconds he would have to act. Darcy shifted in his seat and, pretending to fidget with his cuff, brought out the quill knife.

Was it cowardice that he was reluctant to stab Steamer, or did that make him a decent person? Of course, it was necessary and right to save himself and Elizabeth by whatever means necessary, so why was his hand shaking?

"Get your head back in here." Rather than jump at Steamer's impatient tone, Elizabeth rested her cheek on the window frame.

She had courage enough to play her role; he would have to conquer his fear.

Elizabeth was not a short woman, but she still had to rise from her seat to lean out enough to grasp the handle. The latch gave way, and Steamer swore a vicious oath before leaping across the carriage.

He grabbed her by the shoulder to pull her back inside the window frame, and she gave a shriek of pain as her hat caught the edge, but she managed to push out the door. The momentum of Steamer's hard yank brought them both back toward the centre of the carriage as the door swung open.

Elizabeth scrambled to the side, crawling atop the seat to hold open the door. Steamer was on the floor, facing the open door when he shoved Elizabeth with a sharp blow to the chest. She coughed roughly as all the air was driven from her lungs, and she fell back as Steamer reached to close the carriage door. It rattled lightly with each turn of the wheels while Darcy adjusted his grip on the knife.

Darcy raised a fist and brought it down above Steamer's coat collar, between his neck and his shoulder, driving it down with all the force he could muster. His hand slipped from the knife, and it stayed embedded in Steamer's flesh, blood oozing out of the wound. Steamer gave a roar of pain and in the same breath reached for his own larger knife. Before he could turn around, Darcy leant against the carriage wall and kicked against Steamer's back, forcing him off balance. Steamer fell into the door, but rather than fall through it he held on to it with both hands.

He heard Steamer drop his knife, and it clattered onto the road as they rumbled on. Darcy shoved him again, but Steamer braced himself against the open door, his upper body leaning over the roadway. Elizabeth brought out her broken bottle and drove it into Steamer's hand.

With a scream of outrage, Steamer let go. Darcy gave him a final shove, and he tumbled out.

The rear wheel jolted, and Darcy thought Steamer had been run over. Elizabeth reached to shut the door while Darcy knelt onto the rear seats to look out the window, but it was too dark for him to see if Steamer had rolled free or been crushed.

Darcy turned around, collapsing into the seat with a weary sigh. Elizabeth was pale, and then she gave a little cry of laughter as tears ran down her face. It was as though her body did not know whether to rejoice at being successful or cry at the distress of it. His own relief was short-lived; Conway was not slowing the horses.

"Why do you look like that?" she asked, smiling even though she still clutched the broken bottle. She raised the side-glass and latched the strap back into place. "We did it!"

Astonishment first kept him silent, but anxiety and fear soon succeeded this. "We are not stopping, Elizabeth."

Conway had not stopped to investigate the commotion, and now they would have to deal with him when they arrived in Dartford. He might shoot them the instant he realised Steamer was missing.

She brought two hands to her mouth. "What shall we do? Do we attack him in the inn yard, in front of witnesses?" She looked at the tiny bottle that now had a splash of red on it. "This is not what we planned! He was supposed to stop so we could take the carriage from him and drive it the rest of the way ourselves. What shall we do?"

She was panicking, probably from what they had just had to do as much as the scheme falling apart. She had been struck yet again, she had someone's blood on her gloves, and the hurt of all the other stress of their brutal kidnapping must be near to pouring out of her.

"I don't know," he whispered. "Let me think."

The last bit of colour vanished from her face. "This was not the plan!" she cried. "What do we do when we get there?" Her hands shook, and she was gasping as though she could not breathe. "We were supposed to take him by surprise on the road and steal the carriage!"

Darcy moved across the carriage and took her face in his hands. "We will think of something. Elizabeth, listen to me! We can still get away."

He forced her to look at him, and she calmed. She muttered a quiet apology, but Darcy still drew her into his chest. Her breathing slowed as the carriage rolled on. After another quarter hour, it slowed to make a turn to enter the inn yard of the Bull and George. Elizabeth sat back, clutching the bottle in her fist.

"We should get out ourselves to put as much distance between us and him."

She was right; they should not wait for someone to open the door and lower the steps. "Let me go out first—"

"No, Conway might shoot you as soon as he sees you and not Steamer," she cried. "Let *me* get out first—they might still need me alive—and when he gets off the horse, I can stab him before he draws the pistol."

It was not a bad idea to take Conway by surprise, incapacitate him, and then explain themselves to whomever was in the yard. "Give me the bottle, and let me do it," he said, holding out his hand. He noticed both of them had blood on their gloves.

She clenched her fingers. "No, he will not suspect a woman so I can get closer—"

"I am stronger—"

The door opened, and to his great surprise Kirby peered inside. "Where is Steamer?"

Darcy's mouth fell open. He and Elizabeth shared an anxious look, and she then asked, "Where is Conway?"

Kirby shrugged and folded down the steps.

"Were you riding on the rumble seat?" Darcy asked. He had not thought there was anyone on the back of the carriage.

"No," he said hesitantly, still looking into the carriage to find Steamer. "I was postilion. Uncle said it was time to do more and said if I drove the horses then Conway could load cargo tonight. We are all to meet in Gravesend tomorrow—today, I suppose."

Elizabeth gave Darcy an emphatic look before putting the broken bottle in her pocket. There was no way either of them would harm a twelve-year-old boy.

"Where is Steamer?" he repeated.

Someone came near and called out to Kirby for his tolls and tax tickets, and Elizabeth and Darcy stared at one another while Kirby showed he had paid. After that was settled, Darcy heard Kirby arranging for another team of horses, arguing over the price since now it was Sunday.

"We cannot harm him," she whispered.

"Of course not," he agreed.

"Will he just let us go? He has said that he does not want this sort of life."

"He might be willing to look the other way and leave us here, but what would Markle do to him? Kirby will have to answer for it when he meets Markle in Gravesend later. Or he will go back toward Shoreham to look for Steamer."

"You have to convince him to leave us here, Darcy," Elizabeth said gravely, "and not try to help Steamer. If Kirby goes back for Steamer and he is not injured, they could be back here in an hour."

Darcy had no answer. He got out of the carriage and handed Elizabeth down. They were in the courtyard of the Bull and George, just inside the tall coach gate. The three-storeyed building around the courtyard was galleried. Inside, there would be a hall for receiving guests, a staircase, and through another door was probably the apartment for dining coach passengers. The first floor was arranged around the inner yard, and the rooms were accessed by the open gallery that wrapped around and overlooked the yard.

He saw a few horses in their stalls, but there were no stage coaches, post boys, or carriages in the yard. Not a surprise, since it was near three in the morning on a Sunday.

As the ostler worked exchanging the teams, Kirby returned to them. "Where is Steamer?" he cried again, his face in absolute confusion.

Darcy gathered his thoughts. He could not distress the boy, but he also needed his help. "Kirby, what does your uncle intend for Miss de Bourgh and me?"

He toed his boot against the cobblestones. "Don't know."

"You may not know for certain, but you are an intelligent boy and can guess. Miss de Bourgh and I have done nothing to deserve what your uncle's gang intends for us."

Kirby gave him a pained look. "Maybe, maybe if that other lady pays..."

Darcy held his gaze for several seconds until Kirby looked away. "After he has extorted all he can from Lady Catherine, Markle intends to kill us both, does he not?"

"Yes" was said in a mumbled breath.

"Do you want to be a party to murder, Kirby?"

"No!" he cried, drawing the attention of the ostler who led away their team. "I am just driving the horses. I have nothing at all to do with whatever happens later." His shoulders fell, but then he gathered his confidence as he said, "Now tell me where is Steamer?"

"About four miles before you enter Dartford. We threw him from the carriage."

Kirby looked between the two of them, shaking his head in disbelief. "I have to find him! Is he hurt?"

"I think one of the wheels might have run him over, but he was alive when we tossed him out, which is more than I can say for Miss de Bourgh and me when we get to Gravesend. Now, I need you to leave Steamer—"

"I cannot!"

"—and go on to Gravesend as planned. Tell your uncle that you never looked into the carriage when you exchanged the horses and no one ever got out. Tell him you drove the horses as you were bid and were shocked to arrive and find the carriage empty. You are not an experienced driver and could not tell there was a weight difference."

"No, I cannot lie to him!"

Kirby started pacing restlessly. Darcy looked at Elizabeth. He had no idea how to reason with the boy. He was a good-hearted child, and certainly did not want anyone to be murdered, but he was terrified of his uncle.

Elizabeth gently put her hands on Kirby's shoulders. "He is going to kill me." Kirby looked away. "And I will probably suffer before he does. You don't want to be a free trader for many reasons, but this is one of them. You do not approve of their violent methods, do you?"

He shook his head but would not look at her.

"Kirby, Mr Markle and his gang will murder me, and you will feel guilty about that for the rest of your life."

"I know." The boy rubbed his knuckles across his eyes. "Very well," he muttered. "I, I can go to the house in Gravesend, and, and just be surprised that the carriage is empty and tell my uncle I did not know what to do, so I waited for him to come."

"Can you convince him?" Darcy asked. "He is a shrewd man, and we do not want you hurt."

He blew out a long breath. "I can convince him. It would make sense for you to not get out of the carriage when we stopped here. But as soon as my uncle arrives in Gravesend, he will trace you back to Dartford."

"Perhaps your uncle will simply want to find Steamer, and give up looking for us," Elizabeth said.

Kirby gave Elizabeth that adolescent look that was both pitying and conveyed that he thought her stupid. "He thinks your mother disrespected him. He will find you to kill you, even if it means he does not get any ransom for you."

Elizabeth looked shaken to hear the truth laid plain, but it was as they had suspected.

"When shall you see Markle?" Darcy asked him.

Another vague shrug. "Sometime today. He might arrive first thing in the morning if all went well with the cargo, or at midday if it did not."

"That does not leave us much time to be gone from Dartford," Darcy quietly said to Elizabeth.

"It is better than Kirby finding Steamer right now or explicitly telling his uncle that he left us here."

Darcy hated the idea of sending the boy back to his savage uncle. "Do you want to come with us, Kirby?"

"What?"

"Do you want to leave your uncle? I promised to help you if—"

"No! No, my uncle will find me, and while he might not kill me, he will punish me. He, he does not know that I don't— He thinks I want to be just like him."

By now, the new team was hitched. Kirby took off his hat and removed a few coins from a purse inside it to pay. He then got on the left-side horse and asked, "Are you going home, to Hunsford, from where they took you?"

Darcy nodded, intending nothing of the sort.

"Then you need to be gone from here as soon as you can," Kirby said, in a voice that was far too old and serious for a boy of twelve. "I won't tell them I left you in Dartford, but my uncle will follow the route back and speak to every toll keeper."

"Thank you, Master Kirby," Darcy said, touching his hat as he led Elizabeth away.

"Sir?" Darcy turned back. Kirby adjusted his grip on the reins, not looking at him, and muttered, "Fitzwilliam Darcy, number eight Charles Street?"

Darcy gave a small smile. "Near Berkeley Square, whenever you are ready." He dearly hoped the boy would escape his uncle and the violent life laid before him.

Chapter Twelve

K irby left through the gate, and before Darcy could speak with Elizabeth, the innkeeper and a porter came out. The porter watched the carriage leave and then looked around in confusion at their having not a single trunk.

"A mishap," Elizabeth said with a disarming smile. "The servants and trunks were loaded onto the wrong carriage and are hours behind us. We have not a thing with us."

He gave her an odd look as he touched his hat and went back inside.

"I am Mr Skillman," the innkeeper said, stifling a yawn. "It is gone two by now. What are you doing travelling so late? Did you have to wait for horses somewhere along the way?"

This was asked pleasantly, and Darcy wished he and Elizabeth had sorted out a story.

"A series of delays and misadventures," he said. "Have we missed the night stage?"

Mr Skillman looked surprised. "By several hours, but I have a room."

Darcy thought of the mere eight shillings they had. "Then I suppose we must stay the night. Have you anyone who can carry a message?"

Mr Skillman had been leading them to the door, and he turned back with a bewildered expression. "Now?"

Darcy felt Elizabeth press a hand to his arm. He did not have the influence, the reputation, or the coin to assert what he needed. It was the middle of the night, on Sunday when no one of character travelled, and he did not have the money to pay outrageously for the privilege of sending an express now.

"First thing in the morning, then," he said. "I need a messenger to go to Hunsford, near Westerham. I expect someone to send a carriage for us tomorrow."

The innkeeper gave a brisk nod. "Three pence per mile for the horse and four pence per mile for the postboy to deliver your message."

They would have just enough left to pay for a room and some food until Fitzwilliam could come for them.

They entered the hall, and in the lamplight, Darcy saw Steamer's blood on his gloves. He stuffed them into his pockets. He gestured to Elizabeth to do the same, but she kept her hands clasped behind her. He wished she would take them off; the last thing they needed was to appear like criminals.

"If your own carriage does not come," Mr Skillman went on, "the coaches travel the London-Dover road, and I can book you on Monday. White Horse, Fetter Lane, if you are going to town."

The innkeeper had a quill poised over his book. They did not have the money to go half that far, or the money for two nights in this inn. "We only need the room and meals."

"And to bathe," added Elizabeth.

Darcy held back a smile. "And water for the lady. I am afraid we are without a single thing for our toilette, so whatever you can provide would be appreciated." If they did not use many candles, they should have enough to pay for it all.

"Very good, sir." He came around the counter to the stairs. "My wife will see to it all in the morning. How shall we address you?"

Darcy widened his eyes. He could not use his own name, not with Markle soon to be looking for them. His mind was a blank slate.

"Gardiner," said Elizabeth, putting a hand around his arm. "Mr and Mrs Gardiner."

The innkeeper nodded and led them up a staircase while Darcy exhaled in relief at her quick thinking.

All the rooms were arranged around the exterior corridor. Their chamber was regular in shape, twice the size of the cell they had been in, and not cluttered at all. Darcy assured Mr Skillman they needed nothing but a candle, apologised for interrupting his sleep, and then sent him away and locked the door.

There was a curious kind of anxiety attending to not currently having anything to threaten their well-being. Elizabeth slowly removed her outer clothes and walked into the room, turning in a complete circle, as though not believing where she now found herself. In the dim light of one candle, he could not clearly see her expression.

"Will Colonel Fitzwilliam come for us?" she asked as she tossed her pelisse over a chair.

"I will send a message at dawn. If he does not arrive by noon, then we leave a message here for him and go. We should put as much distance as we can between us and Markle's gang, and we do not know if Steamer is injured or on his way."

Elizabeth gave him a long look. "We have little money, not enough to hire a coach on a Sunday. We shall have to walk."

"And hope that Markle is late to arrive in Gravesend to meet his nephew."

She nodded and stripped off her gloves, murmuring, "Poor boy."

As he took off his own things, he asked, "Why did you not take off your gloves when we came inside? You look like Lady Macbeth," he added lightly.

She gave a rueful smile and took them off. "True, but we would attract a different type of notice if 'Mrs Gardiner' took them off."

She held up her left hand and waved a finger. It took him a moment, but he comprehended her concern.

"Oh." Darcy removed from his pocket the box that Lady Catherine had given to him Wednesday. It had been easier to ignore it in his pocket than resign himself to keeping the dreaded emblem. "This might suit the purpose." He brought the box near enough for her to see. "The band is thin, and the stones do not sit very high. You can turn it round whenever anyone comes in and it will look like a wedding band."

"You typically go for a morning walk with a diamond and sapphire in your pocket?"

He pursed his lips, not wanting to talk about it. However, not sharing the truth with Elizabeth felt worse. "I was trying to forget all about it. My mother designed it after a ring Bonaparte made for his first wife. My aunt gave it to me to give it to Anne as an engagement gift."

Elizabeth had been running her fingertips over the two stones, but she dropped them.

"Lady Catherine had it for a long time," he said hurriedly. "She gave it to me a few days ago, and I left it in my pocket, wanting to ignore it. She was trying to convince me to..."

He did not know why he felt awkward. Elizabeth knew he had no desire to marry Anne. Perhaps it was because she had a few days ago said she did not want to marry him, but her actions these past few days hinted she might now give him a different answer.

"What will you do with the ring, since you will not use it the way your mother intended?"

"I hate to sell it since she did commission it. I suppose I shall give it to Georgiana."

"Thank you for letting me borrow it."

She held out her hand, and he was about to take the ring out of the box and slip it on for her, but the motion was too like a wedding ceremony. If he ever put a ring on Elizabeth's finger, it would be one of his own choosing, not the one his mother intended him to give to another woman. Darcy thrust the box into her hand.

"We ought to get a few hours of sleep. I will find someone to ride to Hunsford as soon as the sun is up."

Silently, they readied themselves for bed. While he took off everything but his trousers and shirt, he could hear Elizabeth untying her gown and lifting it over her head. He absolutely refused to turn around. Before, she had slept in everything but her shoes and pelisse. Darcy snuffed the lone candle. He did not think he could stand to see her in only stays and a chemise without the promise of ever seeing more.

He wanted to kiss her until he made all of her fear and pain disappear, until she knew how urgently he still loved her.

They climbed into the bed at the same time. How often had he thought of their joy in going to bed together, in finally giving way to that urgency of desire? He shook his head to himself as he fell onto the pillow. Over the past two days, he had thought of such things nearly as often as the phrase "now is not the time" crossed his mind.

Still, it no longer felt inappropriate or an unfortunate necessity to sleep next to Elizabeth. It was both welcome and comforting. What would it feel like to him tomorrow evening when they were in their separate homes, and there would not be a single reason in the world to share a bed?

"I have been wearing and sleeping in the same clothes for two days," she said through a wide yawn as she curled onto her side, facing away from him. "I cannot wait to wash them and wear anything else."

"Would it be wasteful of me to give away this entire suit of clothes because I can no longer stand the feel of them?"

"I think in this instance the rich can be forgiven their foibles."

"Then these trousers and shirt might go into the fire as soon as I get to town."

She laughed, and there was a long pause. "There might be talk, Darcy," she said slowly, "insinuations about an improper connexion between us because we were kidnapped together."

"When you give an accounting of our kidnapping, you can leave out any mention of there being only one bed," he said dryly.

When she neither laughed nor spoke, he added more seriously, "The sensation of our being kidnapped by smugglers, about your mistaken identity, will be what has everyone's attention, not that we were alone together. The outrage over what happened to two respectable people will be what captures notice. There is no need for where we slept to become a general concern."

He could mention that if there was any hint that her reputation was forfeit because she was held in the company of a single man, or that she was alone with a gang of kidnappers, he would marry her and damn anyone who spoke against her.

Of course, I would marry her anyway.

Darcy's heart beat faster at the thought of her being his wife, or holding her against him, feeling her arms around his neck again, and her lips moving gently over his. He longed to know for certain if she could love him, but now they were too weary for such a conversation.

Elizabeth yawned and then said, "I can honestly say that as long as we are unharmed, I could not care less about what anyone whispers. But it would hurt you if there is disparaging talk about your character."

"People like gossip if it hurts someone, Elizabeth," he said quietly, "and no mention that we were kidnapped together would hurt me. Besides, after an experience like this, our safety and happiness are more important to me than a few whispers by a tiresome society gossip trying to create a scandal where clearly none exists."

"Are we really safe, Darcy?" she said into the dark.

He knew she was not talking about safeguarded reputations or safe from gossip. Steamer might not have been injured after all and be briskly walking toward Dartford now. Kirby might admit immediately to Markle where they were. He turned on his side to face her back and moved a strand of hair that had fallen across her cheek. "For now."

Elizabeth reached back her hand, and Darcy took it. And when she tugged him nearer, Darcy shifted closer, wrapped his body around hers, and linked their fingers together. It felt like such a natural course of events to fall asleep with Elizabeth in his arms. His heart beat a little fast at her wanting the same thing.

But she might not be as ready to give in to their mutual attraction as he was.

He would have to risk his heart and ask her what she wanted. When this entire kidnapping matter was closed, when she was with her family and could think clearly, he would ask her again to marry him.

"I still don't know whether to feel afraid or relieved," she whispered.

All amorous wishes were driven away at the tension in her voice. "Both, I think. That is how I feel." The sensation of pushing a knife blade into another person would long stay with him, but he would do it again without hesitation. "In a few hours, we will be far from here, and everything about this will be a painful memory."

"Except for us being together."

"Is that because I agreed that your plan of escape was better than mine?"

She gave a little laugh, as he had hoped. "I am not sure what I would have done if you were not with me."

"That is not something you ever have to worry about," he whispered roughly.

Elizabeth yawned again, and then brought his hand to her lips and pressed a kiss to his palm.

Darcy kissed her hair before giving her hand a squeeze and falling asleep.

～

WHEN ELIZABETH AWOKE, STRETCHING HER ARMS OVER HER head and blinking at the sunlight, she had a moment of contentment before panic took its place. Darcy was gone. She leapt from the bed as a bolt of fear coursed through her.

"Darcy?" she called to the empty room.

She went to the window overlooking the courtyard, but, being Sunday, the typically noisy and busy yard was silent. She rushed to find her watch, the chain slipping through her fumbling fingers. It was eight in the morning; where could he have gone?

Gradually, her breathing slowed, and her heartbeat calmed. There was a sensible explanation. Darcy had likely gone to find paper and ink and someone to send a note to Colonel Fitzwilliam at Hunsford.

Elizabeth drew in a breath and slowly let it out as she sat on the bed. There was no reason at all to go to pieces. He would never have left her. Darcy had not been out of her sight for two days, and she missed him. Not simply was his absence noted because they had not been ten feet apart since this began, but she missed talking with him whenever she wished.

Wherever he was, did it feel strange to him to be apart, or did he welcome finally having a moment alone? Typically, she would be delighted to have a moment of privacy, the chance for inward reflection and quiet. But in this moment, she wanted Darcy here. They were safe now, and she wanted to enjoy that feeling with him before they returned home.

Falling asleep with his chest to her back was almost as lovely a feeling as kissing him.

But a kiss was not a vow; several heart-stopping kisses were not a vow. Darcy was the last man in the world who would give any woman the idea of his feeling more for her than he really did. He still loved her, but did she love him in return? What other name could she give to what she felt for him?

But did Darcy condemn his father's godson to penury out of jealousy?

Elizabeth groaned, pressing the heels of her hands into her eyes. Could she trust a man to be her husband, to be the man who would have absolute control over her money and her person, on whom she depended for her very survival, if he was capable of such callousness? What might happen to her, to her children, if her husband turned against her in the same way Darcy had turned on Wickham?

But such behaviour went against everything she had come to know about Darcy these past two days. Aside from his manner of treating Wickham, Darcy was everything she might want in a husband. His situation in life, friends, and his amiable mind, strict principles, clever insight, his kindness and generosity, his affectionate manner—*all* that was really of the first importance.

She could no longer believe that there was a shade on Darcy's character after all she had seen. So whom did she trust more: Wickham or Darcy? She knew the answer, but she still needed to know what had truly happened between them.

Was she brave enough to ask Darcy to explain?

It was a daunting thought. She remembered how contemptuous Darcy had been at the mere mention of Wickham's name. His complexion had turned red, and he paced while speaking in a raised voice. But there was no moving forward with Darcy in affection if she did not find the courage to ask him what had happened. Wickham's account of him seemed so outside his character.

Surely he was sensible enough to understand her concern. Darcy had already shown himself of having a heart and a character capable of improvement and repentance. If Darcy explained what had happened in a way that absolved him of any wrongdoing—and her heart told her that such a good man as Darcy must—then she could trust her future to him.

If he asked her again to marry him.

There was a knock, and the same terror that overtook her every time the door in Shoreham opened held her in its grip.

"Mrs Gardiner?" a woman's voice called. "It is the landlady, Mrs Skillman. Your husband sent me."

Elizabeth exhaled a laughing breath. She was in a respectable coaching inn. Darcy was in the building, and this was a pitcher of water; she was perfectly safe. She turned Darcy's ring so the stones faced her palm, and she was composed by the time the door opened.

Rather than just the innkeeper's wife, who entered with a breakfast tray, two maids—each carrying a bucket and towels—and a footman with a small hip bath entered. The maids deposited their loads and left, and the footman set down the bath near the fireplace, moved the screen, and built up the fire.

The innkeeper's wife set the tray on the table with a heaving sigh and put a small box on the washstand. "I think Mr Gardiner does not expect you to eat again today. He said to send up everything that was not much trouble to make."

There were shirred eggs and a honey cake, and toast and butter and coffee. Elizabeth smiled to herself; she would leave the honey cake for Darcy.

"If you can wait to eat, ma'am, I think it best to bathe while the water is warm."

She had expected only a basin and a pitcher, and said so to Mrs Skillman.

"Mr Gardiner thought you might want more than that," she said as the footman left. "It sounds like the two of you have been travelling a great deal, and with a few mishaps along the way."

This was said pleasantly by someone who was inclined to chat. "Something like that."

"Shall I help you, ma'am?"

Elizabeth nodded. She could likely get in and out without slipping, but pouring the water over herself to rinse would surely spill water all over the floor. It would be miserable to put her dirty clothes back on, but it was a price to pay for finally getting clean.

Mrs Skillman adjusted the privacy screen next to the bath. The hip bath was shallow, just wide enough for a person to squat in, nearly oval in shape, with the front side high and angled to keep much water from splashing.

Elizabeth actually smiled to hold the bar of soap in her hand.

"Will your husband want to bathe after you? Should we save some water?"

He likely would, but where could she go in the inn while he did? A respectable woman did not go into the public rooms, and they had no adjoining parlour. She was not about to walk in the town alone, not with it possible that Markle could be back to find them. "I think he will at least want to shave."

"Yes, he mentioned that, as though I could not tell by the look of him." Elizabeth rather liked the look of Darcy with whiskers, but kept the thought to herself. "Everything is on the washstand. I saw Mr Gardiner in the parlour, writing. He has been there an hour."

How long did it take to write to Colonel Fitzwilliam to say they had escaped and to come get them? "I wonder why he is taking so long to write to his friend."

"Mr Gardiner already hired one of the postboys to take his message. He said he also had to write an accounting of what has happened during your travels."

Elizabeth sat in confusion, holding her hair out of the way, as Mrs Skillman poured water over her. What could Darcy be writing?

"Your husband must be an enjoyer of travelogues if he is down there writing his own."

"He is a great reader," she said vaguely.

"I suppose his writing box and all of your other things are still missing. He asked if I would put it in the post to your home on Monday."

"Oh," she whispered. Darcy wanted to write everything that happened while it was still fresh in his mind, and he wanted to have an account in case anything happened to him. She hoped that Markle had not made it to Gravesend and talked with Kirby yet.

"Your husband seems a considerate man," Mrs Skillman led. "He was as concerned for your meal and bath as he was for making sure he had enough paper."

"Yes, Mr Gardiner is so thoughtful." She paused, thinking on all she felt for Darcy. "I think he is the best man I have ever known."

The door opened, and Elizabeth started, giving a little shriek of surprise and, although she was behind the privacy screen, she folded herself as small as she could.

"Oh!" She recognised Darcy's voice instantly. "I—I thought you would be finished—I can leave. I will walk in the yard."

And be seen immediately if Markle or Steamer arrived? "That is foolish," she said through the screen. "You will want to shave and eat. I am almost done."

She heard slow footsteps move from the door. What could Darcy see now that he was past the screen? Her back, and likely a little lower given how shallow the bath was. With her hand on the tall side of the bath, leaning slightly forward, Darcy would see the side of her breast as soon as he turned his head.

Now that he was in the room, she realised that she did not mind if he saw her naked. Not only did she not mind, she liked the idea very much.

"Did you want to bathe, sir?" Mrs Skillman asked.

It sounded as though Darcy tried to speak, but only managed to make a rough sound at the back of his throat. *Is he looking at me?* She refused to look over her shoulder to see for herself.

"Yes, he would," she answered for him.

She would look to the wall and stay to the side of the screen when he did. Simply because she would be happy to have Darcy admire her wearing no clothes did not mean he felt the same.

The landlady nodded to her. "And you can help him, then?"

So much for not seeing him unclothed. She made some indeterminate sound of agreement and turned enough to look at Darcy. If he looked absolutely mortified, if he seemed incapable of saying this distressed him, she would make his excuses.

The intensity of his eyes when he looked at her made her breath catch. He held her gaze as best he could, it seemed, but his eyes darted here and there across her body. A delighted thrill shot through her.

"Have you been married long, ma'am?"

Darcy went pink and started, and turned to the shaving stand. She heard water splashing and a deep sigh.

"We met last autumn," she said by way of answer.

Mrs Skillman poured water over her one last time to rinse the last of the soap. Elizabeth took her hand to step out of the bath and onto a towel, and wrapped another one around her. Darcy was still at the slim shaving stand in the corner, gazing at the tilted-up mirror.

She could still feel the press of his thighs against hers, the warm sweep of his tongue, his palm stroking her breast. Did Darcy feel the same tension between them that she did? Did he want to relieve it the same way she did? Whatever he felt, there was no way to address it with the landlady in the room.

"Thank you for your help," she said. "I can manage the rest myself."

After the door closed behind Mrs Skillman, Elizabeth finished drying. She heard a final quick scraping sound of a razor and then water splashing. She watched Darcy run a hand over his now-smooth jaw as he turned from the mirror.

She had liked him with whiskers, but he looked handsome freshly shaven too. Their eyes met and the sound of laboured breathing filled the room.

"Did, did you want to dress?" His voice sounded deeper than normal. "Do you need help?"

"Not yet; my clothes are so dirty. I will wait." His eyes moved from the top of her towel down to the bottom. "Unless, unless this bothers you?"

He gave a despairing little laugh that was devoid of humour. "There is no way in the world for me to answer that and still be a gentleman."

She felt her cheeks get hot even as she smiled. He could insist that she dress, and be thought to disapprove of what he had already seen, or he could say that he did not mind at all and be thought a complete cad.

"Your turn," she said, gesturing to the hip bath.

He swallowed so hard she could hear it. Darcy took off his coat and kicked off his shoes. While watching her, he removed his pocket watch and unfastened his waistcoat buttons. She felt the tension between them build to a heretofore unknown height.

Elizabeth turned away before she saw any more. As eager as she was to explore whatever Darcy was willing to do, watching him strip off his clothes piece by piece was too much to handle. She combed out her hair and brushed her teeth, and ignored every fluttering sound of Darcy's clothes being tossed to the floor. When she heard splashing, she felt brave enough to turn.

She had always thought his face was handsome, even when she disliked him. She tried not to stare, but even the stolen half-glances gave her enough to assemble a complete picture in her mind. Broad planes of his back. A lean waist. Muscles here and there. Dark hair on his chest trailing down.

Looking at him made her overwhelmed by a shameful amount of excitement. Maybe not shameful at all, for what could be more natural and necessary given what she felt for him and after what they had been through together? It was only shameful if Darcy was not wanting the same thing. He might be far better at managing his desires than she was.

There was a sudden, larger splashing sound, and she saw Darcy had tried to reach for the bucket himself.

"I can do it," she said, coming near. "Do you want your hair rinsed too?"

He nodded, then went still as she came to where he was crouched on his heels. She poured the water to rinse him and watched it run down his neck and chest. She wanted to lick off each droplet. Her entire body flashed hot at the thought.

He stood, keeping his back to her and wrapping a towel around himself, but not before she had a full view. He wanted her as much as she wanted him. It made her a little faint with pleasure. Not that it meant he would do anything about it with the woman who had refused to marry him.

Elizabeth watched him dry off, a towel slung low over his waist, waiting for him to turn around. He might say they should eat or get dressed, or some other respectable thing.

Darcy turned and when he looked at her, his eyes looked wild and fierce. She felt her heartbeat slamming in her chest. She was aching to hold him tight, but had no idea if he was willing to go to bed with her.

His gaze slid to her lips and then back up; his mouth parted, and he looked on the verge of asking a question. Elizabeth took a step closer and nodded. His eyes went wide, and a shiver moved through him. He slowly walked near, and she looked up at him, feeling the stir of his breath against her lips. They stared at each other for the span of a few shallow breaths.

When he whispered, "I want to do more than just kiss you," Elizabeth nodded again.

He took her mouth in a deep, demanding kiss, exploring it with possessive sweeps of his tongue. Darcy framed her face with his hands, tilting her head for a better angle. She could have laughed from excitement and relief. She moved her hand to the back of his neck, fisting it in his hair, and she wrapped the other around his shoulder.

He wrapped his arms around her with a groan, pulling her tight against him. His mouth moved from her lips, down her throat and sucking hard.

The sensation as he sucked and kissed her made her hot with longing. He tugged away her towel with a rough sound of desire.

When she felt bold enough to push away his towel, his stomach muscles flexed, and she ran her hand up and down him, hard and ready. He whispered her name, and she felt the syllables vibrate against her neck.

She drew his lips from her neck back to her own and kissed him with a frenzied passion. Darcy's hand stroked her breast, his thumb swirling around her nipple. Elizabeth arched against him, gasping out his name.

He gave her a hard look, and then with one arm locked around her waist and the other still working her breast, he walked her backward toward the bed. Or maybe she pulled him with her as she made her own way across the room, kissing him back hungrily.

He pushed her down on the mattress and joined her, drawing one nipple into his mouth, circling it with his tongue. He alternated between his mouth and hands on her breasts until she nearly felt on the edge of release. It was astonishing. Then he sat back and swept his hands over her stomach and down her hips before kissing down her body. What he did next was so shocking and arousing she had no words for it.

His tongue moved against her in long, steady strokes as he brought her leg onto his shoulder. She wanted to close her eyes, but when he looked at her and she saw the ardour in his eyes, she had to watch him as he set his tongue against her faster.

"Darcy!"

Thankfully, he never stopped to speak, but he moved a hand to her breast, kneading it hard. Tremors of bliss overtook her, and she cried out. Darcy's motions slowed, and he pressed lazy kisses to her thighs and fondled her breasts as he moved back up her body, his expression a mixture of pride and fondness.

When he was atop her, he stared into her eyes for a long moment. "I still—" Now his expression looked pained. "I know your feelings do not—"

"I have made a fine beginning to fall in love with you." She smiled and stroked his cheek and kissed him. "I think things are going on charmingly."

"Is that enough for, for this?" Before she could answer, he said in a rush, "If you don't want...me, we can stop."

She made a despairing sound and shook her head. "I want you."

Darcy smiled, and it was the most endearing sight. She kissed him again, giving him all the encouragement she could through the press of her lips and the swift motions of her tongue. The heat of him pulsed against her, and she instinctively tilted her hips.

She gave a cry of surprise, not in pain, but at how good it felt to be with him. He started a slow and steady roll of his hips, staring into her eyes.

"Darcy," she said breathlessly after a few moments, "I think—"

"I think you should give me my name."

How could he speak so calmly while his body moved over her and within her? She marvelled that someone so reserved wanted still more intimacy with her, and she was grateful for it. "Fitzwilliam?" she said purposefully, testing the name.

He smiled, keeping the same languid pace. "Yes, Elizabeth?"

"We can move faster."

"Oh no. Not yet." He looked down at her body before bringing his gaze back up to her face. "I have been waiting for this for a very long time, and I intend to make it last."

Pleasure flashed through her, and she kissed him again. He kissed her back slowly and sweetly until finally his kisses became rougher and his strokes harder. She reached off the bed to meet him, and Darcy wrapped her leg around his hip. Now his every stroke hit her in the right place and she gasped.

His fingers laced with hers, pressing them into the sheets above her head as he thrust deep, over and over. Rapture built as she lost herself in every sensation. The sound of him moaning, lost in pleasure, pushed her over the edge, and she cried his name again. His thrusts quickened and lost all of their rhythm. They had not talked about what to do in this moment, but with a low groan, Darcy withdrew. She pulled him back to her, and he fell against her, calling her his "dearest and loveliest."

Chapter Thirteen

D arcy missed her the moment he left her arms. He immediately drew Elizabeth against him again, and she came willingly, pressing a leisurely kiss to his lips even though he still had not caught his breath. She then kissed his neck and ran a hand over his chest, and it made him wish they had time to do it again. It was dangerous to stay as they were, naked and wrapped around one another, with Markle and his gang possibly on their way.

He would never forget the sight of Elizabeth from a few moments ago. The most beautiful picture he ever saw: head thrown back, face expressive of bliss, figure exquisite in every way.

The tension had built up inside him over the last day, but he had only been partly secure that she felt the same, or rather that her degree of desire matched his. Seeing her naked in the bath had been the height of the mounting anticipation he had been feeling. He had been afraid that Elizabeth had not wanted the same thing, or, worse, that she could not see a future with him at all.

But then their eyes met; hers were dark, full of meaning. He had felt her intently watching him as he bathed. By the time he had dried off, the apprehension and excitement were unbearable. He wondered if she would be hesitant, or need more promises first—promises he wanted to offer. Instead, her mouth had claimed his with hunger and purpose, and they had fallen into bed.

"You have not fallen asleep, have you?" a voice whispered in his ear before a pair of lips kissed behind it.

He answered by folding her in his arms a little tighter. They were not out of danger yet, but just another few moments. Somehow, despite the fear and anxiety of what had happened to them, desire and attraction and —he hoped—love had built between them these past two days. In a moment, they would get up to be ready for whatever happened next.

His body had a different opinion than his mind. Elizabeth smiled, sitting up a little with a flash of interest in her eyes that sent his heart racing. "Maybe we could stay a little longer," she said with the hint of a question.

It seemed to him she already knew the correct answer. "I wish we could, but that would be foolish."

"We are not out of danger yet," she agreed. He shook his head ruefully. "Markle could be on his way, but he would have to search the entire inn to find us, and no one here would stand idle as he tried to abduct me again."

She sat up as she spoke, and Darcy let his eyes wander her body, grateful that he no longer had to hide every longing and appreciative look. "True," he said, dragging his gaze back to her face to see her satisfied smile, "but I sent a messenger to Fitzwilliam hours ago."

Elizabeth let out a long breath of dismay, and Darcy laughed. "You should be delighted that rescue is on its way. I have only three shillings left, and it is a long walk to town."

She got out of the bed and put her chemise over her head before pulling up her stockings. "I am glad for that, and I suppose it would not do to be caught in a situation that would be difficult to explain."

As long as they did not need to justify it to each other, he was satisfied. Maybe what they had done would be considered by some a sin, but it did not feel like a moral failing to him. It was not wrong given their feelings for one another, even if hers did not yet match his. They were going on charmingly, she had said.

But insecurity drove away both his confidence and rational thought. "Do you regret it?" he asked.

She took what felt like so long to answer that he began to feel nervous. She came back to the bed, the corner of her mouth turned up in a hint of a smile. "That depends. May I still call you Fitzwilliam when we are alone?"

"Always," he said through the emotion in his throat.

"Then no." Elizabeth kissed him quickly and went back to dressing. "When can we expect help to arrive?"

Feeling lighter, he dressed. "I hired a messenger around half six, who probably got to Rosings two hours later. It might take Fitzwilliam four hours if he rode in my coach, which would be sensible if he brought help and planned on bringing us back." He checked his watch as he put it back into his waistcoat. "But it is just as likely he ordered a horse saddled while my letter was still in his hands, and he will be here himself in two hours."

Elizabeth struggled with a tie on her gown, and Darcy helped her, running his hands over her hips when he was done and keeping her close. "What time is it now?" she asked.

"Ten."

"So, he could be here in half an hour?"

Darcy nodded, and Elizabeth brought her hands around his shoulders. "I hate the feel of these filthy clothes, you know. I would like to have kept them off for another half an hour."

He felt a grin tugging at his lips. "And how might you have liked to spend that time?"

She immediately kissed him. He nipped her lower lip with his teeth, and then his tongue met hers as a hum of pleasure sounded in her throat. And then her stomach protested loudly at the meagre amount of food she had eaten in the past two days.

"Are you hungry?" he asked through a laugh.

"Starving!"

She insisted the entire honey cake be put before him, refusing to let him take only a slice, and took all the bread and butter for herself. As they ate and drank, their silent and comfortable camaraderie felt different to him. He felt Elizabeth's lightness and playfulness fade, and a stillness replaced it. He wondered if it was real or if his insecurities played with his perceptions. Should he speak into the silence, to ask her what her sudden pensiveness meant, or was he only imagining that her mind had gone some place far from the bed they had just shared?

"Well," she said, setting down her napkin and pushing aside her plate. "I think I have gathered my courage enough to ask you something."

She wanted his assurances after what they had done. He felt a little relieved. Her feelings were only natural, and he was eager to offer himself again.

"My dear, I promise you that my—"

"Please, please let me speak." She idly twisted the sapphire and diamond ring round her finger. "I know you are not on friendly terms with him, but you must tell me what happened with Mr Wickham."

Darcy sat quite overwhelmed by surprise to hear mention of that man's name.

"Fitzwilliam, would you tell me why you did what you did?"

"What I did?" he repeated as his heart rate rose.

Elizabeth gave him a pained look. "I know your father bequeathed him the best living in his gift. He meant to provide for Mr Wickham, but when the living fell, for some reason, you gave it elsewhere."

"Why do you need to know?" He felt extremely shocked. Did she think him capable of some sort of malicious revenge?

"I know you are resolved to act better by those outside your circle, and I *do* believe you." She said this with emphatic entreaty. "But I need to know why because"—she gave a tremulous smile—"my feelings are changed from what they were on Thursday. But Mr Wickham expected your patronage, and you left him with no money and no prospects. Can you imagine how alarming that is to me, as a woman choosing her future partner?" She searched his eyes, but he was still so confused that he could not give her whatever it was she was looking for. "You disapprove of my family, my connexions, my lack of fortune, and you regret having an affection for someone who brings you nothing."

"I was wrong to say all of that," he said, struggling to keep his patience, "and to even feel it in the first place, but what has that to do—"

"I don't want you to resent me," she cried. "I give up everything to become a wife; my very personhood is forfeit. You will have absolute control over me."

Darcy rose quickly, knocking the table and clattering the dishes. "And you think I would do, what? Cut you off from your family? Allow you no money of your own? Abandon you?" His voice raised in grievous anguish as he realised what Elizabeth was afraid of. "You think I am capable of committing some shocking and unheard cruelty to the person I am supposed to love best on earth?"

"No! At least, not any longer. After these past two days, I cannot imagine it at all," she pleaded. "You are generous and kind and, and every-thing that I could want. So, explain to me why you mistreated a man who expected your support. It would assure me that your wife"—her voice broke—"if she was poor and unconnected, with embarrassing relations, would never be neglected the way Mr Wickham was."

For a moment, he was incapable of articulating a single thought. All he was aware of was an indescribable agitation. At her, at Wickham, at himself, at this entire situation.

"What do you feel for me?" he asked as calmly as he could manage. Her mouth fell open in surprise, and she closed and opened it a few more times. "Tell me," he demanded, louder than he ought to have. He needed her to put a name to it.

Elizabeth had gone pale. "I feel a lively esteem for you, a deep affection. As well as gratitude and respect."

"The last thing in the world I want is your gratitude," he retorted. "And what we have experienced together in this terrible situation should not be what makes you admire me."

"I love you on your own merits!" she cried. It should have made him happy beyond measure to hear those words. "How could you think I would love you only because we were locked in a room together? By that estimation, I might have gone to bed with Colonel Fitzwilliam or Mr Bingley if they had been present instead of you!"

She glared at him with a cold fury. It sounded foolish to his own ears. "Do you even want me to ask you again to marry me?"

She now looked on the verge of tears. If she said yes, he would do it in his next breath.

"Not before you explain your history with Mr Wickham."

Darcy scoffed and shook his head, an unfamiliar bitterness filling him. "You love me, or feel that you could, but if you think me capable of cruelty toward him, then you do not know me any better than you did on Thursday."

"I do know you *now*. But before, you were proud, selfish—I just want to know your reasoning for doing such an awful thing to an amiable man."

"That man you trust deceived my sister!" The words hurt to say. His chest actually hurt as the words left his lips.

"Deceived?"

"Deceived, persuaded, cajoled, coaxed, duped. Pick a name," he ground out.

Elizabeth had the same look of shock in her eyes as when she had fallen to the ground after Steamer struck her face. "Seduced?" she whispered.

"No," he said, forcing into his voice a calmness he did not feel. "No, but only by the barest stroke of luck."

"Mr Wickham said Miss Darcy was—but was this before you denied him the living?" Elizabeth stammered every other word. "But he said— what really happened?"

Darcy strode to his greatcoat, wrenched out the letter he had written

Friday morning, and threw it on the table, the envelope filling the air with a harsh snap.

"Read it, since you need to know my history with that man before you can trust me." He gave her a hard look, and he was certain they both felt every other moment in the past two days where she had trusted him. "It defends every unjust accusation you threw at me."

Darcy stormed out the door, his heart fractured and with a cold sweat across his body. He charged down the open gallery that overlooked the yard. Even after all they had been through together, Elizabeth still blindly trusted whatever Wickham had told her. He felt bursting with the need to move or do something. Possibly kick something.

He let out a curse of frustration. Whatever she thought of him before, he should no longer be a stranger to her now. Not after every meaningful conversation they had, after every profound look they had exchanged. After what happened in that bed. She should know him better by now.

Darcy took a few calming breaths as he paced the gallery. Losing his temper did neither of them any good. Elizabeth's accusations about him were formed on mistaken premises, and Wickham was the one he ought to be angry at, not her. He hardly wanted to spend a moment thinking about the worst man he had the misfortune to know. But had he not already decided to defend himself and explain his history with that man?

It churned his stomach to think that Elizabeth might read his letter and still not believe him.

A sinking feeling now struck his heart as it finally began to slow. Their conversation played over in his mind. Had he misunderstood Elizabeth? He was so insecure in what she felt for him, still wounded from her acrimonious refusal, that he did not hear what she was truly asking him. Perhaps she did not think the worst of him; she only wanted to know his version of his history with Wickham.

He leant against the rail, staring blankly at the lone horse in the yard. When he had proposed, Elizabeth had accused him of inflicting harm on Wickham. But just now she had only asked to hear his account of the events.

Her opinion of him might not be as dreadful as he assumed, but with his mistaken assumptions and loss of temper, he might have just ruined any chance he had at redeeming himself in her eyes. Had he ruined everything, or could he apologise and make it right? They both needed to be calm if he had any chance of resolving this misunderstanding he had caused. He would pace the courtyard for a while before going back into that room that now had a mixture of many wonderful and painful memories.

When Darcy approached the end of the corridor, he saw Kirby hiding in the dark corner.

"What are you doing here?" he cried in surprise.

"I heard yelling from your room," he muttered, keeping his head down, "so I thought to wait."

Darcy blinked. "You knew what room to find us in?"

Kirby shrugged. "'Twasn't hard. I said I had a message for the couple who arrived overnight with no trunks, and a porter sent me up."

That they were so easily found was alarming. "Why were you looking for us?" Kirby stepped from the shadows, and he saw the boy sported a purple bruise around his eye. "Kirby," he whispered, tilting up his chin to have a better look, "what happened?"

For a moment the boy looked vulnerable, but then he pulled away, frowning. "My uncle was not pleased that I could not explain what happened." He crossed his arms. "He said I was stupid for not knowing something went wrong during the drive."

His indignation at Wickham and his loss of temper with Elizabeth felt very different from the anger that now simmered in his chest. That Markle would abuse his nephew was unjustifiable. "Did you come back to report to Markle where we are?" It could only be expected. Kirby was just a child, a brutalised child.

"No," he said, scowling. "I came to warn you. I heard them talking yesterday while you were all in the house. They always planned to kill you and Nan. Uncle talked to the toll collectors and thinks you must be here at the Bull and George and sent me ahead to find your room, and then I am to find Steamer. Someone near Dartford probably found him and called for a surgeon. I came to warn you they are a quarter of an hour behind me."

His mind spun with possibilities. Fitzwilliam might come with a carriage and every able-bodied man from Rosings, but possibly not in time. Markle's gang would find him and Elizabeth in the room, murder them both, and flee. Where could they go without being seen? If they left the Bull and George and were encountered on an empty street, two quick shots would go off and Markle's men would be gone before anyone pushed aside a window curtain to peek out.

What are we going to do?

Kirby shoved his arm. "Go, Mr Darcy! Hide in the stable, or in one of the post chaises. I will tell them I could find no one to question, so I left to ask the local doctor if anyone brought in Steamer."

"Will your uncle believe you?" he asked, looking at the boy's bruised eye.

He shrugged again. "He might, but he will still check the rooms for himself."

"Someone is coming for us this morning. Join us?" he asked again. "I hate to leave you to such a violent man."

Another look as though he was the most foolish adult Kirby had ever encountered. "If I disappear the same time you do, he will figure it out and never leave you alone! You need to hide. I found your room in two minutes; anyone could. My uncle does not care about the money. He only wants to hurt the lady who crossed him."

Kirby gave him another shove down the gallery, and then he ran down the stairs without another word. Darcy felt his mind turn in a thousand directions as his heartbeat raced. The likelihood of harm or death that had hung over them for the past two days felt different from this immediate threat.

He had to explain himself to Elizabeth, but this new development meant there was no time for talking.

THE TUMULT OF ELIZABETH'S MIND WAS VERY GREAT. HOW HAD asking for this one reasonable explanation led to such a quarrel? Her agitated reflections gave no answer, so Elizabeth read the letter that Darcy had thrown to the table.

The beginning was angry, and a quick perusal of the first paragraphs showed it reviewed what they had discussed about Bingley and Jane. But the last two pages and the back of the envelope laid bare the full history of Wickham's acquaintance with Darcy.

The extravagance and general profligacy that Darcy laid at Wickham's charge shocked her; the more so, as she could bring no proof of its injustice. How astonishingly different did everything now appear in which Wickham was concerned. His designs on Miss Darcy utterly appalled her.

I was so weak and vain.

Darcy had vindicated himself, and how he must hate her for championing such a man. She never told Darcy that she trusted him and suspected Wickham of withholding some part of the story. How dreadfully had she managed this conversation. She just ended breakfast and demanded an accounting as though she still thought the worst of him. As selfish and proud as Darcy had once been, he had been more just to Wickham than that horrid man had ever deserved.

All this time, only one of them had been a good sort of man, and it had always been Darcy.

The door was thrown open, and of course it must be him. She was not ready to raise her eyes; her cheeks were hot with mortification. She felt depressed beyond anything she had ever known before.

"Get up," he cried.

She started at his harsh tone. She had thought walking away would have calmed his anger. "What? Why?"

"Kirby says they know we are here."

She stood, mute and confused. Darcy grabbed her wrist and tugged her to the door, and with stumbling feet, she followed, grabbing her letter off the table before she did.

They ran down the stairs, Darcy taking them down the exterior staircase rather than lead them into the inn itself. Were they fleeing into the town? The yard was silent, and Elizabeth ran toward the arch that led out of the courtyard when Darcy yanked her hand and pulled her to the stables.

They ran past the horses in their standing stalls and into the adjacent carriage house. Being Sunday, all was quiet. Darcy led her past the small washing station for the carriages and the tack room. There were large windows at both ends, and all the doors and windows were open, as they ought to be. It seemed a foolish place to hide.

"Someone will see us—" she began.

Darcy made a hushing sound as they went to the post chaises not currently hired. They were all the same, but with varying degrees of wear; all yellow, with one inside seat, no box, and no external seats. Darcy opened the door to one and, without bothering to lower the steps, told her, "Get in!"

She did, not very elegantly. Darcy climbed up after her and, using the side-glass strap, tugged the door shut behind him. He closed the forward window blinds with two quick flips and sat on the floor, gesturing for her to do the same. They were crammed in uncomfortably, with her wedged between the seat and wall with her knees bent, and Darcy in pretty much the same position in front of her, his feet touching the door.

All she could hear was her own heartbeat and the sound of their breathing.

"Darcy," she said, her voice shaking, "I did not know Wickham was—"

He looked over his shoulder at her, his eyes wide. "Do not talk," he muttered, enunciating every word.

He silenced her because Markle's gang was here to kill them. It still hurt to be pushed away, although she could not blame him after what she had said. She did not know if she wanted to beg Darcy to put his arms around her, or never lay eyes on him again from humiliation. All of her feelings weighed on her, and were compounded tenfold when she heard several horses enter the yard.

Chapter Fourteen

Her hands shook, and the sound of paper fluttering was what made her realise that she still held Darcy's letter. She was afraid to fold it and put it away lest it make more noise. How many horses had just entered the yard? It must be Markle's gang; no one else would travel on a Sunday. Elizabeth heard voices calling out, but they were too far away to identify them or hear their words.

Sounds above them told her that a groom was making his way down the stairs to tend to their horses. There seemed to be a lot of talk, and she was desperate to know how many men were out there. Maybe they could escape if there were only a few. When she was certain the groom was outside, she leant forward.

"How many?" she whispered into Darcy's ear. He shuddered at the near contact. He held up four fingers, then he raised his shoulders and lowered them. Four riders, possibly more or less. Markle, Conway, Colton? Markle might have gathered others to help pursue them.

She wanted to whimper in terror, but it would not be her fault that they were discovered. Darcy was silent, and she could be too. Someone would likely find them regardless, and Markle would shoot them in this old post chaise. The smugglers would find their room, realise that they had recently been there, and then search all of the Bull and George until they found them.

Elizabeth felt absolutely freezing despite how fast her heart was pounding. She swore the post chaise got smaller the longer they sat.

After some time of quiet, she heard more horses' hooves against the cobblestones and then voices again. Elizabeth pressed her lips together as tightly as possible. She could not cry out. Markle would open the door, shoot Darcy, and then her. The last thing she would know before she died was that Darcy had died too. And he would die believing she still trusted and admired a complete scoundrel.

She heard quick steps enter the carriage house and come closer.

She let out a whimper involuntarily and then clamped a hand over her mouth. Darcy reached behind him and rested a hand on her foot, giving the only comfort he was capable of. Or telling her she had better be quiet.

The top of a hat appeared in the door's window, and then the door opened, revealing Colonel Fitzwilliam's face.

Elizabeth immediately burst into tears.

He started, either at the sight of them huddled on the floor or at her sudden weeping.

"What are you doing in here?" he asked, looking between her and Darcy as he moved out of the way and lowered the steps.

"We are not out of danger," Darcy said, stepping down and then throwing his arms around his cousin. Elizabeth saw the colonel's eyes widen in surprise, but he clapped Darcy on the back in return.

"I should like to see anyone recapture you with me here," he said, smiling.

"I do not think you alone are enough to hold back a band of smugglers bent on revenge," Darcy said. He sounded stern, but he was looking at his cousin and smiling widely.

"Well, it is a good thing I am not alone. Your valet, Mr Easton, and Rosings's coachman joined me. More wanted to come, but these were the men who made ready the fastest. I was not about to wait any longer than the time it took to saddle my horse."

Darcy had said this might be the case, and a pang struck her heart as she wondered who in her life would have faced imminent danger to come swiftly to her aid. It might have been Darcy before she implied that she still believed Wickham.

Darcy noticed her climbing from the chaise and held out a hand to help her balance. But he refused to meet her eye, and she felt disappointed in herself all over again. She folded Darcy's letter and put it away before anyone commented on it.

Ignoring Darcy, she held out a hand to Colonel Fitzwilliam. She could not find the words to thank him, and he smiled knowingly as she gripped his hand. Just as with Darcy, words of gratitude seemed too absurd and inadequate.

"Miss Bennet, Mrs Collins is beside herself with worry for you," Colonel Fitzwilliam said. "Are you well, as well as can be expected?"

It was peculiar to be called Miss Bennet. She had been tauntingly called Nan or endearingly called Elizabeth for two days. "I am shaken and over-whelmed, but perfectly well."

"Hardly," Darcy muttered. "She was hit in the face, yanked by her hair, tossed about, and half starved. To say nothing about the vile threats made against her."

The colonel's eyes widened in shock, and then they softened in sympathy. The look struck her. It was full of pity and a little fury too. She hated the expression and knew instantly this was how everyone would look at her as soon as they knew someone had kidnapped her.

"Darcy was just as knocked about and threatened as I was," she said. "But we are in good health, and there is nothing else to say about it."

The cousins exchanged a look and seemed to agree with her. They left the carriage house and entered the yard to see the two men from Rosings and their horses. At the sight of them, they gave a cry of exultation. They bowed over her and shook hands with Darcy. It was remarkable to be celebrated for not being dead.

"How did you find us in there?" Darcy asked his cousin.

"It was the damnedest thing," Colonel Fitzwilliam said. "A boy with a blackened eye watched me the entire time I was in the yard—"

"Kirby!" Darcy cried, turning sharply from the smiles and handshakes.

"He never said his name," his cousin said. "We asked the innkeeper to go to your room—I gave him the name you said that you used here—but it was empty. No one could account for where you might have gone, not even the innkeeper's wife who had seen you an hour earlier. But as I came back into the courtyard to consult with the others, this boy mutters, 'Check the stables,' as he walked past me and mounted his horse."

"Was he alone?"

"The boy joined men who arrived on horseback not five minutes after we did."

Elizabeth gave a little whimper at realising who the other riders in the courtyard must have been. At the sound, Darcy finally looked at her. She could not read his expression, even as she tried to tell him with her eyes that she was ashamed of herself for not realising sooner Wickham had lied. Whatever Darcy saw in her face, he betrayed nothing of what he felt.

"Did you speak with the other men?" Darcy asked his cousin. "What did you notice about them? What did they say?"

Colonel Fitzwilliam shrugged and shook his head in confusion.

"They were our abductors if they left with Kirby," Elizabeth said.

The colonel's face betrayed his surprise, and then his cursing betrayed his frustrations at not having known.

"I spoke with them," Darcy's valet said, stepping forward. "While Colonel Fitzwilliam was with the innkeeper, there was a slight man with blue eyes and two other men who came into the yard on horseback and were listening to us. I asked if they had seen you in the town. I could not remember the name Mr Darcy used here, but I described you and said that there was a young lady with you."

"What did he say, Easton?" Darcy asked, his voice low.

"He looked us over and said he had not seen you. Then he swore angrily, and they all rode off."

"Markle gave up rather quickly," Darcy muttered.

"Not if he saw the brace of pistols the men from Rosings carried," Elizabeth replied. "He must have realised he could not kill us without being caught."

Darcy nodded, but rather than it be a beginning of a conversation between them, he turned to consult with his cousin.

After having his sole attention during this terrible experience, it was jarring for Darcy to speak to anyone but her. It was not that she was jealous of the colonel. She could not even name the feeling as she stood by herself with her thoughts. Darcy and his cousin were talking in low voices, but she heard, "tell the magistrate," "Lady Catherine's brandy," and "smugglers to justice."

It was a peculiar loneliness to see Darcy confiding in and making plans with someone other than her.

"Are you ready, Miss Bennet?" Colonel Fitzwilliam asked. She was confused, and must have looked it because he added, "You must not have been listening. I have hired a post chaise to take you back to Hunsford."

"What?" she cried. "No, I do not want to go there! I cannot face her ladyship."

Colonel Fitzwilliam nodded placatingly. "You need not, but Mrs Collins is desperate to see you. I had not thought so staid a woman could cry so hard when she learnt you had not eloped—" He looked at his cousin, coughed, and turned pink. "Well, when she learnt what truly happened. You will be glad to see a friend, will you not?"

Ignoring him, Elizabeth strode to stand before Darcy. "I do not want to stay in Kent at all. We wanted to go to London, did we not? I need to see my sister." She forced Darcy to look at her, to hear her. For an instant, she saw in his eyes all the affection for her he had shown her only an hour ago. Then his former reserve took its place.

He nodded, even placing a condoling hand on her arm. She wished he had left it there for longer. "Miss Bennet needs to go to town," he said over his shoulder. "She wants to be with her family. I can trust you to see her there safely?"

For a moment she was distracted by his calling her Miss Bennet and not Elizabeth and did not realise he was walking toward a saddled horse. "Wait!" she cried. "You are not coming with me?"

Was she truly going to part from Darcy here, in this inn yard with strangers watching, without another word? There was so much left to be said, to explain, and she was not ready to be away from him. Was he furious with her for trusting Wickham, and was all of his affection for her lost, or was he simply trying to keep his cousin and the men from Rosings from knowing what they meant to each other?

What she thought they meant to each other.

"I cannot go to town yet," he said, sounding sorry for it. "Fitzwilliam can take you. I need to report to a magistrate in Kent what has happened."

Elizabeth frowned sceptically. "Do you really think in that area of Kent that the magistrate will issue a warrant to arrest Markle, or if he did, the constable would even arrest him?" Corruption and fear might make seeing justice done impossible.

"I have to try."

She suppressed a sigh. Yes, she knew he did; his character would demand no less. Darcy was about to mount the horse when she held out her hand to stop him. "Do you hate me for believing Wickham?" she whispered.

"No."

That hardly meant that Darcy still loved her. "Then why won't you at least escort me to town? You could make a statement to the magistrate at any time."

"I must deal with Lady Catherine," he said in a pained voice. "She has to hear it from me that I know what she has done, and that I will tell the magistrate everything. And it would be a torture to you to have you return with me to Hunsford. You should be with your family."

And Darcy should be with someone who cared about him after their trying ordeal. As angry as she was with him for leaving her, she felt his pain at the thought of confronting his aunt. "I am sorry you have to face her."

He gave a sad smile. "Doing what is right rarely means doing what is easy."

He bowed, but she stopped him again, scarcely believing he would walk away from her. "How can you leave me so easily?" she whispered. She hated how desperate she felt, especially when he looked to feel nothing.

Darcy leant down and spoke softly, looking directly into her eyes. "It is not easy at all."

Elizabeth felt her heart clench, hoping that she was not too late to apologise, that she might still have a future with Darcy. They were standing near together, only a few inches separating their lips. "Will—will you come to town?" she stammered. "Will you come to Cheapside?"

"Yes." His gaze moved down from her eyes to her mouth, and then looked to the side. His cousin was watching. Darcy leant back and held out his hand. Elizabeth took it, and Darcy brought it to his lips, then mounted the horse without another word.

ROSINGS PARK WAS NOW IN SIGHT. IT HAD BEEN JUST OVER TWO days since he and Elizabeth had been abducted from that very place in the lane he had just ridden past. Darcy had parted from Fitzwilliam with promises to join him in town by tomorrow. He could trust him to see Elizabeth returned to her family, but Darcy still thought of her the entire journey back to Hunsford.

He still felt a little betrayed by her, but Wickham was the one who deserved his fury. Elizabeth could only be accused of being ignorant and too trusting. He had not been calm enough to continue any conversation with her in Dartford, and certainly not while his cousin, his valet, and her ladyship's coachman were watching.

It had hurt to be thought capable of such things after what they had been through together, but it was all a mistaken assumption on his side. He would put it to right as soon as Lady Catherine was dealt with.

Even as he rode into the paddock, talking with the men who returned with him, he desperately missed Elizabeth. Part of it might be from having been locked in a room together for days, having to always consider her and never being apart from her. But it was also because she had fallen in love with him. Their morning in the bed at the Bull and George was evidence enough of that, and now he did not know when exactly he would see Elizabeth again.

It was a strange, lonely feeling.

He needed to speak to the magistrate and explain the entire abduction. Before he could do that, he owed it to his aunt to tell her what he was going to do. It was not her fault they were assaulted, abducted, threatened, terrorised, but her duplicitous actions had led to it. It would be cowardly not to tell her he knew about her scheme and that he intended to lay it all bare.

"Mr Easton," he said to his valet, "we will leave after I have seen her ladyship. Will you pack and tell the coachman to ready the carriage?"

"We are not staying, sir?" Easton asked, surprised.

Darcy shook his head. He would never sleep in this house again. "And send someone to tell Mrs Collins that Miss Bennet is safe with her family in Gracechurch Street and to please send her belongings to town."

As he entered the house and went directly to the drawing room Lady Catherine preferred, Darcy took close notice of every uselessly fine ornament, every chimney piece, every painting, and wondered how her ladyship's finances had gone so wrong.

"My dear Darcy!" Lady Catherine cried upon seeing him.

To his great surprise, she put her arms around him as soon as the door was closed. She was not an affectionate woman, and her embraces had stopped even before he had grown up. Now she gripped him close. The hug reminded him of his own mother, and it almost made him change his mind about what he had to do.

She stepped back and held him at arm's length, looking him up and down. "You are in good health? Perfectly well?"

He briefly considered if he would always wonder if the person walking up to him might try to harm him. "Perfectly well. Miss Bennet and I managed to escape."

Her ladyship settled herself on her chair, once again with all the authority and arrogance one might expect from her. "Criminals! It is scandalous that criminals can abduct decent people from a respectable home.

What has the world come to when people are not safe walking at Rosings Park?"

Darcy sighed to himself. He had known it was likely, but it still disappointed him that his aunt would deny the truth behind their abduction. "It was not a random attack," he said in a low voice. "Miss Bennet was targeted because they assumed she was Anne, and I would not stand by and let them take her."

"You cannot believe that." Lady Catherine frowned. "You have the sense to not trust a word those criminals say. The important thing is that you and Miss Bennet are safe. Where is she? I suppose she wished to see Mrs Collins before she called on me."

Darcy blinked once, slowly. He could not allow this wilful self-deception to continue. "Was it all lies, aunt? The cherry brandy, the smuggling scheme to exchange your mediocre brandy for fine French alcohol, bribing to get the certificates to ship your brandy within England?" He gave her a fierce look. "Cheating criminals to save a few guineas? Was that all lies?"

A muscle twitched next to his aunt's mouth, but she was silent. That alone raised his suspicions.

"Be honest with me," he said. "Please, be honest. After all I have suffered since Friday morning, I deserve the truth."

She flinched. "The truth is, those men are criminals, and they have nothing at all to do with me."

"Then I must tell you what happened. I was threatened with being shot and stabbed more times than I can count. The threat of my tongue being cut out particularly stands out in my mind. But that is nothing to what Miss Bennet endured." He watched his aunt turn red in mortification. "Shall I lay out what they did to her, what I had to watch happen to her because I was powerless to stop it?" His voice shook, though he tried to hide it. "You should hear what they did to her and what they threatened to do, and all because *you* cheated unscrupulous smugglers!"

Lady Catherine met his gaze but said nothing, and Darcy felt his temper snap. "She was threatened because they thought she was Anne! They wanted to torment her because Anne's suffering would wound *you*! Now, for the last time, be honest. You entered into a smuggling deal with Markle, did you not?"

"I did," she said with all the confidence he expected from her.

"And then you cheated them. They lost their money and one of them went to prison, and they sought vengeance."

"Cheated!" She drew back. "I did what was best. There was no reason to continue bribing for new shipping certificates for every load when the previous ones were always accepted. It was only one time they seized the shipment, and those smugglers should have been able to evade the excise men."

Darcy scoffed. "You always think you know better than everyone else. Why? Why did you bargain with smugglers?"

She shifted in her seat and looked away. "There has been some mismanagement of Rosings's funds, and I found a solution to restore us to profitability."

"And who mismanaged them?" She was silent, but he already knew the answer. "Why did you never ask for help, or rely on a capable steward?"

Lady Catherine gave him the same look she did whenever he gave his opinion too freely. "I have managed Rosings since Sir Lewis died. Besides, once you marry Anne, it will not matter if I am behindhand. We shall more often be at Pemberley, and only need to keep up Rosings for your second son after he is grown."

He ignored this as another suspicion returned to his mind. "Does Anne still have her fortune? She had twenty thousand pounds settled on her. Is that spent too?"

Her expression was all the answer he needed. He felt his anger rising for Anne's sake, and for all that he and Elizabeth had suffered. "How did you reply to the ransom letter? Were you going to pay?"

"Good heavens, Darcy!" she cried. "How can you suggest such a thing? You are my nephew. Your mother's memory would haunt me for all time if I let anything happen to her child."

"And Miss Bennet?" he asked in a low tone. "You must have realised what had happened once you got the ransom letter, that she was taken by mistake and pretending to be Anne. Did you write back that you would pay for us both, or did you tell them you would only pay for me since they took the wrong woman?"

He did not want the latter to be true, and Darcy searched his aunt's face for some sign that she was not so lost to all decency.

After far too long, she finally said, "It was an outrageous sum for the cousin of my parson."

"They were going to kill her." Darcy's voice broke as disappointment filled him. "Could you have lived with that?"

No matter what Elizabeth believed about Wickham, Darcy could never tolerate any harm coming to her. She could even marry the dreadful man, and Darcy would still do anything for her. Not that he believed she had any affection for Wickham. No, she was simply a loyal friend, one who believed a lie that the man had suffered a grave injustice at his hands.

"It would be a waste of money for me to pay for an unconnected girl, but I did not leave Miss Bennet to a dismal fate," she said comfortingly. "I told them they had the wrong girl, and that with their permission I would contact her family, who would undoubtedly pay for her release."

His aunt's selfishness knew no bounds, and worse, she was so certain of how right she was. "You risked her life," he said sharply. "If we had still been their captives when Markle got that letter, he would have just killed her."

Darcy looked around the ornate room, at the jewels on her neck, at her stylish gown. He thought of the many servants, the horses and carriages. Lady Catherine was born into and married into so much wealth, but somehow it all went wrong.

"All of this will fall around you," he whispered. She wanted to appear as wealthy as ever, but now she had no money at all.

"That is histrionic, Darcy," she said in an angry tone. "I shall have money again when you marry Anne, and we can secure the family fortunes in such a way that—"

"I am not marrying Anne." He enunciated every word. "I have told you and her, but you both refuse to hear me. Your salvation is not coming from Pemberley's coffers."

He would never allow himself to be at the mercy of an insolent, unscrupulous woman even if he did not love someone else. Even though Elizabeth had lacked discernment about Wickham, he still loved her and wanted to marry her.

"I am leaving now, madam. I wish, I wish that I could have helped you before it was too late. I am telling the magistrate what happened, and I will tell him the entire story, including your involvement. Maybe they will not pursue charging you, but I will do what I must to sleep at night." He took a long, deep breath. "And that includes breaking with you."

Lady Catherine stood, her frame shaking with rage. "How dare you implicate your own family in a scandal!"

Darcy threw up his hands. "What has happened to your morality?"

"What has happened to your good sense?" she shot back. "What has happened to your sense of duty to your family?"

"I have a greater duty to my future wife and to my own conscience." If he could resolve everything with Elizabeth, she could never bear to hear mention of Lady Catherine after knowing that her ladyship's selfishness caused her abduction.

"Do you blame me for what those miscreants did?" His aunt looked wounded. "You think I was behind your abduction?"

He shook his head. "You would never have countenanced such cruelty." He fixed his eye on her. "But I do blame you for your choice to go into business with criminals, and then think you could cross them without consequence."

He had turned his back when she called after him. "I need your help to save Rosings. It pains me to admit it." The words came out as though she were choking on them. "But the truth is that I need your help."

"The only help you want is for me to marry Anne so you can close up this house and make it my problem to shore up Rosings for a second son." He saw the truth in her eyes. "I am not marrying Anne, and I have lost all respect for you."

"I am shocked at how you have turned your back on your own family and would sully my name in front of the magistrate by mentioning my brandy."

"You left Elizabeth to die!"

Lady Catherine looked startled. "I told Markle I would arrange for her family to pay for her return."

"Do you think that if we had not escaped before Markle received your letter, he would have kept her alive? And do you honestly think that I would have let a ransom be paid for *me* and just leave her?"

"I will not be lectured for not understanding the inner workings of a criminal's mind." She pursed her lips and exhaled through her nose. "And... I require assistance."

"Ask it of anyone else. I will throw you upon your own resources, force you into responsibilities of economy." He gave a bitter laugh. "Brace yourself for the work. You are a sensible woman, but deficient in the power of organisation, stubborn and arrogant to the point of foolishness, and do not know the details of estate management. But worse than that is your greed, and that you refused to seek advice. You saw a quick way to fill your coffers, but you crossed the wrong people. These smugglers would never simply defer to your rank, and Miss Bennet and I could have died."

As he walked to the door, he heard her stride after him, and he turned round, keeping a thin hold on his patience.

"You cannot make any mention of my arrangements with those smugglers to the magistrate." Her ladyship was highly incensed. "Good society will whisper about me, and I shall be received nowhere. I will not have your misguided sense of duty damage my position."

Darcy gave Lady Catherine a pitying look. "It is not my responsibility to save you from your pride and selfishness." Then he left, hoping he would eventually feel like he had done the right thing by turning his back on his mother's sister.

Chapter Fifteen

I t felt strange to Elizabeth to have no one else present in her bedroom in Gracechurch Street on Monday. Sleeping alone, waking alone, *being* alone was peculiar after having Darcy always by her side during their harrowing experience. Here, it was quiet and she was safe; there was no threat of immediate or future harm. But it was odd to have nothing to consult with Darcy about, not being able to talk with him whenever she wanted.

There was a knock on the door, and she flinched before she realised how foolish she was to be afraid. Steamer or Markle would not be on the other side of it. She hoped she recovered her expression before Jane entered.

"Who came to call?" Elizabeth asked. She was still in a borrowed dressing gown, waiting for her own clothes to arrive from Hunsford. She refused to wear any of the clothes she had worn since Friday, no matter how often her aunt said they could be cleaned.

"Colonel Fitzwilliam returned to see how you were," Jane said, sitting at the toilette table. "I told him you were resting and not up to company yet. He stayed longer than he did yesterday and told us a little more about how he recovered you and Mr Darcy." Jane gave her such a pitying look that Elizabeth had to look away. "You must have been terrified, my dear Lizzy. I can picture you huddled in that chaise wondering if you would be rescued or killed."

"I am well now that I am home with all of you."

Yesterday, Elizabeth could not keep down tears as she caught a glimpse of those dear faces. She was certain she had not been intelligible in explaining what had happened, but between the tears and hugs and her garbled words and Colonel Fitzwilliam's explanations, her family understood broadly what had happened.

"I think Colonel Fitzwilliam was disappointed not to see for himself how you were, but he understood you not being ready for visitors."

It was true she did not want to be asked about her ordeal, but if Darcy called when he returned to town, she would run downstairs in her dressing gown. He was the only person who could know what being abducted could truly be like. "It was kind of him to come in person to wish me well."

"He feels dreadful that everyone at Hunsford assumed you had eloped with Mr Darcy. We did not even know you were missing until Charlotte sent a messenger very early on Sunday morning." Jane turned away, but in the mirror's reflection, Elizabeth could see she was hiding tears. "To think since Friday morning you had been captured by those horrid people!"

Elizabeth smiled wryly. "Lady Catherine thought I had eloped with her nephew, and she must not have wanted that to get abroad after she had been so vocal about Mr Darcy marrying her daughter."

"Colonel Fitzwilliam hinted that Charlotte had defied this Lady Catherine in informing us at all that you were abducted. He implied her ladyship had an involvement with these criminals."

It would all come to light if Darcy followed through on his intentions to implicate his aunt when he informed the magistrate about what had happened. She sighed over how distressing it would be for him.

"Do you want to talk about any of it?" Jane asked gently.

She had already told her aunt and uncle and sister about the salient facts. Somehow, she knew telling Jane that a brute of a man had struck her across the face with the back of his hand and that she was under constant threat of being assaulted would not make her feel better. It was bad enough to see the rage and helplessness in Darcy's eyes every time she was harmed. To see the same feelings as well as pity in Jane's eyes would be unbearable.

"Not now," she whispered. Jane's sensibilities were too fragile to not display her horrified reactions to whatever Elizabeth said.

Jane nodded knowingly. "Shall my aunt write to my mother for you? Longbourn does not even know you are here, let alone that you were ever missing. By the time we had any sense of what we might do or if my uncle was needed in Kent, another rider came from Charlotte saying that Colonel Fitzwilliam was on his way to retrieve you."

"My aunt can write. I am not ready to put it all to paper any more than I am to talk about it."

"Of course," Jane murmured. "In a day or so we can go home. I am sure Sir William would understand and send for Maria himself in May."

Elizabeth started. Going home would put her in the face of her mother's fretting, her father's teasing, Lydia's curiosity, and endless talk in her neighbourhood about her abduction. "No, I will find no comfort at Longbourn."

Jane could not hide her surprise. "Do you not want to be amongst your family at such a time?"

"You and my aunt and uncle are what I need right now."

Returning home would also put her in the company of Wickham, and the thought turned her stomach. What other lies might he spread in Meryton, and what other debts would he accrue? What other young lady might he hurt?

"Jane," she began hesitatingly, "I talked a great deal with Mr Darcy. I know him so much better now. We talked about, well, about our families and our likes and dislikes, and, and how I misunderstood him, and how he realised how wrongly he had been acting—but he always had good principles—and..."

Elizabeth could tell by Jane's expression that she was not making sense. She took a deep breath and then spoke of everything she had read in Darcy's letter as far as it concerned Wickham. All the rest of what she and Darcy had spoken of felt impossible to talk about. Elizabeth was sensible that nothing less than a perfect understanding between Jane and Bingley could justify her in explaining Darcy's interference and Bingley's swift abandonment. She was certain Darcy would send Bingley back to Jane as soon as he could.

And how could she speak of all that had happened between her and Darcy from Thursday night to Sunday morning? That Darcy had proposed and how badly he had delivered his sentiments. And how she not only now saw him in a more amiable light, but that she hoped he would propose again. That she had fallen in love with him, shared a bed with him, and had hurt him deeply by implying that she trusted Wickham more than him.

"Wickham so very bad! It is almost past belief." Jane sighed over it. "And poor Mr Darcy, having to relate such a thing of his sister! I am amazed that he confessed it."

He would not have if Darcy had not been in love with her and wanted to preserve her from an immoral man. He would not have if he had not proposed and she had not thrown unjust accusations at him in return. She felt mortified all over again for what she had demanded of Darcy yesterday. She had known Wickham was a subject that distressed him, and she had gone about it all wrong.

He must have felt so betrayed.

All she could do was shrug and say, "An experience like ours must naturally lead to some friendship." She was eager to change the subject. "I ought to make our acquaintance in general understand Wickham's character."

Jane paused a little and then said, "Surely there can be no occasion for exposing him so dreadfully."

"Jane, he is a wicked man, and liable to do harm. I have suffered at the hands of evil men who might never be arrested for their crimes." She strove to keep her voice steady. "But I can have some control over this. I can make everyone in Meryton distrust Wickham. I do not have permission to relate anything about Miss Darcy, but I can write to my mother about all the rest, his lies, his debt. And I can hint that I have it on good authority that his character is lacking and he ought not to be trusted amongst the young ladies of the neighbourhood. My father might not take any action, but you know that my mother will spread news of it throughout the county."

Her sister agreed. "You know," Jane added, "I never thought Mr Darcy so deficient in all goodness as you did. I hope you did not quarrel while you were together. A lot of your criticism of him was wholly undeserved, if what he said of Wickham was true."

The guilt and humiliation twisted Elizabeth's stomach. "Yes, I was unfair to him. For all of his former self-importance, I formed unjust prejudices against him. I hope, after what happened between us, I hope that is all in the past. I have come to admire him very much, Jane."

Jane smiled. "Even so, it would be difficult for anyone to presume that you and Mr Darcy eloped. Lady Catherine must have been too frightened for rational thought. Any admiration of you, of course, is entirely natural" —she smiled—"but I cannot think you would ever be *that* fond of Mr Darcy."

This wounded too. "Oh." If Darcy appeared at her window with a ladder, she would climb down in her dressing gown.

"Lizzy?" Jane leant forward in concern. "What does that face mean? Do you have an affection for Mr Darcy? You spent some weeks together in Kent before your ordeal."

No matter how much she hurt, she would keep the whole situation to herself. She had no idea how her relationship with Darcy would proceed and, until she did, it was better—it was easier—not to admit to anything. "I was very wrong about Mr Darcy. And...I grew fond of him."

She felt more than fond. It was difficult to fall asleep last night without hearing him breathe from the pillow next to her.

Jane, however, took her at her word. "Well, he took good care of you during your ordeal, and I am glad that you like him better. And we can stay in Cheapside for as long as you need to steady your mind before we return to Longbourn."

That was good, because she needed to be in town when Darcy returned. He would call, and they could resolve everything between them. She also needed the quiet here with the Gardiners. It was not only the mental wounds of what had happened that troubled her. She was certain that time, a sympathetic and unemotional listener, and her own resolve would ultimately heal those. But there was an aching void in her heart caused by Darcy's absence.

～

Darcy had walked the short distance from his house to Grosvenor Street where Bingley was spending the season with his brother-in-law. He used the time walking home to Charles Street to pass over everything that had happened between Sunday and today. Even though he was now safe and could, in theory, be at ease, he found that his mind was always working.

After parting from Lady Catherine, he had spoken with John Wade, magistrate of the large parish of Westerham, to report the abduction and explain his aunt's part in the smuggling scheme that led to it. Mr Wade had put on a concerned expression, but once Darcy had said Markle's name, he knew justice would not be done.

The damned man had been afraid.

This officer of the peace had said all the correct things, but Darcy doubted that the warrant he said he would issue would ever be given to a constable to execute. Either fear of retribution from the smuggling gangs or a resignation to the fact that the constables might never find Markle amongst the tunnels and basements of Kent was clear across his face.

"Kidnapping is not a crime typically prosecuted, you know. Since you and the young lady escaped, unharmed, I think it best to be grateful for that and put the matter to rest in your hearts and minds," Mr Wade had said shakily when Darcy had finished making his statement.

Eventually rumour would lead to the loss of her ladyship's reputation, and Lady Catherine's pride would lead to the loss of the last of her money, but Darcy was furious that Markle and Steamer would remain free.

He yawned as he turned the corner from Grosvenor Street to Davies Street, glancing over his shoulder to be certain no one was too near to him. He had not slept well on Sunday or Monday night. One could say it was due to anxiety over the ordeal, or a busy mind unable to stop thinking, but he knew it was because Elizabeth had not been asleep on the other side of his bed. Between his exhaustion and the exchange he had just had with Bingley, he felt depleted.

My conversation with Bingley could have gone worse. He could have told me he never wanted to see me again.

Darcy first had to confess his abduction to his friend, at least broadly, to explain his conversation with Elizabeth about her sister. He coped with Bingley's alarm on his behalf and answered a lot of questions before he could confess his interference and apologise. Bingley had been rather short with him as he suddenly remembered he had somewhere to be, but Darcy trusted that after a call on Jane Bennet he would be restored to his friend's good graces.

He was past Berkeley Square and Gunter's and turned on to Charles Street. As much as he wanted to see Elizabeth now, Bingley was on his way to present himself in Cheapside. He owed it to his friend to not be there as a distraction. He would call on her tomorrow.

He was still a little irritated that Elizabeth had never considered the possibility that Wickham had lied to her, but he was desperate to settle everything between them. He would not throw away a future with Elizabeth over one misunderstanding. His temper he might not vouch for, but he was not spiteful. And he loved her ardently.

He was about to climb the few steps to his door when he heard a commotion from below. Darcy walked through the wrought iron gate to the stairs below the street level that led to the servants' entrance almost directly below the front door. There was a scuffling of feet and a small cry, and then he heard his housekeeper shout, "I told you not to come back!"

Standing by the coal vault was Kirby, still dressed in his mourning clothes, and Darcy's housekeeper blocked the door.

"Mrs Watson," he cried. Kirby spun round at the sound of his voice, and Darcy saw relief flood his eyes. His housekeeper, on the other hand, looked angry.

"Sir, there is no trouble. I sent this beggar away last night, and now he is back—"

"Master Kirby is my guest," he said, putting a firm hand on the boy's shoulder. "Come inside."

He steered Kirby to the door, and his housekeeper was now alarmed that the master was entering through the basement. "Sir, please, you ought not to come in through here."

"It is still a door to my own house, is it not?" He led Kirby down the corridor, past the housekeeper's room, pantry, and other offices, and into the servants' hall. A maid was forced to stop to curtsey and a footman in dishabille sneaked off at the sight of him, and all the while Mrs Watson fretted over this breach of decorum. Darcy sat Kirby at the table and then asked his housekeeper to bring Kirby something to eat.

Darcy sat across from him and looked him over. His bruised eye was now green rather than purple. Aside from being dirtier than he typically was, Kirby did not look further injured. "What happened?" he asked gently.

Kirby set his shoulders. "You said you would send me to school, help me become a barrister if I left my uncle. Is that true?"

Darcy nodded. "I will oversee your education myself, if that is what you want. No boy should be forced into being a criminal."

"I never wanted to be a free trader, but do I have to tell you where to find my uncle in order to go to school?" Kirby pursed his lips.

He was so sceptical. The boy had likely never been able to trust anyone. "Kirby, you need not make a deal with me. Besides, I am already in your debt."

The boy swallowed thickly and blew out a long breath. Mrs Watson returned with an entire cake; she must have reconsidered her opinion about the boy lurking outside her door. Darcy allowed Kirby to busy himself with the cake and hide his relieved emotions.

"Mrs Watson, this is Master Kirby Ramer. He will stay with us until I can arrange for him to be sent to a school. He will also need a room and a new suit of clothes."

She nodded and smiled in Kirby's direction, but he was too busy devouring the cake. Darcy wondered when he last ate.

"Is Master Kirby to sleep in a servant's room, sir?"

"A guest chamber," he said to make his point. "He is to have free rein of the library."

Mrs Watson curtsied and left, and by the time she did, half of the cake was gone. Kirby wiped his mouth on his sleeve and looked like a weary little boy.

"Kirby, before you rest, can you tell me what happened after you left the Bull and George? What changed your mind about fleeing your uncle?"

He rubbed his eyes reflexively, flinching as his knuckles hit the bruise below his eye. "My uncle was furious when he realised those men were in Dartford to rescue you. His entire plan had fallen apart. He was so angry, like when my father was arrested or when they killed that excise officer."

Kirby leant his elbows on the table and held his head in his hands. Whatever had happened, it was nothing a child should have to bear.

"Why do you not start at the beginning? You arrived in Gravesend without us or Steamer. Your uncle struck you out of anger..."

"And then my uncle and Conway and I went to Dartford to find you and Steamer, like I said. He wanted to kill you both in your beds and be gone before anyone realised he was there. But your friends came, so we left. Steamer had been found along the toll road and brought to a surgeon. His leg was in a fracture box and he had a wound on his neck and was all bruised from the fall, but the surgeon said he would recover."

The boy looked wretched. He was now tapping the fork tines against the plate, and Darcy had to repress the urge to snatch the fork from his hands to make the noise stop. "Kirby, what happened next?" he asked. "What made you leave your uncle?"

"We left Steamer with the surgeon. We could not move him, of course. And then Colton met us in Gravesend not long after my uncle and Conway and I returned. Colton had the reply from the woman who never got the proper papers for the brandy that got my father arrested." Kirby toyed with the fork, pushing crumbs about. "Is the lady who crossed my uncle really your aunt?"

"Yes, she is."

"But she is not Nan's mother?" Darcy shook his head. "That is what Colton's letter said, that the lady would pay for *you* but that she needed time to arrange for the family of the girl Steamer captured to get the money for her ransom."

Tears pooled in Kirby's eyes. "He was so enraged at Steamer for catching the wrong girl and for letting you get away. I have never seen him so angry. He often lashes out, but this was different. When we were done with the cargo in Gravesend on Monday, he and I went back to Dartford."

Tears were now streaming from his eyes. Darcy handed him his handkerchief, his stomach churning as he waited to hear what happened next. "What happened to Steamer?"

"My uncle killed him," Kirby said hoarsely. "He told me to go into the apothecary shop and ask the surgeon to look at my bruised eye. I didn't know what he was going to do!"

"Of course you did not," Darcy said consolingly.

"The apothecary-surgeon and I were in the front of the shop, and my uncle must have gone into the surgery through the back. We heard a horrid sound, and me and the surgeon ran in...and my uncle had slit Steamer's throat!" He dried his eyes and took a deep breath. "There was blood everywhere! He relied on Steamer, said he was the best of his crews, and he just..."

Darcy was horrified, and yet not surprised that Markle's impulse was to turn to violence.

"If he did that to his friend..." Kirby seemed to have turned inward and was talking aloud. "What might he do to me? What would he do to me if he found out I let you go? That I don't want to be a free trader? That I can't kill people? He will kill me too."

After sitting in silence for a while to give Kirby time to calm himself, Darcy asked, "How did you flee him?"

"After he killed Steamer, Uncle met me with the horses and told me to return to Shoreham to await the next load from France. He said he intended to put me to work, that he needed me more than ever with my father in jail, and now that Steamer had failed him." The boy looked green, and Darcy feared he might cast up everything he had eaten. "But while he rode to Gravesend, back to Colton and Conway, I left the horse at the Bull and George and found a man with a cart to take me to town."

"It is Tuesday afternoon. Where did you go between Monday night and now?"

"You mean after your housekeeper turned me away the first time?" he said with a hint of bitterness.

"I am sorry that happened, and from now on you are to come in through the front door."

This seemed to console him. "I wandered about. I slept in Hays Mews just behind here. I tricked someone into thinking I was a new stableboy. I would have found your carriage if you called for it. Since you never asked for it today, I tried the door again."

"You slept in the stables?"

Kirby must have heard the hurt in his voice, because he said, "I have slept in worse places and amongst worse company."

That hardly made Darcy feel better. He wondered if Markle would suspect that his nephew had come to him. "You shall have a better bed tonight. I think it best you stay in the house until we know for certain your uncle is not in town looking for you."

"That is why I did not hire a horse! I did not want him to trace me."

"You were clever. Let us hope he does not find the man with the cart, or even suspect you came to town at all. You may stay here and let Mrs Watson spoil you with cake, and read in the library for a few days until I can enrol you in a school."

"Will you send me to Westminster or Eton?"

This was said so earnestly that Darcy absolutely refused to laugh. "I think you might be out of place amongst the boys there, and bullied terribly. Besides, if your education until now has only been reading stolen books—"

"I went to the charity Sunday school."

"And I am certain that you excelled. However, your Latin and French are probably lacking." Kirby would be incredibly outranked and behind if he went to a public school. And the farther he was from his uncle's business in Kent, the better. "What if I find a gentleman to tutor you privately and you can board with other boys? I will make certain you are ready for Cambridge when you are old enough."

"You want me gone," he said flatly. He sounded disappointed.

"Not at all. Have you ever been north? That is where my home is. I am certain a clergyman will tutor you, and you can come to Pemberley on school holidays unless one of your new friends invites you home."

After everything the boy had endured, Darcy wanted very much to take care of him and secure his prospects. He wondered if Kirby could imagine a future with playmates and studying and with no one hitting him or forcing him to commit violence. He must have felt some hope, because his expression brightened. "Will it take long, do you think?"

Darcy smiled. "No. The Easter holidays are over, and all the boys will have returned to school. We cannot have you be behindhand, can we?"

Kirby gave him the first smile he had seen from him.

Chapter Sixteen

E lizabeth was glad she had not gone downstairs yesterday when Bingley had first called on Jane. Given how he reacted when he saw Elizabeth today when he returned to Gracechurch Street with his sisters, she feared he would not spare a thought for Jane amidst the concern he showed Elizabeth.

He must have repeated, "And you are well? You must have been terrified," at least three times.

Thankfully, Jane was not the sort to be jealous, and she smiled every time Bingley showed her more solicitude. Elizabeth kept her patience and said again and again that she was well until he finally moved to sit by Jane.

"Miss Bennet, you must have been so worried when you heard the news," he said, taking Jane's hand. When Mrs Gardiner raised an eyebrow, he dropped it and said, "And you as well, ma'am."

Mrs Gardiner agreed and then caught Elizabeth's eye. They shared an amused smile. A proposal seemed likely once Bingley could speak with Jane without his sisters nearby.

He turned back to Elizabeth. "Darcy said that you were both—"

"We need not mention the sad affair again," Miss Bingley said through a clenched jaw. "To mention their names together might imply to someone of an uncouth mind that something untoward happened. Besides, you are liable to distress Miss Eliza," she added, forcing a smile in Elizabeth's direction.

Bingley, pleasant and kindly as he was, instantly engaged Jane and her aunt on another topic. Elizabeth was required, therefore, to be polite to Miss Bingley and Mrs Hurst. "Thank you for insisting on a change of subject."

"Of course," Miss Bingley said, mirroring the same empty smile Elizabeth had given her. "I would hate for you to suffer anyone insisting anything improper between you and Mr Darcy simply because you were unfortunate enough to be kidnapped at the same time. Such a harrowing episode. It is best not to discuss it."

She knew what Miss Bingley was doing: she would stifle any mention of Darcy and Elizabeth having been alone together. Elizabeth did not even have to leave out how they had shared a bed because Miss Bingley would make certain no one gossiped about the abduction at all.

She nearly laughed to think that Miss Bingley would preserve Elizabeth's good name because she needed Darcy's reputation to remain intact for her own hopes. Thoughts of him made it hard to pay attention to Miss Bingley's empty niceties and, claiming she was tired, Elizabeth left her aunt and sister to finish the visit.

Alone in her chamber, she idly turned Darcy's ring over in her fingers. She did not care for the desperate, sinking feeling in her heart as another day passed without seeing him. It was even hard to fall asleep without him.

Jane found her soon after and entered her room without knocking. Elizabeth gave a little shriek, and her heart raced.

"Did I surprise you?" her sister asked, concerned. "I am sorry."

She tried to smile, pressing a hand to her chest. Would sudden noises and unexpected visitors always startle her? Would she always feel a little unsafe, or would that improve with time? She quickly assured Jane that she was well.

"I came to tell you that my aunt has had a reply from Longbourn."

"Does my father tease and my mother fret?" Elizabeth asked drily.

"They are as you would expect them to be, but they are both worried about you. My father even added a few lines himself, saying he wants you to come home soon."

Elizabeth raised an eyebrow. "Is that all he wrote?"

Jane's face told her there was more. "He also wrote to come home when you can tolerate being noticed by everyone for being kidnapped and living to tell the tale."

That sounded more like her father's satirical manner. Longbourn could bring her no peace now, and there was certainly no peace to be had if she left London without speaking with Darcy. She continued to turn his diamond and sapphire ring between her fingers.

"I also must tell you that Mrs Hurst invited us to dine in Grosvenor Street tomorrow. I do not recognise that ring," Jane said, sitting on the bed and peering at it. "Was it a gift from my aunt?"

Elizabeth carefully set it in a box on her toilette table and shut the lid. "No, it was more like a property from a play. I have to give it back."

She explained it had been in Darcy's pocket when they were both kidnapped. "When we fled our captors, we had little money between us. It was late, and we needed to take a room while we awaited rescue..."

"And you could only afford one room, so you used the ring to make it appear as though you were married?"

"We had only eight shillings in our pockets when we each went for a walk on Friday morning." Truthfully, if they had enough for two rooms, they would not have taken them. Separating from Darcy would have felt impossible.

"It was sensible," Jane said consolingly, "although hardly the sort of thing to mention in public."

Elizabeth smirked. How could she say to Jane that she slept better when she was in Darcy's arms? "Yes, Miss Bingley would be distressed to think I had to pretend to be his wife."

She was lost in thought, remembering Sunday morning, and it took her a moment to notice Jane staring at her. "What is the matter?"

"It is plain to me that you miss Mr Darcy."

Elizabeth avoided Jane's perceptive gaze. "Of course I do. There is an affectionate sympathy between us because of what happened."

"Lizzy, look at me." She did, with a sigh. "You shared a room while captured, and you shared a bed in an inn with a man you now admire very much."

She swallowed roughly around the emotion in her throat. "Are you asking if Mr Darcy and I, if we—"

"No," Jane said firmly. "I do not want to hear you say it."

Elizabeth felt the heat of shame creep up her neck. "Because you would judge me harshly?"

Her sister instantly came near and put her arms around her. "No, because if my aunt or mother or father asked me, I would be obliged to answer them." Jane squeezed her tightly. "I suppose," she said haltingly, "I would only want to know if, whatever happened, you still judged it the correct choice. Perhaps, in a distressing situation, with heightened emotions..."

Elizabeth laughed. "You think I shared a bed with Darcy because I was afraid and he was there? That there was no affection involved at all? That he forced me?" It was absurd. She had been eager, and Darcy would rather die than cause her pain.

Jane sat back and looked into her eyes. "I want to be sure you have no regrets."

She had no regrets aside from she ought to have realised Wickham had lied to her from the moment they met. "I won't have any if Darcy calls."

"It is 'Darcy', then?" Jane asked with a little smile.

It should be "Fitzwilliam" if they were alone. "We relied on one another in ways no one else could understand. Even if we had not—" She broke off as Jane held up her hand. "Well, I think calling one another Darcy and Elizabeth a natural thing."

"Of course," Jane murmured.

"You really will not mention this?" Her sister would keep a confidence, but this matter was unlike any secret she had ever held.

Jane gave a fond smile. "All I know is that you are awaiting a call from Mr Darcy." After a moment, she added, "I am certain he will do the honourable thing."

Elizabeth covered her face with her hands. There was no way to find the words that Darcy had offered for her before this horridness and she had said no. "Enough about me," she said, eager to talk about anyone but herself. "You are likely to get a proposal before I am."

Jane blushed. "Did Mr Bingley distress you with all of his care and questions?"

"I think we can call him Bingley now, don't you?" she said with a teasing smile. "And no. I was smothered by his concern, but not distressed by it. His sisters will keep any gossip about me in hand, so I must not dislike them as much as I did before. I will reconcile myself to that misfortune as best I can."

Jane rose to leave. "You know you are certain of a willing listener in me. Aside from"—she struggled to find a word—"what happened with Darcy. If you want to talk about the abduction or your feelings for him, you know where to find me."

Whenever she might wish to talk, she could rely on Jane, but the only person she wanted to talk with now was Darcy. If he did not come to

Cheapside soon, she would have to take matters into her own hands. As she knew now, life was far too fleeting to sit idle.

~

DARCY HAD SPENT THE DAY CALLING ON FRIENDS WHO referred him to acquaintances who might know of someone in the Peak taking on young scholars as boarders. Now, Darcy left Brook Street with the name of a clergyman in Sheffield twenty miles from Pemberley who tutored boys Kirby's age. As reluctant as he was to part from him, sending Kirby to where he could settle into a new life far from his uncle was best done as soon as possible.

It was late Wednesday afternoon, but there was time yet to call in Cheapside. It would not be a fashionable visiting hour by the time he got there. Only someone angling to be invited to a family dinner would call now, but hopefully a quarter of an hour alone with Elizabeth would allow him to be included in that number.

He would lose half an hour walking home and ordering his own carriage. He felt impatience build in his chest as he walked to the hackney coach stand at the corner of Brook and Bond. It was worth the money to get to Gracechurch Street all the sooner.

He was about to hail a driver when a voice from behind him said, "Shall we share?"

Darcy spun round to see Markle. The mere sight of him was sufficient to astonish him. Markle was not a tall man, five foot nine at the most, but the ruthless look in his eyes told anyone of sense that this was not a man to be trusted.

Markle's hands were empty, and Darcy saw no obvious signs of a weapon, but he still took a step back.

Markle smirked and looked at the passers-by, riders, and coaches all around them. "My business is of the utmost importance to me, Mr Darcy. Killing you on a crowded street is not good for my business, but I still would not recommend threatening me." He passed a hand over the pocket of his greatcoat where Darcy could now see the outline of a knife.

"Is that why you did not stay at the Bull and George to kill us?"

A shadow darkened Markle's eyes. "Quite." He tilted his head at the coach stand. "What part of town are you going to?"

"I have changed my mind," Darcy said. "The next one is yours."

Getting into a carriage with Markle was a sure way to get stabbed in the chest.

He walked away, but Markle kept pace with him. "Going home, are you? Or perhaps back to your friends? You have been all over Mayfair today."

Darcy had turned down Bond to walk toward Berkeley Square, and he realised Markle had learnt where he lived. Not a difficult task when one rented a house for generations and such things were printed in London directories. What was more alarming was that Markle had been following him all day.

"You have gone to the trouble to find me, but you claim you no longer are interested in kidnapping me," Darcy said. "Or murdering me."

Markle gave the slightest of shrugs. "Lady Catherine will be publicly shamed, and killing you no longer suits my purpose, for now."

While Darcy struggled to breathe normally, Markle added, "Where is Nan?"

"Back at Rosings, I suspect," he said, keeping up the ruse and not showing one symptom of the fear that was knotting his stomach.

"Not Lady Catherine's daughter," Markle spat. "*Your* Nan."

Darcy did not answer. He would walk to Brooks's. Markle would not be allowed inside the club, and Darcy could gather support there to detain him.

"If you do not wish to talk about Nan, tell me where is my nephew."

Darcy saw where this was going, and it twisted his heart.

"Not inclined to talk?" Markle asked as they walked. "Then you can listen: my nephew has been missing since Monday."

"Are you afraid someone abducted him? Terribly frightening when that happens."

Markle's eyes flashed at this taunt, and Darcy watched his nostrils flare. "It is no coincidence that you escaped and Kirby fled the day after."

"Your nephew did not help us. You have only your friend Steamer to blame for that. I do hope he survived the fall from the carriage." Darcy saw a muscle twitch near Markle's eye. "Maybe Kirby left because your business distresses him." The yellow brick clubhouse in St James's Street was not far now. "Regardless, it is no concern of mine, and since you have decided not to kidnap me for ransom or kill me on the street, I suggest we part ways."

"It *is* your concern." For such a slight man, his entire manner was menacing. "Kirby helped you in return for something. He is good at allying himself with people who will aid him. The baker for an extra bun. The vicar for a new book. The squire for a chip of ice."

"Why would I help the nephew of the man who tormented me?"

"If you do not admit it, I will make you. Where is Nan?"

Darcy looked at his former captor with the haughtiest, coldest glare he could give. "I cannot help you, for she is no friend of mine."

"What would Miss Elizabeth Bennet feel to hear you say that?"

He fought against every instinct to react: to wince in resignation, to cringe in fear for Elizabeth, to lash out against Markle.

"Why, sir, your face has lost its colour," Markle said with a chilling smile. "Colton learnt a few things in Hunsford yesterday. A few pints and coins, and he learnt her name, but not where she lives. We traced the carriage from Dartford to Cheapside, but not beyond."

Darcy shrugged and tried not to quicken his pace. "She is just some woman you abducted by mistake. We went along with pretending she was Miss de Bourgh so you would not kill her in anger over kidnapping the wrong woman. She is nothing to me."

Markle barked a mirthless laugh. "No man looks at a woman the way you looked at Nan if she is 'just some woman.'"

"You should return to Kent and look for your nephew," Darcy said as evenly as he could.

Markle made a quick sound of disapproval with his tongue. "My men will follow you all round London. You will cross paths with her at a dinner or a ball or an amusement."

"Unlikely," Darcy said. "I do not know that lady socially, and have no way of seeing her."

"What about your sister?" Markle asked. "I suspect you will see *her* soon."

Could a man faint from terror and vexation? The only way Darcy could open his mouth to take in a breath was from the hope that Markle was only trying to taunt him. It must be a ruse. Surely, Georgiana was safe. "You are mistaken. I do not have a sister."

"Miss Darcy lives in Upper Wimpole Street with a lady named Annesley. Terribly easy to find her. This morning she wore a green pelisse over a white gown and went shopping on Bond Street."

Wrapping his hands around Markle's throat would get him stabbed, and then what would happen to Georgiana or Elizabeth?

"You have two days to bring me my nephew," Markle said when Darcy struggled to answer, "otherwise Miss Darcy will be my guest. For her sake, I hope you have a different answer as to where my nephew is. I am not a patient man."

He had to keep Markle walking and talking with him until he reached the club to get help to detain him. "I thought you wanted this Miss Bennet, and now you are claiming I have a sister you can kidnap. For a man of business, you seem disordered."

"By all means, tell me where Miss Bennet is and I will have no need for Miss Darcy. I suspect a lover might be more encouraging to you than a sister."

"You are wasting your time with me, Mr Markle."

"Two days to bring me Kirby, or your sister will pay for it with her life. And," he added darkly, "when I do find Nan, because I promise you that I eventually will, she will wish you turned Kirby over to me immediately."

His heart was now racing away. "Return to your smuggling and—"

Markle was no longer next to him. Darcy stopped on the pavement and turned round, but Markle had been absorbed by the crowd.

His cousin met him at Brooks's in the Small Drawing Room. Darcy had somehow made it into the club, made himself sensible to write Fitzwilliam a note, and now held an empty glass in a hand that had finally stopped shaking.

"Georgiana and Mrs Annesley are now with her sister, just off Fetter Lane," his cousin said as he sat next to him. "I thought that safer than taking her to my family or to some other friend of rank where Markle might think to look for her."

That was two miles east in a less fashionable neighbourhood, but Darcy was nevertheless frightened. "Was someone watching her house?"

Fitzwilliam shook his head. "She is safe for the present. After removing Georgiana from Wimpole Street, I went to Charles Street. The boy is safe."

Darcy's eyes narrowed at Fitzwilliam's tone. "But?"

"But I asked in the mews, and one of your neighbour's grooms said a man had been there last night asking about where you usually went and how often you ordered your carriage as though he was looking for employment. The same groom told me a different man loitered in the stables this morning."

Darcy rolled the empty glass between his hands. "I have to assume Markle has been watching my front door as well."

"If I were watching a house, I would pay someone in the stables to report to me if your carriage is ordered. But that leaves the front door unobserved. I sent Mr Easton to the neighbouring houses to enquire from the servants if anyone saw someone out of place."

Darcy looked up from the glass. "Your voice says he discovered something."

Fitzwilliam nodded grimly. "By Berkeley Square. A man had been there for hours this morning. Not troubling anyone,, not poorly dressed, just pacing or standing as though waiting for someone. Mr Easton noted you could see straight down Charles Street from there."

"Was anyone near to that spot tonight?" The clock on the mantel across the room said it was almost eight.

He nodded again. "Mr Easton thinks it was a different man. Different heights, different coats."

Kirby had said his uncle had two crews of smugglers, and it took five or six men to manage each ship. "Markle has some of his smugglers watching my house." At least the men were focusing their attention on his home and not his sister's. The brandy had calmed his nerves, but had not settled his fear.

"I told the boy to stay inside and away from the windows. He was shaken that his uncle was looking for him, but he seems to trust you to manage it all."

Did he not always manage everything for those he cared for? Was that not what his father had entrusted to him on his deathbed? Were all first-born children—all first-born sons, especially—naturally responsible, duty-bound leaders who could be relied upon?

"I will," Darcy said, setting his glass on the table. "I just have to reason how."

"That is what you do," Fitzwilliam said, smiling. "You take care of your sister, your friends, me—sometimes," he added with a wink.

"Only if you let me," Darcy said, trying to meet his cousin's manner, but failing. "Lady Catherine never needed anyone's assistance. She mismanaged or wasted her fortune from ignorance and greed, and look what happened."

"I tease, but you do not actually have to care for *everyone*. And certainly not those who do not ask for it."

"A habit," Darcy said drily, as though teasing. There was truth to it, though. Pemberley had hundreds of people within his care, and he had an orphaned younger sister. He had a duty to those less fortunate, a desire to be generous to anyone in need. And of course, he had a responsibility to his friends. But he had not helped Bingley, however kindly-meant he had been.

"What is that pensive look for?"

"I have not taken as good care of my friends and my sister as I could have. I should have done better by them. And I know that I have been selfish in the past as well, and I must make up for that."

"You really take on too much," Fitzwilliam retorted. "This child in your house is a liability."

Darcy drew back. "Could *you* have left a little boy to abuse and neglect? This is the same boy who told you where to find us, who risked a second beating to make sure they did not shoot Elizabeth and me in our—chamber." He had nearly said "bed," but best not to let his cousin think on that.

"And," Fitzwilliam said, as though he had not been interrupted, "his presence in your life is a threat to your sister and Miss Bennet. If you take this on, it is for the rest of this boy's life. Even if it is always a secret managed through other parties, you will be forever entwined with the nephew of the man who tormented you."

"I will take care of him the way his family should have." Darcy was resolved on this. "Markle is not pursuing him through the law because he knows he would be under scrutiny for his other crimes. He only wants him as a future smuggler. I feel no guilt in facilitating Kirby's escape."

Fitzwilliam gave a pitying smile. "You are a good man."

"You look like you want to say meddlesome, interfering, or maybe controlling."

"Only in jest. You are well-intentioned, even if you take on too much." Fitzwilliam leant forward and said in a softer voice, "Are you afraid to go home?"

"No," he answered honestly. He was afraid for his sister and for Elizabeth, not for himself. "Markle needs me alive for the present. I just feel...unsettled."

Fitzwilliam gestured at a waiter and ordered drinks for them. Darcy was contemplative until the waiter returned and then left, his cousin waiting for him to sort through his thoughts.

"I thought we were safe now. And Markle just approached me on the street. It was so...unexpected and exceedingly brazen."

"It was. Sadly, menacing you is not illegal."

"Pursuing a violent smuggler who abducts people should be easier," Darcy muttered, taking a drink. "The magistrate from where we were abducted will never serve that arrest warrant. Mr Wade will say they cannot find the smugglers." He considered the matter. "Maybe they cannot. I know they are always on the move, from one hiding hole to the next. Still, the magistrate would rather fox hunt and sit in his handsome brick mansion than exert himself."

"He may be afraid this smuggler will burn down his handsome brick mansion."

Darcy nodded in concession. "I shall have to go to Bow Street. Sadly, that will involve Kirby, and a court will say I had no right to aid in Kirby fleeing his rightful guardian who beats him."

"It will also take longer," Fitzwilliam said. "Someone who abducts an heiress, or a slave trader, or someone who steals a child," he said, ticking off on his fingers, "these are the cases of abduction that get noticed."

"I cannot wait for the law to act and arrest Markle—if they can even find him in whatever tunnel or basement he hides in. I need to keep my sister safe and get Kirby out of London now. Markle said two days, and today is nearly over."

"Markle must not think you would keep Kirby in your own house. Still, they might soon decide to break into it to search it." Fitzwilliam took a long drink and then stared into his glass. "Or he will break into it to take his frustrations out on you."

"Then I must think quickly, because he is already impatient, and if he cannot find Elizabeth or Kirby, he is going after Georgiana."

After a heavy silence, his cousin pulled a letter from his pocket. "This came for you in the four o'clock post. Your footman gave it to me when I said I was seeing you."

Darcy read it silently and winced. "Mrs Hurst invited me to dinner tomorrow. Bingley must forgive me for interfering in his love affair. I cannot go. Markle's man will follow me."

He had already explained to his cousin how he had convinced Bingley not to marry Jane Bennet and had then admitted all the ways his interference had been wrong. A red-faced Fitzwilliam then confessed to boasting to Elizabeth the day before the abduction of Darcy's saving a friend from an unfortunate marriage.

As though Elizabeth needed another reason to refuse him last Thursday. It was not even a full week since he had proposed. Many incredible things had happened in a short time. Most of them were horrible, but if he could make things right with Elizabeth, then perhaps some of their suffering would have been worth it.

So long as Kirby and Georgiana were also kept safe.

"You might go to dinner," his cousin said. "Miss Bennet and her family may not be invited."

"Oh, I think they are. Bingley has called in Cheapside. I bet that this invitation to 'an intimate dinner of Charles's friends' is his sisters' penance for their role last winter. And if I go, Markle's man will follow me. They will see Elizabeth entering or leaving and abduct her, or follow her home and take her from there."

When he looked up from hanging his head, Fitzwilliam gave him a confused look. "Missing a dinner with the Hursts and Miss Bingley should make you happy. Why are you cast down over missing a dinner?"

"Because I want to see Elizabeth, and now I cannot," he cried, losing all patience.

Fitzwilliam studied him over the rim of his glass. "They said she was healthy when I called on Monday, glad to be with her sister and aunt." Darcy must have had some expression on his face that his cousin did not like because he cried, "What is really troubling you? Georgiana is hidden, and once this boy and Miss Elizabeth Bennet are out of London, all will be well."

"Unless Markle realises Georgiana, Kirby, and Elizabeth are gone and kills me out of spite like he did with his colleague." He had his own personal knowledge of how savage Markle could be, but to know that he murdered his friend in a fit of rage made the matter far more alarming.

His cousin drained his glass. "If you are clever enough, Markle won't be able to trace Kirby out of London, and he won't soon find Georgiana. Once Master Kirby and Miss Elizabeth are gone, Markle will go back to smuggling."

Darcy doubted very much Markle would let this go. "He might eventually find my sister, and I cannot see Elizabeth until Markle is dead or in shackles," he said with a sigh.

"The abduction was a sad business," Fitzwilliam said. "And Miss Bennet has suffered horribly—as have you. What happened must naturally lead to a bond, not unlike between soldiers who have faced battle together, who depended on one another."

"No, our connexion is sincere."

"Not that your friendship is not a real one"—Fitzwilliam held out his hand—"but you do not need to see Miss Bennet as much as you think you do. You can move past this horrid event without her by your side."

He had to believe that they meant ever so much more to one another than the abduction that had bound them together. "I *need* to talk to her," Darcy murmured.

His cousin looked at him for a long while. "What do you need to tell her?" he asked just as quietly.

Under pain of wounding his own feelings all over again, he said, "I asked her to marry me last Thursday, and she said no because she did not respect me and believed Wickham's lies about me." Darcy gave a sad little laugh. "I had assumed she had been expecting my addresses. But you can imagine that time in each other's exclusive company led to insightful and fortuitous conversations for both of us."

Fitzwilliam's expression did not change. He blinked and then gestured to the waiter for drinks.

Darcy shook his head. "I have already had two."

"We are going to be here for a while." They were silent until their glasses were refilled. "You have been calling her Elizabeth," Fitzwilliam said. "I am not certain you realised it. I thought it merely because you had been alone together."

"Well, that is part of it."

"When she left Dartford, I thought her frantic because she was still afraid and she believed she needed you to be safe."

"We kept one another safe," Darcy corrected.

Fitzwilliam shrugged. "But the way she looked at you, it was as if she had been waiting a lifetime for you." Darcy's heart seized. "I did not know there might have been a deeper emotion behind it all."

"And how did I look at her?" he asked, not meeting his cousin's eye. "Like I felt betrayed because I thought that she still trusted Wickham? That I was angry, even though it only meant she was not as discerning as she could have been?"

"That is how you felt?"

"Yes," he answered honestly, "but it did not last." If Kirby had not been in the corridor, he would have paced around, calmed his mind, and gone back to their chamber. Elizabeth would have read the letter, and they would have eventually come to an understanding. They were reasonable people with generous natures. "Did I look it?"

"You did not look bitter. You had your usual reserved expression that convinces everyone that you are steady and above any minor concern." Fitzwilliam took a drink. "I saw something more, though."

"What?"

"The same look you had at Rosings: you basked in her presence like you did when she talked and argued with you."

"Basked?" he asked sceptically.

"Well, basking for you. I thought that look was present in Dartford because you were both relieved to be safe. I suppose the question is, does she only like you a little better, or does she love you now?"

"I have made a fine beginning to fall in love with you" was what Elizabeth had said to him while they were in bed together. "I know that she does."

Fitzwilliam took a slow drink and studied him for a moment over the rim of his glass. His cousin then swore and slammed down his glass. "You did not!"

"What?" he asked, alarmed.

"While kidnapped? You would never—no, in the Bull and George after?" He laughed. "Safe and sound in one another's arms!" Fitzwilliam laughed harder. "I cannot believe it!"

If he had not had so many recent threats on his own life, Darcy was certain he would die of embarrassment. He bowed his head over his glass and refused to raise his eyes.

"Now I see why you need to talk with her," Fitzwilliam said, still chuckling.

"This is not amusing," he cried. "Markle wants to kidnap her again to force my hand. A violent man wants me to trade an innocent child for Elizabeth, or else he hunts down my sister for the same purpose. I cannot even go to Elizabeth and tell her I still want to marry her." Darcy sullenly took a drink while his cousin's expression sobered. "What woman could be secure after what we did, and how we argued, and with my not calling?"

Fitzwilliam gave him a compassionate look. "You will think of a way to solve this. Get the boy out of London first."

"Even when I do, Markle won't let this go. If he finds Elizabeth and cannot trade her for Kirby, he will kill her. If he cannot find Elizabeth, he will kill my sister. And then he will kill me the next time he follows me. I have little time to find a solution."

Chapter Seventeen

The Gardiners hired a carriage to take them to the Hursts' in Grosvenor Street on Thursday evening. Elizabeth saw how pleased Jane was with Miss Bingley's and Mrs Hurst's notice, so she was resolved to be patient with them. They would soon be Jane's family, if Bingley's looks and smiles meant what she thought they did.

"Do you think Bingley will contrive to take a place by yours at the table?" she asked Jane as the carriage slowed. "He used to do that at all of the dinners in Meryton."

Jane blushed prettily. "I will be happy to sit next to anyone."

She might have demurred, but Elizabeth knew Jane felt confident of Bingley's intentions by now. "I am certain you would, but I think he only wants to sit by you."

He showed his interest once they were shown into a grand entrance hall, and Bingley scarcely let his sister do the courtesy of greeting her guests before he bounded forward to welcome Jane. Mrs Hurst's greeting was milder, and her husband only bowed.

"Do you expect others this evening?" Mr Gardiner asked him pleasantly, but Mr Hurst only shrugged.

"No," Miss Bingley answered shortly. In a voice of forced politeness she added, "Louisa has an even number now, so that is the only good thing about Mr Darcy not coming."

Elizabeth's heart sank. "He was invited, but had an engagement elsewhere?"

Mrs Hurst shook her head. "He sent a note saying that he was not well."

Elizabeth shared a look with Jane, who gave her a commiserating smile. She felt such disappointment to have missed the chance to see Darcy.

Bingley immediately came near. He spoke to everyone but looked meaningfully at Jane. "Darcy wrote to me as well," he said in his cheerful way, "and he was glad that I had gone to Gracechurch Street. I wish I had known that Miss Bennet was here all winter, but Darcy says he is particularly glad that I learnt you were in town. He hopes to see you himself soon."

Bingley and Jane were all smiles, but Elizabeth felt wretched. He had all but given his permission for Bingley to pursue Jane, said he wanted to show Jane her due notice, but he would not come tonight. Was it because he was still angry over what she had said about Wickham?

"I suppose it is just as well for Miss Eliza and Mr Darcy not to be seen together so soon," Miss Bingley said. "For the sake of their reputations, you would want nothing to be misconstrued by their being in public together so soon after the incident."

"It is only us here this evening, Caroline," Bingley said. "And no one would misconstrue anything unless you hinted something was amiss."

Miss Bingley sputtered and said how she would never damage dear Mr Darcy's reputation, or her friend Jane's sister's either, and was seconded by Mrs Hurst in her empty pleasantries.

While the others listened, Elizabeth grew furious. What could Darcy mean by avoiding her? Was she simply supposed to wait for Darcy to show up, whenever that might be? Women were to be proposed to, and could never speak first. Jane had been miserable all winter because she could not call on Bingley herself, and now here she was supposed to do the same with Darcy.

How long am I to sit passive and silent and wonder what Darcy's feelings are?

Her kidnappers could have killed her. She had been an active participant in getting her and Darcy to safety, and now she had to return to letting men manage every matter of business concerning her welfare and happiness. She could control not a thing for herself. Elizabeth shook her head as she wandered to the other side of the hall to pretend to look at a painting. It was infuriating to be submissive and patient until Darcy came to her. And what if he never did? He might always assume she still favoured Wickham.

Grosvenor Street was near to Charles Street. Down one short street to Berkeley Square and then onto Charles Street. Number eight, Kirby had said; a five-minute walk. Elizabeth clenched her hands. They had to speak to one another—*she* had to be heard—and Darcy was right there.

"I am afraid I have a terrible headache," Elizabeth said loudly as Mrs Hurst was about to lead everyone into the dining room. "I am sorry to disappoint you all, but I must go home at once and lie down."

Mrs Gardiner and Mr Gardiner exchanged a look that seemed to communicate an entire conversation. Her aunt said, "Then I am sorry to say, Mrs Hurst, that we all must leave."

"Must you?" Bingley cried. "I am so sorry Miss Elizabeth is ill, but the rest of you are welcome to stay."

"It would be senseless to hire a carriage for me to take Lizzy home," her aunt replied, "and then hire another for Mr Gardiner and Jane when supper is over."

As Jane came to put an arm around Elizabeth's shoulders, Bingley looked devastated.

"I would be glad to offer my chaise for the Gardiners and Miss Bennet to return home later this evening," he said to her aunt. "I know if the Hursts kept their own horses, they would be very eager to offer theirs."

Bingley looked to Mrs Hurst, but his sister did not echo this nicety. "And," he said forcefully, "I am sure she would hire a carriage now for Miss Elizabeth, and I will send my servant to see her safely home." Bingley pulled the bell to set all the matters into motion. If he had waited for his sister to do it, he would have had to wait a long while given the indignant look on Mrs Hurst's face.

"Would you rather us all leave and come another time, ma'am?" Mrs Gardiner asked.

Mrs Hurst recovered, although she exchanged a quick irritated look with Miss Bingley. Elizabeth turned away to hide a smile; Bingley's sisters would have to learn to cope with their brother's choice.

"Are you in a lot of pain, Lizzy?" Jane asked. "I want to take you home and stay with you. I can dine with my friends another time."

She certainly could not admit that it was all a lie in order to call on a single man a few blocks away and that Jane's coming would ruin a scheme that was so far going perfectly. "You must stay," Elizabeth whispered, "to hold your ground with his sisters, and to show Bingley how much you like him."

Holding her temple and wincing, Elizabeth then apologised to her aunt for all the trouble she caused, and when she insisted that Jane needed her support more and she was only going to go home to bed, Mrs Gardiner finally agreed to put her into the hired carriage with the servant.

"Take care of yourself, my dear," her aunt said, raising the hood of her cloak. "Straight to bed with you."

Bingley's footman opened the door to the hackney, but Elizabeth paused once the door to the Hursts' home shut. "Before we go to Cheapside, we must first stop in Charles Street."

The driver nodded, but Bingley's servant looked distressed. "Are you certain, ma'am?" he asked. "Mr Bingley expects me to see you safely home."

"And you will." Bingley's servant sighed and climbed onto the back.

She called the house number to the driver and wondered if she could persuade Bingley's servant not to mention this detour. She would not be subjected to society's rules about who could call on whom or who could speak first. She felt nervous, but this matter with Darcy had to be settled, and if he was avoiding her, she would demand to know why.

Had Darcy felt anxious before he came to the parsonage last week? Maybe not since he had been so sure of his acceptance. At least he had the right to show up and speak to her. Men were the ones who were allowed to take action, after all.

They were there in a moment. Charles Street was quiet, but there was a party at Berkeley Square and many carriages were passing. Perhaps it was best to use another name, like they had in Dartford, when she called on him. If anyone recognised her calling at a man's house alone in the evening, not even Miss Bingley's determination would save her reputation.

Bingley's footman came to the carriage door. "Are you calling on Mr Darcy?" He sounded incredulous.

"Please say that Mrs Gardiner is calling for Mr Darcy." Bingley's man shook his head, and Elizabeth tried to keep her patience. "It is nothing like what you fear. This will not take long, and then you can return me home. No one in Grosvenor Street needs to know."

He huffed and went to the door. Darcy's footman looked surprised to have an unexpected caller at half past six and was even more astonished that Mrs Gardiner did not have a card to leave.

From the carriage she heard the words, "not at home," and then Bingley's man turned from the door.

Elizabeth grumbled at yet another man and another rule that kept her from what she wanted. She drew her cloak's hood tightly around her head, awkwardly climbed down with no one to help her, and pushed her way past them both and into a finely appointed entrance hall.

"Madam!" Darcy's man cried. Bingley's footman was actually covering his face with his hand.

What a scandal; a woman had asserted herself. "Please tell Mr Darcy that Mrs Gardiner is here and that she requires a moment of his time."

Darcy's servant looked like he was deciding how to throw out what looked like a respectable woman when the door to the room to her right was wrenched open and Darcy came into the hall. His face snapped to hers, and the connexion between them seemed to intensify. Elizabeth knew he felt it, too.

The servant cleared his throat. "Sir, if you are receiving guests, Mrs Gardiner is here."

Darcy's eyebrows raised, but she could not understand his now shaken expression. "Yes, I thought I heard her voice." He seemed to recognise Bingley's man because he said, "Did you bring her?" A nod. "And does anyone in that house know she is here?" A shake. Darcy sighed deeply, and it seemed as though he thought a thousand things at once. "Is Bingley's chaise waiting?"

"No, it is a hired hackney to return her to Gracechurch Street. The lady said she was ill."

"Send it away—do *not* let it wait in the mews," he said firmly. "You can stay, and we shall hire another when Miss—Mrs Gardiner leaves. This shall not take long."

He was ready to throw her out, and not even call his own carriage to send her home? Elizabeth felt ready to burst into angry tears. She was not leaving this house until she had spoken and until Darcy had explained why he had not come to see her. The servants left them, and he said, "Instead of the drawing room, I think you had better come into the library."

She followed him and saw Kirby on the floor by the fire, wearing a new suit of clothes, lying on his stomach with his feet in the air, a book open before him, and a full plate next to the book.

"It is Nan!" he cried, climbing to his feet to bow. "Although, I suppose that ain't your real name, is it?"

Kirby grinned widely and looked comfortable here, and Elizabeth knew instantly that her situation with Darcy was more complicated than she had feared.

∿

Darcy was certain Elizabeth was about to raise her voice to him until she saw Kirby in the library. He watched the fury fade from her countenance as a thoughtful comprehension took its place. As pleased as he was to see her, the idea that Markle's man had been watching and recognised her made his heart seize in fear.

"Did anyone see you?" he asked. "Was there a man on the street or at the square?"

"I had up my hood," she said, laying her cloak over a chair. "Someone had a party so there were carriages lining up along Berkeley Square, but why—"

"Because my uncle is watching the house," Kirby said through a bite of food. He had returned to sit tailor-wise on the floor by his plate and book. Darcy saw Elizabeth noticed his faded bruise that was a sickly shade of yellowish-green. "I left him and came here. Mr Darcy is sending me to school, but my uncle is looking for me."

Kirby went back to his book and his food, and Darcy tapped the corner of his own eye. "He came here to be safe," he said pointedly. "Markle does not know the boy is in my house, but he suspects I am helping him, and is following me wherever I go."

Elizabeth nodded along. "He thinks you will lead him to Kirby."

"No, he thinks I will lead him to *you*." Even in the warm light from the lamps and candles, the colour drained from her face, giving her a deathlike pallor.

He led her to sit on the sofa. As much as he had wanted to protect her from the truth and the danger, she was here now and had to be told. "Markle thinks I have Kirby hidden away somewhere and that he can abduct you to trade for Kirby. And since he has not yet found you, likely because you are not known in town and are staying with family who does not share your surname, he has threatened my sister instead."

Elizabeth gasped. "Is Miss Darcy safe?"

"Fitzwilliam hid her with her companion's sister. He thought that safer than with a friend known to society. Markle insists he will find her and said he would kidnap her tomorrow if he cannot find you. He knows he abducted the wrong woman; he killed Steamer in a fury over that and losing us, and he is shrewd enough to"—he looked away—"to know harming you would hurt me."

Elizabeth swallowed thickly. "That is why you have not called, and why you did not go to the Hursts'."

He could not speak freely in front of Kirby about everything he had to talk with her about, but Darcy explained what had happened since Kirby arrived Tuesday morning and Markle approached him yesterday. "I had been on my way to Cheapside before he accosted me on the street," he finished awkwardly.

Elizabeth looked to where Kirby was reading his book. "And here I thought," she said slowly, "that you were avoiding resuming our conversation from Sunday morning. I continue to misjudge you." She dropped her eyes. "I am sorry that I trusted every lie that man said."

He took her hand. "I am—"

"Mr Darcy found a tutor in Sheffield for me," Kirby called from across the room as though just remembering. Darcy reluctantly let go of her hand. "He says that on school holidays I can stay with him at Pemberley."

It was true, but now Darcy wished him away so he could talk to Elizabeth. He had too much to say and not much time to say it before he hurried her to safety. But Elizabeth smiled at the interruption. "That is grand, Kirby. You are very fortunate." She turned back to him. "What shall we do? How do we keep your sister safe?"

"I will think of something, but for now, you must return home. We called a watchman, but Markle's men just smile and leave, and a different man takes his place once the watch is gone. If the carriages blocked Markle's men from viewing Charles Street, it shall not last all night. I will hire a—"

"I said *we*," she said, staring at him. "I will not be put to the side any longer."

"We can discuss everything between us once Markle is behind bars," he said so Kirby could not hear.

Elizabeth gave a weak smile. "I should hope so, but I meant regarding Markle and Kirby. Your sister's safety relies on us. My safety is threatened too, and I refuse to be ignored. We can solve this together."

"I need to keep you safe." Darcy hoped she did not notice how his voice wavered.

"And I need to help," she said, forcing him to meet her eye.

"This is a sad business, Elizabeth, and you have already suffered horribly."

"And so have you. Did we not do everything together when we were abducted? I am helping you to solve this. It would seem getting Kirby to Sheffield is the first thing, and then we must keep your sister safeguarded."

As much as he wanted to protect Elizabeth, wanted her as far from him as possible, it felt good to have her with him. It was selfish, though, to indulge in it. "We must get you away before Markle's men resume their watch. If they chose not to loiter because of all the carriages at the square, they will soon be back."

"They do not think Kirby is here?"

"Markle did not hint at it when we spoke. He thinks that he has to find you in order to get to Kirby, and since he has found no hint of you yet, he threatened Georgiana."

Elizabeth looked pensive for a moment. "Gunter's is around the corner in the square."

What had ices to do with anything? His face must have shown his confusion because Elizabeth laughed. "Are you questioning the lady's ability to be useful if she is thinking of confections?"

"I would never question your acuity."

"My aunt has four children under the age of eight." Darcy could not see where this was going, but did not know how to politely interrupt her. "Can you imagine what a rowdy group that is? If not, then you should invite a friend with a large family to ruin your drawing room for a while. Then, before they leave, they walk to the square where they are spoiled at Gunter's. A loud group of children often seems larger than they really are."

Comprehension dawned, and Darcy grinned. "And when they return to Charles Street, who could be certain if five or six children entered the carriage that finally took the noisy bunch on their way?"

Elizabeth returned his smile. "Markle's man does not follow it because you remain here and they are looking for a young lady. I am sure your friend would take your young ward to where your servant will meet him and see him safely to Sheffield."

Brilliant dark eyes that showed the spirit and intelligence exhibited in how she lived her life animated her face. "You are clever," he said.

"But still not cleverer than you?" she asked with a smile, remembering their game to distract them while they were kidnapped.

"If you would like to prove it by also figuring out how to rid ourselves of Markle, please do so."

He had spoken lightly, but her laughing expression fell. "What can Bow Street do?"

"Our abduction is not a priority, and menacing me with vague threats is not illegal. And there is still the matter of finding him." Markle was still in town, but he was as often at sea smuggling, or bringing items onshore and to his inland gang to hide, distribute, and sell.

"So, we need a solution that keeps you, Kirby, Miss Darcy, and me alive for the weeks it might take for the courts to issue a warrant and act on it?"

"There was a warrant issued for him earlier this year, Nan," Kirby called through a mouth full of sweets.

They shared a look of surprise. Kirby returned to his book, and Darcy rose and went to him. "What do you mean he is already wanted?"

"By the excise officers," he said, brushing his sleeve across his mouth. "Remember how I told you about the revenue man my uncle's gang killed? They threw him into a well? I don't know if they charged my uncle for the informant they burnt in the barn, but the Board of Excise would not forget the murder of one of their riding men, would they?"

"Then why was Markle not arrested for the murder?" Elizabeth asked.

Kirby shrugged, holding a finger in his book to keep his page as he answered. "He is always moving about and has plenty of hiding places, and no one close to my uncle will give him up because they are afraid. The smuggling gangs also earn the trust of the locals and the officials. There are thousands of smugglers in Kent, you know."

Darcy's mind turned over what he had learnt. Having procured the necessary warrant, one only needed someone willing to execute it and find the perpetrator. Now he need not wait weeks for Bow Street to act and pursue Markle.

"If there was a way to lure Markle into meeting me, we could make certain that the excise officers were there to arrest him," Darcy said as he paced the room.

"With the threat to your sister, he has no reason to meet you," Elizabeth said. "Unless there was a reason to negotiate for Kirby."

He shook his head. "Kirby is in a carriage to Sheffield as soon as I can arrange the outing with a horde of loud children." He was not about to bargain with Kirby's life when he finally had a way to secure it.

"I agree," Elizabeth said softly, looking at the little boy who had returned to his book and his treat. "But we both know how to draw out Markle and to keep your sister safe tomorrow."

He had been afraid many times in the last week, but the anxiety of understanding what she offered exposed a new depth of terror. The mere hint of what she was suggesting was enough to shock him.

"Kirby," he said as evenly as he could, "say good night to Miss Bennet." He could not overhear the argument that was about to take place.

"But I have not finished my—"

"Take your things and a candle, and go to your room," he said while still looking at Elizabeth. Kirby grumbled as he obliged, and Elizabeth parted from him sweetly and insisted on kissing his cheek. Kirby looked startled and rubbed his face. Darcy wondered if the boy had ever had a single affectionate embrace.

When the door closed behind him, Elizabeth squared her shoulders and crossed her arms over her chest, bracing herself for his objections.

"I will not trade Kirby's life for yours, and I will not risk your life for his. Georgiana is safe in Fetter Lane for the meanwhile. We—and yes, I said *we*, Elizabeth—shall find another way."

"Is she really safe?" she asked, but of course he had no answer. "And what have you come up with? You have been thinking of nothing else for a day, I am sure."

She did not say it rudely. It was not a taunt, but it wounded him all the same. He had thought over the matter for hours at a time and come up with nothing timely, nothing certain, nothing at all.

"I will let his men see me," she said when he looked away, "before Markle can even consider looking for Miss Darcy tomorrow. They will abduct me and force you to trade. We can lay a trap with the customs officers to be there to stop him from getting away."

"He would kill you when he realises his nephew is lost to him. We know how impulsive he is." Darcy had to stop himself from reaching out to stroke Elizabeth's hair. She had made such a terrible sound when Markle hauled her to her feet by her hair. "He slashed Steamer's throat as he lay on a surgeon's table with a broken leg."

She exhaled a long breath. "I know. But Markle wants his nephew. He needs him as a smuggler and for the sake of having what he thinks is rightfully his. Don't you see?" she pleaded. "It is in my control to end all of this and keep Miss Darcy safe. We let his men take me, and he will forget all about going after your sister. He arranges an exchange with you, and before he knows that Kirby is not coming, the customs house officers will arrest him for murder."

Darcy hated this with every fibre of his being. "I cannot risk your safety."

"And you cannot stop me from running into the street right now and letting Markle's man see me."

"I am the one who assumed the risk and responsibility for Kirby," he cried, pointing to his own chest, "not you."

"I am not doing it for him," she said just as loudly before turning pink. "Or, at least not only for him. I am a selfish creature, Darcy. We need to end this, and neither of us is safe until Markle is arrested."

"No. Absolutely not." Her plan to lure Markle into a trap was rational, if still dangerous. And if it was some other person being put to risk, someone he did not love, he would argue its merits. "Elizabeth, I spent three days in acute desperation wanting to keep you safe, and you are talking about willingly letting him take you again!"

"What about your sister?" she cried. "If he has me and thinks he can use me to get Kirby back, he has no reason to find Miss Darcy."

He ran his hand across his eyes, feeling weary. The thought of Georgiana being smacked across the face, kidnapped and terrorised, stole his breath. "She is hidden for the present. Fitzwilliam moved her, and that bought me time to come up with a solution—one that does not put you or anyone else in danger," he added.

"Markle is vicious, vindictive, and violent." She came forward in earnest. "He will not let this go, and London is not as big as you think it is. Neither of us is safe, not here, and not at Pemberley or Longbourn. He said he would take your sister unless you brought him Kirby. Are you going to trade his life for hers?"

She knew he would never do that. It would devastate him to forsake a child. And it would devastate him to not protect his sister. He only had to think of a better plan, one that did not put Elizabeth in danger. "I am not giving Kirby to his uncle, but I am also not allowing you to put yourself in harm's way."

Elizabeth threw up her hands. "Markle will ultimately learn where Miss Elizabeth Bennet with a friend in Hunsford lives. And he will do the same with Miss Darcy. I want us to move forward, and I cannot see another way in the short time we have."

"Time is running out," he agreed, "but I am unwilling to risk your life."

"I could talk myself out of any real trouble with Markle, at least while he wants to get his nephew back and thinks I am the means to do it. And I am more likely to remain calm than Miss Darcy would. I have already been in this situation and have some idea what to expect. I can do this, Darcy, even if you will never ask me to."

Darcy felt his resolve breaking. Georgiana would be haunted forever if Markle kidnapped her. He had seen enough of Elizabeth's bravery to not doubt her mettle, but how was he to agree to a scheme that threatened her life? "There has to be another way," he whispered to himself, looking at the clock on the mantel. His sister might not be taken tomorrow, or maybe Markle had already followed Georgiana and was planning on harming her to get to Kirby. Who was to say Markle would not wait four months, follow his sister to Pemberley, and try to take her from there the same way he had tried to kidnap Anne?

"Darcy, we are in a desperate state, and you admitted that we are out of time. You are not choosing between me or your sister. I am choosing to let Markle take me to keep her safe. To keep all of us safe." She gave him a long look. "And I am not asking your permission."

She might have been prepared for a debate, but he had nothing to argue against the point aside from his own fears. They needed to get an advantage over Markle, and they needed to take action now. If it had been another person, a man, being kidnapped to lure out Markle, he would think it was a good scheme. A dauntless person wanted to exchange themself for his shy sister and an innocent child. It was only a plague on his heart because he loved her.

Darcy put his arms around her. "You are exceedingly brave, although I wish your prudence equalled your courage."

"Some might say I am exceedingly foolish, but I thank you for the compliment," she said, smiling.

Her calmness shocked him, and he dropped his arms. "How are you not terrified of putting yourself through that again?"

"Oh, I am, but I think one can be both courageous and frightened."

"I am the one who is supposed to be courageous." A wave of mortification washed over him, leaving his chest tight and his cheeks burning.

"Because you are a man?" He nodded, a little ashamed. "You would take my place if you could, and you *are* brave, braver than me. You, my dear Darcy, have to watch me do this."

"I don't know how," he whispered. "Every time Markle or Steamer so much as looked at you, I was terrified for you. And this time you would be alone."

She gave a tight nod. "I will be. And I will wish for your strength and company every moment. But there was little you could do for me then too, although not for a want of trying or a want of spirit." Elizabeth gave him a beseeching look. "If I can let Markle take me to lead the officers to him, to save Kirby, to protect your sister, to keep us safe, I must try."

She was resolved, and as much as it hurt to put her in harm's way, he admired her bravery, her strength of mind, her boldness. "Good heavens, your family will absolutely hate me when they find out, Elizabeth," he said, falling into the sofa.

"That is why we won't tell them. Besides, it is my idea, and short of kidnapping me yourself, you cannot stop me."

"You jest, but I am sorely tempted."

She sat by him and put a consoling hand on his arm. He wanted her to put her arms around him instead. "My doing this is the best choice of a poor selection."

He agreed, resigned to the whole affair. He leant back in his seat, looking at the ceiling. "I will get Kirby out of London tomorrow, and then go to the Excise Office on Broad Street and tell them what we plan so they are ready for whenever..."

He did not want to say the words "whenever that hateful, violent man kidnaps you." This could all end in disaster. He looked at her beautifully expressive face, full of determination, and knew that he had to tell her he was in love with her and still wanted to marry her in case he never got another chance.

Chapter Eighteen

Darcy looked at her so sadly that Elizabeth knew he hated everything about this plan, even though he recognised that it was their best choice. She was not about to allow Kirby or Miss Darcy to be harmed, not if she could prevent it. She wanted to rest her head against Darcy for longer, but the Gardiners would make it an early evening to check on her.

She rose. "I should go before I miss my chance to return unnoticed."

To her surprise, Darcy leapt to his feet. "No, if we are resolved to do this, if I am to risk you—"

"I am risking myself."

"Yes," he said, giving her a pained look. "Regardless, you are risking your life, and if anything happened to you, I want nothing left unsaid between us."

She had come here for precisely that conversation, but matters were more complicated than she had known. "Darcy, we can talk when this is all over."

"I told you in Dartford that you should give me my name when we are alone."

Did he have any idea how much he captivated her heart when he said things like that? "Even after I foolishly said I needed assurances you would never hurt me the way you supposedly hurt Wickham?"

"I am sorry I misconstrued what you really needed from me. You only wanted the truth; you were not casting aspersions on my character." After looking into her face for a long moment, he added, "And I am sorry that the truth about your friend pained you."

Elizabeth scoffed. "It is only painful to be convinced that one whom I thought was my friend is unworthy of my confidence."

"I assure you, I have not spoken of him as severely as he deserves," Darcy said darkly. "What did he say to you? That I denied him the living out of jealousy and gave him nothing for it?"

"And that you accused him of forfeiting all claim to the living by his extravagance and imprudence." She felt the burning shame across her cheeks. "I should have suspected earlier that he was an unscrupulous liar, especially after I knew what type of man you really are."

"Mr Wickham is a consummate scoundrel, and has been from his earliest days."

"Your narrative of your history with the man made that clear."

"My father promised the late Mr Wickham to provide for his son. It was a debt of gratitude to *him* for his devoted care of the Pemberley properties, rather than excessive affection for the son. My father was fond of him, certainly, but never in a way that made me jealous."

She felt her heart wrenching all over again. "You must have felt so hurt when you believed that I still thought you had wronged him." Darcy opened his mouth, but she said, "And you deserved better, because what I feel for you is not some mere romantic flight. I love you dearly, and so I should have trusted you without having to hear what happened."

"Any sensible woman would want to be certain that the man she wants to—" He stopped and seemed to gather his thoughts. It struck her that Darcy would not assume she wanted to marry him. "Well, you thought me devoid of every proper feeling."

"But not by the time we were in Dartford," she cried. She might as well have said, "Not by the time we shared a bed."

"Suspicion is not in your nature. I could not see it at the time, but why would you have assumed that you had been lied to?"

Elizabeth lifted her eyes to blink away a few tears of shame. "I should have done better."

"A sentiment by which I live my life."

It was said wryly, but she saw that he felt the truth of it. "You are too hard on yourself. I am sorry I hurt you that morning."

He shook his head. "I made assumptions, blinded by fear over what your feelings were. It was my fault."

Her mistaken judgments, both before and after the kidnapping, must have been such a trial to Darcy because he cared for her so much. "I know that I hurt you. I am sorry that loving me hurt you."

Darcy looked completely taken aback. For a moment, he was silent. "No, it is rejection that hurts, and loneliness," he said carefully. "And being unable to prevent the person you love from hurting. Loving you does not hurt me at all, and I would risk all the rejection, all the loneliness, all the fear, to have love in my life, to have *you* in my life."

He came near and took both of her hands in his, but still did not ask her again to marry him. The open, earnest desire in his expression made it difficult for her to breathe. She had been brave to come here, and she could not stop now.

"I think you have too generous and perhaps too proud a temper," she said, smiling, "to persecute me with what you fear are unsolicited wishes. So, I am here, soliciting them, to tell you to ask me again."

He gave a soft laugh as delight diffused over his face. "You assume I have not been wanting to ask you to marry me since you charged into my house. In this moment, however, I was deciding whether to kiss you before I asked you or after."

"Oh," she said, laughing a little from relief. "Well, the order does not matter to me, so long as both are accomplished quickly."

Darcy let go of her hands and put his on her waist. "I am in love with you, and if your heart is equally engaged, then I beg you to marry me."

Her cheeks hurt from how widely she was smiling. "Yes." She gathered his face in her hands and kissed him, breathing him in and tasting him. Darcy stilled in surprise for an instant before his mouth moved against hers with the same purpose and passion. His grip tightened around her, and she clasped at his neck and shoulders, kissing him with urgency.

When they broke apart, they were both breathing harshly. "You should know," she said, catching her breath, "that giddy violence of desire you just experienced is of course preceded by warm esteem and a rational attachment."

Darcy laughed softly, staring at her with desire. "I never doubted it, dearest."

"Fitzwilliam, I have always wanted someone who believed in my abilities and who would take care of me in all the ways that mattered. Someone who would see me as their equal partner. You are exactly that person, and I love you very much."

To her surprise, the lightness in his face faded, and he leant down to look directly into her eyes. "I plan to be indebted to you for the most blissful moments of my life, so if you let Markle take you, you have to promise to come back to me."

She could not make him that promise, and he knew it. She kissed him again instead, pouring all of her affection for him into it. After a time, he broke the kiss to trace his lips across her cheeks, her jaw, and down her neck before pulling her into his chest.

"I do not want you to leave," he said into her hair, "but you have to get back before your aunt and uncle do. Bingley's footman is likely prowling the servants' hall wondering if this will cost him his position."

He was trying to hide how afraid he was for her. "Do you think I can leave from the servants' entrance and not be noticed?" she asked, still leaning into him.

She felt him shake his head. "If the carriages are now gone, whomever it is has a clear view and will follow anyone in a skirt."

"Then we can set this into motion now," she whispered into his chest. His hold tightened, but he did not disagree.

After holding her for a while, he said, "Colonel Fitzwilliam's brother, Lord Milton, is in town. He has two daughters, and his wife's sister has three or four children; I am not certain. I will invite them in the morning to remove Kirby." He kissed her hair. "Then I will go to the Excise Board and tell them I can give them the murderer of one of their men if they rescue you."

"Do you think they will abduct me now?" she asked, clamping down her fear so as not to alarm Darcy.

He let her go to look into her face. "No, I think the men watching the house must check with Markle. They will follow you and take you from home as soon as they can tomorrow."

"I don't want them to enter the house. I will make a point of walking Gracechurch Street in the morning. I will tell my aunt I have shopping to do and try to be as much on my own as I can."

"While I am getting Kirby away tomorrow, I will ask Fitzwilliam to watch the Gardiners' house to follow whoever takes you."

"That is unnecessary. Markle will contact you to arrange an exchange."

"You cannot think I am letting you do this without learning where they take you." The look on Darcy's face told her how much he hated her plan. "If they don't take you tomorrow, after Kirby is gone and I speak with the officers, I will present myself in Cheapside and they can follow me."

"You can ask to speak with me alone so you can offer your heart and your hand. Should I prepare my family for joyous news?"

Darcy looked like he was trying to keep his patience with her levity. He was hiding the depth of his distress, but she saw how afraid he was.

"I can do this," she breathed. "I am afraid, but your cousin will know where I am. The revenue officers will arrest Markle when he tries to make an exchange, and then we will have the banns read." She forced him to look at her. "Don't look so pained, Fitzwilliam, please. I cannot do this without your full support."

"Of course I am pained. What greater injury could be done to a man than to see a woman he loves be put into harm's way?" He touched her cheek before tucking a ringlet of hair behind her ear. "But your plan to see Markle arrested is a good one, or as good as we have with the time and resources available to us."

"I will not let any harm come to Kirby or your sister," she said determinedly. "We can retake control of this dreadful situation. Markle will take me and arrange an exchange. He wants his nephew, and you will have the officers ready."

"You do not have to do this, my dear."

He must have seen the apprehension in her eyes. "Don't say that. Markle has to be stopped. Besides, I have endured one kidnapping. What is another one? I will be better prepared this time."

"You will be alone."

Rather than acknowledge this, she asked, "Have you slept well this week?"

He knew what she meant. "I missed you dreadfully the first few nights."

"Only the first few?" she said archly. "I miss your arms around me when I fall asleep."

He shrugged. "Markle showed up, and I have been so worried I would not have slept well even if I could hear you breathing next to me."

Darcy suddenly crossed the room to a writing desk and pulled out a large mother-of-pearl pocket knife. "Do not say I do not give my betrothed gifts. It is sturdier than the quill knife I used on Steamer."

She took it and opened it. She could do this, and she would not need the knife. Markle would taunt her and perhaps knock her about, but he wanted his nephew. She would not need to escape; the excise officers would arrest him when Markle appeared to make the trade for Kirby.

"You don't have to do this," Darcy repeated.

Elizabeth put away the knife. "It is my idea, and my decision."

"Any sensible person would stop you from doing this. What does that say about me?"

It said he was terrified for a little boy and his little sister. She knew this was going to be harder for him than her. "It says you know this is the best and fastest way, and you are respecting my choice and admiring my courage."

"Or that I am a damned fool."

"If you don't like it," she said, reading his expression, "we could run away instead to where Markle could never find us. India? The Canadas? Is there anywhere you have always wanted to go?"

"There is the small problem of the hundreds of people at Pemberley who depend on me."

"What a shame. I do wish you were poorer."

"Stop trying to make me laugh." He said it so forcefully Elizabeth flinched. "When this is over you can sport with me to your heart's content, but not now. I feel like every nerve around my frantically beating heart is being frayed."

She put her arms around him, pressing a quick kiss to his lips. "I am sorry. Let us talk about something else. Kirby will be so happy to leave London. You have done a wonderfully generous thing."

Thinking of him made Darcy smile. "Hopefully we can afford him because Kirby eats everything put in front of him." She smiled, but Darcy sobered. "I did not consider your feelings as I ought to have done. You will start your married life with a twelve-year-old ward, and I have already promised the boy that he is welcome at Pemberley whenever he likes."

"In this instance, there was no reason to consult me. You know I would do exactly as you had. I hate to think of him alone and friendless after what he has been through. He will often be at Pemberley with us, and, for that matter, so should Miss Darcy. Once this is over, you must introduce me to my new sister."

"How do you do that?" he asked in wonder. "How do you easily imagine our happy future knowing you are going to be abducted? My mind is imagining every worst possible outcome."

"Don't you see, Fitzwilliam? I am doing this to guarantee our happy future," she said emphatically. "If we do nothing, Markle will lose his patience and kill you on the street out of spite, and he will find me and do the same. Or he will find your sister, and I cannot live with that. There is no one to protect us. I am doing this for us, and to stop a child beater and a murderer."

"I know!" His loss of temper did not surprise her. He knew Markle had to be stopped; Darcy just did not want the woman he loved to be involved in doing it. "I know why," he repeated quietly, "and I wish I could go in your place."

She answered by kissing his lips tenderly. "You cannot control everything."

He bowed his head, as though this truth was physically painful. "He will underestimate you, but comply with him like you did before, and assure him that I will do anything to get you back, that I will bring him Kirby, that I will pay more than what he wanted from Lady Catherine."

"Why would I offer money? He does not want it; he only wants Kirby back."

"Offer him anything, and I will pay it," he said plainly. "He could harm you. He could torture you, do unspeakable things to you. If you need to offer money to stop him, do it."

"He might just threaten me to get what he really wants, which is his nephew."

They heard a noise by the door. Feet shuffling, pausing, and then moving away.

Sighing, Elizabeth rose and pulled him up with her. "Was that Kirby listening, or Bingley's man wondering when we can leave?"

"Probably the latter. I will order my carriage. If the point is to have you followed and kidnapped, we might as well get their attention."

She might have said she would lower her hood and wave, but Darcy did not want her playfulness now.

"Can you endure this?" he asked after ringing the bell.

"Can *you*?" Darcy would have to be just as brave as she would need to be. He nodded. "Will you meet Markle and get the excise officers to arrest him?"

"Of course."

"Then I can endure it to secure our safety, and to stop a murderer," she said firmly. "I am confident this will work."

"I can see that you are, and it is as good a plan as we can make in the short time we have, but the thought of you luring out Markle still feels like the blood in my own veins is being spilt." Darcy then took her face in his hands and gave her a fierce kiss goodbye.

∾

"Did you have a pleasant time with my cousins' children?" Darcy asked Kirby as they stood in the entrance hall Friday morning. He flinched at the sound of a shriek and a crash from above. Five children were running about in his drawing room as though it were a garden.

"I suppose, but I did not get to go to Gunter's."

Darcy tousled Kirby's hair. "I walked the square before everyone arrived and saw Conway. You would have had to walk straight past him." Conway had remained in place while Fitzwilliam went to Gracechurch Street to follow Elizabeth. His worry for her felt like a sickness, but what he could do now was ensure that Kirby was safe. Any moment of inactivity was sure to lead him into a wretchedness of worry.

He pulled Kirby aside because the carriages had been called and it was time for him to leave. "Do you remember what will happen now?"

"I stand next to you to block me from view of the square then join while the other children run onto the pavement and I get into his lordship's carriage to Curzon Street," he recited. "I sit on the floor to be certain no one sees me."

"My footman George will meet you there, and then the two of you are going to Sheffield. Mr Gates and his family expect you in three days." To his surprise, Kirby sighed. "I will be down by the time you have a holiday, and you can come to Pemberley and eat me out of house and home."

Kirby nodded, but still looked forlorn.

"What is the matter?" Darcy asked. "Do you not want to be free from your uncle and go to school?" Darcy feared Kirby's ties to home, however awful that home was, might be too strong to break.

"I do, but what about Nan?"

Darcy did not correct him. From him, it was almost as though Nan had become an affectionate nickname. "What about her?" He smiled down at Kirby so as not to worry him.

Last night, carriages from the party at Berkeley Square had moved along, and it would not have been difficult for someone watching to see a woman leaving number eight Charles Street and follow her to Cheapside.

"She is going to let my uncle snatch her so you can draw him out."

His smile fell. How had he guessed, unless he had been listening at the door after Darcy sent him away? "It is nothing a little boy needs to worry about."

Kirby drew himself up to his full four feet seven inches of height. "What kind of life do you think I had in Shoreham, Mr Darcy?"

"My apologies." Kirby's years had passed very differently from those of the children romping upstairs. He had seen violence and crime and a shameful amount of neglect. "You are perfectly right, Master Kirby."

Kirby set his shoulders and nodded curtly, and Darcy refused to laugh. "Nan gets taken on purpose. You get the excise officers, and they arrest my uncle for killing their man, and then we are all safe. It makes sense, but are you sure I should leave? I can be there when my uncle brings Nan to trade. You might need me."

This little boy and Elizabeth were the bravest people he knew. "You are courageous, but Miss Bennet and I want to put it out of anyone's power to return you to your uncle."

Kirby tugged down his cap and sighed again. "My uncle needs me in his gang. I don't care one way or the other for free trading, but I don't want to hurt people. He is a wicked man," he added in a whisper. "You and Nan are brave to stand up to him."

Kirby had not witnessed his uncle killing Steamer in a fit of rage, but he had seen the bloody aftermath, and Darcy now wondered if Kirby had witnessed the brutal stoning of the revenue man. Or, worse, he might have been forced to participate. He would not ask him the question. Kirby deserved to think about the future.

"Do you want to know a secret?" Darcy knelt down to look Kirby in the eye. "I am terrified that something might happen to Miss Bennet and that I won't be there to help her. But once you are away, she and I are going to make certain your uncle never hurts anyone again."

The boy gave him a solemn nod. "And then the next time we come to town, it will be safe to get ices."

This time, Darcy did laugh. "It will be perfectly safe to go anywhere you like." There seemed a good chance Kirby Ramer could now live a life like any other twelve-year-old boy. Darcy heard the drawing room door open, and the noise spilled into the hall just as the front door opened with the servant to say that the carriages had arrived.

"Thank you, Mr Darcy." Kirby solemnly held out a hand, and Darcy, knowing once again that he could not smile, took it.

"Ready to begin your new life?" Darcy asked as the other children and adults went past them and out the door.

Chapter Nineteen

I t was with a strange mixture of fear and contentment that Elizabeth began her day. She felt absolute dread that she was going to be abducted by a murderer, but she could not stifle the satisfaction that came in knowing everything was settled with Darcy. She supposed it boded well for their future, that any misunderstanding or disagreement could be settled if the two of them just spent enough time in the same room.

She just had to be certain she survived her encounter with Markle so she could enjoy that future.

Whatever she would suffer at Markle's hands, she felt that Darcy would suffer more. He had hated watching her be threatened and hit and provoked, and it would be worse when he did not know where she was or what was happening. He was not the sort to sit and wait, but her plan forced him to be passive while she took all the risk.

Elizabeth checked the window again. Colonel Fitzwilliam was still walking up and down Gracechurch Street. *Darcy has not been entirely passive.* But he would hate the silence, the waiting, the not knowing.

She opened a box from her toilette table and pulled out the diamond and sapphire ring Darcy had in Kent. She ought to leave it behind because the symbolism was horrid, inspired by a dictator who ultimately divorced his wife, intended as an engagement gift for another woman. But Elizabeth had worn it when Darcy saw her in the bath in Dartford, when she ran her fingers through his hair before falling into bed together.

Elizabeth put it on her right hand. Darcy would rather she not wear it, she knew, but she wanted something of his with her other than a pocket knife.

The door opened and Elizabeth managed not to cry out in surprise this time as Jane entered. Her heart still raced whenever someone entered the room unexpectedly.

"Are you ready to visit a few of the shops?" Jane asked. "I am so pleased you are feeling better. My aunt says we can take her man; she would rather stay with her children this morning."

Elizabeth had placed Darcy's knife down in her stocking and tied it with a ribbon. She let out a slow breath and nodded. She had to go outside alone and allow herself to be taken without Jane being harmed. Now to proceed as she had rehearsed in her mind.

"I am not certain what to wear. Do you think I should change into my blue pelisse, or will I be warm enough with this yellow spencer?"

Elizabeth looked out the window to pretend to guess the weather and saw Colton on horseback a few houses down the street. Colonel Fitzwilliam was by a shop window, farther away. Someone must have followed her home last night. Colton could not carry her off unnoticed atop a horse, but perhaps Markle did not care about being subtle at this point.

"Open the window and see how it feels," Jane said, tying her bonnet ribbon.

She had not considered that. "Hmm, I would rather step outside to decide." Elizabeth went for the door, but on passing Jane, she could not help but pull her into a tight hug. "I will be back."

"Lizzy!" Jane cried, laughing. "What is all this?"

There was nothing she could say. Elizabeth smiled and went down the stairs. She nodded to the servant in the hall and said she was checking the weather. She clutched the door handle, but her shaking fingers struggled with it and he came back to help her.

"I can do this," she whispered as she walked onto the pavement. She could be brave to save Kirby's future, to protect Miss Darcy, and to help arrest a violent criminal determined to torment them.

No one came running up to her, and no carriage came alongside her like what had happened at Rosings. Perhaps she had judged wrongly, and Colton would only follow her and abduct her later. After walking a few townhouse lengths, Elizabeth could not pretend she was feeling the air any longer. She was about to turn when a hand wrapped tightly around her arm.

She gave a genuine shout of surprise. "None of that now, Nan," Markle said in a low voice. "Come along with me."

Although this was according to plan, her instinct was to pull away. Markle tightened his grip, turned his cold eye on her, and pulled aside his frock coat to reveal a pistol. "Remember, when I say to do something..."

She did not say, "I do it," but she stopped fighting.

"There's a good girl. You would not want something to happen to that other pretty girl in that house. No, no, don't turn round. I think she came out looking for you, but Colton will put a bullet in her head if you don't get in."

A hackney coach was waiting, and Elizabeth wondered if Jane could see this far or if Colonel Fitzwilliam was near enough to note the number on the coach. She climbed in, and Markle pressed in next to her as the hackney rumbled down Gracechurch Street.

"Who was that lady?" Markle asked. His pleasant tone was an affront. "A sister? Another friend like that Mrs Collins in Hunsford?"

Elizabeth refused to answer. The thought that harm could come to Jane because of what she was doing wrenched her heart. Jane would be so frightened when she realised she had been abducted again. Then she thought of Darcy. He must be slowly dying inside from fear for her.

If anything truly horrible happened to her, would she tell Darcy or stay silent to spare him the anger and regret he would feel? As much as it was her own choice, he would feel responsible. Part of her wanted to keep whatever happened a secret, but she supposed a lie like that, an omission, would ruin something between them. Besides, whatever Darcy imagined might be worse than what would actually happen.

"No answer?" Markle asked again. "'Tis rude to sit in silence when spoken to."

"You know I am not Miss de Bourgh, so why abduct me again?"

Markle gave a dark smile. "Free trading has taught me to adapt quickly. Lady Catherine's nephew has something of mine, and now I have something of his."

She supposed it was pointless to argue that she did not belong to Darcy, or that she was even significant to him. "Mr Darcy stole nothing of yours."

"He knows where my nephew is." Markle looked out the side-glass. "Troublesome boy, not like my sister. Perhaps too like his father, though; too stupid by half, that one. Damned boy needs much correcting."

Elizabeth thought of Kirby's bruised eye and how happy he was to read a book with a plate of food within reach. *That is why I am here.* She was protecting an innocent boy who had no one to defend him. "If he is troublesome, why do you want him?"

Markle turned swiftly from the window to stare at her. "Because he is mine," he bit out.

Elizabeth was too startled by his anger to reply. She clasped her hands in her lap to stop them from trembling. This was the plan, so there was no reason to fall into a panic, but perhaps she could move things along. The idea of another two days as a captive was now more fearful than it was when she talked about it in Darcy's library. Perhaps it could be resolved in hours instead.

"Do you," she stammered, "do you intend to trade me for him because you think Mr Darcy knows where Kirby is?"

Markle did not bother to answer.

"Shall you demand a ransom as well, or do you only want Kirby?" Elizabeth forced her shoulders down and let out a slow breath. "Mr Darcy would pay to get me back." She would not mention a specific amount. She was not desperate yet.

To her shock, Markle snatched her right hand off her lap, his thumb turning the diamond and sapphire ring. "I suppose he would," he muttered, shoving aside her hand again just as quickly. "A betrothal gift, I presume. Was it out of affection or some pompous honour over your good name?"

That did not deserve a reply. "He will want me returned, and you want your nephew. We can settle this, and I am certain Mr Darcy would pay to have it settled swiftly."

Markle smirked. "Well, then everything will be neatly arranged, according to you. Do you think you are clever, Nan? I think you are stupider than that boy."

His calm tone was alarming, but she could not allow herself to be intimidated. The desire to challenge him rose in her. "I am surprised that you abducted me yourself. Usually, it is Steamer who abducts and transports your victims."

Markle's eyes flashed, and in a swift motion, she was struck across the face. He could not draw back far in the hackney, and it did not hurt as much as when Steamer had hit her with the back of his hand. She had only not been expecting this blow, and cried out more from shock than pain.

"I cut Steamer's throat for losing you, and for kidnapping the wrong bloody woman."

Elizabeth forced down her fear. He had lost his temper, and Steamer died. A revenue man had confronted him and was stoned at the bottom of a well. A potential informant was burnt in his barn. She was stopping a child beater, a kidnapper, a murderer, a violent man who could not be trusted.

As she cradled her cheek, Elizabeth wondered at Markle's confession. For a shrewd criminal, even an impulsive one, it was foolish to admit he had killed a man. "You ought not to say such things, Mr Markle."

He barked a laugh. "Who will you tell?"

Elizabeth dropped her hand and looked up quickly. "No one, if you trade me for Kirby, I promise." Markle made no answer. "You want your nephew returned to you, do you not? You need him in your gang?"

"Oh, yes," he said mildly, looking out the side-glass again. "Dearly do I want him back."

His strange manner and replies caused her pounding heart to quicken. Everything was proceeding as she and Darcy had intended. So why did it feel like they had got something wrong?

~

Now that Kirby was gone and Darcy had returned from the Excise Office, now that he had no task before him, anxiety settled into his mind. Fear that Elizabeth would be injured, fear that she would be terrorised and never feel safe again, fear that she would distrust her own decisions and be harmed as a result all mingled and intensified as the day went on.

His cousin had listened to the plan in stony silence, dissent plain in his features, but Fitzwilliam had done as he asked and gone to Cheapside to watch the Gardiners' house. Five hours had passed, and he had not come back, and Darcy could not decide what was worse: that she must have been abducted and he had followed them, or Elizabeth had yet to be taken and this agonising waiting might go on for another day.

Darcy was still prowling in his drawing room when he heard the front door open and his cousin's quick tread on the stairs. Fitzwilliam could always come and go from the house as he pleased. Rather than wait for him to open the door, Darcy ran to it and wrenched it open himself, startling his cousin, who had a hand out to reach for the knob.

"You are a sight when you have nothing to do."

"And when I am sick with worry," Darcy answered, moving aside so Fitzwilliam could enter.

The look on his cousin's face answered his unspoken question.

"He came at nine and took Miss Bennet when she was alone on the street," he said, as though reading from a report. "A slight man put her in a hackney from the stand at Gracechurch and Spread-eagle. I was not fast enough to follow it, so I noted its number and waited for the driver to return. He said he took them across Blackfriars Bridge and noticed that they changed into another hackney at Union Street and Blackfriars."

Darcy inhaled to speak, but Fitzwilliam went on. "Yes, I went there next and asked all the drivers who took that fare. After an hour and a few coins, I found the driver. He said he went down Neptune Place as far as Hatch House, but would take them no farther."

Darcy could not imagine what was on the south side of the river in Surrey. "What are they doing in Lambeth? It is marshes and meadows near to there."

"The driver did not know, but he said the man grew irate that he would not drive down the private road. The driver was hard of hearing. He thinks the man ranted something or other about not being let out where he wanted. If it was Markle"—Darcy nodded—"he then demanded for him to 'take them nearer to the yard.' But the driver just told them to get out in a hurry and presumed that they walked from there."

"The yard?" Darcy repeated, perplexed.

His cousin shrugged and threw himself into a chair. "I don't know what it means, but this is *your* reckless plan."

He should be relieved that Elizabeth was not taken farther, but anxiety of knowing she was with Markle festered in his mind like a wound. "Where could he have taken her?" he muttered, pacing the room.

"Well, I highly doubt they are going to Vauxhall."

He turned sharply at Fitzwilliam's annoyed tone, but his cousin did not look one bit chagrined. "Are you *angry* with me?"

Fitzwilliam lifted his eyes. "You come to my rooms last evening at an ungodly hour, say by the way you are engaged to marry Miss Bennet, and also she is about to be kidnapped on purpose and can I please follow the murdering kidnapper? If you are wrong about Markle wanting the boy, she could die. If you are wrong about the revenue men wanting Markle enough to help you, she could die."

"No, I went to Broad Street after Kirby got in your brother's carriage," he said, feeling breathless. He felt the truth of what his cousin said, felt the sickening fear, but it was too late for second thoughts. "I talked with an officer, Mr Sullivan, and they want Markle for his role in the death of their colleague. They do not have the resources to search every basement and tunnel, but when I tell them where he will be and when, he will have men ready to arrest him."

"Terrific," Fitzwilliam muttered. "Let us hope no one dies in a gun fight."

Darcy felt so ill with worry for Elizabeth that he wavered on his feet. His cousin gave him an apologetic look. "Well, it might all end well with Miss Bennet as a heroine. Now, we wait for a ransom letter and arrange a meeting. It cannot be long; they only took her to the other side of the Thames."

Or Markle might wait days just to plague him. A voice of distress in his head was screaming for him to get Elizabeth back now. "I cannot wait," he whispered. "I thought I could do this. I thought I could arrange everything and wait to hear from him, but this is a torment."

He went to his hat and gloves where he had carelessly thrown them when he returned earlier. "I am going back to the city to see Mr Sullivan. Maybe he knows why a smuggler went to Lambeth, or where Markle might be in Surrey, and they can arrest him now."

"No," his cousin cried. "You two made this stupid plan, so stick to it. Wait for Markle to arrange an exchange and get the revenue men to capture him. And what if Markle sends a ransom note while you are gone?"

"Then someone can chase me down at the Excise Office!" He was sick to death of his cousin's arguing.

Fitzwilliam swore under his breath, but rose and snatched up his hat and gloves to follow. They refrained from quarrelling before the servants and until the carriage was readied.

When they were alone inside, Darcy said, "Your disapproval is rolling off of you."

"I *do* disapprove. I heartily disapprove of her plan, of your agreeing to it, of your not asserting yourself over her." His cousin cursed again.

"Markle threatened to go after my sister," he cried. "What would you have us do?"

"Georgiana was moved—"

"None of us are truly safe. We had no time, and luring out Markle was our only option." He sighed heavily. It was a reckless plan, but what else could they have done in so short a time and with so few resources? "You need not have joined me."

"Of course I did. The plan is already underway, and if you learn where she is, you will need me. If you are going to face a murderer, you won't do it alone."

While Darcy felt the warmth of gratitude push back against his worry, his cousin added, "It is still the worst idea you have ever had."

"Would you have done differently if you were being followed, your loved ones threatened, if someone would kill you when he next saw you unless you complied with his demands?" The plan to trap Markle was a good one. It only hurt him because it was Elizabeth who was in danger and not him.

"I suppose I might have done as you. I would do what I could to see him punished. I might not have even kept it within the law as you have done." Fitzwilliam shifted his weight and looked out the side-glass. "I would not have used a woman, though."

There was the crux of his cousin's fury, that a woman had been put in danger. Elizabeth lacked the physical strength of a man, but Darcy could not doubt her mettle or her intelligence. She had wanted to do this. He had seen in her eyes, in her entire manner, that she needed some control over this situation and was determined to do what she could to preserve them all from further harm from Markle.

"She is brave and clever and capable, and her being a woman is irrelevant." Other than she was the woman he loved.

"You ought to have offered yourself as a trade for the boy and led the excise officers to you."

"Well, Markle did not want me," he said, "and he will underestimate her."

"He might also cut her throat as a diversion."

Darcy sat forward in the carriage and rested his elbows on his knees, his head on his hands.

Fitzwilliam clapped his hand on his shoulder, then gave it a jostle before letting go. "I am sorry, I am not helping. Maybe Miss Bennet will have changed her mind about her scheme, escaped again, and will be walking down Lambeth Road looking to hail a hackney."

He sat up with a sigh. Elizabeth would do no such thing, not when Kirby's and Georgiana's safety as well as their own hung in the balance. She would follow their plan and stay as long as she believed Markle would send for him to make the exchange.

"When this is all over, would you like me to distract the revenue men so you can steal a kiss unobserved? Shall I ride back to Mayfair in a separate carriage so you can have a private moment to talk with your betrothed?" Fitzwilliam shoved his arm with his shoulder. "Or something more?"

Darcy shook his head over his cousin's teasing. "She is just like you in a crisis. Forcing levity and being cheerful regardless of anything."

"It is not how we behave when we are in a crisis," Fitzwilliam said quickly, "it is how we behave when *you* are facing a crisis and seem on the verge of every last nerve wearing to pieces. I am done judging you, and if I cannot amuse you, I can at least distract you. Did my nieces and nephews destroy your drawing room?"

He forced a smile. "It is a good thing I am getting married because Elizabeth will need new wallpaper, carpets, and a sofa after the children spent an hour in it."

Would he marry, or would Markle kill her out of spite? He had no time to enjoy his happiness in being accepted. "I should have gone to Gracechurch Street instead while you saw Kirby off in my place."

Fitzwilliam barked a laugh. "Darcy, it was hard enough for me to watch Miss Bennet get into a hackney with a man like that! There is no way that you could have stood there and let it happen."

What a plague on his peace this was, and he had not even had to watch her be taken.

"Kirby is safely away?" Fitzwilliam asked after some moments of silence.

He was trying to distract him. If he could not be cheerful in return, then he could at least be calm. "The carriages left with the children, and my footman George will escort him to Sheffield. Conway stayed at Berkeley Square. He must not have seen Kirby, but he also did not follow me to the Excise Office. He must have known they were taking Elizabeth today and there was no reason to follow me."

"Do you think the officers will know where Markle is and apprehend him now," Fitzwilliam asked, "or are we doing this just because you cannot sit still?"

"Both," he said, "although they do not have the resources to hunt him down. But if I tell Mr Sullivan where he is, or near enough, maybe we need not wait for Markle to contact me."

"Was it difficult to convince an officer of revenue that you could bring them to the man who murdered their fellow officer?"

He shook his head. "Did you know the revenue office has had to recruit the navy to help them stop smugglers? They are overwhelmed and cannot pursue every infraction, and not when local justices rarely help. But the officer, Mr Sullivan, wants Markle for murder, and he thinks witnesses will come forward once they arrest Markle." Darcy thought over his conversation with Kirby earlier this morning. "Part of me wonders if Kirby saw the whole thing too. He might present evidence against him."

"It is better Kirby is gone then, out of anyone else's power to give him back to his murdering, smuggling uncle."

No one cared about Kirby but himself and Elizabeth. The boy deserved to not be hit, to not be recruited into a life of violence at the age of twelve. They were now in the city, and Darcy thought of Elizabeth's distressed family. "The Gardiners must be terrified. Should I call in Gracechurch Street?"

Fitzwilliam spun from the window. "And say what? That you allowed their niece to be kidnapped to trap Markle, that you encouraged it, that there has been a smuggler and murderer following you and he might kill you *and* her if he does not get his nephew? And that you would like also to marry her, after you have put her in danger? Oh, certainly, that will put them at ease."

Darcy looked at his hands, heat crossing his cheeks. "Yes, but they should know we have a plan to get her back."

"And do you think they will let you marry her if they know you allowed it?"

"I allowed nothing," he corrected. "Elizabeth is a competent woman who makes her own decisions. She was right that this was the way to secure Markle's arrest and free us from having his shadow over us for the rest of our lives, which would be infinitely shorter since we know he will eventually kill us unless we stop him."

His cousin scoffed. "Perhaps, but how many uncles or fathers would accept that? How many men in general would accept that a single young woman made an informed choice to do something dangerous and that you, as a man, did not stop her?"

"Regardless, Mr and Mrs Gardiner must be beside themselves," he said, "and poor Jane Bennet inconsolable."

"You truly want to waste hours patting their hands and answering demanding questions? Better to show up at their doorstep when it is done, with Miss Elizabeth."

"Should I not assure them that I will get her back?" If he said it enough, if he thought it enough, perhaps by his own will he could make it true.

"You want to marry Miss Elizabeth? Then they can never know you were a party to this. I know you hate to lie"—Fitzwilliam dropped his voice —"but you have to, so let us hope we recover the young lady and that they never question your involvement in her being taken in the first place."

Chapter Twenty

The Excise Office in Old Broad Street near the Royal Exchange was a large stone edifice that presented an air of strength and propriety. Darcy and Fitzwilliam walked past the tall ceilings of its Judicial Court with its commissioners to find Mr Sullivan's less lofty office.

Mr Sullivan was a tall man, past forty, with an ill-shaped nose and a smile that was just as lopsided. He sprang to his feet and came round his desk when Darcy entered.

"Back already, Mr Darcy? Has your scheme with your brave lady come to fruition?" he asked, leaning against his desk with his arms folded.

"They took the lady this morning, and we know she is somewhere in Lambeth."

Mr Sullivan's bright expression fell. "I want Markle in custody, but we do not have the men to look door by door. I need a precise location before I can gather the men to arrest him."

"We hoped you might have some idea of what a man like Markle would be doing on that side of the river rather than wait days for him to make contact."

"He was seen near Ha'penny Hatch," Fitzwilliam added, "and the hackney driver said he complained about not being let out where he wanted."

Mr Sullivan started fidgeting with his fingers as he looked at the wall, saying, "Hmm" several times. Darcy and Fitzwilliam exchanged a curious look while Mr Sullivan thought while twiddling and shifting his weight. He then went to the bookcase and pulled out a large folio and set it on a table.

"As custom house officers, we know areas along the river are a smugglers' depot. They sail from Kent to the sea and use small-scale Thames-side quays. We just seized twelve-hundred weight of sugar from a ship moored on the Thames."

The officer furiously flipped through pages until he came to a map of the south side of the river. He bent over it, his face very near the pages, gesturing for them to come near. "You say Markle was by Ha'penny Hatch?" He stabbed the map with this finger. "Say again, what did the driver overhear?"

Darcy feared Mr Sullivan was not capable enough to help him, but said, "We are not certain, but we think Markle was cross that he was not let out nearer to where he wanted to be. He mentioned wanting to be closer to 'the yard.'"

There were more "hmms" and quick taps of his fingers against the map. "Love maps," Mr Sullivan muttered. "An interest of mine. That area is all commercial, you know. Warehouses, manufacturers, breweries, timber merchants, cloth factories." He then stood upright and snapped his finger. "Timber!"

While Mr Sullivan hummed to himself and pulled out another volume, Fitzwilliam swore under his breath. "This is the man who is to retrieve your betrothed from a murderer?"

"Smugglers sometimes have arrangements to hide goods with the legitimate merchants along the river," Mr Sullivan went on, undeterred. "He meant Lett, the name, not 'let' as in permission." He met their blank expressions with a grin. "Lett is a timber merchant in Lambeth." He pointed at the book in his arms. "Come, see?"

Darcy went near, struggling to understand Mr Sullivan until he saw it for himself. In the middle of the directory page he read, "Thomas Lett & Sons, Timber-merchant, Narrow-Wall, Lambeth." He looked up at Fitzwilliam, feeling some of his hope restored. "Markle meant a timber yard along the river."

Mr Sullivan gave a wide crooked grin as he slammed shut the directory. "And now we know exactly which one!"

His cousin's shoulders settled back down and he gave a nod. "Can you assemble men to lay siege to the timber yard and recover Miss Bennet?"

"That is what we will ultimately do, but as far as the business of this office and its nine commissioners are concerned, we are arresting a known smuggler for whom a warrant has been issued for the murder of one of our revenue men."

Mr Sullivan lifted a quill cutter from his desk and turned it over in his hands as he spoke. "Smuggling is theft, and Markle ought to be transported or jailed like his brother-in-law. Magistrates often cannot try smugglers in their own counties, you know. Too many are bribed or afraid. And many people feel they may shun paying any duty on their goods. But killing an officer while smuggling is punishable by death, and that is how we will stop him."

"And there is no force in this country to pursue Markle or others like him," added Darcy.

Mr Sullivan nodded enthusiastically, still fidgeting with the quill cutter. "Bow Street and its policing of this country has hitherto been imperfect, to say the least. We cannot look at every hiding place all over Kent and Sussex nor check every warehouse along the river. Getting your betrothed kidnapped to lure Markle out for us was a grand idea, Mr Darcy."

He bowed. "It was primarily Miss Bennet's idea."

"And not a good one," Fitzwilliam muttered.

Darcy threw him a look. Rather than continue his frustrated asides, Fitzwilliam asked, "All I have seen here are commissioners and clerks. Who can you assemble who is capable of attacking the yard?"

Mr Sullivan grinned. "For surveying and collecting duties, a number of out-door officers are employed in different districts or divisions throughout the kingdom to prevent frauds and losses. There are never enough," he added with a rueful sigh. "But we are not all clerks with ink on our fingers, Colonel. I can have about six capable men assembled, and the Marine Police will help from the water."

He attempted to clap his hands together once, but had forgotten he still held the quill cutter. Mr Sullivan tossed it to his desk with a laugh, saying, "I shall have it all arranged, and the men will attack the yard around midnight."

"Midnight!" Darcy cried. "Miss Bennet cannot wait eight more hours to be rescued."

Mr Sullivan's eager expression faded. "Is it perhaps you who cannot wait, Mr Darcy?"

Fitzwilliam barked a laugh. "This man is not as impercipient as I thought," he muttered to himself.

Darcy felt his hold on his self-control slipping from his grasp. "We know where Miss Bennet is, and I do not want Markle to move her or harm her."

"He does not know you followed him," Mr Sullivan said with a shrug. "The plan all along was to await his summons, correct?"

He could make no reply, but his grudging nod seemed to make Mr Sullivan reconsider. "The sun will set around eight o'clock, and by nine it will be dark along the river and docks." He looked at the map again, tapping his fingers across it as he did. "Two boats on the Thames, and six men—"

"Eight," Fitzwilliam corrected, and Darcy felt most of his frustration at his cousin fade.

Mr Sullivan met his eye with a quick nod. "Very well. You may come, but you follow our directions. The eight of us will assemble at Narrow-Wall Road and move into the timber yard." He looked up from the map, giving it a final tap. "Half past eight, bring a brace of pistols, and follow my orders."

He gave a quick bow and strode from the room, presumably to set their attack into motion.

Darcy exchanged a look with Fitzwilliam as they too left the office. "Curious man," Fitzwilliam muttered.

Mr Sullivan seemed in constant motion, completely unable to be still, with his mind moving nearly as quickly. "Yes, but he appears competent, and arresting a criminal might be more suited to his talents than sitting indoors accounting for excisable commodities."

They made their way outside to hail another hackney when someone called his name. Darcy turned to see his footman George loitering nearby.

"They said in Charles Street that you were here," he said, slightly out of breath as he got down from one of Darcy's own horses.

"Why are you here?" he asked, immediately alarmed. "You are supposed to be one stage to Sheffield with Kirby by now."

"Somehow, I let him slip, sir," George cried. "We were at the coaching inn. Everything was settled and I thought he was in the carriage, but when I went to get in after I checked the trunks, he was gone!" His footman looked beside himself with anxiety.

Kirby was now missing. "Was he abducted?" Darcy asked, fearing the worst.

"I don't think so. I searched the inn yard, questioned everyone. A groom saw him running down the street away from the inn, but no one saw him since. I went back to Curzon Street and Charles Street, but he never returned."

While Darcy was thinking about what might be done to recover him, George held out an envelope. "This came in the four o'clock post."

He opened it to see a lock of brown hair. "It says"—he struggled to swallow—"it says that unless I bring Kirby when told to do so, the next time Markle will send me a finger wearing a diamond and sapphire ring."

If he did not intend to get Elizabeth tonight, if he did not know where she was, Darcy knew that this would be the moment he would break down. He had thought he could endure Elizabeth's scheme, that since it was rational and that she was willing, that since they had no better way to preserve Kirby or Georgiana, that since he would not let her down, he could endure his trepidation for her. This was so much more terrifying than he had anticipated.

He felt the others looking at him, but Darcy could focus only on breathing in and out.

"George, you can return to Charles Street," Fitzwilliam said. "Tell Mr Easton to oil and load every pistol in the house."

When the footman left, Fitzwilliam said in a kinder tone, "Put that away now so we can go get her back."

Darcy realised then that he had been holding the lock of hair, staring at it a few inches from his eyes. He tucked it into the envelope and put the letter in his pocket, then allowed Fitzwilliam to lead him to where they could hail another hackney.

"He seems to have forgotten about my sister, but Kirby's safety is now compromised," Darcy muttered when they were inside. "This is the last thing I need."

"Why are you worried about him?" Fitzwilliam cried. "I think his uncle sent Kirby to you in the first place."

His mouth fell open. "No, if Markle sent Kirby to harm me, he had plenty of chances. He could have let Markle's men into the house to kill me in my bed any night this week."

"Then why did Kirby flee as soon as he was out of your sight? It is highly suspicious."

"I don't know," he admitted. "Kirby was eager to go to school, and he is terrified of his uncle."

Fitzwilliam swore. "You have played into his hands."

"To what purpose?" he cried. "Kirby asks for my help, and then leaves before he gets it? How does that aid his uncle?"

"I don't know, but I don't trust him." After thinking a moment, his cousin said, "Does Kirby know what you have planned with Miss Bennet? Would he tell his uncle your scheme?"

The first inklings of concern settled into his heart. "He overheard me and Elizabeth planning." As quickly as the fear came, it then vanished. "No, Kirby said he wanted to stay and help, but I told him to go to Sheffield. He is *not* aiding Markle. The boy came back to help us."

"Damn it, Darcy! Kirby was sent by his uncle to cause you what further harm he could. Now Kirby has returned to his uncle to tell him Miss Bennet set him up and that we are coming."

"I refuse to believe that," he said calmly. "The boy came back because he wants to help." There was nothing Kirby could do now but be another thing for Darcy to manage in a disastrous situation.

"You refuse to believe it?" his cousin repeated. "Not even the possibility of it? Is that because that would not fit into your perfect little plan?"

"It is because he is an abused child who asked for my help." Truthfully, he had offered to aid Kirby several times before he had been accepted. Steamer's savage death was what pushed Kirby to flee. "You have not seen his fear, his bruises." Darcy shook his head. "Kirby would never return to Markle after he was finally free."

Fitzwilliam clenched both fists as though he might otherwise throttle his neck. "He might have told his uncle that he has been set up to abduct Miss Bennet."

"No, Kirby ran away because he knew Elizabeth was putting herself in danger and he wanted to help. He has gone back to Kent to look for her, or he knows where Markle hides in London and he will be at the Lett timber yard and will need our help."

His cousin sat back and swore yet again. "Then I guess there is nothing to do now but confront Markle and hope he is not expecting us."

~

Elizabeth knew she was somewhere between Westminster and Blackfriars Bridge, and near enough to the river to smell it. She was on the second floor of a building facing the Thames, but from the small, high windows she could only see trees on the other side of the river and, on one side, a tall structure shaped rather like a beehive with a chimney.

The sun was still up, but it would not be up much longer. Markle had dragged her past breweries, iron works, warehouses, and into a building where she had seen raw logs stored and woodcutting equipment. The room she was in now seemed more like offices than a warehouse, but below there had been a row of barrels along one wall. The smell of sawdust held its ground against the stench from the Thames.

She choked against the handkerchief shoved in her mouth and gave her wrists a break. Markle had bound them before he left, and while it had taken no time at all to get to the pocketknife under her skirts, twisting it in her hands to cut herself free was proving difficult.

Conway and Colton were at the bottom of the open stairs, laughing and sharing a flask by the sounds of it. Markle had left a long time ago after he had cut a lock of her hair to prove to Darcy that he had taken her. She feared he did not arrange a meeting with Darcy in that note.

I could be here alone for several more days.

She screamed in frustration into the handkerchief. She heaved a few breaths through her nose, willing herself to calm down. She could not panic just because she was more afraid this time. She and Darcy had a plan, so it was really an easier ordeal than her last kidnapping, was it not? There was no reason to be afraid; this time she knew someone was coming for her.

Of course, the last time was easier because Darcy had been there. Even before they had ever talked, even before she had fallen in love with him, she knew she could trust him. There must, naturally, be something significant in going through a trial with a partner rather than facing a similar trial alone.

I can trust that Darcy will recover me. He just needs to be told where I am.

Then why was she frantically sawing at the thick rope on her wrists and thinking of a way to get past Conway and Colton?

She needed to stay to pretend to make the exchange for Kirby, so it made no sense to flee. Elizabeth rested her wrists and took a long breath through her nose. She just wanted to free her hands to untie the handkerchief from her mouth. She knew Darcy would come with the officers and when he did, this would all be over. They had a carefully constructed plan, and she would abide by it.

It was nearly dark, and she was making slow progress when she heard the voices stop and a steady tread on the stairs. Elizabeth tried to fold up the knife to hide it, but her fingers fumbled—either from ache or surprise—and it clattered to the floor as Markle strode in.

He raised an eyebrow and crossed the room to pick it up. "Pretty little knife, Nan." He folded and opened it as he talked. "No reticule, no pocket that I can see. Where were you hiding it?"

With the handkerchief around her mouth, she could not speak. He reached around her head to loosen it, then yanked it down, the tight fabric scraping at her lips and chin. After taking a gasping breath, she only stared.

"No answer? Have you forgotten already? When I say—"

"In my stocking," she rasped, her throat dry. "After surviving one kidnapping, you could not think that I would leave the house unprotected."

"Little good that did." Markle laughed, but that was better than him presuming she had been ready for him because he was being set up. "I will hold on to this, since this will be your final kidnapping."

"I hope so, since Mr Darcy will bring you Kirby and you will have no further need of me."

"Presumably." Markle continued opening and closing the knife. It was disconcerting watching the blade flit back and forth, knowing what Markle had done to Steamer.

"Why are you waiting to meet with Mr Darcy?" she asked, keeping the fear from her voice as best she could. "Don't you need your dear nephew to work in one of your smuggling crews?"

"I do want him, but not for the reasons you think," he said, thumbing the blade before closing and opening it again. "I have no need of a gangly boy who would rather read than run brandy."

A new fear settled into her heart. If Markle did not need Kirby, he had no reason to lure Darcy into an exchange. Did Markle take her simply in order to kill her as punishment to Darcy for his plans going awry?

She felt all the varying emotions of fear and hope. She did not want to believe that she was about to die, that Markle never intended to trade her, that he did not want his nephew back. But it was a small, desperate hope that she clung to. Every other fact before her told her that she would never be released.

"You must have some affection for your sister's child." She had seen no evidence of this, but she frantically wanted it to be true.

"What I need is for Kirby to be loyal, and I cannot assure myself of that loyalty if he is not with me. So I need Mr Darcy to retrieve him." He pointed at her with the knife. "Hence, my purpose with you. I suspect you can spur him to action."

"Do you not care about Kirby at all?" The question came out even though his behaviour toward his nephew, toward everyone, answered for it.

"I care about loyalty and respect."

Elizabeth thought power and control more apt, but stayed quiet on that point. "And Kirby disrespected you by leaving?"

"If he cannot be trusted, then he must be punished. Kirby has seen things, Nan, and if he was loyal, then I would not be worried. But he has run off with the aid of your Mr Darcy." He came near, pointing at her again with the blade. "He crossed me, and people who cross me are punished."

Lady Catherine would be humiliated for her involvement with the smugglers, but that would not help Markle financially. He delayed meeting with Darcy just to distress him, but that would not satisfy Markle. Maybe he wanted money in return, the money he did not get from her ladyship.

"Then, you must want a ransom since you could get no money for Miss de Bourgh?" she asked hopefully. "Mr Darcy will pay for me. You need only name your price," she pleaded.

Markle shook his head as though he was a tutor and she was a disappointing pupil. "What I care about is watching his heart break as the light goes out from your eyes."

The dread was nearly overpowering. She was so afraid that she was unable to even be absolutely overset. She ought to burst into tears, sob aloud and scream. She was going to die here, but she still held an irrational hope that she could talk Markle out of what he intended to do to her.

She could not fall to pieces. It would only give him more satisfaction. She had not lost her composure when she was abducted before, and she had to believe that it was because of some mettle of her own, and not just because Darcy had been with her.

"You won't exchange us?" she whispered, already knowing the answer and not wanting it to be true.

"Kirby cannot tell tales about me," Markle said, looking at the blade. "Colton and Conway will get him from Mr Darcy when they come. But Mr Darcy wronged me by helping Kirby, just like his aunt did by reneging on our deal. I am operating a business, and loyalty and respect are at its core."

He took another step and held the blade flat against her face. "Lady Catherine will be ruined in her social circle, but how to show that a man like Mr Darcy has no sway over me and my business? Mr Darcy and people like him have a lesson to learn." He tapped the blade against her cheek, and she whimpered. "Maybe I will use this little knife to do it. Pretty eyes you have, Nan."

The terror struck her that Markle intended to cut them out and make Darcy watch.

There was a noise from outside, from behind the building and not from the water. They both started, and Markle cursed and withdrew the knife. It sounded like muffled voices and then loud footsteps rapidly moving away. Elizabeth wondered if, by some means, Darcy and the excise officers had found her already.

She and Markle held each other's gaze for a long moment before Elizabeth opened her mouth to cry for help.

"Dar—"

Markle gave her another swift smack in the mouth. She tasted the blood just as Markle shoved her gag back into place, securing it tightly.

"Colton!" Markle yelled down the stairs. "Go see what that is."

"Likely a dock worker," Conway called back up as Colton went outside.

He held onto the knife for an excruciatingly terrifying moment before folding it. "Expecting someone to help you? How would anyone know where you are?" Markle looked at her, but of course, she could not answer. His dead-eyed stare was frightening, and he seemed to deliberate. Whatever he was considering, Elizabeth knew with horrifying certainty it would not be good for her. "Time to move you a little way, Nan, just in case. Conway, I have a task for you."

He tugged her by her bound wrists to the stairs, and Elizabeth's stomach sank. She and Darcy had got everything wrong. Markle did not want an exchange or money. He only cared about power and control. He wanted to punish the people who had defied him, and he did that by harming those they cared about. Kirby had run and Darcy had helped, and now Markle would see her and Kirby die for it.

Chapter Twenty-One

Darcy and the excise officers were at the end of the commercial road that led to the wood yard. He knew the Thames River Police had a few boats on the water to prevent Markle from escaping, but he still felt like they ought to have twice as many men as they did. Eight men with pistols, daggers, and an arrest warrant no longer felt like enough to get Elizabeth back. Mr Sullivan wanted to wait for it to get darker to make their attack, and the waiting was driving Darcy to distraction.

The dread of some calamity preventing them from preserving her from Markle weighed on him. He looked down the road toward the timber shed. Elizabeth was a quarter mile away. If anything happened to her, he would never forgive himself. They had formed this plan in a sense of desperate urgency, desperate to protect Georgiana and Kirby—and it had made sense at the time—but now he regretted every choice attending to it.

"Give me your pistols," Fitzwilliam said, startling him.

"What?" he cried in a low voice. "Are you mad?"

His cousin beckoned with his hand. "You are shaking with some sort of nervous energy. A pistol in your hands is a bad idea."

"I am a decent shot." Markle would leave here in shackles or laid out in the back of a wagon. Any other option was unacceptable. If Markle walked away, that would mean that Elizabeth had put herself in danger for nothing.

"Could you truly aim and hit anything right now?" his cousin pressed.

"Of course I could." He could hit Markle in the chest and then apologise to the excise men for denying them the privilege of a trial.

Fitzwilliam reached into Darcy's coat and removed one of his pistols. Darcy let him, but withdrew the other and held a firm grip on it.

"You don't need a pistol. Your only job is to talk to Markle, lure him out and distract him so these men can surround and arrest him."

"If Elizabeth—"

"Darcy, do you really think I won't shoot him myself before anything happened to Miss Bennet?" Fitzwilliam gave him a long look. "You will be impulsive because your nerves are fractured, and that could put everyone in danger. And there is no way you are steady enough now to hit the broad side of that timber shed."

Darcy wanted to argue, but he felt his hand tensing on the pistol handle. His cousin hated everything about this scheme, but he was still here by his side and willing to do anything asked of him. Silently, Darcy handed it over.

"Let these men do what they came to do," Fitzwilliam added.

"Not much longer," Mr Sullivan said while coming to them and clapping Darcy on the shoulder. The man was alarmingly pleasant. "I sent a man ahead dressed as a warehouse worker to survey the timber yard and see how many men are about."

"Do you think Markle suspects we are coming?" he asked, afraid to express the whole of his fears for Elizabeth.

"He showed no fear of immediately being traced when he kidnapped the lady?" Mr Sullivan asked Fitzwilliam, who shook his head. "Then we will take him by surprise, and he will surrender. They load timber in an open shed on the water, and with offices above. She is likely in there. All the yard workers are gone. Nearby there is only the river and a large dry-house."

"A dry-house?" Fitzwilliam asked.

"A tall brick structure, an enclosed room where green lumber is subjected to the heat of a fire." Mr Sullivan's voice lifted with enthusiasm. "Fascinating process. It dries and hardens the timber. The furnace fire burns and the dry-house gets hotter, and the hot air and smoke leave through the chimney while cool air enters from the firebox at the bottom. The process takes a few days. It can take a full day for the fire to get hot enough to dry the timber."

Fitzwilliam nodded interestedly. "How do they keep the sawn planks from catching fire?"

"Oh, they stack the timber on a slatted floor." To Darcy's annoyance,

Mr Sullivan sounded as though nothing in this life could be more interesting than drying wood. "The fire is below and is stoked from the outside."

Mr Sullivan not only could not stop moving his feet or his hands, but when he found a subject of interest, he would talk at length. Darcy was of half a mind to be grateful for the distracting chatter and in the next moment was ready to strike him.

Maybe it *was* wise that he not carry a pistol.

Darcy blew out a breath. He could not allow his anxiety for Elizabeth to cause him to lose his wits. He had to be calm for her sake. When it was dark, he would confront Markle. Markle would be arrested, and Elizabeth would be back in his arms.

"The cut timber sits atop the slats, you see, through which the heated air from below circulates more or less freely. Fascinating," Mr Sullivan repeated. "Such an element of danger, though. They are built in isolated positions close to water to mitigate risk."

Just when Darcy felt certain to lose his patience with Mr Sullivan's singular interest, they heard someone coming from the yard. They had not lit their lanterns yet, and it was not until Mr Sullivan's man was near that they saw he was not alone, and was dragging along a small boy.

"Kirby," Darcy whispered.

The man who found him gave him a rough shove into the centre of their group and said, "I found him lurking by the woodshed. Two men were at the bottom of the stairs and were joined by Markle before I got there. I might have seen more had this one not been underfoot."

"Did you see Miss Bennet?" Darcy asked hurriedly.

The officer shook his head, but Kirby answered, "I heard her voice, though. She was talking to my uncle before this one—"

"Markle is your uncle?" Mr Sullivan interrupted.

"We fear the boy is helping him," Fitzwilliam said. "He might have told them we were coming."

Mr Sullivan swore while Kirby gave Darcy a bleak look. "I did not!"

Darcy wanted to believe him, but there was too much at stake to let his decisions be influenced by his wishes. "You were supposed to be on your way to Sheffield."

"I had to help," Kirby said, raising his chin. "I know where my uncle works along the Thames. He stores brandy casks in Lett's warehouse in return for leaving one behind. I came to see if he brought Nan here, and then I was going to tell you where to find her. Then I could help you pretend to trade us."

Fitzwilliam scoffed. "You cannot take Markle by surprise now, Mr Sullivan. Miss Bennet may not even be here if Kirby told them Darcy was coming for her."

"She *is* here." Kirby insisted, a few angry tears in the corner of his eyes. "I heard her voice, and I might have heard more if that man had not pulled me away."

Mr Sullivan idly flipped the shutter on the dark lantern open and closed. He was muttering to himself, and it sounded to Darcy as though he was arguing the pros and cons of pursuing Markle tonight. The man could keep neither his hands nor his mouth still.

The excise officers were huddled together, and Fitzwilliam had his arms crossed and was glaring at Kirby. Out of the side of his mouth, his cousin said, "You thought you could control everything in this situation, and now look where it has got you."

Darcy drew back. "This plan to stop Markle was not about a need for power or my subjugating anyone else." That sounded more like the murdering smuggler than him.

"But you do like to have your own way."

He knew his cousin was afraid for Elizabeth, but to be that misunderstood stung. "No, it is rather that I need to never be out of control."

He could not stand to have things in his life be unmanageable and turbulent, and he was capable of being in authority, of overseeing and directing, of preserving order around him. Sitting idle did not suit him, not knowing did not suit him, and he typically had the intelligence, the authority, and the means to make decisions and act on them.

He was the eldest son, the one on whom all responsibility and duty fell. Had he welcomed it, or had he simply never a choice? Regardless, he wanted to be in control, but now he had to relinquish all of it to get Elizabeth back and stop Markle.

Mr Sullivan came over with his dark lantern now lit. "We will proceed. Markle could move at any moment, and this is still the best opportunity we have had to capture him. The boy is going with you. If you tell Markle that Kirby told you where to find him, it might keep Markle distracted for longer. Then he won't focus on how you found him and grow suspicious." Mr Sullivan looked to Kirby. "Although, if he hints to Markle that he is being set up for arrest, he will rue the day he proved himself a treacherous urchin. Mr Darcy, call out to Markle. Keep him talking while we surround the yard; make him believe you will turn this boy over once you see Miss Bennet. Between us and the River Police, he has nowhere to go."

Darcy took the dark lantern Mr Sullivan handed him, opening the shutter just enough to spread a narrow beam of light on the road. Kirby fell in next to him, wiping a grimy tear from his cheek. "I was looking for Nan for you."

The boy wanted to be believed, and Darcy wanted to believe him, but he had to put Elizabeth's safety first. "Quiet for now. It will all be sorted once Miss Bennet is safe."

There were warehouses and manufacturers, breweries and wharves off this road. The blending of odours, of cut wood, smoke, and the river, was unpleasant as they approached the timber yard. It was after nine o'clock, and there were few lanterns lit near the shed. When they were nearer, he saw wisps of smoke rising from the narrow chimney of the dry-house and no one outside.

"If no one is working, why is that smoking?" Kirby whispered, pointing to the dry-house.

Darcy put a finger to his lips. "If you came back to help, now is your chance to prove it," he said in a low voice.

He put his hand on Kirby's shoulder, but he was not sure if he meant it to be reassuring or to keep Kirby at his side in case he tried to run to his uncle.

He knew the excise officers and Fitzwilliam were behind him, coming up the road and spreading out like a fan to surround the smugglers. Still, his heart pounded, and he felt a cold sweat across his body. If they had misjudged, if any part of this scheme of theirs failed, Elizabeth's life could be forfeit.

From the way Kirby tensed under his hand, Darcy knew he had seen the smugglers at the same moment he did. It assured him that Kirby had been telling the truth. Darcy gave his shoulder a reassuring pat, hoping to convey that he would not turn the boy over.

Conway and Markle were walking toward the timber shed from behind the dry-house. Colton was by the shed, leaning against some raw logs yet to be processed.

Darcy had to swallow twice before he called, "I have something of yours."

Colton and Conway spun round with pistols raised; Markle slowly turned and then stood still, with his head tilted, watching them.

"I received your note," he went on, "but I am an impatient man."

Markle still did not draw a weapon, but his eyes narrowed. Darcy had the impression Markle was calculating.

"You have caused me a great deal of trouble," Markle finally said to Kirby.

Darcy squeezed Kirby's shoulder, reminding him to stay silent. "Then let us put an end to all of this unpleasantness. You wanted to exchange Miss Bennet for your nephew; here he is. Where is she?"

Markle took a few steps nearer, and Darcy wished for the pistols his cousin had taken. Although, his desire to put a bullet in Markle's heart right now rather proved Fitzwilliam's point.

"I don't remember arranging a meeting," Markle said, his arms crossed over his chest. "How did you find us?"

Before Darcy could distract him, Kirby said, "I told him you store brandy barrels here. He insisted on coming directly. He wants Nan back."

"I convinced Kirby to tell me where I might find you," Darcy added.

Markle ignored him and took out a small penknife, turning it over in his hands. Even though his lantern light was dim, Darcy was afraid that knife was the one he had given Elizabeth. The pain in his heart was acute. If that knife had been used against her, Darcy would kill Markle with his own hands.

"Where is she?" he repeated, wondering how much longer the excise officers would be.

"Nan does not have the mettle you think she does," he said carelessly, looking at the knife.

"Miss Bennet is the bravest person I know, next to Master Kirby. You said that you wanted him, so—"

"She seemed certain that you might come for her tonight."

Darcy's stomach dropped. What duress had she been under to confess that?

"Now, I have to wonder if all of this was planned, and with a little help from you," Markle said, pointing at Kirby.

"What matters is that you want Kirby, and I want Miss Bennet," Darcy said quickly. "Your nephew wants to not be a smuggler, but I returned him. Bring out Miss Bennet and end this."

Markle's cold eyes passed over Kirby. "Thank you for bringing him back." Markle's tone expressed nothing close to gratitude. "He has seen much of my business. Come here."

Kirby trembled. He had seen many of his uncle's more vicious crimes, and Darcy suddenly wondered if Markle wanted Kirby with him not as a smuggler but so his right-minded nephew could never present evidence against him.

Kirby had not moved, but Darcy still pressed down on his shoulder. "He is not going anywhere until I see Miss Bennet."

Markle gestured with his head, indicating the two men with pistols behind him. "Nan understands this better than you do. If I say to do something, you do it."

He wondered why neither Colton nor Conway had shot him yet, he wondered if Markle would try to take Kirby from him, he wondered where the hell were the excise men. While his mind jumped all over, he also wondered how to keep Markle engaged until the officers could subdue him and find Elizabeth.

"Why do you want Kirby so badly?" he asked, desperate to divert Markle. "If he does not want to be a free trader, he is more of a liability than an asset. Why not exact his promise not to discuss your business and let him go?"

"Kirby *is* a liability."

Darcy felt his breath fail as a terrible realisation came over him. This was not about wanting Kirby back because Markle felt the boy belonged to him or because he needed him in his smuggling gang. He wanted him because Kirby was a witness to his murdering the revenue man. And then Darcy feared he knew why he had not yet been shot, and why Elizabeth had not been brought out.

"You never intended to trade Miss Bennet for Kirby. You mean to kill both of them." The lantern light wavered as his hand shook. "You want Kirby dead, and me punished for helping him." The way to punish him was to harm Elizabeth. That she might already be dead filled his mind with horror.

Markle smiled, and it chilled him. "You cannot control everything."

This truly was the part of the plan that was out of his control. He guided Kirby to stand behind him at the same moment that Markle opened the pocketknife in a swift motion.

"Lower your weapons!"

Mr Sullivan's voice rang out, and the pounding of running feet told Darcy the excise men were much nearer than he had realised. He saw the surprise in Markle's eyes when the officers closed in. Rather than stand down, he lunged at Kirby. Darcy sidestepped, keeping Kirby behind him, and swung the lantern down on Markle's arm, earning him a string of curses as the knife fell from his hand.

A pistol shot rang out, followed by a loud cry. One of the excise men fell, clutching his arm, and Fitzwilliam immediately returned fire. Conway collapsed, but the curses that followed showed he was injured, not dead. Darcy watched Colton survey the officers, and he immediately bolted toward the river.

Mr Sullivan told them to stand down. "Leave him to the River Police," he called, moving forward and keeping his pistol on Markle.

"John Markle," Mr Sullivan called. "You are wanted for the wilful murder of excise officer Thomas McKeen, on whom you did organise a gang of men to throw into a well and then strike and beat him with rocks, thereby giving him diverse mortal wounds, blows, and fractures of the skull."

Rage filled Markle's cold eyes, and Darcy gave Kirby a gentle push to keep him out of Markle's reach while five of the other officers swiftly closed in. Markle had pistols aimed at him and his arm was fractured, but Darcy would take no chances. An officer placed Markle's wrists in irons while Mr Sullivan continued to list Markle's crimes. Darcy supposed he should feel some relief, some sense of success, but he would only be free from anxiety when he laid eyes on Elizabeth.

"Are you unharmed?" Fitzwilliam asked him. He nodded, still watching Markle's dead-eyed look as he listened to Mr Sullivan state the reasons he was being detained. "I hope you agree I was right to take your pistol."

Darcy was silent, but he knew that in his tense and frightened state of mind he might very well have shot Markle during their tense conversation, and no good could have come from that.

When Mr Sullivan was done, Darcy pushed through the excited band of officers to glare at a furious-looking Markle. "Where is Miss Bennet?"

Markle smirked and said nothing.

"We will find her. He just wants to torment you," Fitzwilliam said.

"He does that by hurting Nan," Kirby muttered.

Fitzwilliam nodded, seeming to accept that Kirby was not an enemy. "A few of the excise men and I will search the timber yard for her."

Two of the men went with Fitzwilliam, while two others hauled a wounded Conway to his feet and another dragged a cursing Markle down the commercial road to the wagon.

Mr Sullivan remained with them. "I heard what your uncle said, young man," he said to Kirby. "Am I correct in suspecting you know things about his smuggling?"

Kirby nodded.

He bent down to look Kirby in the eye. "And a few things about his other crimes, too? Some of his more violent ones? Something that might have happened at a well?"

"Yes," he whispered.

Mr Sullivan rose and tousled Kirby's hair. "You and I will speak another time. A judge will want to be assured that you understand right from wrong, but then we will all want to hear what you have to say about your uncle's crimes. Can you do that?"

Darcy watched Kirby's gaze drift to where his uncle was being led away. "Absolutely."

"Congratulations, Mr Sullivan," Darcy said. "Although it took you long enough to come to our rescue."

He laughed. "If three minutes from the time you walked down the road is long!"

"It felt longer."

Mr Sullivan picked up the dropped dark lantern and fidgeted with its shutter. "A trying situation for you, certainly. Me, I prefer to be active than be a clerk behind a desk. Sadly, the job requires more of the latter. In any event, your plan worked beautifully."

"Miss Bennet deserves the credit," he said. "And it worked except for the part that Markle always intended to kill them both, and I sent her right to him."

One of the excise officers came up to them. "There is no one in the shed or the offices, and no one in the yard. Colonel Fitzwilliam is looking again, but there are no signs of her."

Darcy felt terror grip his heart. Where had she spent the last ten minutes? Was Elizabeth still alive?

"Where could she be?" Mr Sullivan mused. "Could she have never been here at all?"

"She was in there," Kirby pointed to the offices above the woodshed. "I heard her talking to my uncle. She said that Mr Darcy would pay for her. And that was right before your man found me."

Markle might have stabbed her and they would find her body somewhere amongst the sawn planks and raw logs. Or he drowned her in the river right before Darcy arrived to negotiate for her release. Darcy bent at the waist and tried to breathe in and out as a wave of terror washed over him.

"We will find her," Mr Sullivan said with his typical enthusiasm that did nothing to comfort him.

Darcy stood upright again, catching sight of the tall chimney of the dry-house, visible over the roof of the shed. Markle and Conway had been walking from the direction of it when he and Kirby arrived. A sick feeling settled in his stomach, and it took him a moment to find his voice.

"Mr Sullivan, you said drying the wood can take days. So, someone has to feed the furnace?"

His expression brightened. "Yes! Fascinating process. It can take several days for the fire to even get hot enough. I tend to learn all about the things that I find interest—"

"Shut up. If no one is working in the yard, there is no one to keep the fire going. Who is tending to the furnace? Has it been burning this whole time?"

Mr Sullivan shrugged, shaking his head. Darcy turned to Kirby, who looked pale. "I don't think that it was smoking when I first looked round," he said, "but it's been smoking since we talked with my uncle."

Darcy exchanged a horrified look with Mr Sullivan, and then they both ran to the dry-house. Kirby screamed for help, and Colonel Fitzwilliam and two of the officers came running.

"Go round the dry-house and put out the fire!" Mr Sullivan cried.

Kirby and the others went to the firebox and began filling buckets from the Thames. Darcy came to a wide door that was carried nearly twice as tall as he was. There was no lock, but a large hewn log had been placed before it. It took him and Mr Sullivan far too long to work together to roll it away.

He wrenched the door open to run inside and nearly tripped. Elizabeth was sprawled on the slatted floor amid stacks of wood directly before the door. The fire was now out, but the room was oppressively hot and filled with a smoky haze. Darcy picked her up to take her clear of the smoke as his cousin came from around the dry-house, the look of horror on his face likely matching his own.

"Is she...?" Fitzwilliam asked in a cracked voice.

There was soot all around Elizabeth's nose, but she was breathing. "Go for a surgeon! Then ride ahead to Cheapside to prepare her family!"

As his cousin ran off, Mr Sullivan opened the lantern shutter, and Darcy saw Elizabeth's mouth was gagged and her wrists were bound, and in that moment, he knew the blazes of hell were not hot enough for Markle.

Chapter Twenty-Two

E lizabeth heard voices all around her long before she felt capable of joining the conversation. She was saved from the furnace and knew she was now in an open carriage. The handkerchief had been removed from her mouth and her wrists were cut free, and from the feel of the shoulder and the arm around her, she knew she was now leaning against Darcy.

"Her hands are red and swollen," she heard him say.

"She might have been pounding on the door." A quick, eager voice she did not know answered him from across the carriage.

"Oh my God," Darcy whispered in a tone of anguish.

The other man tried to comfort Darcy. "There was no way any of us could have heard her. The chimney carried most of the smoke out, and the fire had only just been lit. She was probably in there less than a quarter of an hour."

It had felt longer. It had felt as though she was being smothered as the fire built and smoke filled the room. Although it was hotter on the floor just above the firebox, it had been easier to breathe down there, and she had banged and kicked at the door until the smoke had suffocated her and she drifted to sleep.

"Markle is a shockingly cruel man," Darcy said, his hand gently stroking her hair.

"He will be punished for it," said the other man. "Well, perhaps not precisely for this, although he certainly should be. We shall see what the

230

courts decide to prosecute. With Kirby's testimony, Mr Markle will hang for his murder of my colleague. Messrs Conway and Colton will be punished for their part as well."

That was a relief, that all of her fear and injury had been worth it. She wondered if Darcy saw it that way. She had been hurt, so of course he would think of that and not about their success.

"When we get there, should I come in with you?" This sounded like Kirby, who sat across with the other man. Why was he not far away from all of this?

"No, the Gardiners will have enough to manage. Mr Sullivan will see you to Charles Street. I will be with the Gardiners for a long while. There will be much for me to explain."

Darcy sounded distressed. Elizabeth tried to tell him he need not confess their scheme, but began wheezing instead. Darcy started in surprise and then sat her up. "Don't try to talk, dearest."

He took out a handkerchief and dried the soot from around her nose. He then handed it to her as she coughed harder. She was still coughing up grey saliva when the carriage stopped.

She felt better now that she was removed from the smoke and was almost cheerful by the time they reached the Gardiners. Her family must have been told to expect her, because as soon as the steps were folded down, Jane and her aunt ran out the door. Elizabeth tried to walk into the house but doubled over from wheezing. Darcy picked her up and carried her up the stairs, and everything after that was hazy disorder. Her aunt and uncle asked a thousand questions as he carried her past them, and in her confusion, she thought she glimpsed her father in the vestibule.

Then everyone was gone, and she was changed out of her smoky clothes. A surgeon examined her, and Jane sat by her side with tears in her eyes. Why was Jane distraught when Elizabeth felt overjoyed? Her elation built as she looked round the room, trying to take in a full breath. She was home, and aside from a little smoke, she was perfectly well. Markle was arrested; everyone should be as elated as she was.

The surgeon opened the door to let in the Gardiners. She heard Darcy behind them, and she thought she even heard her father's voice. How absurd to imagine that when he was at Longbourn?

When she saw Darcy's concerned face, Elizabeth cried out cheerfully, "We did it!"

Everyone gave her a strange look, except for Darcy, who turned pink and stayed by the door. Her voice was hoarse, but that was nothing to be worried about. Markle could never hurt anyone again.

"She is not burnt, but the consequences of smoke often show up hours later," the surgeon said to the men in the room rather than to her. She had just helped to preserve them all from a murderer, but she was not addressed directly about her own injuries. "Fine particles in smoke are irritating to the air passages."

"What will her recovery be like?"

It was her father who asked this, looking grave as he moved through the crowd to take Jane's place by her side.

"What are you doing here?" she exclaimed, taking his hand. Her father hated London, and hated exertion even more.

"When one receives an express that one's daughter has been kidnapped a second time, even I must leave the comfort of my library. I came to do what I could to recover you. And then not a few hours after I arrived, a frantic-looking colonel burst in to say to expect you directly and that a surgeon was coming."

"It all worked out—you need not have come—but I am pleased to see you," she cried before coughing. "I have news, Papa."

She looked at Darcy with a wide smile, but rather than return it, he said, "Perhaps we ought to let the surgeon finish." He gave a cautious look to her father. "There is time for that later."

The surgeon resumed. "She may suffer from continued catarrh and colds for a time, but overall, she is fortunate."

"I feel perfectly well," she cried before clearing her throat. "A little hoarse, perhaps, but well. It worked, Darcy! Markle is arrested and Kirby is free from him, your sister is safe, and we can all move forward. My dear Darcy, why are you not glad?"

No one in the room met her wide smiles.

"After all she has been through, why is Miss Elizabeth giddy?" Darcy asked the surgeon. He sounded dreadfully worried, and the rest of her family was sharing concerned looks.

"Euphoria, as she recovers from the smoke inhalation, is not uncommon," the surgeon said kindly. "It will not last."

He spared a few words for her father and then left. She felt quite jubilant. Markle was arrested; Kirby was free; her scheme had worked. Darcy had brought the excise men before any lasting harm could be done. Her father was here, and now she could marry Darcy. Everything was settled, so why did everyone look sombre?

"Thank you for recovering her, Mr Darcy," her father said insistently while bowing. Darcy, his expression tight, said he deserved no thanks and that he would return tomorrow to call on Miss Elizabeth.

She would not tolerate Darcy being dismissed. "No, Darcy must stay!" she told her father. "I need him to stay." She held out her other hand to Darcy. He stepped forward, but after a cautious look at her father, he bowed instead.

"It is midnight, Lizzy, and you have been missing since this morning." Her father sounded weary. "For now, you must rest. You will have many questions to answer tomorrow about what happened and who is responsible."

"Markle was responsible. He wanted to hurt us, but now he will never harm anyone again." She laughed. "I knew you would come," she cried, looking at Darcy. "I lured him out so the officers could find him! Our plan worked, Darcy!"

Darcy winced and lowered his eyes, and Elizabeth felt everyone's attention turn sharply to her.

"*Your* plan? Did you get kidnapped on purpose?" her father asked, incredulous.

Rather than answer, Elizabeth watched Darcy cover his face with his hands.

"Did you not want to tell them how it came to pass?" she asked him. "Oh," she said slowly as she realised why Darcy looked like he wanted the floor to swallow him up. "My family won't hate you," she called to him. "The scheme was my idea, Papa."

When everyone now looked at Darcy, he grimaced. "If your father allows it, I will return in the morning."

"No, stay," she pleaded. After all she had gone through, she needed a moment alone with him. At the least, he ought to stay because everyone who loved her best was present, although they were all giving her horrified looks except for Darcy. She looked around and fixed her eyes on her sister. "Jane, *you* know what he means to me. You know why Darcy must stay!"

Jane's cheeks turned red, and she brought a hand to them. "I–I know that, that Mr Darcy and Lizzy have...an affection for one another."

"Yes, we do. Darcy and I are to marry."

She grinned at her family expectantly. After everyone stared at her in silence, her father said to the others, "The surgeon did say a lack of air could alter her mind for a little while."

"No, she is telling the truth," Darcy said quietly. "I asked her to marry me."

"Twice," she said, laughing. "I refused the first one, but I was eager for the second proposal. It has been an eventful week." She counted on her fingers. "A terrible proposal, a kidnapping, escaping, falling in love with Darcy, a better proposal after days of wondering if it would all come to nothing, and then finally a scheme to lure Markle into an arrest. I did fear I would die, but Darcy came after all."

Why did Darcy look stricken? "Oh, did you not want to tell them about your first proposal?" she said in what was certainly a whisper. "Or did you not want to explain our plan? I take full responsibility for the scheme to trap Markle, you know. But we can tell my family whatever you like."

"Not now," he muttered while giving her a fond smile. "And I cannot dissemble for my life, anyway. Mr Bennet, I know it is very late, and you are worried for Miss Elizabeth, but may I speak with you?"

Her father let go of her hand and rose. "I insist on it."

Darcy and her father left, and her aunt and uncle exchanged a curious look and they, too, left the room. Only Jane remained, giving her a look as though she saw something peculiar.

"Why did my father sound grim?" she asked.

Jane fell into a chair. "Oh, Lizzy, what did you do?"

~

THE ENTIRE STORY—SAVE FOR THE SPECIFICS OF THEIR morning at the inn at Dartford—took the better part of an hour to lay plain to Mr Bennet, and Darcy felt exhausted.

In Meryton, Elizabeth's father had always struck Darcy as indifferent to everything, and nothing she had told him over the past week about him changed Darcy's opinion. However, the clock had struck two, and he still asked questions about every choice and action he and Elizabeth had taken from when Steamer kidnapped them from Hunsford through the moment Darcy carried Elizabeth from the dry-house. He even pressed him for details as to what Mrs Gardiner had hinted at in a letter regarding Wickham.

Darcy stifled a yawn as Mr Bennet asked, "And she actually agreed to marry you, but after your abduction?" This was asked in a tone of exasperation.

"We came to mean a great deal to one another during that time, but I

234

believe her affection to be sincere and not a result of our tragic shared experience."

"I was rendered spiritless when I arrived in town, afraid for my dear Lizzy, and now I find myself in a dilemma." He sighed. "On the one hand, you let the woman you claim to love put herself into mortal danger, but she is restored to us by your doing and her captor will be punished. And Lizzy has accepted you—although I am still uncertain why when I thought she hated you and you only looked at a woman to find a blemish."

He ought to feel mortified, but he was too tired to care. "I hope your daughter will tell you I really am the object of her choice, and I will give you whatever assurances you need that my affection for her is not the work of the few days we were together."

Mr Bennet still looked grave, and Darcy asked, "Do you intend to withhold your consent?"

"Well, I will have no relief from my wife if I oppose the match. Ten thousand a year is not forsaken lightly."

"Elizabeth would say differently," Darcy said flatly.

"Yes, she would need to truly esteem her husband." He looked at him with new intensity, considering him for a long moment before he spoke. "The first proposal was before the first abduction?"

Who had conversations like this, counting the number of kidnappings and marriage proposals? Darcy nodded, hiding another yawn behind his hand.

"I am surprised that you condescended to ask the same woman a second time. Did you offer again because you were afraid that some misguided family member would assume you had taken advantage of her and she needed the protection of your reputation and name?"

"I asked her again because I still loved her, and I had reason to believe she would say yes." He dearly hoped to avoid direct questions about what happened in Dartford.

Mr Bennet must have had an equally trying day, but he showed no sign of ending his questioning. "My concern, Mr Darcy, is that Lizzy is quick and lively, and not passive like some men might expect a wife to be. She could lose herself if she marries unequally," he said heavily, looking him in the eye.

"I think Elizabeth will be just as much herself when she is Mrs Darcy as she is now, just as opinionated, just as charming, just as confident," Darcy said, leaning forward in his chair. "We are equals."

"I suppose you must see it that way if you allowed her to proceed with this reckless scheme," he coolly replied.

"I would have gone in her place if I could have," he said, struggling to keep his patience amid his frustration and exhaustion. "Besides, would you want her to marry a man who would subdue her, control her, disagree with her simply because she is a woman? Would you want her to marry a man she felt compelled to defer to?"

"In general? No. But in the case of offering herself up to be harmed to lure out a murderer, then yes."

Darcy dropped his head. As much as she had made her own choice, as much as she needed to be a part of the solution, it still hurt him that she had been in danger. "We thought he would trade her for his nephew and the excise men would arrest him," he said quietly. "We never considered that he would kill a child."

"He might have killed Lizzy; what would you have done then?"

"I would have gone after Markle and brought hell with me," he said darkly, raising his head to stare at Mr Bennet. "And blamed myself for her death for the rest of my life."

Darcy was prepared to spend the rest of the night conquering Mr Bennet's incredulity until he reconciled himself to the match, but the older man nodded and said, "I give my consent. My blessing I reserve for after I see how you are with one another at Longbourn. I am taking Lizzy home as soon as the surgeon says she can travel. You are welcome to follow us, and you might as well bring your friend Bingley if all the hints the Gardiners have mentioned have any value."

It took him a moment to realise the matter was at a close, that he could marry Elizabeth. "I will do what I must for you to approve of me," he said earnestly.

"Well, you have secured Lizzy's approval, which will go a long way to securing mine." Mr Bennet held out his hand, and Darcy was grateful to take it.

"May I say good night to Elizabeth?" he asked as they walked toward the door.

"And tell her the good news, I suppose?"

If he was already saying their engagement was good news, Darcy supposed Mr Bennet's reservations might not be as strong as he had feared. "With your permission."

"Very well." They left the drawing room, and he gestured vaguely toward the stairs. "There was no good to be expected when I left Longbourn today, but now I return to it with a rich husband for Lizzy and possibly another for Jane. Mrs Bennet will be pleased."

Darcy thought Mr Bennet a strange mixture of caprice and sarcastic humour, but he would have to take the pains to get to know him and all of Elizabeth's family. When he knocked and entered her room, she was lying on her side away from him, but she lifted her head when he spoke.

"Your father said I could—"

Elizabeth laid back down and reached her hand behind her. When he hesitated, she beckoned him with her fingers.

"This is a terrible idea," he said, smiling as he pulled off his boots. "I would like the Gardiners and your father to not hate me more than they already do."

He laid on the bed behind her, above the sheets, and when he took her hand, she wrapped his arm tightly around her. The tension in his shoulders relaxed, and he felt her give a long sigh of relief.

"It feels right to lie in bed together."

"It does," he agreed, meaning it more deeply than those two words could express. "How are you feeling?"

"Now I only have a throbbing headache," she said in a voice that was still hoarse. "And I am mortified that I announced everything in that dreadful way."

"It was not your fault," he said into her hair. "Besides, it was only natural for you to be glad to be alive."

"I had fifty alternations between hope and terror during the time I realised Markle intended to kill me and the time I fainted from the smoke."

He felt tears in his eyes, and he squeezed them shut. "Tell me what happened."

"Markle suspected you were coming. I had just learnt he was going to kill me no matter what, that he would punish you by killing me. When I heard someone outside, I called your name, and in an instant, he decided what to do. The smoke filled in slowly, but I felt dizzy and confused and boiling. I remember staying low on the floor because it was easier to breathe, and slamming my hands against the door."

"You must have been terrified."

"I am certain you were too," she said softly, giving his knuckles a quick kiss. "The whole time I was with him, you must have been terrified."

Why was she trying to comfort him when she was the one thrown into a furnace? "It was all over with Markle and the officers in five minutes, but then we could not find you—" His voice broke. "I was afraid we would find your body somewhere amongst the wood piles or once they dredged the river."

This time, he could not stop a few hot tears from falling. Darcy clutched her tighter, pressing his face into her neck until he could feel that she was alive and whole, until he could convince himself that Markle was never going to hurt her again. Everything had gone wrong, and yet here she was, still willing to be in his arms.

After a while of enjoying the calmness of lying peacefully with Elizabeth, he said, "I need to go before your sister or someone else comes in to check on you."

"It feels more natural to have you here with me than to send you away. I enjoy sleeping in the same bed with you."

"Me too," he whispered, dropping a kiss to her neck.

She turned in his arms, putting a hand on his cheek and lifting her head until her warm mouth touched his, carefully, as though to test his willingness. He kissed her slowly, with all the tenderness he felt for her and his heart nearly beating out of his chest. She breathed an endearing little sigh that vibrated against his lips.

This kiss was far gentler and less urgent than their embraces in Dartford. It was a calmer moment of contentment amid all the turbulence and terror of the past week.

"Now is hardly the moment for anything more," he said when Elizabeth gave a little frown as he pulled away.

"Did that thought cross your mind as often as it did mine last week?" she asked, smiling and keeping her fingertips along his neck. "I thought 'but now is not the time' so often."

He gave a little laugh. "It did, and I think it best to keep that thought in mind until we are married."

"Be prepared for a very sincere fuss to be made when we announce our news at Longbourn."

"Be prepared for a very long season of courtship to satisfy your father."

Her bright expression faltered. "Did my father not give you what you asked for?"

"What I want is for the love of whom I love best on earth to be wholly mine, under any terms you set. You have already agreed to that." When she pressed him, he added, "He consented because he did not feel that I was a man he could refuse, but he hardly approves of me."

Elizabeth shook her head over it. "He must have been angry after what I did, but he is wrong to blame you for it. It was my choice."

"He was afraid for you," Darcy said, understanding completely. "And quite confused as to why you would want to marry me at all."

"Then I will have to tell him, tell everyone, that I love and admire you, that I am challenged by you, and that as confident and clever as you are, you are also able to listen to me and respect me as your equal."

Darcy closed his eyes and held her close. To think all that force of character, all that subtle kindness, might have been wiped out in an instant.

"Won't you kiss me before you go?" Elizabeth said when he sat up to leave. "I need a reminder that you love me if I am not yet allowed to sleep next to you."

Darcy bent his head to kiss her, lingering over her lips as he whispered, "I shall love you until the last breath leaves my body."

Epilogue

Four months later

Elizabeth had thought that by living in such a large and fine house as Pemberley that she would never feel stifled, trapped, or confined. The rooms were lofty, there were many windows, and she was the mistress of it all. She was the happiest creature in the world, and Darcy was a devoted husband.

But every once in a while, a sudden and forgotten fear struck her.

She no longer started when someone knocked on the door. But sometimes an immobilising fear came over her. It had happened while she was at Longbourn, but it had happened only a few times in London after she finally married Darcy. Her father had insisted on a long engagement—much to her mother's dismay—but she and Darcy married on the same day in June as Bingley and Jane.

Now that she was finally at Pemberley, now that she was Mrs Darcy, she should be feeling all the elation and joy a new bride typically felt.

When an episode came, the fear was uncontrollable, unpredictable, and completely without cause. There was no reason to feel afraid in this neglected sitting room. It had once been a favourite of old Mr Darcy's, rarely used and never changed. She only entered it because Mrs Reynolds had previously shown her the miniatures above the mantelpiece, and Elizabeth intended to rearrange them to make sure Wickham was hidden from view. Georgiana was now at Pemberley, and Elizabeth wanted nothing to distress her.

Wickham's reputation had been diminished in Meryton. Hints to her mother and sisters about his debts and dalliances, without any mention of Miss Darcy, had been enough to ensure neither shopkeeper nor young lady trusted him. Elizabeth would never lay eyes on him again, and she would purposefully misplace this small portrait so no one at Pemberley would have to look on him either.

As she removed his miniature, she looked round the room. It was small with a lovely view of the garden, but with the curtains drawn and the door closed, with only a smoky candle for light, Elizabeth's mind went back to the night they had captured Markle. What Elizabeth felt now was akin to panic—even though nothing was wrong.

"Elizabeth?"

Two hands were on her shoulders and it took her a moment for her gaze to return to see Darcy in front of her, giving her a soft, concerned look.

"Did it happen again?" he asked.

She nodded, taking stock of how she felt: rapid heart, quickened breath, and a sensation of being frozen with fear. But as swiftly as the feeling of dread and incapacity had hit her, now it was fading.

"You make it sound as though I am always being carried away by some strange old fear," she said, forcing a smile so Darcy would not worry. "It rarely happens now."

Darcy gave her a knowing look and held out his arms, and as much as she wanted to show that she was brave and healthy, she would not say no to a hug. She put her arms around him and he held her tightly. The feel of him breathing against her was calming. "Where did you go this time?" he said into her hair.

"I don't go to the house in Shoreham anymore. It is the dry-house memory that provokes such a reaction. Maybe because when I was in Shoreham, I was with you, and not as frightened as I was that night at the timber yard."

Darcy kissed her forehead before letting her go. He opened the door and led her back into the brightly lit hall and then blew out the candle. "Maybe it was the smoking candle along with this dark room that prompted the memory."

It might be true, and it made her angry. Why could she not walk into any room of her own beautiful home and not be reminded of something terrible? "I am tired of these intrusive and distressing symptoms hitting me when I least expect it. The same events happened to you, or nearly so. Why are you not suddenly and inexplicably sent back to some dreadful experience?"

He looked as though he wished he had an answer. "What is it like for you when it happens?"

She thought about how best to describe it. "It is like my body is reliving the feelings of that moment, when I knew Markle wanted me dead, knew he wanted to hurt you by killing me, and then the dry-house was getting hotter and not enough smoke cleared the chimney so I could breathe." She felt embarrassed under Darcy's concerned look. "I know it is foolish to be overtaken by the memories, especially now so many months after, when we are finally where we belong."

Although they had lived together in the house in Charles Street, bringing Elizabeth home to Pemberley last month had been the culmination of months of unease for the both of them. She wanted to enjoy it, and for Darcy not to be preoccupied by concern for her.

"You are not weak, you know," Darcy said gently. "You are the bravest woman of my acquaintance."

"Well, I did handle town society and keep my patience with the gossip about your aunt, but we can call that a virtue rather than courage."

Lady Catherine had called in Charles Street, but Darcy refused to let her in the house. She had been forsaken by every reputable connexion even though the magistrate did not issue a warrant for her treasonous smuggling. She was still a woman of rank and connexions; no man of equal rank was willing to prosecute the daughter of an earl. The only justice served was of a social nature.

She was ostracised in Kent and shunned in London for her part in the Markle scandal. Even Mrs Jenkinson had left them, unable to tolerate living in a house with criminals and social outcasts. Her ladyship's money was gone, her land and possessions sold bit by bit until Rosings itself was sold to satisfy her creditors. She had not a friend to help her, and in order to preserve his only living sister from penury, Darcy's uncle Lord Fitzwilliam allowed her to live in a small establishment on his estate, where she was visited by no one.

If Lady Catherine could never be truly punished, it had satisfied Elizabeth and Darcy to know that her ladyship no longer had any influence. She had no one on whom to dispense advice or hold power over, not even her daughter, for Anne de Bourgh was removed from her mother and the laudanum to live quietly with the Fitzwilliams.

The spectacle of Lady Catherine's fall from grace lessened the gossip about Elizabeth and Darcy regarding the abduction, the smuggling, and Markle's trial. They had been a curiosity rather than a scandal, but it still tired her to have her first month of marriage visits not be about the new bride and her happiness but requests to say what was it like to survive a kidnapping as though it were a grand adventure.

Neither of them discussed the matter in public, and it turned out that Darcy had been right: since gossip could not hurt either of them and they contributed nothing to the story, people soon tired of it. New crimes, assassinations, and town talk took its place.

"You know very well what I mean, dearest Elizabeth," he said pointedly. "To be seized by the occasional bad memory cannot be unexpected, given what we experienced."

"You don't struggle in the same way, though." She had never come across Darcy in tears in a dark room.

He gave a rueful smile. "I still don't like it when someone surprises me from behind, especially while on the street. It takes my mind back to when Markle accosted me and I thought he would kill me then and there. And, as your father noted during our courtship, I do not like to let you out of my sight."

She laughed. "You have become much better at that, especially now that we are truly home."

Darcy turned a little red, but he held her gaze. "Well, I cannot keep you on a leading string."

"Fortunately for you," she said, pressing a quick kiss to his lips, "I do not mind being close to you." She stroked her fingertips along his jaw. "It must have been hard for you to not be in control of everything that awful night."

"No harder than it was for you to endure it," he said, turning his head to press a kiss to her palm. "It was difficult because people I love could have been harmed and there was nothing I could do to stop it. I am not ashamed to seek counsel, although I still prefer to have the power of choice."

"I would expect nothing less from you. The Gardiners and the Bingleys will be here soon," she said brightly. She did not want any unpleasantness to disrupt their families' visit. "Let us find Georgiana and wait in the drawing room."

She turned to go down the stairs, but Darcy took her hand and held her back. "Do not judge yourself harshly, my dear. We had both been badly frightened, and such a deep terror could not possibly instantly disappear."

. . .

Four years later

DARCY OBSERVED THAT ALTHOUGH HIS WARD WOULD NEVER BE tall, at sixteen Kirby no longer had a gangly and underfed appearance. He applied himself to his studies, was well-liked by adults, got reprimanded for playing pranks with the other boys boarding with Mr Gates, and rode too fast for Elizabeth's liking. All in all, he was everything a sixteen-year-old boy ought to be.

"She can hold up her own head now," Elizabeth said, laughing at Kirby's frightened expression while staring at the infant on her lap. "She is much stronger than when you last saw her."

Darcy watched his daughter gnaw on her own fist as she stared up at Kirby with large brown eyes like her mother's. Little Anne seemed open to being held by this blond stranger, but Kirby had reservations.

"I think I prefer the other Miss Darcy's company," Kirby said with a polite nod to Georgiana. "She is less likely to cry."

Darcy stepped forward and picked his daughter off of Elizabeth's lap. "It will be a long Christmas school holiday if you are afraid of a four-month-old." He held her out and forced Kirby to take her. They had waited a long time for Anne, and he could admit to himself that he was eager for others to admire her.

"You can even call her Nan, if you want to," Elizabeth added.

Kirby smiled a little. "But what will she think of me?" Kirby asked, shifting Anne in his arms to look into her face. "She will someday ask who I am to you and why I am here."

Darcy often wondered how Kirby had felt when he heard his uncle was to be hanged at Tyburn the Monday following the trial. It was Kirby's testimony of how his uncle arranged, encouraged, and participated in the brutal revenge stoning of the excise man that sealed Markle's fate.

But Kirby refused to mention his life amongst smugglers and murderers. At the age of twelve, he had divorced himself from his past and spoke only of things that happened after the moment they left the Old Bailey and Elizabeth put an arm around the boy and said, "Let us go home."

He needed Kirby to know beyond a doubt that Pemberley would always be his home. "Miss Darcy is twelve years my junior," Darcy told him lightly, "and I know from experience that sisters are fond of their older brothers, and that they look up to them. And it is an older brother's responsibility to care for his sister, even when she is fully grown," he added, looking at Georgiana.

Kirby ducked his head and turned pink. Darcy noticed Elizabeth give him an approving look for how he put the boy at ease.

Anne was not actually Kirby's sister, but they were still a family. When they visited the Bingleys and their children, when the Gardiners visited, when they travelled to Longbourn, Kirby was with them. He came to Pemberley at every school holiday, and Darcy would support him at Cambridge when the time came.

"Will we have to tell her someday..." Kirby asked, stretching to keep his mouth out of Anne's curious reach. "Tell her how I came to be here?"

"I should like to," Elizabeth cried, earning a surprised look from Kirby. "You saved our lives, after all. You are a courageous young man."

Kirby looked as though he wanted to never speak of it, so Darcy said, "For now, she will accept you as you are, not where you came from. You are her family, and she will love you. But if you want to tell Anne that Mrs Darcy and I found you on the roadside and brought you home because you looked hungry, that is just as well and rather close to the truth."

The room laughed, including Anne, and this first giggle made everyone spend the next quarter of an hour trying to elicit another.

~

"I HAD NO IDEA KIRBY WORRIED ABOUT HOW TO EXPLAIN HIS past," Elizabeth said to him late that night after the baby was finally fed and asleep. "I don't blame him for his uncle, so I never considered that he might feel guilty by association."

"Some will judge him for it, so we must do better to assure him that no one here holds it against him."

"His history could make for an inspiring story when he is a barrister someday, upholding the law."

Darcy agreed and then yawned and tried to hide it, knowing that until only recently Elizabeth was awake much later with Anne. Elizabeth still laughed at him, shaking her head as she readied for bed.

"Now that our family is coming for Christmas and Kirby is here, you will have to stay up later than is your wont."

"My inclination is to retire either to bed or my study room after candle-light, something I am willing to put aside for the sake of good society." The

Bingleys and the Gardiners were good society, and he wanted them here for Christmas as much as Elizabeth did.

"That is why you need two cups of coffee in the evening, without sugar," she added. "Plenty of cakes with honey, though."

"That reminds me," he said while taking off his waistcoat, "I must reduce your pin money. I cannot afford both that and to feed that boy."

She laughed as she brushed out her hair. "He is only here on school holidays."

"They must not feed him at Mr Gates'. Mrs Gates is taking the money I send and burning it."

"Fitzwilliam, you have a droll sense of humour," she said, smiling at him in the mirror's reflection. "I wish everyone could see that." As Darcy watched her, he saw the amusement fade from her expression.

"What is the matter?"

She shrugged and stood. "What Kirby said today had me thinking about the abduction. The second one," she corrected. "Markle wanted to hurt you, but he never meant to kill you. He intended to murder me because he thought nothing could hurt you more. What kind of person even thinks like that?"

The rigour of his resentment for Markle had long been relaxed, but it was still something they rarely spoke of. "A person who will never harm anyone again because of your courage."

"Do you regret agreeing to the scheme to lure him out?" she asked, putting her arms around his shoulders.

"Sometimes, when I see how it haunts you."

"It has been a long time since one of those attacks struck me," she said, giving him a firm look.

"It stays with us, though." He had underestimated the fear they would both experience, the danger, the impact it would have. "In how we look at a room full of strangers, in how we observe our surroundings when we walk down the street, in how we always note the hackney number the other gets into, in how we always have money and a knife on our person when we leave the house."

"I truly believe we had no good choices and Markle was determined to harm us, so we should think on the future rather than the past, and be grateful that we have that future together."

Then she kissed him with such enthusiasm that it almost took him aback. His hands cradled her face as his tongue entered her mouth, stroking deeply. Darcy pushed his hips hard against hers, and what followed could only be described as spirited kissing as they took off the last of their clothes. When they fell into the bed, he urged her onto her side, her back to his chest, wrapping an arm around her body to tease her nipple.

"I thought you wanted to sleep," she asked as his hand caressed her breast, her hand stroking his thigh.

"Should I let you sleep?" He kissed along her neck, nipping just hard enough to elicit a moan.

"Not now."

"I can let you sleep," he lied as she pressed back against him, seeking his touch. He had learnt where to circle slow, when to stroke gently, and when to finally rub faster until she came amid wild cries.

He waited until her breathing slowed for her to tell him she was ready, but after a moment Elizabeth tilted back her head and panted, "If you have fallen asleep, I will be very disappointed."

He smiled at the frustration in her voice amid the desire. As he took her slowly and steadily, she rocked back against him, his name falling from her lips as they moved together. When her gasping breaths came faster, he gripped her hip harder, trying to control himself to make it last longer. Her body held him tightly, and Elizabeth urged him so much that he pressed her onto her stomach beneath him. Sensation crept up him, driving his hips in a fast, erratic rhythm until he said her name and went tightly still over her.

Even after four years, he still enjoyed both the quiet contentment and the blood-warming feeling that came with holding Elizabeth in his arms. Entangled, naked, and entirely satisfied, he held her against him. "You know," he said thickly, still trying to catch his breath, "being with you like this in bed is one of the best parts of being married."

She gave a satisfied sigh. "That was the only good part of being kidnapped. Sharing a bed with you began terribly awkwardly, but it led to many hopes and wishes on my part by the end of it. Thankfully, you were eager to satisfy all of them."

"Only you could find a silver lining on a sable cloud to being abducted and surviving a terrifying situation," he said, laughing.

He felt her laugh softly in reply. "It was quite the bright side by the end of that situation, you remember?" After a few moments, he thought she had fallen asleep, but she said, "It hardly matters now, but at the time my father thought that our relationship was only built on our being near to one another in a distressful situation."

"Did you ever wonder about that?" he asked quietly. The foundation of his love for her preceded everything that happened in Kent. Elizabeth, however, had certainly begun to love him in that cluttered room in Shoreham. "That it was because we were confined together that you could give credence to what I said and care for me?"

Elizabeth turned over in his arms. "You think I mistook gratitude and companionship for love?" The subtle lines of her face were taut. "That if any other man had been kidnapped with me, I would have been waiting and wishing for their proposals after I left Dartford with an aching void in my heart?"

"No," he said quickly. "Whatever we were to each other when we were locked in that room, we still are, dearest Elizabeth, and I am convinced that we would have been eventually even if that horrid event had never happened."

She smiled, her whole expression brightening once again. "We would have found one another finally, I know it. Being forced together only hastened what was certain to happen."

Lowering his head, he kissed her. She slid her hand up to his nape, holding him as she leant into his embrace.

THE END

Newsletter

Subscribe to Heather Moll's newsletter for a free story.

In *The Wedding Guest,* Darcy arrives in Hertfordshire to meet his friend's bride and Elizabeth expects Bingley's servant is on his way to help with Jane's wedding planning.

Mistaken identities lead to a happy ever after in this meet cute available available only for newsletter subscribers.

Subscribe for sales info, new release updates, exclusive excerpts, contests, and giveaways.

www.HeatherMollAuthor.com

Coming Soon

My Dear Friend
Available Autumn 2024

They never get along whenever they unfortunately cross paths. But when a matchmaking service anonymously links them up, will they pen a romance?

Elizabeth Bennet is an excellent judge of character. Eager to prove to her brokenhearted sister that worthy men do exist, the spirited and witty young woman subscribes to the new matchmaking service taking London by storm. And she's pleasantly surprised when the female-empowering agency anonymously connects her with a fascinating correspondent.

Fitzwilliam Darcy is determined to move on from unwanted feelings for the alluring but inappropriate Bennet girl. He hopes his captivating prose partner from the matchmaking service might be the distraction he needs. But when he reveals his inner thoughts, he can't keep the letter-exchanging relationship from becoming something more.

As Elizabeth starts to fall for the mysterious man, her dislike for Mr. Darcy only grows whenever they meet in person. While the man in question still admires Elizabeth, he realizes in alarm that he may have also given his heart to his anonymous correspondent...

Have their letters opened an unexpected path to happily ever after?

Acknowledgments

As always, this book would not exist without the support of wonderful people. My fabulous proofreader, Katie Jackson, who is always willing to schedule me no matter how early I ask her. My brilliant editor, Sarah Pesce, for her wisdom, encouragement, and friendship.

My utmost thanks to Cathie Smith, who helped make this book better. My gratitude also goes to my early reader team. I can't launch a book without them.

Thanks to my family for supporting me in every possible way.

About the Author

Heather Moll writes romantic variations of Jane Austen's classic novels. She is an avid reader of mysteries and biographies with a masters in information science. She found Jane Austen later than she should have and made up for lost time by devouring her letters and unpublished works, joining JASNA, and spending too much time researching the Regency era. She is the author of *An Appearance of Goodness, An Affectionate Heart, Nine Ladies*, and *Loving Miss Tilney*. She lives with her husband and son, and struggles to balance all the important things, like whether to buy groceries or stay home and write.

Connect with her on social media or on her blog, and subscribe to her newsletter for updates and free stories.

facebook.com/HeatherMollAuthor

x.com/HMollAuthor

instagram.com/HeatherMollAuthor

goodreads.com/HeatherMoll

bookbub.com/authors/heather-moll

Also by Heather Moll

An Appearance of Goodness

Can a Derbyshire meeting lead to love or will Pemberley be plunged into mystery?

An Affectionate Heart

Are love and affection enough to overcome the pain of grief and anger?

Nine Ladies

How can Darcy and Elizabeth overcome 200 years of differences in this time-travel love story?

His Choice of a Wife

His letter destroyed her assumptions. His actions are winning her heart. But when scandal looms, is their love strong enough to survive?

Loving Miss Tilney

She's forbidden to wed a nobody. He's nothing in society's eyes. Will their desperate schemes backfire before they find a way to be together?

Mr Darcy's Valentine

Will an exchange of secret valentines lead to love?

A Hopeful Holiday

Is the holiday season a perfect setting for a second chance at love?

Made in the USA
Thornton, CO
03/01/24 08:27:17

746da062-2a55-428b-a285-0c8be8b5b998R01